THE KING OF FASSARAI

THE MACMILLAN COMPANY
NEW YORK · BOSTON · CHICAGO · DALLAS
ATLANTA · SAN FRANCISCO

MACMILLAN AND CO., LIMITED
LONDON · BOMBAY · CALCUTTA · MADRAS
MELBOURNE

THE MACMILLAN COMPANY
OF CANADA, LIMITED
TORONTO

THE
KING OF FASSARAI

by DAVID DIVINE

THE MACMILLAN COMPANY

NEW YORK · 1950

The King of Fassarai was published in *The Saturday Evening Post* somewhat condensed under the title *The Doctor of Unknown Island.*

Printed in the United States of America

THE KING OF FASSARAI

CHAPTER I

≋≋≋≋≋≋≋≋≋≋≋≋≋≋≋≋≋≋≋≋≋≋≋≋≋≋≋≋≋

1

THERE was hardly any noise from the reef. For three days now the trade wind had failed, and the sea to the northeast was a flat and oily calm. Even the everlasting swell had died away, and the first darkness was utterly silent, so silent that they could hear the creak of the ungreased blocks on the davits of the Japanese ship in the lagoon. They could hear even the rustle of the rope running through them. She was a full three-quarters of a mile out from the landing place, a dark bulk looking infinitely larger, infinitely more ominous, than her daylight self. Four lights showed in a row from the ports close down to the water line, five more in her superstructure. Where the boat was being lowered they had switched on a cluster which showed a wide triangular segment of her side, grey and formless in the main blackness of her bulk.

On the high terrace of the All Men House, the Council house of the island, the men sat quite silent, waiting. They knew with a deep, unquiet certitude what this portended. It had happened before, if not with this ship then with others, and there was nothing that they could do—less than nothing. On Falalop, the island to the west, the men had clubbed a Japanese petty officer two years ago. Three men had died in the fight that followed, and four had been shot after.

There was nothing they could do. There was nowhere even that the women could hide. The islands were so small, so very small.

Behind them in the darkness the village was silent also, and yet it seemed alive with a quivering apprehension. The dogs themselves were quiet, and twice when a child whimpered the sound struck off abruptly as sound ceases when a hand is placed over a small mouth.

The boat was coming in now. The splash of oars was regular and grew loud with a remorseless upward movement of sound. They could hear the looms of the oars thudding with each stroke against the thole pins. After a little they could see it—a shape darker even than the survey ship with bright patches on either side as the blades of the oars came out and brought with them the bright glow of phosphorescence. It came straight for the landing place. No stranger could have found the landing in this deceptive darkness, but the men of Asor knew that from the high-reaching gable of the All Men House a long bamboo stretched up far above the highest palm and on it a flag hung, an enormous white square that was the base point of the Japanese Navy's survey of the lagoon. They had themselves helped to lash it there this morning. The Japanese would be steering for the darkness of the flag against the glow of the stars.

The Japanese came straight in, and with a last two extra-powerful strokes ran the boat up on to the beach. From the *ailiuth* they could see a man jump from her bows and, turning, begin to pull them further up. Two other men dropped out and began to drag her. In a moment they were all out; the boat was up on the dry sand; and they stopped for a minute, talking quickly in Japanese. The sound was high-pitched. The men sitting on the *ailiuth* could find no just comparison for it—a quick chattering that had something of a whistling in it, sibilant, staccato.

They turned and came in a compact group up the slope past the All Men House—the *falu*—and the light from an electric flash leapt out and swept over the brown figures seated on the terrace, licked up at the thatched sides and high, ship-like roof. Even under the impact of the light no man moved. They might have been bronze figures seated in the council place.

The Japanese disregarded them utterly. They seemed to know

precisely what their object was. The very compactness of their group was at once defensive and contemptuous. They disappeared past the canoe sheds up the main path of the village; and on the path they halted while the torch leapt from house to house seeking identification.

Still on the terrace no man moved. The voices of the Japanese were silent now, and for a brief moment the night was still again; it was as if the solid, formidable little body of men had somehow been swallowed up in the stillness and had ceased to be.

Then they heard a single voice, and once or twice they caught a familiar word. He was speaking in the tongue of Yap, and for the most part they could understand it; but what he was saying, they could not hear clearly enough to understand. They heard a woman's voice, protesting and then angry. They heard another woman's voice, and then a wild babble of protests and a child shrieking—and this time its voice was not silenced. Dogs began to bark in the village; in the huts that lay out beyond it dogs answered, and they could hear chickens and then the sudden, harsh squealing of a pig. More women's voices were joining in now. For a few moments there was a babel of sound.

It died slowly, with little upward protests and short gusts of anger. And then in another of the dark, forbidding silences they heard the thin wail of a girl's voice rising very high—strange, sad and hopeless. It cut off abruptly, even as the child's voice had ceased, and then it began again, lower but still full of a curious pain. And on the terrace of the *falu* the men sat quite still.

2

The survey ship lay five days in the lagoon. She was clearing up points left obscure in the running survey of the atoll the Japanese had made when they took over the islands from the Germans in the first war. The Japanese had used the lagoon since. The pearlers had come and gone because the few small patches had proved poor in quality and had been swiftly worked. The Japanese fishing boats used it for bonito and for bêche-de-mer, and the Nanyo ships, the ships of the great combine that administered the Mandate, came irregularly and at intervals to collect the islands' scanty copra that was all their trade. They used the northern anchorage.

Ulithi lagoon was made up of a great bow of reef that faced the north, and from it hung a narrowing loop of coral that trended towards the southwest for twelve miles and then changed its direction in a great swirling curve and headed southeast for another seven—a vast lagoon fringed with green islets strung together on the curving chain of the reef. The three main islands lay on the northern bow: Falalop, the biggest of them all, to the eastward; Asor at the beginning of the main reef; Mogmog in the centre of the bow. The rest of the islets on the bow were uninhabited. To the south Fassarai lay in the arc of the reef as it swept off to the southeast halfway along the chain. No other islands in the south had men upon them.

The anchorage that the Japanese used was inside Asor, sheltered superbly from the northeast trade. All the Japanese used the northern anchorage, even the bonito fishermen, and the northern islanders were exposed to their swift angers and to their slow, deliberate rapes. They had grown to acknowledge the harsh sexual necessities of the Japanese away from home. It was not as if they could have done anything about it. The blind, cold ruthlessness of the Japanese on Falalop had shown them long ago the impossibility of protest. Now they accepted inevitability, and on the nights when the Japanese ships came in they sat on the terrace of each island *falu,* waiting.

It was not cowardice. It was only a rationalisation of the old endurance of the islands, the philosophy of resignation. This was a thing as bitter and a thing as strong as the typhoon, the great wind that swept the islands. There was nothing that the men could do about it. Moreover, like the typhoon, men knew even in the darkness of the heart of the storm that the sun would shine again on the morrow. They had in them nothing of the depths

[4]

of European resentment against rape, for virginity had no currency amongst the islands. Yet still the villages quivered in the darkness on the nights when a Japanese ship lay to her cable in the northern anchorage.

Things were different in the south. Things were different on Fassarai.

CHAPTER II

≈≈≈≈≈≈≈≈≈≈≈≈≈≈≈≈≈≈≈≈≈≈≈≈≈≈≈

1

THOUGH the chair was deep and comfortable, he sat on the extreme edge of it, his body crouched forward and his chin resting on his thumbs. He sat so that he could see out of the great plate-glass windows that made the whole wall of the bar five hundred feet above the city. He sat as if he were waiting in the balcony of a theatre, in the front seats, in the moment of suspense before a play begins. It was dark too, though the bar behind him was tactfully lit; dark over the edge of the stonework beneath the glass, dark until far away he could see the lights of Berkeley running up into the hills to the northeast, and the lights of Oakland, and then the nearer lights of the Bay Bridge, and at last, closer below and around him, the blazing lights of San Francisco.

Alderman said: "You've seen those God-damned lights two-three times a week every week for the last six months. This is supposed to be a goodbye party. For God's sake look back at the bar once in a while and finish your drink! They're just lights."

Reis nodded without turning, and his reflection nodded back at him in the glass of the great window, very faint and ghostly against the lights. "The point is," he said quietly, "that I won't be here to see them tomorrow night. And I like them."

"You've been cursing San Francisco for the last six months," said Alderman, "and now you've discovered that you can't do without the lights."

"Not San Francisco. It's just being stuck here. I'd have cursed any place I'd been stuck at. When I moved here from Norfolk I thought I was on my way—and that was February. Now it's August. Six months is too long for any place with a war on."

"Not for me," said Alderman.

"I joined to fight a war," said Reis.

"Sure. So did I. I'd like to fight my war from Twelfth Street, Owensboro, but if I've got to leave home I'd settle for the Top of the Mark." He looked cynically round the bar.

Reis refused to be drawn. "Oh, I like the Top of the Mark myself!"

"That's big of you," Alderman said tolerantly. "You know I've been working out a plan for having the Navy Department take over the whole hotel as a rest camp—the Mark Hopkins Home for Tired Medics. All I want for the idea is an apartment about the fifteenth floor and the concession to pick the hat-check girls. You stay with me, Reis. I'll make you house physician."

"By this time tomorrow night, I'll be a hundred and fifty miles out to sea. You can have the Mark!"

"How d'you know you'll be a hundred and fifty miles out to sea?" asked Alderman derisively. "You're probably going to move down the coast to San Diego and rot there for another six months."

"No, I'm going to sea. I've bitched and howled and moaned for five months to get to sea, and now I'm going."

"Next stop Tokyo," said Alderman, his voice still derisive. "Did you ever see a movie called 'What Price Glory,' or were you too young?"

Reis disregarded the question, leaning forward again to look down over the nearer lights.

"You know," went on Alderman slowly, "you ought to have joined the infantry. The amount of chances a medic has for a Silver Star don't make a big stack." He paused for a moment. "Aw, hell, have it your own way. But the way I look at it is that a medic does his job any place so long as he does a job."

"Sure," answered Reis soothingly.

Alderman's nostrils tensed like those of a nervous horse. "You don't think highly of the suggestion?" he demanded.

"Listen," Reis answered, "I want to go to sea. I joined the navy . . ." He whistled the opening bars of the song. "You don't. If you were just sitting on your ass maybe I might think something, maybe not; but you've got a full-time job, and somebody's got to do that job. For myself I've got to move out. I don't know why, but you know what I feel about it. You've had to listen to my belly-aching long enough. I've got to get into a combat area or I don't square up—that's all there is to it. Mine's a highball." He held out his glass.

Alderman went over to the bar. When he came back Reis's forehead was still resting against the pane; but his eyes seemed to take in Alderman's reflection in the glass, and he asked, "Have you picked up any poop about where the ship's going or what she's doing?"

Alderman said: "I don't know. She was in at the docks a month ago, and she's here again. I didn't know that till an hour after your orders came. I thought maybe you had to go down to San Diego to join. Hell, she's just another attack transport! Don't you go working up any emotion about one of those damn' scows. I suppose you reckoned on a cruiser or at least a destroyer—sucker!"

"I don't care," said Reis doggedly. "I'm going to sea in her, and that's all that matters. She's an attack transport. They've got a job to do. They're built for it."

"Destroyers rate higher with the girls," suggested Alderman sardonically.

"I'll stick to my transport," said Reis. He held out his hand for the drink, and added with a brief impetuousness, "I'd go if she was a mud-dredger." He looked at his hand and noted the faint motion on the surface of the drink and said, "I believe I'm excited."

"You believe!" exclaimed Alderman scornfully. "I've seen kids—" He looked across Reis's shoulder, and his eyes lit up.

[8]

"Here come the girls," he said. "For Christ's sake stop emoting, and let's have us a goodbye party to end goodbye parties!"

2

Reis saw the unlovely bows of the ship high over the cab almost with a sense of shock. A moment later he was fumbling his way out opposite the gangway. He went on board and asked for the officer of the deck and explained himself. He was taken along to the executive officer and explained himself again. Neither the officer of the deck nor the exec seemed particularly interested. He felt faintly damped.

He was taken down to the untidy cabin he was to share with the navigator, who greeted him from his bunk without rising and, after greeting, said: "I hope you've got a better brand of pick-me-up than the last pill-roller. I need it. By God, I need it!"

"You too," said Reis unfeelingly. "Where were you last night?"

"We started at the St. Francis," answered the navigator. Reis had discovered that his name was Wombacher. "We started at the St. Francis and then we went to Fisherman's Wharf, and I think we took in the Top of the Mark on the way back."

"I was there," put in Reis.

"Pity it was so late," asserted Wombacher with a deep solicitude. "Pity it was so late or I'd have noticed both of you. Yeah," he said, exhausting all the breath in his lungs in one quick exhalation, "I was stinking!"

"Well, it was the last night in." Reis spoke indulgently. "I reckon it's fair enough." He made his voice elaborately casual, too casual. "Any idea where we're going?"

"Pearl," said the navigator laconically. He shut his eyes as if to discourage further conversation.

Reis went on unpacking, stowing his gear in the steel drawers and the wardrobe space that Wombacher had indicated. When he had finished, Wombacher seemed completely asleep. Reis looked round the cabin irresolutely for a moment and then found his way out to the deck.

The stream of people passing up and down the gangway had ceased. There was a knot of shore-side men at the foot of it, and there were men at the great mooring bollards. The deck along the rail was crowded, but he found a space and elbowed his way into it. The well deck aft was dense with enlisted men, and they crowded around the landing craft and the boats. It was clear that the ship was getting ready for sea. He watched the ritual with the eyes of ignorance, and presently he heard Wombacher's voice behind him say, "My God, I believe we really are going!"

Reis turned. "At ten-thirty," he said. "They told me ashore that that was sailing time."

"And you believed them?" asked Wombacher. "Most times they say that for three successive days and then sneak us out at nine o'clock at night. It's the only thing they can do to amuse themselves."

There was a sudden clamour of talk along the deck, and Reis, craning over, saw that the gangway had come away from the ship and was being lowered.

"Would you believe it?" said Wombacher. "Would you believe it? They've caught me again, and I had a date for tonight." He rubbed his forehead and his eyes, murmuring, "Down with drink. I'd better be getting up to the bridge. They can't sail without me. Take a good look at Alcatraz as we go by." He went away singing, to an old English setting, "Stone walls do not a prison make, Nor iron bars a cage," and the heads of a dozen Marine Corps officers along the rails turned and followed him.

They slipped out from the pier in a drizzle of rain and began to edge slowly down the water towards the huge overhanging bulk of the Bay Bridge. Reis found his way up to the boat deck. It was less crowded there. He watched the high sky line with the towering hotels on Nob Hill, the brisk water front, the piers and the ferry slips. Then quite suddenly they were under the vast inverted rainbow of the Golden Gate Bridge balanced on its roadway, and there was nothing ahead of them but the empty sea and far off on the edge of it a patrol boat hurrying; and Reis was conscious of an immensity of relief. He went below and asked his way to the exec's office.

The exec wore the three rings of a commander and a sour smile, but he was more human than he had been earlier, less harassed. He said: "You've no need to worry. We start with a clean bill—no leftovers. You'll have a few cases of clap develop in the next few days. The old doc used to reckon on eight between here and Pearl."

Reis seized the opportunity. He asked, "Where do we go from Pearl?"

"We don't," said the exec comfortably. "We come back—here."

"You mean this is not an operation?"

"It is not," answered the exec happily. "It's a ferry service. We're the Honolulu ferry. Peacetime we'd carry honeymoon couples. You'll be safe enough here, my lad, unless the Japs show up with a submarine, which ain't likely."

"Oh," said Reis vaguely, "it wasn't that . . ."

CHAPTER III

≈≈≈≈≈≈≈≈≈≈≈≈≈≈≈≈≈≈≈≈≈≈≈≈≈

THE terns wheeled intricately in the twilight of the Fassarai palms in a wild ecstasy of mating flight. They had the mystery of bats and the same effortless precision, the same tirelessness. They had been weaving their arabesques for an hour now. Sebastian came down the path from the north village, and they heard him though his feet were silent on the silent dust. Unhurried, their flight curved upwards through the blue gap between the palm crowns: they cleared it, and instantly became luminous in the sunlight. In the same moment they were caught by the wind that streamed across the palm tops, and swirled out across the lagoon in a meteor brilliance.

Sebastian did not see them, nor did he see Teresa. The child had sighted him first, and she slipped behind the bole of a palm while the tall gaunt man went silently past. Sebastian's temper was uncertain. He was a big man in the islands, a travelled man, with the aura of the outer world upon him. He had been "Japan side" —though actually it was no further than Takao in Formosa. What was more important, more miraculous, was that he had come back to Fassarai. Many men disappeared from the islands "Japan side," going off with the occasional fishing boats or with the pearlers who had worked the northern end of the lagoon, but none of them had come back. Sebastian, then, was the great man, the Ulysses.

When he was gone Teresa turned off the path through the fringing scrub to the white blaze of the beach. For no reason at all she walked down through the still water till it reached two-thirds of the way to her knees and stood quite motionless. The ripples threw amber loops of gold along the bottom of the coral sand, and out beyond her she could see a shoal of surgeonfish swaying together in the faint sweep of current like wheat in a summer breeze.

After a little she was aware of canoe sails up to the northward. The young men had gone north to Asor on some men's business with the Asor king—food business, she guessed, but without envy. She had eaten well this day. Her stomach was contented, and she was contented, and in the still air behind the breakwater of the island trees the world was utterly perfect.

Three small fish came away from the main shoal and swam round her feet. She watched them speculatively, but they did not touch her: they were suspicious. They and her feet seemed to dance as the ripple light crossed them, but the crinoline of her grass skirt hid from her eyes all but the outer jointing of her toes. She bent forward once to watch the fish, and the sudden letting in of light scattered them sharply to the distance of a yard. They came back. The terns were coming back too, or perhaps another pair, tacking against the wind, high up now and wary.

For no reason at all she grew tired of the water and walked slowly up the beach. She kicked through the coconut-husk trash that lined the tidemark and plunged suddenly into the cool of the shadow again. There were two worlds in the islands—the world of the sun and the world of the shadow. In the warm half-darkness she walked up to the path and, turning on it, began to walk down in a parody of Sebastian's pontifical stride.

Sebastian had passed on to the south village. He went down between the rows of huts and the discouraged-looking papaya trees without looking to either side of the path that went to the All Men House, walked along its cool side between the low-hanging thatch and the dark shades of the great canoe house beyond, and joined the small group of old men who sat in front of it. No greeting passed, nor did he seem to expect one. They sat on in the hot shade under the fringe of the low palms and the scrub along the beach. The sunlight returned to them from the water glitter in patches that played across the outward-leaning eaves of the All Men House and the stones of the square coral terrace in front of it. From time to time one of the men spat a great red stream of betel-nut and saliva; but there was no conversation.

Behind them in the village they could hear the occasional contented, sleepy clucking of a hen, and once somebody or something stirred the pigs and there was a swift crescendo and decrescendo of grunts and squealing. A bird, accustomed to the silence, ran up and down the edge of the overhanging eave that pointed straight to the face of the southwest trades. The All Men House was oriented like any Christian church, but not towards any problematical Jerusalem in the east, only towards the practical factor of the trade wind and the typhoon. The vast, overhanging, prow-like ends served to counterbalance the weight of the wind, to anchor the long house against the lifting force of it. It had a high Gothic air about it, but inside, with the enormous driftwood logs that formed its main supports, some of them three feet in diameter, it was more Romanesque than Gothic, a parody cathedral with no altar and the high rafters given over to nets and fishing spears.

They heard the voices from the canoes over the still inner water long before they saw the canoes themselves, but no one rose. In the canoes were the young men, and there was dignity to be considered. The leading boat came into view between a bush and a palm bole. It appeared suddenly in a pale flame of sunlit pandanus sail, the exquisitely shaped outrigger float high out of the water as she heeled to the down-striking force of the wind, heading up, close-hauled, for the beach. Then suddenly she ran into the calm lee of the palm trees; the outrigger dropped back with a splash to the water, and the canoe glided in swiftly and in absolute silence. The birdlike bow, high-reaching and eager, came up to the sand like a mallard taking off from the water, and the pure, swift lines of the canoe came up behind it. The sail came down rustling, the bird's wing at the clew violently agitated in a sudden eddy. The two youths who manned it slipped into the water and ran the canoe up with a quick splashing movement. They began to laugh easily and in unison, but there was nothing to give the reason for their laughter.

Astern of them another canoe came in by itself, and after that three—all of them larger than the first two—in a little fleet manoeuvring together. The men were all excited and gusty with laughter, and over them was spread something of the distinction of travel, of communication with the world, for Asor was the gateway to the outer world. A gateway that hardly ever opened, it was none the less a gate. They came back with their invisible travels bright on their oil-bright bodies, and the blue bands of tattoo, regular, symmetrical, and perfect, seemed to shine more vividly because of their voyaging.

They brought back eight tins of sardines, a gallon kerosene can open at the top and filled with fish oil that had spilled over the sides on the passage down, a small pile of taro, and a basket of lemons. They brought also a canoeful of mullet, for, while they were there, the Asor people had taken the chance to hold a mullet fishing. The fish came covered with palm fronds and splashed liberally with water, but already they looked limp.

The fishing was described with a high wealth of detail and, as it went on, with pantomime. Four of the boys and one old man got up together to show how the mullet had been driven at last into the circling nets. They all shouted together—the high, almost hysterical notes of the human being in sea water. One of the old men who had been seated beside Sebastian rose and joined in. There was an imaginary massacre of mullet on the soft sand beneath the terrace. The children had come from the village, attracted by the noise, and they joined in, shrieking, thumping with sticks on the sand to frighten the fish, calling a high warning note as an imaginary silver streak leapt clear of the circle to catch against the non-existent net. The thing became almost a dance. There was a rhythm in it, a central thread to the chanting.

And then it died suddenly; and in the quiet a voice said that Atienza, the Chamorro, who had come from Yap to take over Veldhausen's meagre store on Asor when the Japanese deported the emaciated German trader after the visit of the Nanyo ship eight months ago, was killing himself with liquor. Veldhausen had left his gin supply behind him in the swiftness of his going. The store was fading out, and rapidly. No new stuff had come since Veldhausen had left.

Not that they were really interested: the people of the atoll of Ulithi were a sufficient people, their lives perfectly attuned to the qualities of their surroundings. They had a craftsmanship justly and exquisitely balanced to their needs. Iron they liked, rough adzes and an occasional axe and knives, but only because these things were easier than the laborious tools of clam shell that needed regrinding after half a morning's work. They were useful because they preserved, they even weighted down, one side of the balanced lassitude that was their way of life. And because they needed little from the white man they had no need for trade except for the trade that was a social function, the excuse for visits, the reason for far-going adventuring; the trade in superb loincloths that the men of Mogmog, for instance, carried on with the kings of Yap when they took the yearly tribute down. The men of Mogmog were the tailors to the aristocracy of Micronesia; their patterns, their materials, were beyond comparison, and a voyage to Yap had all the mystery and the excitement that the world could furnish them.

The king had been inside the All Men House throughout the uproar and throughout the silence of the afternoon. He came out now, a man of medium height with the blue tattooing across his chest and belly in the outline of an old-fashioned bathing costume with loopholes for the arms and straps running across the shoulder to the elaborate patterning of the back. Down his arms there were long, broad stripes and a design that might have been a Maltese cross upon the biceps. There were broad bird symbols on his thighs. He was close-bearded, a thin, wiry growth of white hair straggling across his chin and halfway up the mandibles. His face was seamed, deep-lined, the face almost of a deep-browned countryman of Central Europe, hardly native save that the nose was broad across the base. The brows were heavy, and the forehead furrowed. He wore an irregular earring charm in the left ear.

For a moment he stood blinking in the sunlight after the dark

[16]

of the house. Then, looking at the fish with a slight scorn, he said abruptly, "Cook it!' and went inside again.

No one moved. This was only the preliminary order. The talk, endless, incessant as the surf on the reef outside, went on. Every possible aspect of every possible subject was threshed out to its last inessentials. The dusk came suddenly, no one noticing the sunset, and the talking went on.

The king had come out again and was sitting with the others on the *ailiuth*. He said again, pushing his foot over to the pile of fish, "Cook it!" and some of the boys scattered, whooping, into the darkness for driftwood.

Late in the warm darkness they ate fish and some of the taro and bananas from the straggling plantation that ran with the papayas through the village. It was not until the very last fragment of the food was eaten that José, the youngest of the boys, said across the murmur of conversation at the far end, "The Yellows are coming again."

Instantly there was a hush, complete and absolute, a hush so still that the night wind in the palm trees sounded almost staccato as the fronds moved across one another and the surf that no one had heard for many hours boomed in the dark distance. No one spoke at all for a long and pregnant minute.

Then Sebastian said contemptuously, "They come for the bonito."

From the darkness a voice said, "No."

Sebastian shrugged. "Or for the pearls. What does it matter? We will not tell them of the patch by Pigelelet."

And again a voice from the darkness said, "No."

"Who comes then?" asked the king.

"Warships," said the voice.

Again there was silence.

CHAPTER IV

≈≈≈≈≈≈≈≈≈≈≈≈≈≈≈≈≈≈≈≈≈≈≈≈≈≈≈≈≈≈

1

THE swift, warm pelt of the rain had stopped, and the deck was steaming. The cloud hid the whole summit of the mountains beyond the town, hid even the deep cleft of the pass of the Pali. Overside there were hot pools on the surface of the quay through which the enlisted men splashed, carrying bags and equipment towards the trucks. There seemed to be an immense number of them, infinitely more than could have been accommodated in the *Penasco*. Reis leant over the rail watching them. The officers had gone already, dispersing to the army barracks, the Marine Corps headquarters and the Air Corps fields according to their orders. Behind him the ship felt curiously empty. His two hospital cases had gone off in an ambulance first of all. The rest of the men on the sick call had minor troubles, nothing that could not be dealt with on board.

Wombacher came up behind him and said morosely: "Would you believe it? Only the bastards on the staff could think this one up. I told you you should have gone ashore to the hospital with the ambulance."

"I've seen a hospital," said Reis remotely.

"You ain't seen a hospital in Honolulu. The bastards—and I had a date tonight ashore at Lousy Chow's!"

"How come?"

"She's a cipherine: she sees all the signals. First night in she's ready for me eight o'clock to take her to Lousy Chow's. She always knows." Wombacher looked sourly at the men below him. "Did you ever break up an ants' nest when you were a kid?" His mind went back again to the grievance. "You've got to have special qualifications to be on the staff. You've got to have a sour belly and a mind like a sewer. Nobody else could have thought up this one—no shore leave, and ready for sea by five o'clock! Did you ever hear of anything like it?"

Reis said reasonably: "Well, perhaps it's urgent. Perhaps the men we're picking up have got to get over to New Georgia or some place fast."

"New Georgia, hell!" Wombacher held up a crumpled signal. "San Francisco for leave, and a lot of sods going back for courses. Ain't no hurry at all, just that some bastard on the staff's got a hangover." He became even more morose at that and added: "I won't have liquor enough to last me the passage back. Jesus, what a war!" He went grumbling along the almost empty deck.

Reis looked after him. Wombacher's wounds were superficial. He would bitch for a day or, this being an extra-large wound, perhaps for two days, and then forget about it. Somehow or other he would organise enough liquor around the ship to provide for the necessary evening sessions in the cabin during the passage back. Two days out he would have forgotten the delights of Honolulu in the anticipations of San Francisco.

Reis smiled wryly. His eight days in the *Penasco* had taught him that she was a ferry. She might be listed as an attack transport, but she was a reluctant dragon. It happened to some ships that way.

They sailed at six o'clock. The new passengers were wild with release, wild with joyful anticipation of the mainland, immensely eager and full of energy. There was a lot of liquor on board the first night.

Wombacher levied a contribution. He said to Reis late that night: "I've been this way before. These guys are so thirsty ain't nothing left after the first two nights unless you're careful. Me, I'm careful." He slapped a bottle of rye affectionately and slipped it into the wall safe.

Alderman was changing into his newest uniform. He said, "So you didn't even see Waikiki?"

"Only from the bridge through a pair of glasses," answered Reis.

"No hula-hula girls?"

"No hula-hula girls."

Alderman looked up quizzically. "No war?"

"Just the usual submarine alarms," said Reis, elaborately casual. "They have 'em every trip. Don't mean a thing."

"Still want to be a hero?"

Reis flushed angrily and then smiled. "Sure, I still want to be a hero. I thought for a minute when we got the poop about leaving the same evening that we were going to push straight over to the Solomons or some place. I might have known! They made a landing at Vella Lavella while we were on the way back. I'd got the scuttle-butt about that from the Marine Corps boys."

"And now?" asked Alderman.

Reis shrugged his shoulders. "My pharmacist's mate, first class, says we leave Thursday for Pearl again. He seems to know."

"And the exec?"

"Oh, he wouldn't know!" replied Reis. "He's past caring." He looked up and met Alderman's eyes. "It's all right. She was built for an attack transport, and she'll work as an attack transport. Vella Lavella was a little show. They've got to put on a big show soon, and the way I figure it is that when they do they'll need every goddam attack transport they've got. There's plenty of other ships can do this ferry job."

"What's she like?"

"Like any other attack transport," answered Reis maliciously.

"No, what's the crowd like?"

"You'll meet Wombacher later," said Reis. "He'll probably be stinking. He likes it that way. Oh, they're all right! Just an average sort of bunch. The exec is a crusty old bastard half the time, and half the time he's honey. I've been working on his liver. Gin. Captain's a bit of a bastard, but he's the sort of bastard you can get on with. Most of the officers haven't got enough to do."

"And you?"

"I wouldn't have had anything to do the passage out if it hadn't been for an appendectomy, and a guy who fell off a landing craft and bust his femur. Just enough to keep my hand in— that and the exec's liver. It's not a bad life so far as it goes." Again he looked at Alderman. "It's all right. I've got a hunch that I'll get to where I want to go in her, and I'm not worrying. I'd have gone crazy in this town. At least I'm at sea."

3

The last of the procession of Corps men went out of the office and shut the door behind him.

Alderman put down his pen. "They're a helpless lot of bastards," he said. "Let's go get us a cup of coffee. You don't really want all that stuff this morning."

"I do," Reis snapped. "What the hell d'you think I came ashore for?"

"Just to come ashore," asserted Alderman, with an air of unbelief.

"No, I want it all right, and it'll take until next trip to get it out of the supply depot. I've a hunch that we're going out early. This is a different crowd we picked up this time—one unit, not just a bunch of mavericks."

"You mean—"

Reis threw up his hands. "I don't mean anything, but it wouldn't surprise me if we were going on beyond Pearl this time."

Alderman snorted. "Bet you five dollars!"

They walked down the long green and white corridor towards coffee. Two nurses passed them, and then a third. Two Corps men came up wheeling a stretcher towards the elevators. The place was busy and pleasantly cheerful.

They were drinking their coffee when a Red Cross girl came in. She waved airily across the room and called out: " 'Lo, Doc Reis. I haven't seen you around."

"You see," Alderman's voice was scornful, "you go off to the war, and nobody damn' well knows. There's no future in it."

Reis chuckled.

Fanshawe from the Ear, Nose, and Throat came in, and another doctor whom Reis did not know. They talked ships for a moment out of courtesy to Reis, and then they talked parties and hard-court tennis and the possibilities of winter sports. No one mentioned the war. It was all very friendly and very cheerful, and Reis felt strangely detached from it and a little superior. It was as if this single voyage to sea had put him beyond the reach of these men, as if he had acquired stature. Then Fanshawe began to talk of a sinus operation, and he felt suddenly professionally humble again.

Fanshawe was dealing malignantly with another doctor's diagnosis when a Corps man came into the room. His voice unaccountably restricted to the nasal levels of a bellhop's, he asked: "Is there a Dr. Reis in here? There's a call for him."

Reis went over to the telephone in the corner of the room. The talk hushed for a brief moment as he made the connection, and they heard him say, "Christ!" and then very curtly and abruptly, "I'll be down." He came back to the group and said, "I've got to beat it."

Alderman looked at him with his eyebrows climbing up towards his hair line. "Nimitz sent for you?" he demanded.

"Cut it out, and call me a cab!" Reis growled. "I guess I can finish my coffee."

"I'll run you down," said Alderman. He nodded to Fanshawe. "Just tell them to suspend all work in the hospital till I return," he said. "At all costs Lieutenant Reis must be there."

"One of these days," Reis murmured mildly, "I'm going to fetch you a crack. Go get your jacket on. I'm in a hurry."

As they drove down he said quietly: "I told you I'd a hunch something like this might happen. The exec knew I was coming here." He was oddly happy with again the same young, almost boyish excitement that he had felt on the first drive down to the ship.

He found Wombacher in the cabin. "What's the score?" he asked.

"Sailing noon," answered Wombacher from the depths of his bunk.

"Why?"

"The last party can't make it before Thursday, and they want the berth," Wombacher informed him uninterestedly, "so they shoot us out at noon. Those guys on the staff wait till they find out about my dates every trip."

"If we're going without some of the party—" began Reis speculatively. Then, changing his mind, he said, "Where are we going?"

"Pearl," snapped Wombacher. "Where the hell did you think?"

CHAPTER V

〜〜〜〜〜〜〜〜〜〜〜〜〜〜〜〜〜〜〜〜

1

THE enormous high-piled cumulus rose and re-formed as the Japanese watched, with a speed that was beyond believing. When they saw the islands beneath it they were like a dark pencil line to mark the bottom of a pattern, a hard bar of palms across the horizon. As they approached, the bar grew deeper until it was underscored with the white of the surf.

The rain came long before they reached the northeast passage, transmuting the sea from lapis-lazuli to a slate and ugly grey. It lasted for six minutes, and then the air beyond was clear and the sea lapis again.

The Nanyo ship led in for the passage. She was angular and ugly like all small Japanese vessels, with an exaggerated superstructure. Normally she worked the islands from Tobi to Eniwetok, a combination of trader and tax-collector, political visitor and floating home for the Kempeitai, the Japanese secret police. She was acting as pilot now to the destroyer *Hinoki* that followed astern of her and the elderly transport that followed the *Hinoki*. They came up to the north of Gielap and headed in towards Falalop, making for the Dowarugui channel and the anchorage inside Asor.

There were no canoes on the fishing grounds. They had scattered for their islands when the first smoke of the *Hakodate Maru* was seen above the horizon. There was no one on the beaches. There were only eyes. The islands might have been desolate or at best inhabited only by the dozen of cormorants that flew, hard-winged, across the bows of the *Hakodate Maru* as she turned up to anchor. The water here was no longer blue but green, green in a hundred superb shades and nuances of light.

The three ships anchored, and a motor boat dropped from the davits of the *Hakodate Maru* and presently, loaded, put in to the beach. Atienza met it alone upon the beach. He was spy as well as deputy storekeeper for the Nanyo, the enormous politico-trading outfit that administered the Japanese mandate. Today he wore trousers and a shirt to mark his appreciation of the solemnities. The first two Japanese who came ashore from the boat ignored him. It was as though he did not exist. They went up the beach sniffing noisily, and one of them cleared his throat and spat. The third man barked at him in Japanese, and Atienza cringed. He waited until the spate subsided a little, and then he explained that the people of the island were mostly over at Mogmog at a feast— the young people, that was; the old people were over on the seaward side. He could think of no good reason why they should be over on the seaward side and offered no explanation.

The Kempeitai officer barked again, "How did they know we were coming?"

Atienza had an answer to that one. He explained that the king's son from Fais had come over two days before with the news —come over by canoe.

The Kempeitai man shrugged his shoulders and said, without turning his head, to the man behind him, "Must have slipped out on the first night we were there." Then to Atienza he said, "No canoes will leave these islands from now on—nothing outside the lagoon, nothing to Yap or to Fais. Is that understood?"

Atienza nodded.

The Japanese quickened his step and caught up with the two naval officers in front of him. He said, with the inevitable salutations: "Most of the people have gone from here, sir. They knew we were coming. The storekeeper says they are on Mogmog Island, five miles across the head of the lagoon. Do you wish to go across to it?"

Neither of the officers answered him, and he fell back, faintly discouraged. They walked on until they reached the tin-roofed store with its heavy over-roofing of pandanus leaf. There were no people about the store, no loungers. They sat down on the verandah, and the junior one said, "Get the rest of the people here quickly!"

Again the torrent of words fell on Atienza. With half a dozen Japanese sailors behind him he headed off through the palms, hurrying. He continued to hurry. The old people were at the furthest end of the island, and Asor is a shade under a mile in length. Olimarao, the Asor king, brought his people back at a pace calculated to achieve a precise balance between the delay that would make the Japanese seriously angry and the shortest time that it would be necessary to endure their presence. He miscalculated slightly. The Kempeitai man was in a furious temper when the first of them reached the store. For three-quarters of an hour the three of them had sat, not speaking, on the hot verandah.

When the old people had come in he harangued them from the head of the steps. The time of the old nonsense was past, he said. From today the Japanese would live on the island. They would put up buildings and wireless masts. The people of Asor and the nearer islands would provide the labour—at once. He would hold the king responsible. No canoes would leave the lagoon. Fishing could go on as usual, but nothing was to go outside to Fais, to Yap and, above all, to Guam—nothing. They would provide women for the men who would live ashore, and coconuts and fish as they demanded them. The rest of their food, the Japanese would provide themselves. Labour, women, food, and no canoes outside the reef: again and again he hammered the points in. The face of the Asor king showed no emotion whatever, only a sort of benign understanding as each point was made.

Suddenly the Kempeitai man gave up. He dismissed the gathering contemptuously and turned again to the naval officers, who had not moved. Bowing, he said, "Is it your wish to go to Mogmog?"

The senior of them, who wore the stripes of a *chu-sa*, a commander in the Japanese Navy, said: "It may be that the captain of the *Hinoki* will wish his men to go ashore there tonight for recreation. It is necessary now to decide the site for the meteorological post, somewhere away from this filth."

He waved his hand, and the flies that he had borne indifferently for an hour rose like a cloud. They moved off down the smooth island path.

Asor was highest towards the eastern end. The coral build-up had been greater here against the spray of the northeast trade. Two petty officers had come with them, and they broke into a sudden solid activity as the site was decided upon. It would be necessary to clear a hundred or so palms. The wood would be used for the shelters, and the leaves also. The Asor king protested amiably. They were good bearing palms, he said. The naval officers appeared not to hear the protest, as if it were too far beneath their dignity. The Kempeitai man stiffened and drew in his breath, but not in politeness. Philosophically the old man fell silent again.

By the time they came back to the store there was an accumulated pile of equipment and material in front of it. A chain of men was busy working up and down between the store and the beach, carrying gear inshore. The meteorological station and a small wireless communicating post were to be set up to provide weather news for the aircraft on Yap and Palau on the one hand and Woleai and Truk on the other. It would have a guard of six marines. They had decided not to garrison the island. There were no advantages save anchorage, and the anchorages at Palau, at Yap, and at Truk were better. It was not possible to garrison every island.

Stiffly the two officers sat on the verandah again enduring the flies until the stream of gear diminished. Eight men came up the path staggering under the weight of a small petrol motor on bamboo poles, the motor for the generator of the radio set. Already they could hear the sound of axes coming dully from the far end of the island.

When it had passed they rose and went down to the beach, and the Kempeitai man followed them repeating over and over again to Atienza and the Asor king, "Remember, labour, women, fish, and coconuts," as if it were in some strange way a litany.

As they got into the boat the Asor king asked softly, "When will the priest come?"

"Never," said the Kempeitai man in a sudden vicious spurt of anger, and put his foot on the gunwale.

2

The cheap bell that had been cast in Barcelona, and that had too much iron in it for an honest note, sounded irregularly amongst the palms. Each of the four islands had a bell. Asor's was the oldest. It had come from Lima in Peru with the Capuchins to Luzon, and when they spread from there to Samar it had gone to the old church on Guiuan and from there it had gone, when the new church was built, with the missions to a score of islands; and because the missions had stopped it rested on Asor. It had a better note than this bell on Fassarai. The people had a special regard for it. At first they had rung it at all hours of the day and held brief services in the palm-thatched church with the open sides; but the habit was not seemly, and they had been broken of it.

Theirs was a tolerant Christianity, a Catholicism without gall in it. The early fathers had come to the islands through a long generation of the tropics, their zeal unblunted perhaps, but its corners, its sharp edges, softened; and they had come seldom. It was seven years now since a priest had passed through the group on his way to Fais, coming by canoe; bearded, enormous, and humorous, the undoubted left hand of God, but kindly. So their Catholicism was wound through and patterned with old custom, shaped and reshaped by tribal memories. The fathers had a wide tolerance, so that the women knelt bare-breasted to take the Host, bareheaded even in defiance of St. Paul, and the grass skirts rustled through the prayers.

Skillfully and with human understanding the fathers had

woven in the tribal taboos to make a complex of Christianity that would endure through their absences. The kings held the services through the years. They married, they baptised, and they buried; and the fathers married, baptised, and said a general prayer above the graveyards when they came again. They had a simple ritual of melodic prayer and singing that was more social than religious, and that was become as much a part of the island life as the ritual of giving the first fish back to the gods of the sea and the rituals of the women at their monthly periods—a loose, warm intermingling of paganism and of Christianity that was settled now into the tradition of the palm trees and the surf, and that had the air of having been there always.

Atienza took the services now on Asor. With a voluble enthusiasm he had filched the place of the king. He was an aggressive man, but he led a new energy in the singing, and if he imposed something of the purer ceremonial of San Mateo of Colonia into the services that were their own tradition, at least he brought a new music also.

The bell of Fassarai tolled on. Nobody stirred. It was a convention that one waited for a couple of bells before setting out for the church. There was a certain schism between the other three inhabited islands—Falalop, Mogmog, and Fassarai—and Asor in this matter of new practices. It was said that on Asor, Atienza even demanded that they should come to church promptly on the second bell.

Teresa took no notice of the bells. She was making a fresh wreath for her father's head, using the yellow-hearted white flowers of the *pomaria*. The size of it and the shape of it were dictated by an unshakable tradition, and the weaving had a ritual significance almost as old perhaps as Christianity. From time to time she licked her fingers for the sweet honeydew so that she could get it before the hungry flies. The smallest pig of the litter, too full of food, pushed stertorously against her thighs and rumbled intestinally. She could hear the men talking in the shadow of the king's house. They were talking of the Yellows who had gone out the previous evening just on the edge of sunset, having completed the siting of the post within a single afternoon. So far there was no news from Asor, and the men speculated only. This was something different from the ordinary visits of the Japanese trading steamer that collected copra irregularly from the store at Asor, different from the fishing luggers that came there for the bonito fishing or from the pearlers who had grown discouraged over the wide floor of the lagoon, uninformed of the patch of enormous pearl shell by Pigelelet and the other and lesser patch below Songetigetsh.

The islands had known the Japanese for fifty years now as occasional traders in the last of the Spanish Empire, as fishermen and aggressive trading competitors in the brief domination of the Germans, as overlords since the beginning of the mandate in 1918. They liked them least of three dominant races, but they had an indrawn, inward-keeping philosophy that accepted them as it had accepted the others, making due allowances for their sexual characteristics even as it had made allowances for the sexual characteristics of the others.

Teresa finished the wreath and took it humbly to her father, kicking the small pig with indifference as she went. With the innate politeness of the island children she handed the wreath to him with both hands, bowing slightly. Then she backed away, watching him critically as he put it on, giggled for no reason at all, and headed off towards the church.

The bell of Fassarai began to ring again. Over on Asor the service was already coming to an end. There they were singing the final hymn, Atienza's voice leading the singing with great booming organ notes. It ended, and the last complicated amen ended also; and Atienza, standing before the altar made and polished out of hardwood driftwood logs, said: "And there is yet another great sin. Last night there were not enough women for the Japanese. Six more women will go to the camp this afternoon. Choose them among yourselves."

Asor sent over to Mogmog for three more women for the Japanese. They called them a complicated name which meant "women who would have been slaves but for the priests," and they found three more in the village. Another canoe went south to Fassarai to tell them the news and to carry the ukase about going outside the reef. The reef was interpreted to include the outer triangle that stretched from Asor to Gielap and back to Feitabul as well as the uncertain shallows of the lagoon.

The young men had not been at church. They were cutting palms under the quick-fire directions of the Japanese petty officers. The site was almost cleared, and three considerable huts were beginning to rise. The boys piled the nuts for the Japanese in the shade and stripped palm fronds for the thatching. The Japanese worked with them, but with a surer energy. There was no undue harshness save when the Kanakas drifted off to rest after the island custom, and even then they understood the Japanese mode sufficiently not to resent it. Broadly that was the pattern of the occupation.

With immense energy the meteorological station was completed in forty-eight hours, the instruments set up, and the recordings begun. The radio masts went up erected between derricks of still-rooted palm trees within the same time, but the installation of the equipment took a little longer. None the less the first signals went through to Yap on the third day.

Thereafter Ulithi settled into a quiet routine, punctuated by nothing more than an occasional rape; nor could the rapes be always described as punctuations. There was a certain continuity of cooperation. The young men fished, and the canoes went soaring like low-flying birds in and out of the coral heads between the passages. The Japanese appetite for fish was insatiable. The stench of their fish curing was incessant. Otherwise with rice and coconuts their appetites were not inordinate. There was even a certain amity within the circle of the surf.

Gonorrhea spread slowly across Asor village and jumped the water barrier to Mogmog through means into which no one enquired. Oddly enough there were no pregnancies from the time of the Japanese coming, even before the gonorrhea took its effect.

Vaguely the conception of war took hold of the native mind. The Japanese were fighting somebody. The people of Ulithi had a tradition of war, but it was obscured in an old and half-forgotten past. There had been no war for most of two generations except for the intervillage conflicts on Yap, and those were too far removed from them to be of account. This war was something different. The Japanese were fighting alongside the Germans. For many months the assumption along the islands was that they must be fighting the Spaniards, for those were the third of the white peoples whom the islands knew. Atienza told them over and over again that they were fighting the Americanos, but only those who had been to Guam had any real conception of Americanos. The rest of the islands preferred to consider them as Spaniards of another sort since it saved the trouble of thinking. They understood that it was a war between ships and between the immense birds that flew in the sky under the control of man.

Six weeks after the installation of the meteorological station a Mitsubishi float plane landed on the anchorage inside Asor. Canoes from each of the four islands raced out before the spray of the landing had died away. The nearest ones from Asor were driven off first by shouting and then by shots in the water that ricochetted past the bows of the leading canoe. They fled hurriedly to a safer distance and gathered, sails down, in a curious knot to discuss the phenomenon. They were not particularly worried by the shooting, which was natural enough from a thing so outlandish. Atienza came out with the chief petty officer who was in command of the detachment, using one of the bigger canoes, and picked up from the seaplane a *sho-i*, an acting sublieutenant. The command of Ulithi was upgraded. His arrival made no difference to the island life. Except in so far as a faint increase in acerbity was observable, the pattern in three islands was unchanged. In the fourth it was no more than a grafting upon an ancient vine.

But, curiously, after this day aircraft began to appear frequently over the atoll—long-distance planes on reconnaissance flights, training planes out from Yap. Twice a month or so float planes would come in, and fishing vessels and small nondescript patrol vessels began to use the harbour in greater numbers. The men came ashore occasionally after women, but there was no great trouble. The main pattern was undisturbed.

This was March of 1944.

CHAPTER VI

≈≈≈≈≈≈≈≈≈≈≈≈≈≈≈≈≈≈≈≈≈≈≈≈≈≈≈≈≈≈

1

THE exec looked at Reis sourly. "I expect this means they've got a job for you."

"I know," Reis agreed, "but if the ship's going on this time . . ."

"You've been bitching for three months about getting a job to take you up to the war zone," said the exec evenly. "The things you've said about the Honolulu ferry!" He grinned with a quick friendliness. "Hell, sometimes even the staff takes one at one's word!"

"I know, but if the ship's going up there I've got the sort of job I want. I'd like to stay with her."

"You've got to report at Cincpac this A.M.," said the exec definitely, and Reis looked round the untidy little office as if it were a trap. The exec began to laugh. "You'll learn; you'll learn the hard way. This war ain't being run for anybody's convenience —except maybe MacArthur's. Easiest thing is to do what they tell you to do and ask no questions. You can get combat fatigue just as quick by kicking against the higher brass as any other way. You'd better go pack your bags." He looked down again at the signal on his desk. "You'll get your travel orders at Cincpac."

"And if the ship does go on west?"

"She goes on west," said the exec. "Ain't nothing you can do about it. Me, I'll have to find out if the new doc knows more about livers than you do."

Reis went back to his cabin with his forehead wrinkled. Wombacher was on his back in his bunk, and Reis said, "D'you know the first time I came on board you were lying in your goddam sack and now you're lying in your goddam sack?"

"What of it?" asked Wombacher.

"Well, this is the last time I'm on board."

Wombacher sat up so rapidly that he hit the underside of the bunk above him. "You don't say! What's happened?"

"Got to report for orders at Cincpac."

"What the hell? Who told you?"

"The exec," Reis answered. "It's official. There's a new doc coming on board this afternoon, and as far as I can make out the ship's going west."

"Sure we're going west," said Wombacher. "I've been working over the charts for the Gilberts and the Marshalls and the Marianas. Way I figure it is that Nimitz has got to go in sometime in the centre. Island hopping's all right in the south, but we got to make a move sometime in the middle. I been talking to the Marines. Maybe we'll take back Guam sometime, or maybe we'll start at Wake."

Reis shook his head. "It all sounds like it adds up," he agreed, "and I've got to go ashore. Jesus, did you ever hear anything like it! I've got to pack."

Wombacher listened to his complaints. After a while he interjected: "You can't gripe. You've been at 'em every time we've been in for a job that will take you on. You can't blame them if they take you up on it now."

Reis was rueful. "I know, but I got so goddam sick of the ferry business."

"It don't pay to bother the high brass," said Wombacher sententiously. "Now and then it wakes up. Me, I'm like Brer Rabbit. I lie low and say nuffin. If we got to go in with an attack, we go in with an attack. If we don't, we don't. Ain't nothing I can do about it."

"That's what the exec said."

[35]

"Jesus, I better find me a new angle," Wombacher sank back on the pillow. "I can't run in double harness with that old bastard." Reis laughed and went on with his packing.

2

The terraced buildings of Cincpac headquarters on the hill above Pearl Harbor were settled-looking and curiously quiet. Reis found his way without difficulty to the Personnel office.

The young ensign at the desk turned over a file. He said in a slow, maddening drawl: "Reis—Reis—Reis, John W. You're going to the Submarine Service rest camp. They lost one of their regular docs week before last in an automobile crash. He was a nice guy. I knew him."

Reis put his hands on the desk and leant forward. "But I wanted—"

The ensign looked up dispassionately. It was clear that he had heard protests before. He took out a wad of papers. "Here's your orders. They're all made out."

Reis shook his head as if to free himself from something that hung close. There was no point in arguing with this boy. "Where is the rest camp?" he asked.

"Waikiki. Some guys get all the luck!"

"But . . ." Again Reis recognised the futility of argument. "You mean—"

"The Royal Hawaiian Hotel," said the ensign. "What more can you ask? Three hundred bedrooms, hot and cold running women in every bedroom. You docs always get the good jobs."

Reis shrugged his shoulders and, oppressed by a sudden futility, asked only, "What do I do about transport?"

"Oh, I'll fix that!" The ensign nodded, relieved at avoiding what had looked like being an argument. He picked up a phone. "Never get the number first time," he said cheerfully.

[*36*]

The long, cool room was quietly lovely. Almost all the southern face of it was one tremendous window that looked out past the great koa tree to a low terrace wall and past that to the sea. They were high over the water here, but the sound of the surf with the south wind blowing came up ceaselessly.

Mrs. Deering came in with the cocktail shaker, and Reis and the other man rose. She said: "Sit down, it's all done—or would you rather sit outside? It's dry now."

Willard—he was the captain of a submarine—said: "I'd like to stay here. I haven't been in a room like this since I left Boston. Your silver is wonderful!"

Reis's eyes followed his over the dark wood of the tables as Mrs. Deering said: "It's English. It came from my husband's family. I love it."

"My mother had a few good pieces," said Willard, and stopped. He seemed to be reaching back into some undefinable past, something that was almost forgotten, obliterated under the press of war.

Mrs. Deering said: "Look at anything you like. That's the best over there." She pointed to a superb pair of candlesticks. "They've got the London mark for 1730, if dates interest you." She turned to Reis. "Do you like silver?"

"I like it," he answered candidly, "but I don't know anything about it. We could never manage much in the line of silver in our home." He checked himself, realising suddenly that there was almost a hostile note in his words. "But I've always liked good things—books, china . . . I haven't had time to learn much yet."

Mrs. Deering reached over and filled his glass again as if she thought that liquor was the quickest sympathy. "How long have you been at the rest camp?" she asked.

"Not three weeks," Reis answered.

And Willard, looking up from the candlesticks, said, "Freshman!"

"You don't like it?"

Reis realised that this woman was very quick, and he told her with a swift honesty: "I'd like it if there wasn't a war on. There's nothing much for me to do there."

"Just what do you do?"

"Sit in the office for the morning sick call."

But Mrs. Deering wanted more. "What do you get?" she asked.

"Requests for hangover remedies." Reis's voice was acid. "If they get more than a stomach-ache I send them on to the hospital. A Red Cross girl could do it!"

"Better," Willard interjected cheerfully. He came over and sat on the edge of a table. "His trouble is that he still thinks he's an individual. All individuals ceased to exist on December 7th."

"Surely not," suggested Mrs. Deering lightly.

"Surely yes," said Willard. "You try to argue with the Personnel department! He's just beginning to find out that he's a cog in a machine, and he doesn't like it."

Reis smiled wryly.

"Tell!" demanded Mrs. Deering.

"I've been trying to get a posting to a combat area ever since I finished with indoctrination." He looked round the room and said with a sudden little realisation of humour: "And look where I am—at the Royal Hawaiian! It's a combat area all right!"

"And your ship?" asked Mrs. Deering.

"She went on to the landing in the Gilberts."

"The Navy Bureau," explained Willard, "goes in for irony in a big way." He turned to Reis. "You've got about the slickest job of the war in the Pacific. I know men who'd pay a fortune to buy you out."

"I'd sell," said Reis briefly. He eyed the koa tree for a moment as if he expected to find in the foliage some solution of his trouble. Then he went on, "I'm young, I'm healthy, I've got no family ties; I may not be a hell of a good doctor, but I'm no worse than most—I ought to be in a combat area. There must be lots of guys up in the islands that ought to come back. Why can't they send me up? There must be lots of men in ships that haven't been out for a year—two years, some of them. That's what a job like this at a rest camp's for. I don't need a rest."

"From all I've heard of the Royal Hawaiian you won't get one there," said Mrs. Deering grimly.

Willard agreed cheerfully. "It cuts two ways. Either you're knifing the other fellow to get the girl you want, or you're beating off the girls you don't want with a club. Submarine officers are *so* romantic." There was no malice in his satire.

Reis said: "Romantic is one word for it. What they need in my place is a psychiatrist. Most of you guys are nuts."

"That's the first qualification," admitted Willard.

Mrs. Deering turned to Reis again. "My brother was wounded in North Africa," she said, apparently at a tangent, "at a place called Station Sened. I'd never heard of it before." Reis shook his head in agreement. "He said he'd never seen anything finer in his life than a jeep coming up through the firing with a Red Cross flag about a yard wide on a staff on the front of it." Reis looked at her with a quick, deep interest, and after a moment she finished, "I don't think he would have come out otherwise." In the brief story he seemed to sense all the sympathy that she had left unsaid, all the agreement that she had with his viewpoint.

Deering came in five minutes later, and the talk became general. When they left she addressed Willard. "Bring him with you next time you come." She seemed to take it for granted that Willard would come again.

"I'll try, ma'am," said Willard, "but he's not sociable."

Reis smiled. "I'd like to come."

"Then come any time you want to. You needn't bother to call me. If I'm not here you can just sit around and be quiet—and you'll come for Thanksgiving anyway."

She watched them leave and went back to her husband. "If that boy doesn't get to a combat area soon he's going to do something silly," she said.

"He'll soften down," answered Deering. "Wait till the island gets him!"

CHAPTER VII

THE village children were building a small *falu,* a small All Men House, in the shallow cove at the south end of the island. They worked in spurts of immense energy, lashing driftwood together in a noisy concentration with tremendous coming and going between the seaward beach and the lagoon beach; the girls carrying wood; the boys going up the palms for new fronds, choice, small young ones to make the perfect thatch.

It all came to nothing. Halfway through they turned it into a fishing expedition instead, splashing out, shouting, into the shallows. The elder girls sat behind in the shadow and discussed the proceedings on Asor with a certain regret that they were not old enough to participate. Teresa listened respectfully because the other girls were at least near to being old enough. They had none of them dropped the grass skirt for the lava-lava. Four girls from the island had been up to Asor by canoe three nights before—that was already known throughout the village. Atienza was preaching the doctrine of *force majeure*—an acquiescence to accepted authority. He had explained that the fathers would understand everything and would approve a proper bowing before the overlords. The *sho-i* had a considerable appetite for girls and a great catholicity of taste. Teresa ran her fingers through the strands of the skirt, combing out the tangles, and considered the possibilities of going up to Asor herself against the regretful background of her age.

Sebastian and four others of the older men had been working on a canoe. For four days they had debated the desirability of putting in a new plank where the top-side curved away from the solid dug-out bottom to replace one that had split and warped in the hot sun. They were still in the betel-nut-chewing stage. It might, with fortune, last for another two days. It never paid to rush the work on a canoe. A rat, emboldened by a longer silence than ordinary, came out from a pile of undergrowth, watched them with a sardonic gleam in its eye, and went back when the scarlet betel spittle plopped on the dust near him.

In the village the women were cooking, and thin smoke from the coconut-shell and fibre fire drifted up through the silence between the palms to be caught by the oversurge of the wind and snatched away.

They heard the drone of the aircraft first at the canoe, for in the village there was the noise of the chickens and the pigs and the buzzing of the flies about the cooking; and at the cove small boys had come out of the shallows again and were torturing a young land crab that they had captured. They were going to cook it shortly and offer it as a sacrifice to the Virgin Mary.

Even when the women and the children heard it only the small boys looked up into the sky. Aircraft were common enough. The drone grew heavier and it was patent that this was not a single-engined plane. They assumed only that it was one of the big four-engined aeroplanes that came past them occasionally on reconnaissance flights. But gradually the drone grew heavier and then, quite suddenly and without warning, they heard a high, thin whistle that grew in intensity, in urgency, and with an appalling speed. And even as it ripped across the silence underneath the palms there was a noise out of all men's knowledge. It was followed instantly by another and another and another—a brutal thundering that filled the air with sound even as the explosion filled it with fragments of palm tree and blown sand, and with smoke and a foul and acrid stench.

Eight bombs dropped in a stick straight up the spine of the island; and then they heard the drone of the plane diminishing across their shattered ears, and instantly the steady roar of the reef came back to take its place. Over it they could hear to the northward the intermingling roar of planes as the aircraft attacked the three Japanese fishing boats that lay in the harbour, and then they heard the rumble of bombs in the distance.

Curiously the children did not scream, but they came drifting back through the palm boles and the settling smoke, furtive and ghostlike. No one was hurt, and in the afternoon the children picked up the green nuts that had been brought down and looked admiringly at the splintered boles of the broken palms. One of them found a fragment of bomb, and immediately a vast treasure hunt for iron developed. By nightfall it had become a game, and Teresa ran down the path making a high-crescendoed "Whee-ee!" while Mau, the king's son, came in at the end of it with a pent-up explosion of breath that almost burst his lungs.

The women were cooking again.

That night in the *falu* the men drank a vast amount of palm liquor, for great occasions called for great drinks.

The king himself stayed sober or almost sober, save that he kept saying over and over in a plaintive threnody: "If they shoot to practice, they should tell us. They might have hurt somebody and they have killed hundreds of the best palms, the very best palms—certainly the best palms."

They assumed, of course, that it was the Japanese. There was no reason even to question it. But on the next day when, according to island custom, they went up to Mogmog and to Asor to discuss the implications of this thing and to exchange sensations, they met a frightened and angry Atienza. The bombers had concentrated on Asor and on the anchorage. The two Japanese fishing luggers lying off the landing beach had been sunk: the one by a direct hit from a bomb that had disintegrated her and killed the whole of her crew; the other riddled by cannon fire in a strafing run to sink an hour later in a slime of Diesel oil and foul bilge that poisoned the lagoon for half a mile.

Atienza had no threnody. He had only an angry exclamation with which he punctuated every sentence, "Damn' Americano!"

Curiously enough no one on Asor had been hurt, though three times the American planes had laced the village with light bombs and though they had blown two of the Japanese huts to fragments. The Japanese themselves were excited, angry, and voluble. The air was full of ringing axe strokes as new palms were cut to make good the damage, and fuller still of cursing and objurgation. The Japanese are a polite people only when custom demands politeness. The young men from Fassarai were pressed into service on the rebuilding—the rebuilding of the Japanese encampment, not the village: that could wait.

That night in the big *falu* on Asor there was no toddy drinking; but Atienza came in foully drunk on brandy, and the slave girls were called in.

Within three weeks the bombing had receded into the past of legend. It had become a date mark so that men measured a catch of fish as fifteen days after the bombing and a girl child born within the week was called by the onomatopoeic word for the shriek of the typhoon in addition to being called Maria. The children still played the noise of falling bombs, but the game was growing old.

The pattern of island life was whole again, and the war was a thing talked of only in the *falu* or on the terrace outside in the intervals of brushing off the ever-hungry mosquitoes. Fishing, canoe building, island visiting, betel nuts, and palm toddy—the men's cycle was again as it had been in the past when there was only the occasional seasonal excitement of the voyage to Yap or the long reach down to Fais.

Presently on Mogmog, on Falalop and on Fassarai the war ceased to be even a subject of conversation. Only on Asor was it kept alive under the staccato whipping of the Japanese talk and the choleric irritability of Atienza. The green nuts went over to Asor according to custom, and the copra when it was dry; and the people of the other islands kept away, so far as was possible, from the Japanese. Even the woman position stabilised itself, and the rapes became less frequent. The night darkness under the palms became less tense, less nervous. It was possible to walk safely swinging the traditional torch of smouldering coconut leaves. The still air was fragrant with the smoke of its burning, and the Japanese stayed within the confines of their own encampment. It might even be that to some of the girls the night darkness was less pleasurable.

CHAPTER VIII

1

THE enormous room that went clear athwart the ship was crowded to a noisy suffocation. Between the lines of tiered cots groups of men sat playing poker, bridge, and gin rummy. One group was singing, a group in which a bottle of rye circulated slowly but methodically. On some of the beds men were lying reading in a complete and perfect detachment from the uproar. Now and then a man half nude would pass on his way to the shower room. The temperature was about a hundred degrees.

On the *Penasco* the ship's officers kept away normally from the sleeping quarters; but Reis had been pulled in tonight in return for the hospitality of his cabin. He sat with two others, one of the Marine doctors and a lieutenant.

The lieutenant was talking. He said, "You should've been at the briefing this morning."

"Ship's sick call," Reis explained. "I couldn't get away."

"We got the dope on Saipan," the lieutenant continued. "It's a mess. They meant to land on Guam last month but they've had to hold it till now. Everything they had up there was tied up in Saipan. Those yellow bastards know how to hold a rugged bit of country. The colonel says 'Howling-Mad' Smith's—howling-mad. We weren't meant for this show, but they reckon after Saipan maybe they'll need more Marines for Guam, so we're the floating reserve. Ain't no landing plans because we don't know where we're going to land. Geiger's commanding." He grinned for a moment and said, "He knows his own mind."

"Jesus, yes!" agreed the doctor reminiscently.

"They've been bombarding since the 8th of July. Reckon they ought to have softened up the beaches by now."

Reis said: "Twelve days—I guess so. Where's the main force going to land?"

"Two beaches," the lieutenant answered. "D'you remember where the Orote peninsula is? They're going in north and south of it. They want to clear the harbour first thing."

"And we?"

"We go on as far as Point A, and then we mark time till we get orders—according to how bad Geiger wants us."

Reis nodded slowly. "Wombacher told me that."

There was a little silence in the heart of the tumult of the great room while the three men considered the possibilities. Then the Marine doctor said, "You never told us how you got away from the Royal Hawaiian."

"I don't know myself," answered Reis comfortably. "I think the Personnel office reckoned Waikiki Beach would wear me down; but they calculated without the exec's liver."

"Meaning?"

"Every time this scow came in to Pearl I used to go down and bitch about getting back to sea. They had to change docs twice after me; and the new man, he didn't understand the exec's liver, or the exec didn't understand his bedside manner. You ask Wombacher! He'll give you a blow-by-blow account of the campaign. This time when they came in to Pearl the doc was asking for a survey and the exec was looking for a shotgun! Next thing I knew was a call from the Personnel office giving me one hour to get on board. I got. I reckon it's broken Personnel's heart."

"Did you know we were coming this way?"

"Hell, yes!" said Reis happily. "I've kept track of every movement west that's been made since I went ashore." He yawned. "And a lot of good it's done me till now!"

The other doctor shook his head at him. "One of these days you're going to shout, 'Let me out of here!' like the rest of us."

"Maybe, but I've got to wait till that day comes."

The other shook his head again. "The Royal Hawaiian. Did you ever reckon what that would have cost you in peacetime?"

"My room rated ten bucks a day," said Reis. "Work it out for eight months—that's two thousand four hundred bucks for the room. You can make your own guess for the food and drink."

"And he griped!" murmured the lieutenant.

Reis looked round the big sleeping compartment with a fine-drawn excitement. "Sure," he said, "I griped."

2

With the Japanese at the meteorological station the temperature of excitement seemed to rise and fall like the barometer when a typhoon was building in the vicinity. The fishing boats brought in rumour, and the wireless clawed portents out of the empty air. But for weeks at a time they would be all but somnolent, sending off three times a day the coded weather messages and reporting the rare, high-flying reconnaissance planes that soared, specklike, across the trade-wind sky high above the trade-wind clouds.

The children called all high-flying aircraft "Americanos" now, but they did not take cover when they appeared: first because they had no conception of shelter against high explosive, and second because it was quite clear that the Americanos did not wish to hurt anybody. Otherwise they would not have dropped their bombs where they had. Even the Asor people bore no grudge against them for wrecking a dozen of the village houses. A single typhoon did more than that—and they had a philosophy that covered all such acts of God.

The second bombing came while the men were out on the fishing grounds. They saw the neat alignment of the carrier planes very far off, this time in the half-light of the earliest morning. It was a dawn attack, this, part of the general attack that covered Yap and the Palaus, well off to the southwestward, to neutralize them at the critical moment of the recapture of Guam. The canoes were scattered in the southern part of the lagoon. Atienza and the Japanese had been angry over canoes that went out of the lagoon to the southward. Since good fish were running inside now the canoes were obeying instructions. The fish were biting well and there was little time to watch the planes coming in.

The whistle of the bombs carried downwind to them this time, attenuated and faint. The one stick that was released over Fassarai fell on the edge of the reef, and they saw monstrous plumes of water roar up far above the dark green bank of the palms. Clearly the Americanos were just practising again. They went on with the fishing.

No one was killed on the islands in this raid.

3

Reis came out of the alleyway on to the deck and blinked at the new-risen sun. "We're heading east," he said. "Why?"

The exec grinned at him maliciously. "Haven't you heard?" he asked. "We're going back. Geiger, he don't want us. The landing went off according to plan."

"You're kidding," said Reis.

The exec shrugged his shoulders. "All right, but we've been steaming east since four o'clock. Maybe the Old Man just likes it that way." He turned and stumped off down the deck.

Reis went forward and climbed the ladder up to the bridge. Wombacher was in the charthouse. Reis demanded: "What's the score? The exec says—"

"The exec's always right," said Wombacher mockingly. "We're going back. Maybe the Royal Hawaiian needs you."

"But how?"

Wombacher flicked over the flimsies on the signal pad. He said, "The beach landings went off all right after they got over the hold-up on the reef—you knew that." He paused at a signal and then went on: "No air opposition. Jesus, I wouldn't expect it after what they did off Saipan! The air boys raided down in the Gilberts Friday—no opposition. They raided Yap and the Palaus and a place called Ulithi atoll." His hand flicked over another series of signals. "Geiger ran into trouble at the base of the Orote peninsula; he talks about heavy mortar fire, but he reckons he can hold it. He's got enough troops ashore and with the ships off Apra to handle anything he's likely to come up against, so he don't want us. So we go home. The Marine boys are mad. You know"— he studied Reis's face for a moment—"you ought to have gone into the Marines. You've got the same ideas."

CHAPTER IX

≈≈≈≈≈≈≈≈≈≈≈≈≈≈≈≈≈≈≈≈≈≈≈≈≈≈≈≈≈≈≈

1

THE third raid hit the islands on September 6th. A stick of bombs dropped neatly and with exquisite direction clear across the village on Mogmog. Seventeen houses were obliterated, but because most of the people were down at the beach or at the women's bathing pool in the swamp part of the island only the king's daughter was killed. They found her, completely disembowelled, lying across the main pathway to the inside of the island. It was not a pretty death.

The raids lasted intermittently for two or three days this time, and the Japanese achieved a chattering level of excitement that transcended everything that had passed before. Their women told the village that the Japanese would go soon, and Asor spread the news through the islands.

The Nanyo steamer came in on the third day after the raid. The deckhouse had disappeared, and there was only a crumpled girder left to show where it had been. Red lead patches on her side showed new welding, and her funnel was sieved with holes from a fragmentation bomb. She came in at dusk and anchored above Asor in the shelter of the reef, and Japanese from her came ashore in a boat at darkness. All through the night there were lights inside the stockade of the meteorological post, and long before dawn the Japanese came down to the All Men House and called the young men and the old alike to carry down to the landing place the instruments and equipment of the wireless station, the petrol motor and the dynamo, the instruments of the meteorologists, the gear, and the guns.

The Japanese were going. A certain elation spread through the village as the loads pulled out to the waiting steamer. The Japanese were going, and now the last of the war would go from Ulithi and they would be able to talk again in the flickering interior of the *falu* at night without arousing the jealousy of the gods or of the Virgin Mary.

2

Eight men staggered down with the petrol motor of the generating set and, walking crab-fashion four on either side of the boat with the long bamboo poles between them, dropped it, panting, on the bottom boards. This was the last load. Japanese marines, who had formed the guard for the meteorologists, stood with their rifles on the beach.

The *sho-i* came back from the ship with a paper in his hand. He called Atienza to him and spoke for a minute, brusquely. Atienza in turn called the king, and the old man came up slowly, his torch of young fruit leaves waving from side to side. Atienza reeled out a list of names. In the darkness the men were found. Under the barking orders of the Japanese petty officers they climbed into the boat and squatted on the bottom boards round the engine.

The motor boat started up, and the tow line between it and the big lifeboat tightened with a jerk. Some of the men fell over and laughed. Clearly it was necessary for them to go out to the Nanyo ship to load the engine up her side. They would have preferred to go in their own canoes. It was of course possible that the Japanese would not provide a boat to bring them back. They could swim, but they would have preferred to have their own canoes.

In the darkness behind them the *sho-i* held the torch while

Atienza called out names from the list. He read laboriously, stumbling over the names. The night became full of the red glow of torches as men and girls whirled up and down the paths calling names, laughing, excited. It was not clear what was happening, but they expected another address—perhaps on the subject of taking their canoes out beyond the reef again. The Japanese were given to public lecture. It made no difference—they were all awake anyhow. The whole island had been awake, even the youngest children, ever since the Nanyo ship came to her anchorage. There was almost a gaiety about, compound of the departure and this excitement of the names in equal shares.

The list went on and on. It included all the girls above puberty, all the young women, all the boys and the young men—forty-three names, all told. Ten of them had gone in the first boat with the petrol motor.

Now in the darkness they could hear the motor boat chugging back from the Nanyo ship, coming in through the quiet of the phosphorescence. Those up beyond the torches could see the pallid green light of the bow wave coming in towards the beach. The motor boat ran up for the landing, slipped the lifeboat and left that to run in under its own way while she curved out to keep the depth of water under her.

The young girls were all together now, giggling and laughing. The air round them was heavy with their body scent and with the scent of flowers, frangipani cutting across the sweat reek and the smell of stale oil. Atienza told them angrily to be quiet, and they laughed all the more. The *sho-i* spoke to him again and, as if he were an automaton moved by the controlling figure at his side, he barked out an order for them to go down to the boat. He spoke in their own tongue, but the accents were Japanese. The words had a harsh crudity.

Out of the darkness the voice of the old king said, quietly, "Why?"

Atienza pivoted and said, over in the direction of the king, "It is the order."

A little beyond him a boy said, "Perhaps the Japanese are making a feast on board the Nanyo ship."

And another voice, faintly sardonic, said, "When do the Japanese feast?"

For a moment or two the girls were silent. Then someone began to laugh again. They went down obediently and clambered over the clumsy sides of the Japanese lifeboat, splashing and calling out to one another in the shallow. The boys followed them, and the remainder of the young men. The late comers pushed the heavily loaded boat off the sand until she floated before they climbed in. The *sho-i* went last of all. In the flicker of the torches of the old men they saw that he had drawn his revolver and held it nervously in his hand.

Again the motor boat started up. The deep, solid mass of the lifeboat hung for a moment with the foot of the keel scraping against the sand. Then with a grating noise it pulled off. The girls were still laughing, and some of the boys with them. The thing had the air of a picnic.

Only the old king, standing on the silent beach, said, "Where do they go?"

And Atienza from the edge of the palms higher up the beach, said blankly, "It is the order," and, turning, went back to his empty hut. His girls had gone also.

In the darkness no one else spoke. The older women had gone back to the huts; but the men sat along the shore fringe, and a few of them on the platform of the All Men House. The dawn came up behind them, filtering through the palms. They were still in shadow when the new sun caught the Nanyo ship and made her, for an instant, almost beautiful against the luminous spray haze of the reef. They saw the steam jet from the old steam windlass on the fo'c'sle spurting out from the flare of the bows and then, losing its energy, drift slowly upwards, brilliant in the new sun. After a little they heard the slow clank of the cable coming in. The Nanyo ship crept forward the length of the scope of the chain. The anchor came aboard with a final angry flurry of water, and she turned with a whistle and headed slowly across the lagoon towards Mogmog. She towed the lifeboat and her motor boat, and it was plain that she was not going out to sea.

The king said, "They take them to work on Mogmog. They will put up the put-put engine there."

The old men accepted his version, nodding. They went back slowly to their homes.

3

The village was empty and strangely silent, for the children were with the old women in the shadow of the huts. Uncertainly they kept a watch on the Nanyo steamer. Four miles away off Mogmog she had lost a little of her height, but she still bulked large against the line of the palms. There was a faint smudge of smoke over her high, ungainly funnel. In the middle of the morning she steamed away from Mogmog. The old men came down to the beach to watch her movement. Behind them came three or four of the women, standing well back in the deep shade. The Nanyo steamer turned in a slow wide half-circle and headed down the lagoon, picking her way delicately between the shoals and the coral heads. They watched her for a long while, growing first a little larger as her course came near to Asor, then diminishing again as she headed for the southern half of the lagoon.

Again only the king spoke, and he said, "Perhaps it is Fassarai."

No other word was spoken, but the old men sat before the All Men House and chewed slowly and a little anxiously. There was no sign of the Chamorro.

The Nanyo steamer lay off Fassarai for two hours, and then one of the oldest men said, "She comes."

They saw her swing away from the anchorage and head north again. In that far distance she was no more than a funnel and a superstructure and the thread lines of masts above the even, lovely blue of the lagoon. She headed due north for a little to dodge the shallows and then went out through the channel north of Mange-jang. Clear of the main reef she turned again. For a little they thought that she was heading back for Asor, but her course straightened out and it was clear that she was steaming for Falalop.

She did not anchor off Falalop but lay stemming wind and current with her screw turning slowly. She was high out of the water, in ballast, and they could see the threshing of the blades as the propeller turned, and the white splash of water between the rudder and the stern. The motor boat went in towing, this time, both lifeboats. Three times the ship fell away from the island and steamed back to her position before they came out again.

The king and the old men had followed her up the Asor beach. From where they sat on the high shoulder of the island above the beach they could see her in a stark clarity, the pitiless light of the westering sun brilliant on every red patch and every bomb scar on her sides and on her funnel. Behind them and quite silent in the trees the old women of the village gathered. They could see people moving between the palms on Falalop and the turmoil round the great *falu* that stood beside the landing place.

And suddenly they heard, very faint but clear across the water, high screams and in the middle of them three shots—slow, deliberate at this distance, without anger or malice—three sharp, staccato breaks across the steady susurrus of the outside surf. The two boats were pushed off a little after that and they could see that they were loaded as the single lifeboat had been when it left Asor.

Again they heard the screaming and the deeper note of men's voices, a harsh bass shouting. But the motor boat chuttered on indifferently and the lifeboats followed. They watched them from the high coral bank as they went alongside, one to port and one to starboard of the Nanyo ship; and they watched the stream of brown bodies go up the ladders. The roar of voices came to them from across the water, a roar that was punctuated by sudden startling silences.

The last brown body went up, and the lifeboat on the port side hauled forward till she was underneath the dangling falls.

They saw steam from the ship's winch. Below, the Japanese of the crew hooked on, and the lifeboat began to rise from the water. Wordlessly they watched it crawl up the battered side of the ship, swing inboard, and come to rest on its cradle. They saw the flutter under the stern speed up as the ship began slowly to move ahead. She swung wide, heading almost towards them for a moment, and then turned out through the channel between the two islands.

No one had spoken through the two long hours of her waiting, but now Elato, the oldest man in the village, said, very slowly, his voice almost indistinct: "Where can she go now? There are no more islands."

And behind him the women began softly to pray, the strange, phonetic, un-understood but immensely potent "Ave Maria gratia plena . . ." It grew faster, more urgent, louder, as more and more of the old women joined in it; a hoarse, desperate appeal—and over it two of the older women began to moan.

Again came one of the swift gusts of noise from the Nanyo ship. She was very close now in the narrow passage, barely half a mile away. And suddenly they saw a man running on her deck and heard louder shouts, and a brown figure leapt to the rail, poised for a second and then dived cleanly to the water. Instantly another figure followed him, vaulted clumsily and fell. They heard the stutter of machine guns and a single terrible shriek. But the ship went on. It was not possible to stop there in the passage between the islands with the strong tide running through and the trade wind beating.

They saw the head and shoulders of the diver come up and again there was the staccato *tut-tut-tut* of the machine gun. They could see the quick spurts of water as the bullets struck, fountains that rose six feet and more and feathered in the low sun. Each time as the swimmer came up the feathers grew about him, but each time the Nanyo ship was further away. She was almost through the channel, almost clear of the islands. The swimmer was heading in now for Falalop, rounding in with the out-splaying of the current. He came up for the fifth time and no bullets splashed: the gun was silent. The Nanyo ship went on.

The old men had moved round to the trade-wind side now, round the shoulder of the coral bluff. With the wind in their faces they watched the Nanyo ship turning in the offing towards the west, and with the wind in their faces they sat and the women prayed behind them, "Pater noster qui es in coelis . . ." The words were unclear, elided one into another, but they made a pattern across the low background of ceaseless moaning.

The ship had gone: the sun had gone with her; the darkness was over them before the king said, slowly and heavily, "There will not be enough to send the canoes out to the fishing." And, rising, walked under sentence of death towards the village.

CHAPTER X

≋≋≋≋≋≋≋≋≋≋≋≋≋≋≋≋≋≋≋≋≋≋

1

THE five children walked slowly in single file down the path towards the south end of the island, Teresa leading. Once she broke
into a trot, skipped a little, and then, seeing that the others were
not following her sudden brief joyousness, slowed down again.
They caught up with her and went on. At the little bay where,
long ago, the bigger boys had begun to build the toy *falu*, there
was only the wreck of splintered trees. The last two of a stick
of bombs had fallen directly athwart the beach. Some of the posts
of the *falu* were still standing but the rest was a wreckage mixed
with shreds of palm leaf and broken nuts. The other four children
began aimlessly to search for iron, but the play had no life in it.

Teresa moved away from them and sat by herself looking out
over the reef shallows towards Lossau, the next island. Here and
there heads of coral stuck up above the water, but for the rest it
was a green and lovely wilderness, pellucid as aquamarine over the
sand, darkening through all the shades of olivine and emerald to
the crisp clarity of bottle glass over the deeps. Little runnels of
surf came over from the swells outside to perish, half-hearted, in
the embossment of the coral. The sea outside looked higher than
the rest—was higher in the long succession of uplifted crests that
broke and savaged themselves to a nothingness of spray on the
reef edge.

Far away, down off Lossau, she could see the sail of Falifi's
canoe. Falifi and Jesus were fishing the inner edge of the reef.
Theirs was the only canoe out today. There were no sails on the

outer grounds to the northeast either, no sails from Asor or Falalop or Mogmog. Her mother had said that the dried fish was all but finished. No taro had come from the northern islands for a week. She was not hungry, but neither was she full. The happy content had gone, and over the shimmering silence of the afternoon there spread a strange, uncertain disquiet. She could feel it, and the other children could feel it. It was heavy over all the village, and there were only children's voices—no voices of the marriageable girls laughing, no voices of the young men making indelicate proposals from the shadows of the *falu,* no sound of adzes at the damaged canoe. The houses that had been wrecked in the bombing were unrepaired still, the damaged rafters naked and indecent to the sky.

The four children behind her began to hold a funeral. Maria, the wife of Eate, had died two days after the departure of the Nanyo ship. Eate himself was dying, the village said. He was not sick: he was just dying. It was not because he had loved Maria either; notoriously he had been unfaithful as a young man and as an old. He was just dying.

After a little she became suddenly angry with the play, with the intonation of wordless psalms and the garbled prayers. She walked over to the little group, kicked aside the log of splintered palm trunk that was serving as the body, and, stubbing her toe, swore abruptly. Then, suddenly frightened either at the sound or at the sacrilege, she began to gabble the phonetic paternoster of the islands as a charm against ghosts.

She left the scandalised children and walked back towards the village. In the distance she saw Sebastian coming down the path, but now she did not hide. She was the oldest girl on the island. The fact came to her with a quick insight. There was no one older than she except the old women, the long-married women who no longer counted. She walked straight down the centre of the path swinging her hips as she remembered the older girls had swung them, her grass skirt swinging provocatively to their motion. Sebastian was flinging his arm out in the remembered gesture, muttering to himself as he walked. For a long second it seemed as if there might be a collision. Then her grown-up moment fell from her, and Teresa flinched from the centre of the path. Sebastian stalked on, his eyes heavy and unseeing—or perhaps looking out on some farther prospect that she could not visualise. She did not look back at him, crushed by the nonrecognition, but walked slowly until she reached the outskirts of the houses.

Four of the old women were gathered in the shade of the straggling banana palms, talking slowly and desultorily. Ordinarily the men would have broken up the meeting. They did not approve of gossip outside the *falu*. That it could happen was in itself symptomatic of the sickness of the island. Teresa made to join them and was driven away by low, acid vituperation—and that again was a symptom of the sickness of the island.

She went at last to her own home and slipped in at the low door out of the glare of the sun. She felt unwell, her head aching and her abdomen griped with quick pains. Sitting in the house darkness with the flies buzzing round her head, she began to sweat and, sweating, moved into a quick, childhood terror—supposing the paternosters had not been enough to appease the ghosts, supposing the ghost of Maria was pursuing her! Maria had been malignant in life. What powers would she have after death? Suppose she was poisoned! She crouched down on the sleeping mat too frightened even to brush away the settling flies.

Back at the little bay the children were still playing—were still holding their funeral.

2

As soon as the sun had taken off the night chill Falifi and Jesus pushed out the canoe. They were not fishing this morning. They headed north for Asor instead, the wind taking them easily across the smoothness of the lagoon. The trades had fallen light the last few days. Some of the way they had to paddle. Jesus was very old: the work was hard.

They came to Asor a little after noon. The canoes from Mogmog and from Falalop were there already, and they joined the group on the terrace of the All Men House, sitting in respect to the Asor king. A canoe manned by Fernando, the only other boy who had escaped the Japanese—hiding in a pile of palm trash after his name had been called on Mogmog—and Tonio, brother of the Mogmog king, had brought the summons the day before. Each island was to send two men to a council. The summons did not tell the purpose of the council.

The *falu* was strangely unreal without the young men and the boys, like a caricature of its purpose. The seamed faces of the older men, the predominance of the blue tattooing that the younger men were forgetting, the wasted arm muscles, and the flaccid bellies gave the place an antique air, as if this were a thing done for show, not deriving of life and purpose.

Atienza was on the terrace. He was not drunk. He was cold-sober. His dark eyes were bloodshot in their darker sockets, and they moved wildly at times around the faces of the group. No one spoke to him directly.

Olimarao, the Asor king, who was king of Ulithi, began to speak an hour after the men of Fassarai had come, and the others were silent to hear him. He spoke of the legends of the islands, of the coming of the people and the making of the nation. He spoke of the wars on Yap and on Guam; and he spoke of the Spaniards, calling out of race memory a long tale of god and of slaughter, of rape and of religion, of trade and of disease. Spaniard and German—the name of the conquest changed, but the conquest changed not at all. Japanese—and still the pattern was unaltered except upon the surface. He spoke of the padres, the Spanish fathers, who had come in great ships or in canoes. And each time he mentioned the name of the Virgin he crossed himself resolutely, crossed himself even as he said again that their lives had been unaltered, crossed himself even as he would have made the signs and spoken the words for the avoidance of the island ghosts.

And he came slowly and painfully, so that all the men on the terrace, even Atienza, grieved with him and for him, to the story of the Nanyo ship. He described it haltingly, but in a vast, almost a grotesque, detail—the slow voice rumbling on and on while the men round him chewed their betel nut and spat; a voice as endless, as repetitive, as the surf itself, giving the gesture of each one as the name was called; echoing, pitifully, the pitiful laughter.

"They went to a feast," he said over and over again. "They went to a feast."

And he told the story of Fayu, the boy who had dived from the rail of the Nanyo ship and who had come ashore on Falalop with a machine-gun bullet in his rump and was now ill with a fever. He left no smallest thing out of that telling that he knew, and they listened wordlessly, not supplementing him, not correcting him, but listening—for this was the great telling that followed disaster. This was the placing on record for the annals of the island, the memory-making story.

Utterly dispassionate, without blame or accusation, he told of the part of Atienza. It was as if a disembodied spirit spoke, a voice of judgment; and Atienza sat on in a stony silence, muttering sometimes under his breath.

The long afternoon passed from short shadow to long and from long shadow to sunset, and still he talked. And still they squatted, their positions unchanging, the terrace of the *falu* red with the splashes of the betel nut and the unheeded birds scuttering up and down on the many-fronded leafage of the thatch. The light went, and the great prow of the gable end of the *falu* grew threatening and dark above them. It seemed to reach out over them with the gesture of an upraised arm. The coolness of the evening crept in and in, and the trade that had been blowing through the afternoon died off, and the trees were still. The silence about them was absolute: the women withdrawn and silent; the children silenced; the whole island pregnant with a dark foreboding.

The story ended in the full darkness with the gable of the *falu* like the bow of a dark ship riding against the phosphorescence of the stars, like the bow of a dark ship advancing, soundless and awful, on a motionless canoe.

"Our young men," said the Asor king, "have gone from us, and our girls. Therefore we are already dead. There are not enough to man the canoes for the fishing. There are not enough for the gardens and for the cooking. There are not enough for life, and we are dead. Let us then, as dead men, kill this man," and he bent his head very slowly in the direction of the dark, indistinct shape of Atienza.

The Chamorro made no movement but they heard his lips begin a prayer, "Sancta Maria," and falter and begin again, "Sancta Maria"—and again and again like the cracked record of a phonograph, "Sancta Maria, Sancta Maria, Sancta Maria . . ."

Then suddenly, without moving, he began to scream, high-pitched and wordless, an agony of sound. The men next to him rose and took his arms; but no one placed hand across his mouth, and the screaming went on. Birds fluttered frightened from the thatch, but they could not hear the wing-beat for the dreadful shrillness of the scream.

The king spoke again, and they jerked him to his feet, threw him brutally on to the smooth coral slabs of the *ailiuth*. The shriek broke to an atrocious, bubbling groan and then came free again, smothered now by the harsh proximity of the stone. In the darkness, moving catlike and absolutely sure, one of the men grasped his hair, another ripped away the collar of the European-style shirt that he wore; and for the third time the king spoke.

"Kill him!"

The heavy knife whistled briefly. There was a thud that had something in it of the quality of a paddle blade hitting the water and the scream ended in a soft inexpressible exhalation. The men who had been holding Atienza's arms released them, and the body heaved convulsively twice and was still. With a short knife one of the older men severed the neck muscles and the windpipe and drew the head away.

In the utter silence the king said slowly, "We are dead men, but he also is dead."

CHAPTER XI

〜〜〜〜〜〜〜〜〜〜〜〜〜〜〜〜〜〜〜〜〜〜〜〜〜〜〜〜〜〜〜〜〜

1

THE ship was silent, the strange silence of a tension that Reis could feel through the nerve ends under his skin. There were no crap games, there were no poker games going on in the sleeping quarters when he passed through them. The few men who were lying out on the deck were quiet. Only in the dining hall was there a low ordered murmur of voices. He went to it through the thwartships alleyway, and the alleyway was full of men standing and silent and the voices were within. He pushed through them. O'Brien, the Catholic chaplain, had set up his altar at the far end of the dining hall. He had been hearing confessions, and now he was talking to the men, taking messages, making curious improbable promises. He was going to hold mass at midnight. Reis stood and watched him for a little. More and more men were crowding into the room.

After a little he passed out again into the darkness and stood outside against the rail. Under the forefoot of the nearest ship he could see the crash of phosphorescence, a green light breaking intermittently; but there was little sea.

He remembered the details of the briefing. They were landing on the east coast of the atoll because the experts hoped that under the shelter of the outlying islands there would be less surf. If the sea was too heavy on the reef, then they would try to get in through the openings on the east side. But against opposition that would mean running a perhaps impossible gantlet.

Again his eyes went over to the ship in the next line. He wondered where her troops would land. They could not all be going in on this eastern side: the islands on the circuit of the atoll were very small. Tarawa had been small also, he remembered—small and bloody. He tried to count the other ships, but in the deceptiveness of the night it was impossible. They had joined the ships from Angaur at dusk. He had not counted them then, but it was of no importance. There were a lot of them—enough, as Colonel Costello had said, to do the job twice over. Again Reis remembered the stories that he had heard of Tarawa.

He wondered what it was like in Angaur where the other ships came from. The fighting there had been lighter than at Peleliu. Angaur was far over the other side of Yap towards the Philippines, five hundred miles away at least. He began to think of the immensity of the Pacific operations, the bland, blank vastness of the water spaces between the islands. They were fighting up in the Aleutians, and that must be five thousand miles from here, and they were fighting away off to the southeast in the Solomons. There were still Japanese-held islands in the Marianas. He saw this attack on Ulithi as part of a spearhead thrust in against the Philippines, a gigantic spearhead whose barbs went back to the Marshall Islands, and whose shaft sprang from Hawaii. This attack seemed overwhelmingly important to him—it must seem as important to every man in the convoy, to every man in the ships making ready to go in to the assault at dawn—and yet it was so small on the plan of this colossal battle of an ocean. He felt intolerably insignificant for a moment, and, turning from the rail, he went in to try to sleep.

Wombacher came in as he climbed into the bunk. He said: "I've got the latest poop. Intelligence don't think the islands are strongly held. They're sending in recon units first. The general assault's been postponed."

"Do we still go to General Quarters at four-thirty?"

"Sure. There's no change in the main plan. We lie off ten miles out while the lead ships go in." Wombacher walked over to the chart on the bulkhead. "We mark time in a square somewhere about here"—he traced it out with his finger—"and then as soon as the general assault is ordered we go in. There's no point in closing before. You can't anchor anywhere except inside the atoll. You've got five hundred fathom of water right up to here. Jesus, am I tired!" He switched out his light and lay down dressed.

2

The landing craft roared in over the green and lucid shallows, the schooling triggerfish racing away from it in threads of scarlet light. With twenty yards to go the sergeant stood upright in the exiguous shelter of the door and fumbled with a hand grenade. Ahead of where the boat would hit the blinding strip of sand beach was a pile of logs and palm trunks, and, timing the thing coolly and exquisitely, he shot his arm up and pitched the grenade with all the ease of the diamond behind him. With a slow-dropping curve it soared through the clarity of the outside air, passed through the overhanging fronds of the beachward palms and was lost in the shadow. He counted slowly and then dropped head and shoulders beneath the shelter of the door. The sharp, brutal crack of the grenade cut across the island stillness, across even the harsh roar of the landing craft's motors.

In the same instant, and even as the smoke and the sand and the broken leaves rushed out across the purity of the beach, she hit the sand. The door dropped, and the sergeant led his men forward in a stumbling rush through three feet of shallow and up the softness of the beach. They dropped on the sandward side of the logs. Behind them other men carried the tripod of a 50-calibre machine gun and lurched with it across the uncertain footing to where they lay, their rifles thrust across the logs into the settling smoke. The barrel came up and clicked into position, the ammunition case followed. They lay sprawled across the sand, unconsciously dramatic, impersonally intent.

Behind them they heard the roar of the landing craft's motors as, freed of their weight, she pulled away from the beach. The roar' passed in a soft decrescendo. They were by themselves.

The dust and the smoke had cleared utterly now and they could see up the long aisles between the palm trees. Nothing stirred.

Rucinski said: "Jeez! The air boys was right. No Japs!"

And from the far end of the little group another voice said lazily, "No battle stars."

"Shut up!" said the sergeant, and they lay silent. Down the beach they heard the quick typewriter rattle of tommy-guns. He cocked an alert and expert ear. "Ours," he murmured.

There was still no sound from the island. Rucinski rolled over on to his back and breathed deeply. "Where's Dorothy Lamour?" he asked in the reasonable tone of one who expects an answer.

The sergeant said sharply, "Straighten up!"

Rucinski muttered reproachfully, "Aw, sarge," and levelled his tommy-gun again.

The sergeant looked at his wrist watch and said, "Give it another minute, and we go in."

"Technicolour, just technicolour," breathed Rucinski.

"Right," said the sergeant, "we go in."

He rose to his knees, putting up one hand automatically to brush the sand from his shirt. Instantly he dropped again.

The man next to him said: "It's a nigger, sergeant. Shall I let him have it?"

The guns moved till their muzzles converged on a point far back in the cathedral darkness of the palms. The brown figure was coming towards them slowly, not hiding behind the boles but walking openly with a slow dignity, one arm gesturing— Sebastian coming down unhurriedly to the noise.

"Kanaka," said the sergeant. "The orders was to let them be. Keep him covered."

They lay there utterly silent, watching the old man approach. He moved easily, normally, superbly innocent of a sense of danger. When he was twenty yards from them they heard the splutter of machine guns again out towards the south of the island but there was no answering fire, no echo of defence.

The sergeant came up in one quick lurching movement, holding his gun at the ready, the muzzle level with Sebastian's paunch. "Halt!" he barked.

Sebastian jerked, threw up both hands palm outwards to the level of his waist as if someone had prodded him in the stomach, and stopped. The other men were rising now, and he looked along the line of them, half seen through the fringing palms and the bush, looked wonderingly at the rounded helmets, his eyes puzzled, clouded behind with old memory. His hand swept over his mouth, and he said slowly, pulling out the syllables, "Guten Morgen."

"Christ!" said Rucinski. "No Dorothy Lamour, and a nigger that speaks German!"

The sergeant took no notice but began searching in his own memory. They had told them at the briefing that some of the natives might understand German. He asked slowly and ponderously, "Wo sind die Japaner?" Sebastian's eyes dulled in an effort of concentration, turning inward over the obscurities of thirty years. The sergeant said again patiently and with clear enunciation, "Wo sind die Japaner?"

"Japaner," said Sebastian suddenly eager, clutching at the identifiable word. "Kein, kein Japaner."

"No Dorothy Lamour, no Japanese. How d'you like that, Rucinski?" said Fleming.

"But technicolour," said Rucinski obscurely.

The sergeant wheeled round, suddenly angry. "Don't any of you bastards speak German?"

"Frendberg speaks German," said Fleming. "He's with the lieutenant."

"You sure he speaks German?"

"Lives round First Avenue and Ninth. You gotta speak German if you live around there."

The sergeant said, "You wait there," the asperity oddly gone from his voice, and stepped to the beach.

The second boat had gone in a hundred yards down. He could see the men still lying on the naked sand. He called out, his powerful voice booming across the rustle of the wind: "Lieutenant, can you send Frendberg? I've got a guy can speak German. He says no Japs."

"Sergeant," called a voice urgently, "something up in the trees."

Again the rifles flung up. "Christ," said Rucinski disgustedly, "kids! An' we got up at midnight for this."

Mau, the king's son, and two other small boys ran down the soft aisle between the palms. They ran past Sebastian, disregarding him, and then stood, suddenly frozen and abashed, their chests heaving.

"All right," said Rucinski, "I give up. I'll go quiet. What goes on here?"

The lieutenant was running along the beach with Frendberg. They arrived sweating and breathless.

"Sind Japaner auf der Insel?" demanded Frendberg, panting.

Sebastian eyed him bewildered.

"Slowly," said Lieutenant Hartwell, "slowly! He doesn't get it."

Painstakingly, giving each word its full value, Frendberg repeated, "Sind Japaner auf der Insel?"

"Kein Japaner," said Sebastian again, "kein." And then slowly, painfully, as if he were tearing the words out of a forgotten fastness of memory, "Sie sind fort."

"Wann?" demanded Frendberg harshly. Suddenly the Prussian was uppermost in his accent.

Sebastian flung back a step and said, quickly and without effort, "Vor zehn Tagen."

The lieutenant said, "Don't scare him, don't scare him!" But even as he spoke the memory of the harshness faded, and the old man stood naturally again. The lieutenant said, wonderingly and to himself, "And the Germans went out thirty years ago!"

Frendberg tried again. "Wohin sind sie?"

"Fort," said Sebastian slowly.

"Haben sie auf der Insel etwas hinterlassen?"

Sebastian shook his head.

"Ask him where the people are," said the lieutenant.

Sebastian wrinkled his forehead for a long minute, not answering. Then, wordlessly, he extended his hand towards the unseen village.

"We'll take a chance," said the lieutenant. "Sergeant, you and Frendberg take him along with you, and four men spread out. We'll bring the gun up behind. Fleming, go down the beach and tell Sergeant Rettak to cut in through the trees and wait for us, and take one man from him and go and tell Sergeant Marker the same. Watch your step!"

The children dropped their terrors abruptly. It might have been the fact of Rucinski winking at them, or a sudden surge of overwhelming curiosity. Mau, the king's son, came up, stepping delicately on the balls of his feet, and touched the heavy webbing belt admiringly. It was the one item of equipment that had a near familiarity; it had a cousinship to the coarse coir fabric that they made for matting.

"Any of youse guys bring any candy?" asked Rucinski, and shook his head. "Make a note of it, Berndorff. Remind Rucinski to bring candy on his next invasion." He pulled out a packet of gum, stripped one piece to demonstrate, and tossed the others round.

The children were swarming all round him now, poking at his hand grenades and at his gun.

"Beat it!" said the lieutenant, and began to move forward forty yards behind Sebastian and his guard.

3

The hut was old and dishevelled—not that it had ever been remarkable. It stood on the inward slope of the faint ridge that marked the lagoon shore, and the ground around it was obscure with dead leaf, old husks, and a vague and indeterminate rubbish. The flies were heavy round it. The sergeant stopped at once, the muzzle of his gun drawn towards the hut like a lodestone.

Sebastian shook his head violently. *"Tapu,"* he said, and again, *"Tapu."*

The lieutenant came up and from twenty yards away called, "What's the trouble?"

"Native hut or something," said the sergeant. "Shall I put a round through it?"

Frendberg spoke quickly in German. "He says the house is taboo," he said over his shoulder as Sebastian answered.

"Take a look at it," ordered the lieutenant.

A look of horror came over Sebastian's face and he raised his jerky arm again. *"Tapu,"* he said for the fourth time.

The children ran forward, deserting Rucinski, to stand looking wonderingly at the puzzled faces.

"Take a look at it," ordered the lieutenant again, and the sergeant walked forward. "Cover him!" said the lieutenant.

Six guns trained on the meagre palm leaf of the walls. Five yards from the door the sergeant said harshly, "Come'n out!"

Nothing happened. He walked up to the low door, stooped, poking the barrel of his gun into the dark shadow behind. Then he straightened himself. "Jeez!" he said. "It's another kid! Come on!"

Teresa came out, bent double, and straightened, blinking in the sunshine. The men came up, Rucinski last. Looking over their shoulders he said: "Hula-hula! Say, kid, have you got a big sister inside there?"

Sebastian, brought up by Frendberg, saw the child beyond the khaki. His hand came up to his mouth in a pious horror and he spoke swiftly in the island tongue. Teresa gave a look of terror and disappeared incontinently into the darkness again. The children scattered, squeaking.

Frendberg asked a question and, turning, said to the lieutenant: "I can't make it out. Maybe she's sick or something."

"All right," said Hartwell. "Get on with it."

They moved away from the hut. Behind, Teresa, with one eye glued to a hole in the palm leaves, watched them go. She was shivering all over in an immense apprehension that was close to terror, but that was overlaid and obscured by an absorbing curiosity. She had violated one of the heaviest taboos of the island—shown herself to men in the terrible period between childhood and womanhood, the banned period, and she merited Sebastian's curse. But the menstruation hut was intolerably hot. There were no girls in it a little older than herself, for they were gone. There were no young women in it in the monthly observance of the custom. The old women who were left were beyond menstruation and beyond sympathy. For the last four days they had brought her food and torrents of old, useless advice as empty as their empty breasts.

The last party of men, those carrying the barrel of the 50-calibre, went by and disappeared. Sebastian had crossed on to the main path, and in a little they came to the outer huts of the village. The sergeant stopped and waited again for the lieutenant to come up.

Frendberg was browbeating Sebastian as he arrived. He turned and said: "Lieutenant, he says the men will be down at the big house. He says there are only women in the huts."

"Tell him to call them out," ordered the lieutenant. "Johnson!" He called the signaller up to him while Frendberg and Sebastian wrestled with the intricacies of understanding. "Take this down: 'Red Fox to Huntsman. Have reached south village. Natives declare no Japanese on island. No signs occupation. Out.'" He took the pad from the man, scanned it for a moment, shook his head, and struck out the word "declare" and substituted "say."

There was a rustle and a shimmer at the door of the nearest hut as Sebastian called. A child came out, and another, both wearing the grass skirts of the young girls; then a small boy came; and after them an old woman, wrinkled, slightly bent, with her flaccid breasts hanging pendulous and a wreath of flowers, incongruous, round her neck. Others came out of the farther huts, and one very old man, bent, lame and covered with great ulcers.

"Still no Lamour," muttered Rucinski softly.

[72]

"Looks all right," said Lieutenant Hartwell. "Sergeant, send three men round the back of the village to the left and tell them to work round the outside of the huts and come down to the beach. Fleming and Rucinski, you go round to the right till you reach the beach, and then cut along it and meet us there."

Frendberg said over his shoulder: "He says the king's at the big hut. He calls it the All Men House. His German's improving." To Sebastian he said, smiling, "Sie sprechen sehr gut."

Not a muscle moved in the old man's face, but he nodded slightly.

"Tell him to take us down there," demanded the lieutenant.

They went off with Sebastian leading, with no pretence now of a guard. The women and children watched them in absolute silence, but as they turned the corner of the path where it branched down to the sea a low murmur broke out behind them. Looking back, Hartwell saw two very small children creep cautiously along the path in their rear.

They passed down the rows of bananas and stunted papayas and came between the king's house and the canoe sheds to the *falu*. It was utterly still there; even the dogs had been silenced: nothing moved. There was a strange expectancy that hung over the place like a shadow in the bright light—a tense, nervous, immanent sense of crisis. The lieutenant had slipped his tommy gun negligent under one arm. Slowly he brought it round his body so that his finger rested on the trigger guard and his left hand held the hand-grip ready. The sergeant seemed to feel the same tension. His rifle had been almost at the ready all the while, but now he raised it still further. Even Frendberg, his long, painful cross-examining silent now, walked with a curious spring in his step, looking quick-eyed from point to point, his head questing like a hound. Sebastian alone walked on unmoved, unalterable, strangely stately except for the jerky movement of his arm, his head high; and, so moving, he led them to the front of the *falu* and the *ailiuth*.

Silent, unmoving as if they had been carved out of a blue and umber stone, the old men of Fassarai sat to wait upon fate. If there were within them forebodings, they showed nothing. They showed neither fear nor apprehension—nor even hope. There had been death out of the air. Now death was come upon the ground, walking and terrible. And death could not touch them, for already they were dead men: the king of Ulithi had said the words long since, and they waited only the final moment of dissolution; and that had no scintilla of importance.

Hartwell stopped, held by the potent immobility, the mute unpassionate stillness of the group. It was not in him to know that they sat in expectation of death, but yet doing honour by the seated position to death himself. He could not know that to them he was death.

Sebastian, who had stalked ahead, came to the edge of the circle at an empty space and stood there.

Frendberg said under his breath, "Christ! What goes on here?"

The faint whisper shocked Hartwell into speech. He said, "Which is the king?"

Frendberg translated. Sebastian raised one hand to point to the man who sat a step above the others at the doorsill of the *falu*.

"Tell him—" Hartwell's mind clawed desperately back through forgotten childhood memories, through into the ancestral race memory of America. Then the words came almost without volition, almost without consciousness: "Tell him that we come in peace."

Frendberg stared for a moment, trying to fit his German to the phrase. He spoke slowly to Sebastian, and the king nodded without the need of further translation. "Looks like he speaks German too," said Frendberg.

"Right. Tell him that if the people behave themselves nobody will be hurt, and ask him where the Japanese are."

Frendberg translated slowly, and after a long, uneasy silence the king spoke, his voice so low that Frendberg could hardly catch the uncouth, half-remembered German. "He says the Japanese have gone. They were never on the island."

"Ask him where they were, and how many."

Again there was the struggling silence as if a man desperately sick were trying to evoke words out of an uncertain consciousness.

Then the king said, "They were on Asor," and stretched out his hand towards the northern island. "There were a few only." There was another long pause, and then he added, "Sometimes ships and the ships that fly."

"When did they go?" insisted Hartwell.

Sebastian had dropped out of the complex of the invasion now, melting into the circle of the old men in the simple act of seating himself.

The king fulfilled his office, spokesman for the island. He said, "Twenty days perhaps."

Hartwell accepted the information with a nod. He was staring, doubtful, at the circle and, his suspicions crystallised, he asked: "Where are the young men? We've only seen old folk, old men, old women and the children. Where are the young people? Ask him, Frendberg!"

Frendberg was too swift, too voluble in question. He had to wait and simplify his question and wait again while the king found words for answer. Finally he translated the slow, soft syllables to Hartwell. "He says they went away with the Japanese."

"Went away with them!" said Hartwell explosively. "That's the hell of a note. Intelligence said the islanders don't get on with the Japs much. What the hell would they go away with them for? Ask him if they went of their own free will."

The finer shades of meaning were too much for the tenuous link between Frendberg and the king. They struggled desperately, floundering in words. And then Hartwell saw comprehension come to the old man, and with comprehension a look of such intense grief as he had not before seen in a human face—a sudden agony that wiped out all the impassive sterility of his eyes as rain wipes out the steady blue of the sky. There was a long wait, and no man in the little group behind the lieutenant moved.

Then the king spoke, and Frendberg said, "They were taken."

Teresa, her eyes to a ragged hole between the battered palm fronds of the wall, watched the Americanos disappear towards the island path. The air around her became still again, freed of the noise of heavy boots scuffing through the leaf trash, the clatter of accoutrements, and the harsh, rough voices.

The ghosts of the island walk by day as well as by night. They began to close round her again in the stillness, and she remembered Sebastian's curse. She was *tapu,* and she had shown herself to men. To have shown herself to the other children of the village would have been sufficient evil, but to Sebastian it was crime beyond crime. What would the ghosts do to her, the offended tribal deities?

She was a Christian, though she could not remember the priests, the last Spanish fathers who had come in the canoes from Yap. She had only a vague memory of much singing and enormous excitement. Yet she was a Christian: she believed in the Virgin and in Christ.

And she believed in ghosts, in the ancient spirits of the island people, in the more recent spirits of the newly dead, in the terrible ancestral shapes of the sky, of the sea, of the day, and of the night—and they were crowding round her. She began to tremble violently. Somewhere out of an idle memory she brought back legends that had been told her when other girls went to the women's place. In the old days if the *tapu* was broken the girl died. She died not for her own sin, but to protect the island from the just wrath of the gods and the ghosts. The fathers had put a stop to killing—or believed they had—but girls had died even as men and boys had died, and there was no showing how they died except that the old women talked of the ghosts.

They were pressing round her now—the ghosts. She put her hand against her mouth and moaned. Sebastian had called to the ghosts to come and kill her for the violation of the *tapu.*

She still stared out of the hole in the thatch through the aisles of the palm boles to the point where the last khaki of the Americanos had shown in an unremembered glimpse. She saw nothing. She could see nothing. Her eyes were turned inwards now; but she kept her face held against the light as if there might be succour in the light, or as if she dare not turn and look into the half-darkness of the hut.

Terror came over her in mounting waves. It was like an epilepsy. She began to drool at the mouth. The quivering of her body grew and grew. She was in a paroxysm of fear. Half consciously she began to pray, the Latin syllables running agitatedly off her tongue; but there was no comfort in prayer, for the fathers had not come for many years and the Virgin was very far away; and there was comfort in singing only when voices sang together in a kindly companionship—in the warmth of human presence.

Her eyes focussed without volition on a piece of colour on the drabness of the ground, a tiny bit of purple and white. It had an hypnotic attraction. For a moment, unseeing, her eyes wandered off it and were drawn back to it and focussed again. It was a foreign colour, a colour not of the islands. Again she remembered the Americanos. It was as if their coarse, heavy personalities penetrated again into the silence of the palms, as if something of their extrovert energy lingered round the hut.

The shivering diminished and died. The prayers went on mechanically. She watched the paper with a strange fixity as if it too might disappear after the Americanos. And then, without conscious effort, without relaxing even, she shrugged the ghosts away and, slipping out of the hut, walked hesitantly towards the colour. It was the wrapper of the piece of chewing gum that Rucinski had dropped, and she stood staring at it, knowing now that she could escape the ghosts—that she could take refuge with the Americanos as she would have taken refuge with the fathers.

She put out a tentative toe and touched the paper, turning it over. Its glory diminished at once to a plain and sterile white. She turned it back again, looking half fearfully over her shoulder to the doorway of the hut as if expecting the ghosts to come issuing. The shivering was almost completely gone now. A gamin

[77]

resoluteness was overlaying her fears, compound of equal parts of curiosity and Christianity. She was not self-consciously defying tradition, not of her own volition making challenge to the ghosts —she had not reached so far yet. She was only seeing in the Americanos refuge and security.

She began to walk, first slowly and then with a gradual quickening of her paces, towards the village.

5

The three men who had been sent down the left flank of the village came striding through the beachward screen of bush. Rucinski and Fleming came in from the right, Rucinski voluble as ever. They gathered beyond the terrace of the *falu,* and Rucinski surveyed the seated circle of men and the half-dozen old women he could see beyond the *falu* still seated by their huts.

"When I get back to the States," he remarked, without heat, "I'm going to Hollywood, and I'm going to slap Dorothy Lamour right on the sarong. You can have these tropical islands—old men and old bags!"

The master sergeant wheeled on him with a deep suppressed ferocity. "You big-mouthed bastard, shut up, and keep shut up!"

Rucinski stepped back a pace. "Christ, sarge!" he said.

Hartwell jerked himself out of the aura of old pain and grief that shrouded the *falu.* He said: "Sergeant, send a detail—six men will do—down to the south of the island. Take that man we had first with you and another half-dozen men and go up to the north village. Frendberg, tell him"—he pointed to Sebastian—"to tell the north village to send all its men down here. Spread wide as you can and look through everything. They may be lying even at that." And then, as if to himself, he added, "No, they're not lying. Where's Johnson?"

The signaller came over to him, weighed down with the walkie-talkie apparatus.

Hartwell said, "Get Huntsman," and Johnson began to whine into the microphone, his voice metallic and impersonal as if by association with his instrument. He made contact and passed the microphone and headpiece over to Hartwell at an impatient gesture. Hartwell spoke into the microphone. He said: "This is Hartwell. The king of the island says the Japs left twenty days ago. There were only a few, and they were on Asor Island. I say again. Only a few on Asor Island. They left twenty days ago. I am in the south village and have sent out search details over the rest of the island. Over."

Thin and metallic again the voice came back: "Red Fox, this is Huntsman. Okay. White Fox reports Mangejang empty. Am sending in mine sweepers. Out."

For a moment Hartwell regarded the dead microphone. Then he said: "Sergeant Marker, put out eight men round the village. I'm not taking any chances—nobody in or out. We'll make camp somewhere up to the right here. Find the clearest space you can, and make it far enough away from the village to get clear of the flies. I want eight men in couples to go up and have a look inside each hut, check up on everything and report back to me. Get moving!"

The two sergeants fell to work in a vituperative rumble of words. The old men sat on silent save when one or other of them leant over and spat out a bright red stream of betel-dyed saliva. The wind went cool, and a cloud came up over the sun.

Hartwell was left with Frendberg and four other men. He stood waiting as if for something that was bound to happen, but there was only the rising sough of the wind in the palms and a far-off fringe of rain seen between palm fronds as the main squall missed Fassarai. The wind reached its climax and fell away in steep gusts, and in the silence between two of the gusts he heard the voices of women scolding, a sort of Kentish-fire of shrill objurgation that came closer and closer, passing from hut to hut down the pathway towards the *falu*.

"See what it is!" ordered Hartwell, and once again his gun came up to the ready.

Frendberg and one of the other men went forward round the side of the *falu,* moving quickly and with a certain grimness, their fingers at the trigger. The shouting was very close now—shrill, menacing, ugly—and as they came to the end of the *falu* they saw the women, their arms waving, the words pouring out of them, screaming from the doorways of the huts. And down the path between the papayas they saw Teresa, her head down, her shoulders relaxed and fallen, walking with a diminishing resolution towards the All Men House.

The nearest women ceased when they saw the two soldiers. And in the comparative silence Frendberg called back, "It's a kid, lieutenant—a girl."

"Bring her here!" Hartwell's voice was remote from the far end of the *falu.*

The women's voices ceased, and, shepherding the child, the two men came back to the terrace. Two of the old men put their hands in front of their eyes. The rest stopped chewing. The king did not even turn his head, but looked from the Gothic arcade of the leaning palms to the shadowed surface of the lagoon.

"What's it all about?" demanded Hartwell.

"God knows," said Frendberg.

"Ask him!"

Frendberg turned to the king. Again there was the conflict between the two of them. Finally from the mass of misunderstandings Frendberg emerged with the words, "He says the women are angry because she has broken the taboo—and the men also."

"What taboo?"

The intricacies of tribal custom were too much for the king's German. No logical answer came to that question, only the reiterated assertion that she had broken the *tapu* and it was very evil.

"For Christ's sake!" said Hartwell angrily, brushing through the exchange. "I came to clear this island of Japanese, not to get mixed up in this sort of thing. Tell him to ask her what she wants and get an end of it." The itching impatience held him while he listened without understanding to the exchange of syllables of

German and of Micronesian, and the girl's reluctant answering of the king's indifferent anger.

Then Frendberg said: "She is afraid of the ghosts—I think he means ghosts—and the Virgin Mary, and she will be safe with the Americans. I don't get it."

"Nor me," said Hartwell. "Take her along to Sergeant Marker. Let him sort it!"

Frendberg went off with the child, but the old men's eyes did not follow. They had resumed the chewing of the betel nut again.

6

The captain was stooped over the high desk at the end of the chartroom. The Marine colonel was looking over his shoulder. Both men's heads were bent towards the signal flimsy on the desk.

The colonel spoke first, savaging the words, "I might ha' guessed it from the intercepts." There was a harsh note of disappointment in his voice.

The captain said, without turning, "Lieutenant Wombacher, I shall want a course for Eniwetok."

Wombacher jerked his head and said abruptly, "Sir?" as if it were a query.

The captain repeated the name again with a touch of irritation, "Eniwetok." Wombacher reached for a small-scale chart of the Western Pacific and pawed casually to his side for the parallel rules. After a little the captain's voice rose again: "We'll have an escort of three D.D.'s. Alter course after 11.00 by flag signal. Well, if there ain't no Japs—"

"Four months' hard training!" said the colonel of Marines.

The captain answered him comfortingly, "It won't be wasted."

The colonel snorted. "They start all over again every time—back to basic training. God damn!"

Wombacher finished his calculations and made a small pencil note. He handed this over to the captain, who said vaguely, "Thank you." It was a matter of form anyway. They would take their time from the nearest ship of the convoy. He slipped out of the chartroom and went down to his cabin. Reis was sitting there with two of the ship's officers and four of the Marines. He poked his head in at the door and said: "Break out the bourbon. We're going home!"

"What the hell d'you mean?"

"No Japs on the islands. No Japs, no invasion. No invasion, no Marines." He looked at the disgusted faces of two of the Marine lieutenants and said, "Blame that guy. He's the jinx." He nodded at Reis. "They began to call us the reluctant dragon when he was with the ship first. Now he's come back, and we don't even get to see the goddam islands that we're supposed to be going to capture. We're going back to Eniwetok." He let the curtain fall and listened sardonically to the rage of talk that broke out behind it, and went back to the chartroom.

Reis alone made no contribution to the splutter of indignation. He sat there wondering if by any chance Wombacher was right. It was unbelievable how the fates conspired.

CHAPTER XII

~~~~~~

1

THE big chart was sprawled over the mahogany table of the commodore's room. The sliding rule held it down at one end, and a fragment of shell splinter that had come on the commodore's ship in some forgotten engagement weighted it at the other. There was still an irritating bulge in the centre which gave under the commodore's hand and sprang up again when he lifted it. He rested the twin point of the dividers on Falalop.

"This is the only place where you can get a long enough runway on the line of the wind," he said. "Fassarai is just off the line and it wouldn't be big enough in any case. It'll have to be Falalop, and Asor will have to be the headquarters island."

There was a murmured suggestion from the far end of the table.

"No," said the commodore, "I will not have my headquarters on top of an airfield. You know what the air is—always bitching about space—*Lebensraum.*" He rumbled the German word reminiscently. "Besides there is no anchorage off Falalop and we'll need small craft. Stores on Sorlen here." The dividers worked up the line of the reef and came to rest on Sorlen. "D'you think we can put enough ashore there?"

"It'll do," said the commander sitting next to him. "Just!"

"Mogmog—" The points of the dividers hovered above the island like the sword of Damocles and then stabbed down. "Recreation," he said, "bathing, liquor, beach." The dividers moved slowly round the reef—Potangeras, Sorenleng, Pigelelet and right round the barrens to the southern anchorage—till, coming back, they hovered over Fassarai. "May have to make a second stores island for the southern anchorage," he said ruminatively, and the points descended, stopped suddenly half an inch above the paper and rose again in a sweeping circle. "Not now, not now," he said half to himself, and the points moved north again.

At the far end of the table the captain who had spoken first asked, "What do we do about the natives?"

"The natives—the natives." The commodore hummed a little. "The natives are friendly." He looked up belligerently, something breaking across his train of thought. "Have you got the figures, Kemp?"

The officer addressed fumbled for a moment and said, "Four islands inhabited: Falalop, Asor, Mogmog, and Fassarai—eighty on Falalop, seventy-six on Asor, sixty-six on Mogmog, fifty-eight on Fassarai. Total as of yesterday afternoon, two hundred and eighty—ten of them sick, Doc Higgins says, most of 'em likely to die. That'd bring it down to two hundred and seventy. A hundred and fifty of 'em are old women, and fifty-seven are children."

"What was the population before the Japs shifted?"

"Four hundred as near as I can make out," said Kemp.

"We can't have them on Asor," said the commodore slowly, "and we can't have them on the air-strip."

"If you're going to have drink on Mogmog," said a new voice, "you can't have them on Mogmog."

"Children and old people," said the commodore, tapping the dividers against his lips. "Take 'em all down to Fassarai!"

Captain Ernst spoke again. "They're pretty sick, Commodore," he said, "and short of food as far as I can make out."

"Have the medics look 'em over before you ship 'em. Burgess will let you have the landing craft you need and make whatever arrangements you think fit about food—but get them clear tomorrow. Bulldozers from the *Katlan Bay* can go ashore on Falalop this afternoon—start on the air strip at dawn. And, Kemp, start on Sorlen at dawn and clear enough palm trees for the Quonset huts you will need. Cap'n Ernst, you and Kemp settle your requirements for men between yourselves. You can go. Price, I want to talk to you about the anchorage. I've sent for Macgregor."

2

The beach outside the Falalop All Men House was high, rising steeply from the still water. On it were gathered the women and the children. The children were alert, expectant. They sat still, but in the quick nervous gestures and the sharp movement of their heads and eyes they showed high excitement. The women's faces, wrinkled, old, showed nothing—not even resignation. The old men were over against the terrace of the *falu*.

Above them stood the interpreter. He was a half-caste Chamorro from Guam who spoke the island dialect. His voice was harsh and mechanical, as mechanical as the bulldozers that rumbled up the far side of the *falu* over the opened drawbridge of a landing craft with a harsh thunder of exhaust and the snapping crackle of back-fire. He had to raise it at times over their roaring so that he shouted at the men of Falalop. He did not address the women.

Awkwardly and cumbersomely he tried to make clear his explanations to the king. He said: "The Americanos must have all the island, for there will come many of the great birds that fly in the air. They must have a place to come down to the earth, and it will take the half of your palm trees and your taro patches and the bananas and the papayas."

The old man nodded slowly, a nod that registered conprehension only and gave no hint of emotion.

The interpreter said: "We will take you to Fassarai. There are empty huts on Fassarai. We will take your canoes and your cooking pots and your mats and your nets and all your household needs." Again came the slight dispassionate inclination of the head. "Anything you wish you may take—anything."

The head nodded again like the mechanical head of a porcelain mandarin, a meaningless acknowledgment unconnected with humanity.

The interpreter was uneasy, as if he felt that his mastery of the tongue was not sufficient to communicate with automata, as if he could not pass his ideas, his meanings, his own emotions across the gulf of the alien words. He said, suddenly angry, "What do you say?" And, as there was no reply, "Speak! Speak, I say!"

In a thin, quavering old man's voice the king of Falalop said, "There is nothing to say." It was like the voice of a corpse speaking, a disembodied whisper that, diminishing at the end, was lost finally in the resurgent roar of a bulldozer going up the slope.

The interpreter began to work himself into a fury of half-Spanish indignation. He said: "You must leave your island—you must take everything with you—and all you can say is that there is nothing to say! Are you a fool? Are you mad? What is it? What is it, I say?"

And again that disembodied voice that was firm behind its quavering, and that had power in its sibilant whispering, said, "There is nothing to say."

The interpreter turned to Ernst, his face working and furious. "He will not talk," he said. "He will say nothing—nothing! I cannot make him. He understands and that is all. Nothing will make him talk!"

"All right, all right," said Ernst warningly. "He doesn't have to talk if he doesn't want to. Will they go without any trouble?"

"Yes," said the interpreter, himself suddenly calmed. "Yes, I think they will go."

"Ask him how long they want to get ready."

The old man stared up past Ernst towards the sea. He lifted his shoulders and considered for a long while and then said softly, "When you will."

"He is hopeless, hopeless!" said the interpreter, with the quick, angry disgust returned to him. "He will not speak."

Ernst watched the old man's face for a moment, looking beyond the Chamorro's words, and then, as if with a sudden insight, he said, "Maybe you're right at that." His eyes seemed to draw in to himself and he stood there quite silent while the last of the three bulldozers roared over the top of the beach slope and moved down between the palms, the shocking impact of their sound diminishing until it became no more than an angry competition with the surf.

The interpreter began to move uneasily, shifting his weight from one foot to the other, his right hand fiddling with the band of his trousers as he waited for Ernst to speak.

The old men showed no impatience. They sat there as if their spirits were disembodied, wandering above some other island or some far lagoon with only their bodies there against the platform of the All Men House, looking neither at Ernst nor at the Chamorro, utterly without interest, utterly still.

With a quick compassionate insight Ernst said: "They can have all the time they want, but they must begin now. Tell them that!" And then hurriedly he added, "And for Christ's sake, don't bully them!" And then he turned and began to walk up through the soft, yielding sand to the shade of the palms as if he could not look any longer on this unexpressed and inexpressible misery.

Between the palms he met Higgins striding down towards the beach. The little doctor was angry too. Everyone on the island seemed angry save only its own people.

He said: "Those three in the huts—they'll die all right. I don't know why."

"What's the matter with them?"

"Hell! How should I know?" said Higgins irritably. "Nothing wrong with them so far as I can see. I'd say it was old age, but they ain't so old."

"What are their symptoms?"

"I'm telling you," said Higgins, "I'm telling you! There aren't any symptoms. They're just dying. Pulse is going, heart is going, breath will start to go next. Temperatures are normal—no pains that I can discover. Nothing to see on the outside."

"Starvation?"

"Hell, no! Malnutrition perhaps, but there's no sign of starvation. It's unscientific"—he shook his head irritably again—"it's unscientific, but I'd say they were dying just because they wanted to die. And how the hell am I to put that into a navy report?"

The captain sheered away from the implications. "The commodore says we've got to get them all off today. Can we move them?"

"Won't make any difference," said Higgins. "Might even give them an interest in life—and that's an admission. D'you want the rest of the sick report?" Ernst nodded. Higgins fished a paper out of the pocket of his thin tropical trousers. "Ninety-two— Hell! Call it a hundred per cent yaws," he said. "They've most all of them got open ulcers. I haven't had time to make any tests, but I should say there's about sixty per cent hookworm—maybe more. They're underfed, and there's a good deal of deficiency troubles, but you wouldn't be interested in that. Five cases of T.B., seven of gonorrhea, three filariasis cases—you'd call it elephantiasis— there's probably a lot more that's not developed; bit of rickets amongst some of the small children; one boy with a bullet wound in his bottom; and two old men with poisoned feet, probably sting-ray poison. There's some other small things—couple of prolapsus cases amongst the women; one of them's got a tumour in the breast. Two of the children have got bad jaw infections—I haven't had time to go into it properly yet. No malaria, no dysentery, and no leprosy."

He waited for a moment. "Aw, hell, what's the use?" he said. "That's just statistics. The whole island's sick. I don't know what it is: it's not disease. There's no life in 'em," he said, "no life at all. They won't talk, they won't move—they're just not interested." He became explosive. "Damn it, don't look at me like that! I can't help it. I don't know what's the matter with them. They're just sick—not as individuals; they're sick as a community. Can you understand that?"

Ernst watched him, remembering the thin voice of the island king. "Yes," he answered slowly, as if he were speaking against his own wish, "I think I can."

Higgins snorted. "Well, I can't!" he said, and stumped off through the shade.

There was a sudden clatter of axes far up the island, and Ernst turned away from the huts of the village and began to walk towards it. In a little while there would be an air strip straight and level and firmly bonded with live coral across the island, and the fighters and the torpedo planes and the bombers would come roaring in out of the trade wind and settle in the long shadows of the remaining palms; and the war would go on.

He remembered that he had come ashore to determine the placing of the enormous fuel tanks, petrol, bombs, pipe lines, bomb stores, ammunition stores, messroom, a club—there would have to be a club. And he thought at once of the *falu*, of the village club, and of the old men sitting there beside its terrace, immobile and with the life already out of them, like dead men sitting upright, like dead men speaking. Yesterday, when he had told the island king that he and his people would have to move, the king had said: "It does not matter. We are already dead."

3

"The Seabees are starting in here"—Ernst placed his pencil on the chart—"about the middle of the morning. No particular snags."

"Why only the middle of the morning?" demanded Commodore Keldon acidly.

"Difficulty of getting the bulldozers there. They had to cut through the palms. You can't run landing craft in here," he moved his pencil up the line of the beach, "because of the reef, and you can't get them along the beach because the bank is steep to here and here. They had to cut a way through. They didn't lose much time."

"Kanakas gone?"

"They've gone," said Ernst, his face not moving.

"Trouble?"

"That depends on what you call trouble. They didn't say anything—they just went." He paused for a little, and then said in an almost conversational tone, "You know they're going to die."

"Rubbish!" said the commodore. "See that they're fed and housed. They'll come round. Hell, what've we got doctors for?"

"You ask Higgins," said Ernst grimly. "He doesn't know either."

The commodore was silent for a brief moment. "What can I do?" he asked. "We've got to have the island. Have you seen Kemp?"

"I've heard him," said Ernst. "He was using explosives on the island an hour ago."

"Good!" said Keldon, and added, his thought processes clear enough to Ernst: "There's another hurry-up signal from Cincpac this afternoon. Paulsen is working out a berthing plan for the Eniwetok convoy. I want you to look it over and go through the survey reports. Let me know which of the niggerheads in the anchorage ought to be dealt with first. They've bitched up the loading of the *Sanco Point.* Kemp says they'll have to land two hundred tons of stuff they don't want before they can get at the girders he needs for his piers. Look into it first thing in the morning! He wants water tanks too. And get Doc Higgins to give me a plan of the sick-bay accommodation he wants and where he wants it. I want a meeting—all heads of departments—at eleven o'clock tomorrow, and I want progress reports." He hummed for a minute, tapping his teeth with a pencil. "I say again, progress," he murmured absently. "Goddam admirals!" Some old acerbity was plainly rankling. "I want a report from the stores too." He tapped his teeth again. "Why should they all die?" he asked, not expecting, perhaps not wanting, an answer.

4

Higgins leant back in his chair and said, "I wonder if the English landlords ever felt like I feel when they evicted the Irish."

"Commander Higgins," said the commodore acidly, "I asked for progress. I don't want an historical discussion."

"I still wonder if they felt like I feel," said Higgins. "There's nothing in navy regulations to stop me wondering." He grinned ruefully at Keldon. "We've cleared Falalop and we're clearing Asor. If we had any Christianity we'd put the whole lot into hospital. There's not a single one in the whole pack of them that I would certify fit—not even the kids."

Ernst asked, "Did they talk on Asor?"

"The old king talked a bit," said Higgins slowly. "As far as I can make out he's the king of the whole atoll. The others are just subkings. He says that when the Japanese took away the young men and the young women they cut the throat of the islands; and his view is that they are all dead now, and so it doesn't matter anyway. They'll just sit around till they die."

"Nuts!" said the commodore. "People don't do that sort of thing."

"These people do," said Higgins bluntly. "One did in the boat starting down to Fassarai. They want a priest to bury him—and that's another thing! You'd better get a priest down there. They're Catholics, these people."

"That's just what it wanted," said Keldon. "I can hear a Catholic Congressman on his feet already. Is there a Catholic chaplain in the anchorage?"

"There is not," said Higgins, with an obscure irony.

"Can we send an Episcopalian?"

"Jesus!" said Higgins, his voice charged with feeling.

"All right, all right!" said the commodore. "We can't send an Episcopalian. What the hell is this anyway? You are the medical officer here. You keep them alive! Ernst, you keep them fed! What the hell else can we do? Nimitz is squalling for the air strip. Hell, who wants my job? You can leave the Mogmog people for a week. Ernst, how is the strip going?"

CHAPTER XIII

≈≈≈≈≈≈≈≈≈≈≈≈≈≈≈≈≈≈≈≈≈≈≈≈≈≈≈≈≈≈≈

1

HARTWELL watched the men striking the pup tents with a faint air of regret. To the young naval lieutenant he answered: "Oh, hell! They're all right. There's just no life in them, that's all. The only bit of trouble's been over that kid." He nodded towards Teresa, leaning against a tree, and already sleeker, more solid, more filled out than she had been on the day of the first landing. "I haven't sorted all that out yet. She's broken a taboo of some sort. Christ! I wouldn't know what—something to do with women's ceremonies. I've had to get it through the old man's German—and that's lousy—and Frendberg's translation, and I'm not sure that that isn't worse! I think a little while ago they'd have killed her for it, but they don't seen interested enough now. All the same I'd keep an eye on it and, if your interpreter is any good, try to get to the bottom of it. I've told them that I'll come back and hang the king if they touch her, and it wouldn't do any harm if you took the same line." He paused.

"I'll try," said the naval man. "Glad you're going?"

"I don't know," said Hartwell, "I don't know. If it wasn't for the flies and the mosquitoes and the dirt . . . Where do we go from here anyway?" He shrugged his shoulders. "Back to the ship . . ."

Rucinski was packing close to the child and keeping up a flow of talk. "Now you listen," he said for the fifth time, "you'll find the stuff in a gasoline can over in the bush at the back of the little shack." He meant the *dopal*, the women's house. "The last

quart of medical alcohol— Jeez, what a waste! You take it along
to the king. It'll be the finest palm toddy he's ever tasted. Jeez!
What a kick it ought to have—and I won't taste it! Don't let
those goddam navy boys get a sight of it. They drink"—a virtuous
horror spread over his face—"like fish. I mixed it yesterday morning. It ought to be good and hot by tonight. Jeez, what a waste!
Honey," he warned her, "you hop along there and grab it before
those navy boys get ashore. They'll smell it out otherwise. Hound
dogs, just hound dogs!"

The child watched him uncomprehendingly, smiling when his
face lightened up, sobering when it darkened, understanding an
odd word here and there without its context and without its
import.

Rucinski knew that she could not understand, and yet he was
perfectly serious when he looked up from the musette bag. "Now
listen," he said. "It's a two-gallon can, and it's behind the little
shack, and it's got the last of the medical alcohol in two gallons
of palm toddy; and it'll make the old king and the rest of that
goddam All Men House stinko for a coupla days. They'll let you
off after that, you see."

"Okay," said the child, screwing up her eyes as if with effort
over the unfamiliar syllables. An onlooker might have thought
that she understood the whole of his charge, yet she understood
nothing—only, from his tone, that he wished her to acquiesce in
something and that the stark syllables meant acquiescence. "Okay,"
she said again, and the children close to her giggled.

Frendberg, without looking up from the work of cleaning
sand from the cradle of the machine gun, said: "You'd better let
me tell Sebastian. Ain't no point wasting it if it's as good as you
say. The kid don't understand."

"The kid," said Rucinski mildly, "understands a goddam sight
too much." He rocked back on his heels. "I think I'll go hand the
lieutenant my resignation. I ain't got no more interest in this war,
and what's more I'm gonna cancel my subscription to the *National
Geographic*. Tropical islands!" He spat widely, and Teresa laughed.
"Hokum!" he said.

Hartwell came back to the naval lieutenant from a quick, nervous walk round the emptying encampment. "I don't know why they left us here so long," he said. "Couldn't think what to do with us next, I suppose. Well, it's been a change from shipboard anyway. Tell the medics when they come that one man has died while we've been here and one old woman. They'll know— they saw them the first time they came down. They're just dying," he said vaguely. It was as if he found in the cool darkness under the palms a daylight horror, as if for him there was a pall over the loveliness of the island, a darkness that was not of the palm fronds. He said suddenly in a rush: "Damn it, I don't know what's wrong with the place! It gives me the creeps. Where d'you come from?"

The lieutenant named a little town in Vermont.

Hartwell said, "Have you ever tried to think what Morrisville would be like with nobody over twelve or under sixty in the place? Gets me down," he said after a little pause, "the poor bastards." He jerked his head over his shoulder and called out angrily, "Come on, let's go!"

And the master sergeant echoed his words, "Come on, men, let's go!"

"Goodbye, sweetheart," said Rucinski to the child. "You're the only woman I've ever loved. And if you can't be faithful to me when the navy boys come in, try to remember me once a week. Jeez, kid," he let out an enormous hand and slapped her shoulder, "why couldn't you have been your elder sister?"

He humped the musette bag, picked up his gun, and followed Frendberg towards the beach. Teresa and the children pattered after him.

2

The first of the landing craft hauled off the beach, thundering. Frendberg was aware of Sebastian standing rigid and expressionless beside a palm. He shouted out above the noise as he went past to the drawbridge of the second, "You'll find a can behind the women's hut—palm toddy! Hooch," he added in English.

"Right," said Hartwell. "I don't know whether I'm sorry to go or thundering-glad." He hesitated for a moment and then said again, "The poor bastards," and walked over the drawbridge.

The second landing craft went astern, and a swirl of water and sand flooded over her forefoot, and then she was clear over the green depths, and he could see the frightened fish streaking in arrows of scarlet and silver. They turned to starboard and swept past the *falu*, and on the terrace he could see five of the old men sitting as they had sat almost without interruption, it seemed, almost without relief, since he came; and he remembered the pregnant and awful silence of that place—the utter negation of emotion. "The poor bastards," he whispered again, inarticulate.

The landing craft swept round in the wake of the first and headed up to the north for the anchorage. The chopping spray came at times over the square corner of the starboard bow. The men were huddled amidships with their ponchos over them, squatting on the wet steel of the deck. They grumbled ceaselessly: Rucinski remembering his laced palm toddy; Johnson remembering only the halcyon quiet of the little cove to the southward with its inexplicably splintered palms; Frendberg remembering the flies, the mosquitoes, the squalor, and the ulcers.

Hartwell, standing behind the quartermaster in the steering shelter, did not look back as the palm trees exchanged their individuality for a part in a solid bank of green and changed from trees into a bar of malachite on the cloud-flecked blue of the lagoon. He looked forward all the time, forward to the formless huddle of hulls and the stark, up-thrust spike of masthead and derrick and funnel in the anchorage. The task force had lain outside the reef when he came in, but now it was at anchor and peaceful in the calm of the lagoon, and it was enormous. It had been joined by convoys and by single ships until the whole basin of the north was covered with huge, square shapes and the palms of Asor and the northern islands were almost blotted away by their potent ugliness.

They had left the island almost an hour when they saw, heading from the eastern fringe of the anchorage, a small procession of landing craft like their own, four of them in line ahead. And as their quartermaster altered course in curiosity or in friendliness the two lines came together, the northern one growing with every moment of the passage until the bar of spray under the drawbridges and the splashing plumes on the side became enormous and somehow ominous. The first of the landing craft swept by, and Hartwell from his eminence saw in her crouching figures and dark heads and the blue of tattooing. They passed the second, and when they passed it over the roar of the engines came a faint wailing, a thin threnody, tenuous and ghostly above the noise. There were more figures and the masts of canoes in the last two landing craft. The people of Falalop were passing to a new island and to a new age.

3

There was a song that was sung in the islands when the kings went visiting, a song of welcome, the song of a sovereign people to the ruler of another and friendly people. It was a song that had its prescribed and delicate ritual, that began when the canoes first hauled their wind to shoot in under the lee of the sheltering palms, and that grew as they approached and had its precise moments for the touching of the prows on the harsh coral sand; that went through its traditional syllables as the first feet touched the water and that grew in its chorus, full-throated and powerful, to a swift crescendo of welcome as the king put his foot upon the dry land. And the kings of the other islands played their own part in the ritual, waiting their movement to fit the rhythm, suiting their actions to the ordered words.

The people of Fassarai gathered now about the landing by the

All Men House; the old women silent, the children anxious and abrupt in their movements as the inshore fish, the old men sitting. They began the song as the landing craft came in, but in what should have been the ghostly silence of the inward sweeping of the canoes, in what should have been no more than the soft whisper of the water under their razor bows over which the voices would have carried, plaintive and sweet, there was the thunder of the Chrysler motors—deep, threatening, angry, drowning out melody with the overtones of war.

The landing craft swept in roaring to a finish and ran, grating, up the shallows one after another, and not until the last engine cut was there a silence; and even then the silence was scored across and disfigured by the cries of the seamen and the shouted orders.

The song went on, gathering in volume—and yet ignored and somehow ignoble. There came the moment when the king should have placed his foot with ceremony in the friendly water and the tenor and the rhythm changed. They had not thought of it, these old people—they had forgotten the inwardness of this ceremony— for in this moment the young voices of the island took the full burden, the young and vigorous heart of it, chanting the melody and scoring the rhythm. The older voices faded here, yielding place to the young. And now there were no young, and slowly the song faltered and broke, and the melody was lost. Where the great crescendo of welcome should have come there was only silence and a seaman shouting, "Get out of the goddam way then, and let me get it clear!"

And slowly the people of Falalop began to move ashore, forlorn, uncertain and deafened by the long noise of the motors. The king of Fassarai moved forward to greet his fellow king.

CHAPTER XIV

1

THE white sides of the two hospital ships were like open and lit windows against the blackness of the coming squall. Vast sheets of water hung pendent from the belly of clouds that, too gross to support themselves, fell in immense swags towards the sea. The whole of the southwest was black, and the nearer edge of the cloud was over Ulithi; but the morning sun still struck in from the eastward and flooded the lagoon with light.

The battleships turned in the dog-legged passage of the entrance and swept up very slowly past the anchored transports and the store ships, the L.S.T. with the open bows that was the Fleet post office, the seaplane tenders and the depot ships, the tankers and the ammunition ships, the L.S.I.'s, the tank landing craft, the tugs, the salvage vessel, the whole incredible host of small ships that ministered to the Fleet. Ulithi was no longer a lagoon. It was a Fleet base, the base of the American Pacific Fleet—the base of the most tremendous concentration of maritime power in the world. Out of the ring of the atoll, broken by the entrance channels, breached by the high-tide surf, green and white and exquisite from the air, white and green and lovely from the sea, Keldon had made a secure and magnificent harbourage.

And now the Fleet was come. One after another the battleships made the turn and moved in to their anchorages. The vast perspective of maritime might grew with each deep reverberation of the anchor cables. And after them came in the great carriers of the "Essex" class—immense, ugly, hostile, suggesting with the ranked aircraft on their flight decks an intolerable anger. Cruisers, destroyers—the anchorage absorbed the endless procession of them. Line after line of ships built up across the grey-green waters under the rain squall, lines that blotted out the islands, that seemed to join and coalesce until the outer edges of the lagoon—the break-waters of the harbour—were lost in a floating wall of steel.

Higgins, on the beach of Asor, stood ruminatively under a primitive shower. To Ernst, who was waiting his turn, he said, "Here's the Bull." He stooped to soap the lower part of his legs and groaned slightly as he straightened himself up again. "It's the end of a quiet life. I wonder what he's got up his sleeve now."

"You've got nothing to bitch about," said Ernst brusquely. "I'm the one that catches it. I'm low man on the totem pole. You wait—Kellie'll be in a hell of a temper this morning. He always is when there's superior brass in the offing. Nice ships, those 'Essex' class."

"Thank God I'm only a poor damned medic!" said Higgins, rolling his eyes piously. "Wash behind the ears!" He vacated the shower, and Ernst moved in. "You'll just about make it before the rain hits you. 'Bye."

2

The canoes came in from the fishing in the late afternoon—three of them, all that could be manned now. And because the blight of the island seemed to have spread also to the sea, they had with them only a few poor baskets. The blue and yellow stripes and the silver were bright for a little as they carried the fish through the sun to the shaded sand beside the *falu* and put them down.

Teresa came stalking down the village path to claim the share of her hut. She was developing swiftly with the hot sudden tropical growth that came partly on the onset of puberty and partly with the sudden change from the meagre diet of the past to the

American canned goods that she stole from the indifferent king. Her breasts were jutting out now, and her shoulders broadening. Her skin glistened with oil, and she swung her hips provocatively as she walked. Fayu had brought in the first canoe, and of the two eligible boys now on the island Fayu was her choice. She had acquired already the dubious prestige of a taboo-breaker against whom the gods had not taken just revenge. On that single day of the coming of the Americanos she had passed from childhood to more than womanhood. She had acquired stature. Fayu himself had the attributes of heroism—he carried the mark of the Japanese bullet in his bottom.

Fayu looked up and laughed as she came. Fernando, the boy who had hidden on Mogmog, was behind him, and he was making clear his proprietory rights. He dropped the last basket at her feet, contemptuously shrugging his shoulders.

"Jesus is old," he said, "and the lines are rotten, and I think the god of the sea is angry with us."

Teresa nodded, picking out the two best fish. "These," she said calmly, "are mine. Tell the old men to make new lines."

"I have told them," said Fayu.

Teresa began to walk away with the fish. Over her shoulder she said, "We will ask the Americano doctor for fishing lines."

"Perhaps."

Fayu began to sort out the fish, and Olimarao, the Asor king, came from the *falu*. The other kings had abdicated now in a general acknowledgment of his sovereignty. If he had heard Teresa's arrogation of his authority or Fayu's implied criticism he gave no sign. He looked only at the fish and at the succeeding basket that Fernando and Falifi of the third boat brought in, and spat widely an enormous red quid of betel juice.

"The fish are sick," he said slowly.

Other women came down, and he apportioned fish gently and without enthusiasm until the inadequate heap was gone. The men had intended to work at the canoe near the southern cove, but obviously it was too late already in the afternoon. They sat around the terrace of the *falu* until close upon sunset when the women called them to eat, and then they went slowly. Fayu and Fernando had long since disappeared.

In the night they drank toddy in the *falu*. The laced toddy that Sebastian had found behind the women's hut had long since been used up. There had been enough of it only to bring to the *falu* a false memory of the past, a brief access of a spurious joy; and now there seemed to be no body in the thin liquor that they drank.

That morning thirty-four new ships had come in to the southern anchorage—attack transports, most of them, with four tankers and eight of the nameless misshapen necessary ships that went to feed, to repair, to maintain the vast fleet of the northern anchorage. To the north there were eight battleships, nine heavy carriers and a round dozen of escort carriers with cruisers and destroyers beyond counting. Up by Asor the water was heavy with the burden of two vast floating docks, seaplane-base ships, ranked rows of Catalinas hovering like drinking gnats upon the water, and cluttering patches of anchored small craft. The twelve-mile stretch of the two anchorages was forested with masts almost as thick as the islands were with palms, a malignant, ominous foresting.

In the *falu* the men discussed the new ships, but only in terms of their appearance, their beauty or ugliness, their size and shape and colour. They had no conception of the ships' meaning, no conception of the thousands of men cooped in them in preparation for invasion, no conception of the fantastic elaboration of machinery, equipment, material that went to their creation. To them they were shapes on the water, and to them it was more important that their presence might be an offence to the sea god than that this incredible assemblage was like a slingstone poised against the Japanese and ready for release. They could remember only that today the fish had been wary and the sea god not kind.

The coconuts came thudding down, the green and olive husks bloated and almost sinister in the shadows; and the children, under Teresa's direction and with her quick help, stacked them in piles beside the island path. There was no fishing today. Fayu and Fernando and two of the biggest of the small boys were cutting nuts for the two villages. There had been no direction. Sebastian and one of the old men had indeed spoken the previous night of a shortage of nuts, and two of the women had complained in the morning; but it had not seemed necessary to them to do anything about it. The nuts came when they were wanted—that was the tradition of the islands. Fayu had made his suggestion in the morning, and Teresa had backed it; and she had brought in Filomena, who came from Mogmog and was almost as old as herself.

Slowly, very slowly, the two groups that made the society of the island now were dividing, the young people from the old. It was as if the two boys and the older girls could see the death in the eyes of the old people, and fearfully and with a delicate apprehension were edging away. They broke ritual and tradition in every move they made, and there was no retribution. Unconsciously, and at the behest only of a recognised necessity, they were making a new pattern of life; but the lines of the pattern were unclear, and the edges ragged.

So now, when enough nuts had been cut, they indicated a rough division and ordered the younger children to do the carrying. The four walked down towards the beach where the Americans had landed first and sat in the near shade, staring out at the new ships and at a convoy that even now was threading its way in through the gate between the reefs in a long chain like a necklace widely spaced. The leader of the escort vessels that preceded it was heading up towards the north, the new accretion to the southern anchorage.

"There'll be no fishing tomorrow either," said Fernando.

"The fish will be there," said Teresa, faintly scornful. "The old ones do not wish to catch them. Falifi's canoe brought in one basket only."

"We must catch more then," said Fayu with a ready complaisance. "I like fishing," he said abstractedly. "When does the Americano doctor come again?"

Teresa folded up three fingers one after another. "In three days," she said. "More stick medicine." She meant injections, and injections were popular on Fassarai.

"More candy," said Filomena, and rolled her eyes. She used the English word. They were all of them picking up English now—a few words every week remembered and sometimes practised amongst themselves.

"Why does he come?" asked Fernando.

"To give the stick medicine," said Teresa again.

"Yes, but why?"

Teresa was silent, and Fayu said, "Because it is an order."

"Elato is sick," said Teresa, apparently without connection. "He will die today."

"Then the doctor will be angry again," said Fayu. "He doesn't wish people to die."

"Elato is very old," suggested Filomena, a faint compassion and understanding in her voice.

"It doesn't matter," said Fayu. "The doctor will still be angry. It is an order that the old people shall not die."

"Why?" asked Fernando again.

Fayu took refuge in the phrase he had already used: "It is an order."

"The Yellows did not care," said Fernando.

"The Yellows were different," agreed Fayu, "and there was no order."

"I like the Americanos better," said Teresa.

"Women do," said Fayu thinly, remembering the dictum that he had heard in the *falu*.

Behind them they could hear the shrieks of the children carrying nuts to the north village. There was more noise today than there had been for many days on the island—not for any just cause or reason, but spontaneous noise, a reflection perhaps of the sudden access of energy of the older children. Fayu stood up and, striding down to the beach, slipped into the water and swam out, his body lithe and graceful in the lucent green of it. The white terns were circling over them, mute and exquisite. After a little Fernando and Teresa and Filomena joined him, and they swam out to a sandy shoal on a reef that they remembered. Teresa, sitting on it with the water up to her breasts, began to laugh for no reason at all except that she was happy and happiness was a precious commodity on Fassarai. They splashed and played in the water for an hour and swam back again to the beach to dry in the soft air of the trade wind.

There was a faint scent in the wind now that was another new thing in the islands, a scent of mingled Diesel smoke and fuel oil, a new scent that the keen island nostrils had not known before.

When they were dry they crossed the island, breaking through the seaward undergrowth, and walked along the ocean beach looking for flotsam.

4

The trade wind died with the sunup and was succeeded by variable flaws that chased one another over the glass calm of the lagoon in cat's-paws of corrugated darkness. The day became hot and sultry long before the middle morning, and the air was heavy. Outside on the reef the sound of the surf grew and grew in the silence, though the waves were no higher than they had been. Everything magnified itself in the stillness, and Teresa, walking down past the women's hut towards the north village, could hear the beat of the terns' wings among the palm fronds, a sound unheard in ordinary times.

The cat's-paws died away in the end, and on the mirror surface of the lagoon the ships of the southern anchorage were piled in high, fantastic shapes, the further ones lifting in the hot shimmer in great cubes of blue and grey steel—distorted cliffs of darkness.

The canoes came in early and frightened, like sea mews seeking a crag against the gale. The sounds of ordinary movement, of ordinary life, that were lost normally in the incessant susurrus of the palm leaves, were sharp now against the dull continuous background of the reef thunder. Even Sebastian's mutterings as he walked along the path were clear and had the form of speech.

The big wind hit the island in the middle of the afternoon, coming with no more than the warning of a single squall. It came in from the southwest, battering and snatching instantly at the seaward palms and then leaping to flow over the rampart of the island with a roar infinitely greater than the surf itself. It hit at low tide, and the seas that came with it and grew with it, and that became enormous in an instant with it, thundered against the sheer outer face of the reef and leapt in upward waterfalls of spray that were seized by the wind and hurled bodily against the palms. The space between the palms that was still under the thrashing of the trade became now a whistling, roaring wind-tunnel charged with so heavy a spray that it was scarcely possible to breathe in it, and the boles of the palm trees ran with salt water to the girdling leaves at their bases and the salt ran into the fresh-water reservoirs that stood below them.

By five o'clock the air was dark, and inside the palm trees it was blacker than the night, for no stars shone between the fronds that snapped and broke and whistled away in the roaring. The high tide came with the fall of night, and over the southern end of the island the seas that marched across the shoulder of the reef grew in a ranked and brutal combat until they raced across the white sand beach and lifted beyond that to the soil under the palms and, in a little, were racing, unchecked, across the southern horn to rustle down into the cove.

In the huts where they were when the wind hit them, the people stayed. The two boys were at the All Men House with the Asor king and five of the old men, and they too stayed. There was nothing that any man could do. This was the *tai-fung* of the

Chinese, the great wind, and nothing that man could do was of importance. So they lay while every palm frond of the roof became a snapping, crackling banneret in the wind, and while they heard palm branches and fronds flung against it from the seaward line and heard the crash of whole palms in the distance and the endless *thud, thud, thud* as the nuts came down. Once they heard a woman shriek in the darkness, and once they thought they heard the rush of water close beside them. But this was not the heart of the typhoon, only the outer wind of it, and the seaward bank along the centre of the island was still rampart enough against the wash of the sea. Only at the northern and the southern ends was it swept; and at midnight the wind veered steeply and began to die.

At dawn Teresa, crouching and wet from the spray that still drove through the palm trees, came to the All Men House and called outside, not daring even in this crisis to go inside it. Fayu and Fernando went wordlessly to her and, doubled and gasping against the wind and the spray, followed her up into the village. The hut of Jesus had collapsed and the old woman was pinned under the fallen beams. They worked to get her out in a fury of terror and excitement, afraid of the ghosts of the typhoon and the wrath of the god of the sea, and afraid physically of the tearing, relentless weight of the wind.

At sunup there was a brief calm. After it the wind blew again for an hour, but almost without malice. The searching spray had ceased between the palm boles and it was possible to stand and breathe again without fear. At noon Sebastian and the king walked down towards the southern end, and Teresa and Fayu and four of the children followed them. The damaged canoe was gone, swept down the wind into the empty ocean. One of the good canoes was gone with it. Sixty trees at the southern end had had their roots washed clear of soil and had gone over with the wind weight. A score of others near them had lost their crests and stood naked as flagpoles and as useless. All through the island there was a ruin of palm fronds and green nuts. In the village Jesus's hut had ceased to be, and the roofs of two others of the huts were stripped and the rafters were naked and obscene in the fitful sunlight.

The rain came heavily, but the water jars were full—full of salt water that had run down the palm boles.

In the northern village three houses were wrecked in part, and the second of the canoe houses. A canoe had swept clear here too, and the sails of another were shredded into fine threads of pandanus.

No one was hurt. Even Jesus's wife was only bruised and angry with fear. The sun came out in the midafternoon, and the island was steamy-hot with everything in it wet and salt-coated and sticky. When they looked out over the lagoon the ships of the Americanos were still there.

CHAPTER XV

≈≈≈≈≈≈≈≈≈≈≈≈≈≈≈≈≈≈≈≈≈≈≈

1

ERNST'S face was grey with fatigue. The khaki shirt and trousers that composed his uniform looked as though he had slept in them; only he had not slept. All through the brutal night he had been on the water with a tug giving help where he could, trying to bring some order into the fantastic chaos of the anchorage.

The small craft had begun to go early, some of them swamping at their moorings, some of them parting cables or breaking adrift from the ships at which they lay and dragging down to crash in ruins on the reef. Some of them fetched up on Mogmog beach and were safe. Some of them fetched up against Sorlen. Some of them battered and thrashed their way as the tide rose out over the reef shoals and, sinking or floating precariously, passed into the open ocean on the heels of the typhoon.

The bigger ships in the soft patch up at the northeast of the northern anchorage began to drag about eight o'clock in the evening. Most of them steamed to their anchors and held their positions after a fight. One L.S.T. broke down and finished up stern on to the reef and heeled over at a wicked angle. Odd craft followed her.

Keldon, rustling through a sheaf of reports, looked over at his second in command. "She blew," he said noncommittally. "Is this the lot?"

Ernst nodded. "Eighty small craft, mostly L.C.P.'s and L.C.T.'s. Jesus, how fast those things can move on a wind! We damned near lost the tug chasing one. She was half across the reef before we knew it."

"Eighty," said Keldon again, and tapped his teeth with the pencil end. "That about put us out of commission." His voice became suddenly angry. "Christ Almighty! Why did it have to come now?"

"The Lord sent a wind, and they were scattered," said Higgins profanely and unhelpfully from the depths of his chair. "The Bull'll start howling for boats in an hour or so."

"He will," said Keldon grimly. He tapped his teeth again. There was a little silence. Then he said: "Should have the recon reports by now. Get through to Air Command again. Have you got the first report there?"

Kemp passed the paper over.

"Three still afloat at fifteen miles," said Keldon slowly; "wreckage, two patches. Two more at twenty miles. What time will the destroyers get there?"

"The *Lawson* should be right there now," said Kemp, "and the *Warren* in about half an hour. There's three tugs on the way. We'll want the rest pulling stuff off the reef."

"Make a signal to the *Warren*: tell her to leave the five that have been sighted to the *Lawson* for investigation and to go on to a position thirty miles out, same bearing, and wait for the recon reports. Tell the *Lawson* not to attempt to tow, but just to check each craft and see whether they're in immediate trouble or not. The tugs can pick them up. Has anybody worked out what the maximum drift is likely to be?"

"I calculate sixty miles," said Ernst thoughtfully, "if any of them floated that long. If we work on a basis of seventy miles it should clear everything."

Keldon nodded. "The *Melotte* is due to sail for Eniwetok and Pearl Harbor Tuesday. Take all her landing craft except two. What's the report on the *Harmon*?"

"Starboard turbine still on the blink," said Kemp, thumbing over a sheaf of papers. "Feed-water troubles and a lot of small stuff: the engineers say that she ought to go back also."

"Take her landing craft—leave two as before. Let me have a list by noon of all attack transports that aren't involved in the next operation and we'll skim them too."

"Cincpac will howl," said Ernst.

"Let 'em"—Keldon's voice was curt—"and give me the list of craft afloat." He scanned it rapidly. "One L.S.I., two L.C.T.'s to the *New Jersey;* L.S.I.'s to the carriers as far as they will go; L.C.T.'s to the rest of the battleships and the cruiser flagships. Won't be able to cover all the cruisers—can't be helped. Hell, they've got their own boats—let 'em use 'em for once! Keep a pool of five for our own use and two for Falalop."

Ernst was pencilling hastily. "That makes six more than we've got," he said. "All the same, with luck we'll have enough off Mogmog beach by tonight to fill it out."

"Don't worry me with details," said Keldon irascibly. "Get it done! And send one L.S.I. down to Fassarai."

"Commodore"—Ernst's eyebrows went up—"we can't spare a boat. McNally's due to go down Friday. I'll try to raise one then."

Keldon disregarded the interruption. "Send down one L.S.I.— at once! McNally goes with it, and tell him to take all the supplies he needs. That island may have been swept. I'll not have that on my conscience as well." He slammed down his pencil on the table. "That is all."

2

Filomena saw the L.S.I. approaching in the midafternoon and ran up the path from the canoe sheds, calling. The doctor had said that he would be back in seven days—in other words, on the fifth day of the full moon. It was not possible to say what this arrival three days early portended. Teresa and four of the smaller children followed her back to the beach. The boys were away at the north village, looking at the destruction there. The northern part of the island had been swept also. There were many trees down, and all across the narrow spine of Fassarai was a ruin of palm fronds and green coconuts, and the ruin was coated with a thin crystalline salt. The air itself seemed salt; their skins were salt; the food seemed impregnated with salt.

On the beach near the All Men House the children waited the arrival of the L.S.I. She anchored clear of the shallows, and a dinghy came in. At once the children recognised the lank form of McNally. Teresa had hoped that it was the soldiers coming back again. They treated her more familiarly than did the austere McNally. But the children waited for him politely at the water edge. Teresa and Filomena even sang prettily as the dinghy came in. McNally splashed up through the last shallow and greeted the children quietly.

"You're still alive, huh? The old man ought to know better than to think you can kill a Kanaka with a typhoon. Where's the king?"

Teresa caught at the one word that she recognised clearly, "king." "King," she said, imitating accent and tone as nearly as she could, "king there." She pointed to the All Men House.

Sebastian and Jesus were sitting at the door. They remained seated as McNally went up, but Sebastian said, "Guten Abend."

The pharmacist's mate, who followed McNally, was German-speaking. The painful cross-examination of Sebastian began again.

"He says the wind blew."

"Yeah. We know. It blew. What I want to know is, What did it do when it blew?"

Humourlessly and faithfully the pharmacist's mate translated, "It blew terribly."

"Fer God's sake! Look here, ask him if anybody has been killed and if any bad damage has been done."

"No one in this village," said the interpreter after a brief interchange, "only the wife of Jesus—she is hurt."

"How?"

"The house fell on her."

"All right—so we've got one injured and one house gone. Anything else?"

"He says no, not in this village."

"What about the north village?"

"He doesn't know. He thinks maybe it's all right, maybe it's not."

"If I was to stay in this island I'd need a psychiatrist to look after me," said McNally in exasperation. "Who is Jesus? Tell him to get Jesus and take me along to his wife."

"This is Jesus," said the interpreter, indicating the passive figure next to Sebastian.

The Asor king emerged suddenly from the door of the All Men House. He greeted McNally with a half-salute and sat down respectfully.

"Ask him what happened."

"He says it blew," said the pharmacist's mate stolidly.

"Christ!" said McNally. "Tell Jesus we want him and we want his wife, and tell the king I want to know just what happened in the north village and I want it chop-chop. Where's the woman?"

The wife of Jesus was cooking on the fireplace that had survived the wind. McNally examined her rapidly, disregarding her protests. She was heavily bruised on the left side and there was an ominous tenderness over one rib. It was a little while before he was satisfied that it was not broken.

Then he said: "Well, that's a relief anyway. If I'd strapped her up we'd have to leave it for ten days, and God knows what would happen in this climate. Give her some liniment and tell Sebastian to tell her how to rub it on. Maybe she'll drink it. It don't signify much anyway. Get your gear ashore, and we'll run 'em over again. I don't suppose we can do anything about hookworm specimens since we're three days early. We'll fix them here first, and then we'll go up to the north village. When you are getting your gear, tell the L.S.I. to go up and wait for us off the north anchorage. Tell the dinghy to come straight in as soon as she gets there. We've got to get the L.S.I. back quick." To himself he said, "One old woman chipped about the ribs. Ernst is going to be mad wasting an L.S.I. over that, but I suppose it's all right as long as it keeps Kellie's conscience steady. Maybe it is at that.

"Hey, you kids, come on! I'll get on with you first. What's your name? Teresa? Yes, Teresa, come on, lift up your arm." He stooped and began to examine the yaws ulcers underneath the armpit. "Hurts a bit, don't it? Well, you can't have a tropical paradise for nothing. Kid, if you take my advice you'll learn enough English to answer back and learn it quick. First word you want to learn is no."

He slapped her bottom and chased her away, and she ran giggling and then turned to watch him as he caught one of the smaller children and began a second quick examination.

3

Keldon rubbed the rough deal table with the butt of his dividers. "As far as this base is concerned, this is the position," he said. "Task Group 38.1—McCain's Task Group—comes in according to plan. Their return will not—repeat, not—be cancelled. Everything will be ready to store, fuel, and ammunition them according to the schedule." He looked belligerently round the table. "And if you don't cut twenty minutes in every hour of the schedule, somebody's going to be shot around here. The Bull may need 'em, and he may need 'em bad before this thing's finished. Task Group 38.4, return cancelled. The Bull keeps them with him —and by God he'll need 'em!"

He pushed back his chair and, walking over to the wall, stood in front of the small-scale chart of the Philippines, studying it intensely for a moment. Then he half turned towards the men at the table.

"This is the position as I see it. The submarines attacked here." He indicated a point in the Palawan Passage. "Since the attack they have moved to here." The dividers stabbed in immediately south of Mindoro Island. "The dawn search from the *Intrepid* reports them heading up here." He jerked the points out and moved them towards the Sibuyan Sea. "Your guess is as good as mine. I put it that the Japanese are heading for the San Bernardino Strait; that's the main force, no carriers. There's another force. The dawn search from the *Enterprise* sighted a second force southwest of Negros Island"—again the dividers stabbed in, pulled out, and moved northeasterly—"at least two battleships, heading this way." He put both hands up to the chart and the dividers fell, points downwards, into the floor. "Crab's claws," he said, "what the army calls a pincer movement. We've got about three hundred ships off Leyte Gulf besides small stuff."

Keldon shrugged his shoulders. "That is all. I don't know anything else. Maybe we'll know tomorrow, maybe not; but, by God, if McCain is not clear as far as this base is concerned within forty-eight hours at most, I'll do the shooting myself!"

Ernst leant back in his chair. "The Bull's got the ships," he said, "and they're in the right place; but it looks like the big show-down to me."

"Please God!" said Higgins. "Then we can go home."

Keldon was still staring at the chart. "Halsey," he said, "will go north towards San Bernardino. He'll leave the Seventh Fleet to look after the Gulf. I wonder"—he paused for a moment—"I wonder how much bombarding the Seventh Fleet's done."

Again there was a little silence in the room, a silence through which the drone of an aircraft coming in could be heard above the dull noise of the reef.

"I wonder how Kincaid's off for ammunition."

4

Elato was dying. By Teresa's reckoning, he should have died long since, should have died even before the typhoon. She waited outside the hut and listened to the old women grumbling in the interior. From time to time she scratched at the bites of some malignant insect. They stretched in a line up her thigh and across her belly to the navel. The women had sent her out of the hut. The men seemed to ignore her breach of the ancient taboo and the lesser breaches that had followed it. They treated it as if it had not happened, ignoring it because they could not deal justly with it according to the custom of the islands. It was easier to ignore it. But the women neither forgot nor forgave, and now they had driven her out of Elato's hut where she had been watching death in the company of others where the ghosts could not frighten.

She was morbidly curious about death. She had not seen it come, before. She had seen only the bodies after death, the bodies over which tradition and religion quarrelled in a wordless, voiceless combat so that the Christian dead of Fassarai went to their graves covered with the paint of saffron and coconut oil in whorls and arabesques, in stripes and odd convoluted patterns. So the service at the graveside—truncated, distorted, strange-sounding to a European ear in the uncouth syllables of phonetic remembrance —was followed by feasting and a dance. There would be no dance after the death of Elato; there would be no feasting; but if they could keep the body until Friday—she remembered that on Friday the father would come, Adamello, the Catholic chaplain of the submarine depot ship—they could have a proper burial, a thing of flowers and singing, the whole strange excitement of gravesides and of death. She listened to the sounds of the hut. If Elato would last over till tomorrow it was certain they could keep the body. If he died this afternoon perhaps the Asor king would order his body into unhallowed ground.

Filomena joined her silently, and, in a little, Fayu. They sat, the sun striking on them, motionless outside the hut listening to the struggle within. Elato was dying of his own will, and yet his body struggled within. They could hear gasping and the horrible throat noises of the old man under the steady rustle of the women's talk. The whole village was aware of Elato's imminent end. It had held him to be dying for all of a month now, and yet it was instantly aware of the imminence of death. It was as if the shadow of the wings were across the sun, as if there were a chill over the island.

A thousand miles to the northwest there was a battle, the greatest sea battle of the war, a vast thing covering all the Philippines and spread far out into the open depths of the Philippine Sea. One by one the intercepts were coming into Keldon's office on Asor: the *Princeton* hit mortally, the new threat from the northeast where the carriers dropped down from Japan in their last fantastic banzai charge across the sea, the night battle in the Surigao Strait, the dawn surprise of the Japanese as they fell athwart the escort carriers off Samar, the desperate, swirling calls for help across the crepitating air.

But here in Fassarai all the world was Fassarai, and all the world was indrawn and concentrated on the death of a single man. It was not that they had emotion for Elato. There was no pity in it and no sympathy. It was only that with it came an awareness of their own condition, an awakening again to the knowledge that they were a dead people in a dying world.

The children sat on fearfully while the sun dropped down and made of the seaward palm boles the bars of an angry furnace. Fernando joined them, and some of the smaller children; but there was no giggling, no laughing. It was as if they could feel the agony of the soul within the hut fighting against the coil of fate. The sun went down, and in a little the darkness came up from the west and flooded across the island as the tide flooded across the reef. Elato still lived, and the strange body of fear across the island persisted. The ghosts of the darkness were malignant, and the children cowered together for comfort in a hot, uneasy huddle.

He died at midnight.

5

Though the great windows looking out over the sea were open there was not movement enough in the air to flicker the flame of the twelve tall candles on the table. They stood like a coronet of light on the dark pool of the mahogany, and the silver and the lace of the table mats shone under the brightness of them.

Reis watched alternately the faces of Mrs. Deering and her husband. They were very full of the Leyte battle, full of the tremendous story of the victory. But they discussed it quietly, gently almost, as if in that shadowed room there was small place for violence.

Deering delivered himself of the final judgment. "Admiral Seager says it's the end of the Japanese Navy as an effective fighting force."

Reis looked up. His voice was quiet too. "That's all right," he said, "as long as we don't build too much on it. It may be the end of the Japanese Navy, but it's not the end of the war. You know how they fought on Saipan. They didn't do so bad on Guam if it comes to that. We were sent back on D plus 3; but it took our men three weeks to clear the island, and they had to kill seventeen thousand Japanese before they finished. I don't know what they've got in the Philippines, but they'll fight—and there's a hell of a lot of islands still before we get to Japan."

Deering nodded in agreement.

"And then there's Japan," Reis continued. He waited while the soufflé was served and then, when the room was quiet again, said almost wistfully, "I suppose it's just about the biggest sea battle in history." He hesitated for a moment and went on, "You've only got to look at the chart." Again there was the little faint hesitation. "And I was in an empty transport coming back from Kwajalein!"

Mrs. Deering said tartly, "You can't expect to get the whole navy into a battle!"

"I asked for that," said Reis, "but I like being sorry for myself every little while. It helps." Mrs. Deering snorted involuntarily and Reis laughed outright. "I can't help it," he said. "I got away —I didn't even have time to say goodbye to you. I went on board with everything so Top Secret I was afraid to cough. I was back

[117]

with the old crowd, and when we got out of the harbour she headed west. And what happened? We steamed to Point A, and you can take it from me that Point A when it's in the open ocean looks like Point B or any other damn' point you like to name! You are there, and there's a hell of a lot of sea round you, and Wombacher says this is Point A—and I never believe what Wombacher says anyway."

"What did happen?" asked Deering. "We never heard."

"Nothing happened, sweet damn' nothing! Geiger he decided he'd got enough men to do the job and he didn't want the extra reserve that they had scraped up; so we came back again, but we went to Molokai instead of here. Then we went to San Diego, and then some guy made a mistake so we went to San Francisco and back to San Diego. Hell, I guess I know the coast of California! And just about the beginning of September they went all Top Secret again and rushed us to Kwajalein empty and in a hell of a hurry, and we picked up Marines and raced down all excited as hell to take a place called Ulithi atoll. And we got ten miles from Ulithi, just near enough so as not to see the islands, and they found there weren't any Japs on them; so we went back to Kwajalein. Now we're back here and my pharmacist's mate says we're going to San Francisco again. I wouldn't know. The boys say I put a hoodoo on the ship."

Deering very quietly from the end of the table said:

> "I am become a name;
> For always roaming with a hungry heart."

Reis pricked up his ears. "I don't know that one."

"Somebody said it about Ulysses." Deering smiled at him.

"Tennyson," interjected Mrs. Deering.

"Hell, no!" Reis challenged it. "Ulysses spent most of his time in combat areas."

"Except when he hid amongst the women," put in Mrs. Deering.

"I'd include that," said Deering.

[*118*]

Reis put down his fork and said unaffectedly, "It's nice to be back here all the same."

Mrs. Deering almost exploded.

They took coffee under the koa tree on the terrace. The night was like all the island nights, ineffably soft and gentle. They sat in long companionable silences, and finally Mrs. Deering spoke. She said, "You're not worrying so much about it now, are you?"

Reis shrugged his shoulders invisibly in the darkness. "Eels get used to skinning, so they say."

CHAPTER XVI

≈≈≈≈≈≈≈≈≈≈≈≈≈≈≈≈≈≈≈≈≈≈≈≈≈≈≈≈≈

1

THE one-roomed hutment with its neat verandah facing inward over the lagoon looked bare and austere in the new clearing of the palms. Inside, it was comfortable enough, with deep chairs and a radio set and a drinks cabinet in the corner. Behind it, and standing back from it on the coral road that the Seabees had made in the first five days, stood the headquarters mess, and beyond it the "hotel" for transients. They were still working on the Quonset huts for the headquarters staff. Behind the area, tent lines stood in ordered rows. The air-strip had been functioning for three weeks now, and the daily flow of planes from Guam had been straining Falalop's resources to the utmost. The base was in being.

Doc Higgins, almost sunk in a deck chair on the verandah, looked out over the water and said, "Looks like the Bull means business again."

They could see the shape of Admiral Halsey's flagship far out in the main anchorage.

"Looks like it," said the commodore.

"Clam face," said Higgins sourly, "clam face Kellie!" He tried the more direct attack. "When's the Bull moving?"

"I am only the commodore of the base," said Keldon drily. "I wouldn't know. All the same if the fleet anchorage was empty Saturday midday it wouldn't surprise me."

"Huh!" Higgins raised his voice a little, called, "Jasper, my glass is empty."

"Yassir." The negro mess boy appeared instantly with a fresh-poured rum and coke.

Higgins lifted the glass and said: "I hear you got the floating dock connected up yesterday. Here's to it!"

"You hear everything." Keldon took a fresh glass himself from the mess boy and drank in turn.

Higgins murmured impersonally, "It's a wise admiral that keeps his sources of information lubricated."

"I'll buy it," said Keldon lazily.

The two were old friends in the Service. They understood each other.

Higgins said, "There's a Roman Catholic bishop coming visiting with us Saturday."

"Yeah."

"What are you going to do with him?"

"Feed him and pass him on through channels to Halsey. Bull's got more rings than I have. Why shouldn't he have his headaches too? What d'you want me to do—go to confession?"

"No. No. It wouldn't do much good now. But, if you want my advice, don't send him down to Fassarai."

"Why?" Keldon sat up with a jerk. "What's wrong there?"

Higgins watched the bubbles rising through the maroon fluid in his glass.

"Come on!" demanded Keldon. "What is it? What's the trouble?"

"No trouble. No trouble at all. Docile"—Higgins considered the word as he had considered the bubbles—"docile, that's what they are. They don't give any trouble. They just die. I think they die rather than give trouble. Have you seen Chaplain Adamello?"

"I've been dodging him for two days," said Keldon gruffly.

"Keep right on dodging."

"What's it?"

"He's got himself into a state of mind," said Higgins judgmatically.

The commodore in his turn considered his drink as if in the

pattern of the bubbles he could see, somewhere, a solution. Finally he asked, "Which of your boys went down this week?"

"McNally. He's been down every Friday with the rations since we put them on the island."

"Where's he now?"

"His quarters or swimmin'—I wouldn't know."

Without turning his head Keldon called out: "Jasper, go to the base. Tell Ensign Gabrielski to send a messenger to find Dr. McNally. Tell him I want him for a drink, pronto." The mess boy's head disappeared through the door. "Wait a minute!" called Keldon after him. "Tell him when he's done that to find Chaplain Adamello and bring him on here half an hour later. You got that? McNally first and then Adamello."

Higgins finished off his drink and rose ponderously. "Since Jasper's gone I'll mix me another drink; and I'll mix you a double. You'll need it if you're going to talk to Adamello!"

2

McNally was young, enthusiastic, new. He sat rather too much on the edge of his chair. But he answered Keldon's questions quickly and clearly. He said: "There's nothing wrong with them barring the ordinary list of tropical diseases. By and large I wouldn't say they were any worse than any other atoll that we've struck yet—yaws, T.B., hookworm, and a bit of gonorrhea. They're better off than some: they haven't got any syphilis—that's because of the yaws, probably. There's a bit of malnutrition, but that's ironing out now with the rations, although they don't use much of the stuff we've sent them."

"Why?" interjected Keldon sharply.

"The old king says they don't like it, haven't any use for it. His line is that the only things that are fit for a man to eat are yams, taro root, fish and coconut— Oh, a few other things for trimmings, but that's about the list. They don't know what to make of canned peas and asparagus and dehydrated onions, and they hardly touch meat."

"He's not trying to make a corner in the stuff?"

"Good God, no!" McNally exploded. "How could he? They don't use money in these islands and they all live together anyway. No, they just haven't any time for the sort of things we like. But it doesn't matter. It's not malnutrition that's the trouble with them. I wish to God it was! We could force-feed the lot of them if it came to that."

"What is it then?" Keldon was growing irritable.

"Search me," said McNally, more as if he was speaking to himself than to anyone else, not meaning to be flippant but indicating complete and conscientious failure. After a long silence he continued: "There isn't a name for it in the textbooks, but you might as well call it combat fatigue as anything else. That covers most things these days, and I'm not sure that it doesn't cover this. Combat fatigue—they're just too tired, as I see it, to fight for their own way of life, so they're going to die. They prefer it that way."

"So what?" said Keldon, not rudely but in a soft regretful tone.

"So they die."

Keldon shrugged his shoulders. "You're my medical staff. It's no use my saying I'll court-martial you if they die, because it wouldn't be any use—and you know I wouldn't anyway. But we can't let them die."

Higgins spoke over the rim of his glass for the first time in half an hour. "You can't stop them if they want it that way. Short of picking the whole lot up and farming them out in small groups in a couple of dozen islands so that when they die it wouldn't be noticed, you can't stop 'em. It's not a medical problem. I doubt if it's a psychiatrist's problem—or at least I doubt if a western psychiatrist can reach their minds. There isn't any easy way of putting it, but to me it looks like this. If you cut the guts out of a man you can't expect his head to go on talking or his feet to go on walking. That's what the Japs did to this atoll. It's lost its heart and its lungs and its stomach, and what it's got left is not worth while going on with." He waited for a long moment and then said, "If you look at it realistically, it isn't." He nodded over at Keldon. "You are the last straw, you and the bulldozers."

"What the hell d'you mean?"

"Tell him, McNally," said Higgins.

"It's just something the old king said to me last time I was down. He said, 'Even if you go who will give us back our taro patches and our lime trees and our breadfruit?' You see, they know you have filled up the central depressions in Falalop and Asor, and they know they won't be able to grow any of the deciduous stuff that they need—palms, yes, but nothing else, and they can't grow it on Fassarai anyway. They never have been able to—the island's too narrow. So as far as they see, they haven't got anything to hope for anyway."

3

Chaplain Adamello came across the sandy path awkwardly. He had a belligerent Christianity that was aroused always by authority, a strange and not always lovely compound of his life in a New Jersey slum and three years' schooling in the narrow seminary of the Marist brothers in Rome—a mixture of obsequiousness and arrogance. He was not liked, yet because of an intransigeant sincerity he was respected.

Keldon watched his approach ironically. "Ha! Chaplain, sit down, sit down. Drink?"

"Thanks, I'd like a coke," said Adamello.

"Little rum in it?" asked Higgins from his corner. "Keeps the sun from desiccating you, you know."

Adamello shook his head. "Straight coke," he said.

Keldon waited until the drink had been served. "Sorry I was busy yesterday. You wanted to see me about something?"

"Yes," said Adamello, "yes, I wanted to see you." He had prepared a speech, almost a sermon, but the circumstances were not appropriate. It was a speech for the quarterdeck, or at worst the office, not for the verandah and the rum and coke. He said abruptly, almost blurting it out, "Fassarai, Commodore—you've got to do something about Fassarai!"

Few people under the rank of admiral, and not all of those, said "You've got to" to Keldon, but the commodore's face did not move. Adamello began to search for eloquence, and there was an awkward silence.

"Commodore," he began again, "those people are dying like flies. You've got to do something about it."

Patiently Keldon waited. After a moment he said, "Yes?"

Suddenly words came to Adamello. "War's hell, but this—" He made a quick Latin gesture. "These people—they're innocent, a primal innocence. They've always been innocent. They have nothing to do with this war, nothing to do with us and the Japs. But they're between us and the Japs, between the millstones, and the life is being ground out of them. I know you've got difficulties. I know it's a big job. But can't you see the human problem? Can't you see what we've taken away from them? Everything—they've got nothing left. If they only had one of the big islands . . ."

His mind suddenly reached out at a tangent. All the while he had been caught by the lack of a real plan, and now between word and word a plan had come to him. He said: "Give them back Mogmog! You haven't really started work there. You've done nothing except make a pier and a couple of shelters. You haven't even started on the softball diamond. Give it back to them! If they had two islands they could see a chance of life. Nothing will grow on Fassarai that's any good to them except coconuts, but they could grow things on Mogmog. There's not more than two hundred and fifty of them now. They could get along with two islands. You can do without Mogmog."

He paused. There was no comment either from Keldon or from Higgins, and he looked almost fearfully from one to the other. His plan seemed all of a sudden to have no weight after all, no validity.

His voice rose three notes. He said: "You look at this thing as an administrative problem; you look at it on paper; you look at it as statistics. It's not statistics—it's a human problem! These are people, and they're dying; and they're dying because nothing is done for them. No, I don't mean nothing is done for them. I mean that nothing that is done gives them any hope. They're my people. They're Christians, they're good Catholics—" He paused suddenly in an access of honesty. "Not all good Catholics, not all Christians, but most of them—good Christians and good Catholics though they haven't seen a priest for seven years. And because we want an island to play softball on you're going to let them die! It's not human, commodore."

He leaned forward, disregarding his drink, and glared under his bushy eyebrows at Keldon.

"Commodore, what are they going to say back in the States if we eliminate an island community to get a softball field? What are people going to say? What are they going to say in Washington? It's a paper thing; it's not a thing of necessity; it's not even a thing of war. It's inhuman." Again his voice rose. He was losing control of himself. He stood up shaking all over. "It's murder!" he said.

Higgins's eyes moved from the Italian to Keldon. Keldon's face had gone dark, a choleric gathering of blood in his cheeks. Without moving he barked, "Chaplain Adamello, sit down!"

There was a brief silence like the pregnant hush before thunder, but when he spoke his voice was grim only.

"Chaplain Adamello," he said again, "you are under naval discipline. For what you have said I could call in an escort and have you taken away. What you have said is a court-martial offence. Now you will listen to me! You know as well as I do the medical aspect of these islanders. You have had access to Dr. McNally's report and to Commander Higgins here. These islanders have had full medical attention: they have all the rations that the king asks for; and they have adequate shelter, medicines, food. It is not for you, Chaplain Adamello, to designate the requirements of this base. I am the commander of this base. My mission is to provide facilities for the requirements of the Fleet, to provide an air base, a command island, a stores area, and a recreation area.

Are you prepared to balance two hundred and fifty native people against the necessities of a hundred thousand American seamen? Cincpac has outlined his requirements. I am here to fulfil those requirements—and, Chaplain Adamello, I will fulfil them come hell or high water, whether I have one chaplain or the whole Catholic Church and the Pope himself against me!

"I am not going to take any action against you, because I believe you to be sincere, but I suggest, Chaplain Adamello, that you examine other points of view besides your own. These people have all the medical attention that they can be given. They have food and they have shelter. If they are still dying it must be for a reason unconnected with those three things. There is only one reason that is unconnected with those three things—the spiritual reason. If they are dying for spiritual reasons, Chaplain Adamello, that is your share of this tragedy. I think you have appreciated that. I think that is why you have attacked me as you have. I think that you have failed, Chaplain Adamello. I think you and your Christianity have failed these islanders, and I shall so report to your bishop. That is all."

Adamello stood up abruptly. He swayed very slightly as he stood. Then he passed his tongue over his dry lips and said, "Yes, sir—yes, commodore," and, turning, stumbled down the steps and walked off across the sand.

Keldon watched him, the colour fading out of his cheeks. "He's quite a good boy at that," he said reflectively.

Higgins raised his glass. "Here's to the best ward boss outside Tammany Hall. Christ, what a crooked politician you'd have made, Kellie! You had me guessing for three minutes. Are you going to report to his bishop?"

"Hell, no! I'll wait till his bishop reports on me. I can't afford to get excommunicated before this job's done. Nimitz wouldn't like it. Damn Fassarai to hell!"

"Amen!" said Higgins, emptying his glass.

≋≋≋≋≋≋≋≋≋≋≋≋≋≋≋≋≋≋≋≋

1

McNALLY sat in the deep shadow under the roof of the empty canoe house at the end of the north village. The sick call was over; it had involved every inhabitant of the north village, and there were few that had not qualified for inclusion. He wiped his handkerchief across his face, sweating in the still, breathless heat of the afternoon.

"It gets worse," he said, "worse instead of better. I don't know that I do any good coming down once a week like this. You've got to keep after these fools all the time—go chase the pills down yourself. It's getting me down. Did you see what that kid of Pedro's wife was wearing?"

"The li'l girl with the coral sores in her left foot? Yeah, I saw." The pharmacist's mate began to laugh. "Hell, there's times I think stringing them on a necklace is as good a way of taking 'em as the next!"

"I gave them for her mother to take," said McNally caustically. "It's no good. They don't understand half the interpreter tells 'em, and they just say Yes to please me. What can I do? 'Tisn't as if they wanted to keep well." He began to draw with a light piece of bamboo in the dust of the floor. 'Some of the kids—" He hesitated, and after a minute went on: "Yes, I think that's fair enough. Some of the kids are coming on, the bigger ones especially: the boy Fayu now that that wound in his bottom has cleared up; and Fernando's okay, and the girl Teresa; one or two of the younger ones too. But what the hell? What's the use? A dozen kids in a whole community!"

The third man, who had come down with him out of curiosity —he was from the staff on Guam—said slowly, "What's the alternative?"

McNally considered the picture he was drawing in the dust and added another stroke before he said: "Search me! I'm not God. If there was another atoll hereabouts I'd say lift the lot of them and transplant, but there's nothing here except Fais down to the southeast, and we ain't cleared the Japs out of that yet. Suppose we sent 'em up to Guam."

The other man considered in his turn. "Military Governor's got enough on his hands already with the Chamorros," he said at length. "There's little enough spare land in Guam, and what would you do with them, anyway? What can you do with a community that's out of balance? I didn't follow what you and Higgins were talking about the other day—that's mostly why I came down; but I'm beginning to see now. If you pushed 'em up to Guam: wouldn't do any good. You'd have to feed 'em same as here— more perhaps. They can't make themselves supporting anyhow, and it would be a strange place, and they would probably die faster—homesickness."

"Nostalgia," said McNally. "There's times when it's a real disease. I think you're right. Here at least they're on the same atoll; and what there is left of the old life, they've got. I don't know. There's not an alternative—but, hell, it hurts my professional pride!"

"What does it hurt in Kellie?"

"God knows!" said McNally frankly. "Maybe it hurts his pride. He's got no conscience about medicine."

"He's got no conscience—period," said the man from Guam. "Kellie was born out of his time. Last piece of American history he could have flourished in was the Alaska rushes." He chuckled. "He's a lively old devil."

"He's more than that," said McNally. "He's done a hell of a job over this base. He's quite ruthless, but he gets things done.

Seems like you've got to have it that way in war. I believe Kellie would as soon shoot a man as recommend him for a Silver Star if he thought it was justified either way. And yet the mistake you people in Guam make—and half the people down here too—is that you forget that he's human as well. Aw, hell! I don't mean just that he throws parties and gets lit—we all do that at times—but Kellie's worrying about these people. Crops up unexpectedly at times. He'll be talking about the trouble he's had with logistics and worrying about the dry docks and screaming his head off about personnel replacements, and he'll say suddenly, 'How are your damned Kanakas going, McNally?' and everybody'll laugh. But he worries about them. I don't know why. He's never seen them, and yet, by and large, I think he sees 'em bigger than most people except that cynical old bastard Higgins.

"What's this damned kid want now?" He looked up as a child, her head ringed in frangipani blossom and a long wreath round her neck that came down to her little bare navel, came up and smiled at him ingratiatingly.

"Candy," she said softly, separating the syllables so that it sounded like "kan-ti."

"A dose of jalap would do you a damned sight more good," said McNally grumbling. "You don't belong to this village. I've seen you already today. Aw, hell, take your candy! Hey! I missed that sore on your arm this morning. Come here!" He pulled her towards him and examined a big flat scab on the upper arm. "Probably fell on the coral some time and scraped it," he said over his shoulder to the other man. "That's coral's god-awful stuff. We've been having a lot of trouble with the men on Asor. Every bathing party there's a casualty. We don't know enough about it yet. This one's all right though: it's healed up by itself." He pinched the child's arm well below the scrape, and she yelped with delight and pulled away. "Scat!" he said.

"Here's that bastard Sebastian! He's got gonorrhea again, and I can't get at the source of infection. You can't do it with one day a week and two hundred and sixty people to look over. One of the women has it, and it hasn't shown up in examination. 'Tisn't his wife, because I looked her over pretty carefully. He's been keeping somebody else's bed warm, the old ram! If I can't find out next time I come down I'll tell his wife. She'll find out all right. Aw, hell! You see what we're up against. I may not be able to get down next week with the Fleet coming in—be as busy as a bobcat next Friday. There's no continuity."

2

The *Penasco* was third in the line of the convoy as it threaded its way between the buoys that marked the swept channel into the vast harbour of the atoll. Reis leant over the wing of the bridge, watching Falalop slide slowly past them. Aircraft were hovering in the circuit above the air strip, enormous in the part of the circuit that came out over the channel, infinitely small to the north.

Beyond Falalop, Asor was opening up with its richer palms, its deeper foliage, its clustered small craft lying in the anchorage in its lee. And beyond them he could see the stupendous congregation of the main anchorage. It was bigger than Eniwetok, bigger than Kwajalein—the most gigantic concentration of shipping that he had seen ever in one place, something that beggared all imagination. He crossed over the bridge and saw that the tangled mass of shipping extended clear across their bows, thinned out a little, and then began again in the south; and his eye went round until it came again to islands—the little diamond of Mangejang and below it Lolang and then the long line of Fassarai.

Wombacher came across the bridge to him. "You've made it," he said derisively. "I've been waiting for an order to turn back for the last three hours."

Reis smiled at him. "I've made it," he agreed, "and I might just as well have made Pearl by the look of it. Hell, this ain't a combat area!"

"It never was," said Wombacher caustically, and went back to stand close behind the captain.

Mogmog was divided into two parts, one part for the enlisted men to get drunk in and the other for the officers. There is a democracy in alcohol, but there is no democracy of the sea.

The men's half was to the north: dusty softball diamonds between the dusty palms, and horseshoe pitches in the exiguous clearings. The men were spread over it in a diffuse saturnalia. They bathed on the ocean side with a guard boat hovering inside the reef. They sprawled under the palms and scrambled up the boles in disregard of stringent rules. The loud-speakers barked metallic orders and instructions across the complex sounds of relaxation. Men queued for beer, and on a heady combination of canned Milwaukee and the unaccustomed feel of earth beneath their feet, grew drunk almost without benefit of alcohol. It was not always friendly, for old rivalries had a habit of coming to the surface and new spleens developed quickly in the vigorous air.

The officers' half of the island was different. It was quiet or, rather, the noise in it was concentrate. The officers drank at three points: the admirals and the captains in the old *falu*, cleaned out and sprayed and garnished; the best *falu* in the islands, a magnificent structure like a parish church, its superb columns stabbed through by the teredo, sea-washed and come from some infinitely distant mainland. The sennit work was exquisite, beautifully patterned in a strict economy of means. The place was high and had a grandeur of its own. They had spoilt it only a little in the conversion. It was the least noisy of the three.

The senior officers' bar for lieutenant-commanders and above came closer to earth. It was an open shed with benches and with tables ranged about it on either side, and two refrigerator units to keep the beer cool and to make ice. The noise was centred mainly in the junior officers' bar where the pilots and the young lieutenants, the ensigns and the youngsters of the Marines grew flushed and excitable round the crap tables and drank endless successions of bourbon and coke.

McNally went to the senior officers' bar. He was hunting old friends. He found them at a table outside the main shelter: a commander from one of the carriers in the anchorage and two medical lieutenant-commanders from the cruisers. They had been there a long while already.

"Coney Island Pacific style," he said as he slipped in to the bench. "How d'you like it?"

"We think it stinks," said one of the lieutenant-commanders. "Jeez, McNally, what've you done with all the beautiful women from this island? You guys at the base have it all your own way. Got 'em hidden down the south somewhere, haven't you? Damned old Mormon!"

"That's right," said McNally, "lashings of beautiful girls in sarongs with ukuleles! I spend six days a week with them and come up and make excuses to Higgins on the seventh."

"Not the Higgins that was at Norfolk, Virginia, in '36."

"Same Higgins," said McNally.

"The old bastard! You know, commander, I think he's lying about the women. Give us the right dope, McNally."

"Get me a bourbon and coke, and I'll give," said McNally lazily.

One of the lieutenant-commanders went off, faintly erratic, towards the bar. McNally watched him sardonically. Then he said: "We're making a good thing out of alcohol on this island, but I'm going to write to Ernie King and ask him to let me set up a honky-tonk here. We'd make a living then! By God, we would! If you watched those bloodhounds coming ashore with their noses down looking for a bit of a tail, you'd know."

"What's wrong with that?" asked the commander.

"Nothing," agreed McNally, "but I'm not letting you guys loose on the native island."

"Damned pasha!" said the other.

The first man came back with the drink—four paper cups of it—held precariously in his hands. He reached the table without disaster. "Knock it back," he said. "Here's hoping! You old ram, why didn't you leave the best-looking girls back here when you took 'em off?"

"Just selfishness," said McNally, "just selfishness! I thought of leaving half a dozen for the big brass—an apple for the teacher; but then I changed my mind. I've got to think of admirals' wives too!"

They were singing noisily down at the junior officers' club now—"Drinking rum and Co-co-Co-la." The strange, wailing Calypso song came badly out of the tumultuous assault of the beer garden.

Over the noise of it broke a metallic voice on the squawk box, "Lieutenant-Commander McNally is wanted at the medical tent," and repeated itself, disembodied, dispassionate, empty of all feeling.

"Now, what the hell!" demanded McNally. "I thought I was clear."

"Someone's going to have a baby," said the commander caustically.

"That's about the only thing that's not likely," answered McNally. "But the most probable thing is that some guy's stuck a knife into some other guy. They will do it. Aw, hell, it's a recreation island anyway!" He put down the paper cup and said, "Be good," and walked off wearily towards the landing place and the medical tent.

It was curious that he had told them nothing of Fassarai. There was a strange inhibition operating against it, as if he could not associate that sorrowful place with this island of shouting and loud voices, and unsteadiness and drink. He shook himself suddenly and said half aloud, "That damned place is getting on my nerves." Then he remembered the rasping voice of the commodore after he had presented his last report on the island people. "It's getting on everybody's nerves, even Kellie's."

4

The paths were full of people walking towards the church. The sun that dropped golden bars through the palm canopy caught in brief flashes the dark, honey-coloured bodies of the younger children, the deeper mahogany of the women, and the blue-patterned tattooing of the men. They passed in a regular syncopated pattern of shifting light from sun to shadow and back to sun again, so that it was as if innumerable shuttles were weaving a rich texture across the warp of the soaring palm boles. The children were heavy-wreathed, and the men also; and the girl children had for the most part new grass skirts smelling of the sap of the young palm fronds, weighted and dragging at their hips and making a deeper noise than the soft, high rustle of every day.

Chaplain Adamello, waiting outside in the shadow of the banana palms with the Asor king, could see the unhurried, graceful progression of his congregation. They seemed to come from all quarters, not, as would have been expected, straight from the north village and from the south. They came in from every angle as if they came from the long ocean beach and from the lagoon, as if this Christmas service had broken across the pattern and the continuity of the island life.

For no reason at all he remembered an ant heap broken open in the home woods and the scattered ants coming in from every point of the compass to make good the damage, to make holy the desecration. Perhaps that was what this coming together signified, perhaps this was the culminating point of his work, perhaps this community was about to become whole again. Always his services had been crowded—the weekly rival to McNally's ministrations. But this was not a crowd only: it was the whole community. They had come from the further half of the north village, from the outlying habitations of the south. They were all there, the youngest children at breast and the old men, the three kings and with them the agnostic, Elingarik, the *machamach*.

Adamello eyed him almost resentfully. He was the sorcerer, the witch doctor, the devil king—or perhaps only the priest of the older gods, the forgotten ones. He had not come before to the services, and Adamello as he watched him saw how the women moved a little from the straight line as they passed him, deviating as in deference or in fear.

He was disturbed by a sudden doubt that was like a shadow across the larger belief of victory, a sudden suspicion as to the depth, the profundity, of his contact with these people. He had worked desperately hard to get the words of their language. They were few, he knew, the limited vocabulary that sufficed for un‐limited needs only by an elaborate play of nuance and fine-shaded meaning, that compounded an enormous elaboration of allusion and syllogism, of transferred epithet and of synecdoche. There had been a time when he hoped to make his Christmas sermon in their own tongue, even if it were halting and lame; but he had known for weeks that he would speak again through the interpreter and listen to the simple truths he offered, tortured and twisted in incomprehensibility. His eyes passed from Elingarik to the inter‐preter, but the look of resentment went with them, the resentment of the skilled man for the imperfect instrument.

The open-sided hut that made the church was full now; the rows stretched out beyond the eaves and at the back until all the clear space about it was full also, and the men stood ranged beyond the seated rows. Looking round, Adamello saw that the shifting pattern of light amongst the palm boles had ceased and the pattern was come all together; and, moving from the shadow, he passed towards the flowered altar.

McNally, who had stood a little distance from him, moved forward also and stood beside a low seat made from a palm log. He listened to the Introit with approval. He was not a Catholic: his forbears had come from Belfast. Long since, the warmer South of America had unfrozen the austerity of a cold and desolate Presbyterianism; but there still lingered some ancestral memory that scrawled across the walls of his conscience, "No Popery."

Yet he could admire Adamello's sonorous voice, the command that seemed to descend upon him in the deep and real conviction of his duty. This was the priest militant, the commander of souls, and an authority seemed to strike into these people and to lift their voices as they began to sing the old and familiar hymns in strange and unfamiliar words, in a rhythm stranger still. Outside and curiously withdrawn, he watched the slow unfolding of the service and the power and dignity of the man; and, without watching, he sensed its reverence in the women behind him.

When it was over and the singing women unwillingly had broken up, and the children had come out of the trance of fervour and passed from it to a restless curiosity that shuffled in the dust around them, McNally spoke to Adamello. "When are you going to conduct the funeral services?" Immediately he was sorry that he had spoken, for he saw in Adamello's eyes a quick quenching of light as if the virtue had suddenly departed and the glory died.

But Adamello said only: "Yes, I must go now. Three?"

"Flarik and Jesus's wife—I've forgotten her name—and the old woman that lived with Tonio's wife; and you asked me last time to tell you if anybody was likely to die before the next trip. Well, Urzula, Kirak's wife, is in a pretty bad way, and that old fellow José in the north village."

Adamello, who had grieved for some time about the impossibility of giving extreme unction, only said, "So many." Looking up suddenly with his eyes hurt, he said again, "So many."

As he passed out of earshot McNally said softly, "You'd better get in first, or else that old devil Elingarik will be there before you." He looked at the *machamach* speculatively, but the old man was preparing a new quid of betel, rolling the nut and the lime in a fresh leaf of *Piper methysticum.* He walked off and turned up the path towards the north village, singing softly to himself, "Silent Night, Holy Night." It wanted three days to Christmas, but this was the last chance of getting the boat down before the actual day. After a while he changed the tune to "Good King Wenceslas."

5

Keldon's parties had a certain reputation, a reputation not in the atoll only but over the wider reaches of the Pacific. It was not that men got drunk at them so much as that there was in them an inherent loosening of the bonds of discipline. They possessed all the strange democracy of alcohol. To this party Keldon brought Halsey and his staff and the war correspondents with the Fleet. The inevitable alcoholism of newspapermen evaded something of the stringent dryness of the ships, but the half-dozen who came ashore on Asor were thirsty men. By four o'clock they were no longer thirsty; but the drinking went on. The competition of the staff was admirable.

Higgins watched it from his favourite chair sardonically as he had watched many parties. Brindon of the *Tribune* sat with him for a long while. Brindon's drinking followed a steady and normal course from the cheerful to the thoughtful, from the thoughtful to the maudlin. He was about to become maudlin. Without looking at Higgins he said, "How many of your damned Kanakas are dead now?"

"What do you know about my Kanakas?" asked Higgins.

"Plenty. What's happening on that island?"

"They're mostly old folks," said Higgins thoughtfully, "so you'd expect the death rate to be higher than ordinary."

"I've heard they're dying like flies. They might be worth a story at that. Kellie's just pushed them out of the way down there." Brindon watched the commodore moving from group to group. "Heartless little bastard!"

Higgins said from the depths of his chair, "He's done quite a lot for 'em."

"Huh!" Brindon grunted. "Has he done enough?"

"Now that," said Higgins, with a careful, deliberate softness in his voice, "is quite a question. Suppose you go ask him."

"I will at that."

Brindon got up so suddenly that he spilled his drink, and moved, very slightly unsteady, between the groups towards Keldon. Nothing in Higgins's expression changed, even when he heard Brindon's high-pitched voice say, "Commodore, are your Kanakas all right?"

One of the other correspondents made an obscene pun, and it was received with a gust of laughter.

Keldon asked belligerently, "What the hell d'you mean?"

"Dying like flies," said Brindon, "that's my information—dying like flies." Then he became earnest, a crusading note entered into his voice. "Commodore, are you doing all you can for them?" He caught his breath in something that was not quite a hiccup, that had even less dignity about it. "It's a human story," he said vaguely.

"Hell, yes," said Keldon, "it's a human story! They're human beings at that." A little pool of quiet had developed around him, and Higgins heard his voice again. "Yes, I've done all I can for them, and I'm doing more: I'm going to put a doctor to live on the island in the New Year."

"The hell you are!" said Higgins softly in the depths of his chair.

CHAPTER XVIII

≈≈≈≈≈≈≈≈≈≈≈≈≈≈≈≈≈≈≈≈≈≈≈≈≈

1

WOMBACHER had staked out for himself a section of deck under the wing of the flying bridge, which gave shadow so long as the ship's head pointed to the northeast. When it swung, the sun slipped in under the bulk of the bridge and burnt fiercely at his legs. He had spread a blanket there to make a little insulation against the conducted heat of the metal. Wind came in through the space at the head of the well-deck ladder to keep them cool. Reis lay on half of the blanket. He seemed irrationally content. The heat did not affect him as it affected Wombacher.

The navigator was in a bad temper, the result of his most recent battle with the exec. "I only asked if we could have a landing craft to go up to this place Mogmog, but he says 'No!' So I asked him if we could have a motor boat to go ashore to one of the islands down that way." He flopped up a limp hand to indicate the eastern side of the atoll. "And he says 'No!' You'll have to let him take to gin again. He ain't bearable the way he is. If he wanted a drink we'd have a boat to go ashore quick enough, you'd see!"

Reis remained silent.

"For Christ's sake," demanded Wombacher, "ain't you got any sympathy? Don't you want to go ashore yourself?"

"Sure, but I don't want to go drink. I've got enough alk in my cabin and in the sick bay. It's too hot to get drunk."

Wombacher half sat up indignantly. "It's never too hot to get drunk," he protested. "Jesus, that's heresy! Twelve days we've been here, and that bastard won't let us even go for a walk on the beach."

"You've been on the beach on Eniwetok," said Reis equably. "Did you like it?'

"No, it was hell."

"Well, then?"

"It was a different kind of hell from this goddam hell ship," said Wombacher. "I like to swop hells sometimes. Any hell's better than the one you've got."

"That's reasonable," conceded Reis aggravatingly.

They heard feet on the decking, and a voice said, "Lieutenant Wombacher, have you seen the doc?"

"I see him now, and I still don't like the look of him. What d'you want?"

"There's a signal for him."

"Wheel it on," called Wombacher.

Reis sat up. "Why a signal for me?"

Wombacher stretched out an arm to collect the flimsy as the signalman said, "They want you ashore."

"God damn it, don't I get any of the breaks?" asked Wombacher.

Reis took the message and looked at it sleepily. "What the hell's this?" he demanded.

Wombacher, looking over his shoulder, read out loud: " 'Have all gear packed ready boat 17.00. Posting will be notified Asor. Duplicate to captain.' They can't do that to me!"

"It's not you, it's me," said Reis.

"That's what I mean," Wombacher grumbled. "You're my mascot—you're the ship's mascot. When you're with us we don't get no trouble. Hell, I want to live! You stay here."

"Who signed it?" Reis looked again and said, "Who's Commodore Keldon?"

"Kellie Keldon, he's the atoll commodore," explained Wombacher. "How come he's got a sudden yen for you? Hell, you can't go! Supposing I get a stomach-ache on the way back to Honolulu, what do I do?"

"Die, I hope!" said Reis savagely. "What the hell's it all about?"

"And now we'll get another doc, and I was just getting used to you again. The last one he smoked my cigarettes, and he drank my bourbon, and he had no conversation, and I suppose the next one will be worse." He sat bolt upright suddenly and said: "Christ! The last time they did this to you we got beaten up in the Marshalls. Tell him you can't go!"

"For God's sake shut up and let me think! Hey, I don't come under any local commodore! How come he's ordering me around?"

"You don't come under *any* local commodore—but this is Kellie Keldon. If I was you I'd leave it to San Francisco or whoever it is you do come under to do the belly-aching."

"Who's Kellie Keldon?"

"Kellie Keldon's an ornery son of a bitch. The base navigator told me all about him Thursday when he came on board. If only seven per cent of the stories about him are half near accurate you can go kiss the captain goodbye and see that you're ready for the five o'clock boat. If you don't he'll like as not stake you out and leave you for the land crabs. Hell, you don't know the stories about Kellie? Every morning, if he's had a jag on the night before, he gets up early looking about ten per cent sane and jumps in a jeep and tries to run down the negro mess boys. They got steps carved up the palm trees in Asor. The mess boys don't mind— they like him. He don't mean any harm—but, hell, a jeep's a lethal weapon anyways you look at it! Can you climb palm trees, doc?"

Reis slid out into the sun and stretched himself. Wombacher murmured sarcastically: "Maybe he's heard you're a good surgeon, and he wants his alcohol bump flattened out. The exec is always playing up what you do to his liver."

"More likely he's got a duodenal," suggested Reis, "and wants somebody to hold his hand. Oh, hell! I suppose they're short of medics for their hospital setup and I'm the dogsbody." He searched his conscience for a brief moment. "I haven't done anything lately that he's likely to know about," he yawned. "Yes, I'd better pack at that."

He walked along to the captain's quarters to make his position clear.

2

Higgins stared quizzically over the table. "You know nothing about tropical medicine," he said, "apart from the stuff they crammed into you in the course. You are weak on obstetrics and women's diseases, and you don't know anything about negroes, Indians, Chinese, Japanese, or any other men of colour. You'll learn! You will leave for Fassarai at ten o'clock tomorrow—we're shifting the weekly boat to Wednesday. You'll get your travel orders in the office. I have put up a reasonable amount of the drugs you are most likely to need and an instrument kit. Make a list at the end of the first week of the stuff you want in addition, and I'll see you get it. Any questions?"

"Yes," said Reis quietly. "May I ask why Commodore Keldon selected me?"

"Can't answer that. I can tell you how." Higgins chuckled as if remembering the interview. "With a pin! There are three attack transports going back to Honolulu this next week, and the only doctors we could find that were in any ways spare were on them. He picked you with a pin. He likes sticking points into things."

He leant forward suddenly, the banter out of his voice. He said: "He'll stick a mighty big pin into you if you don't make good. I've only told you the formal set-up of this thing. Now listen! These people have been ripped apart by the Japanese. We'll talk to McNally tonight. He'll tell you all they've got is a head and feet. The body has been ripped out of them, and so they reckon they are dead and it's not worth bothering about anything; so they die. McNally can't stop 'em, and I can't stop 'em; and if you see Keldon he'll tell you the priests can't stop 'em either. They're Catholics. By the way, are you a Catholic?"

"No," said Reis.

"Don't matter," said Higgins. "You've got to be a doctor to them, and a damned good doctor too. There is a lot of disease that we can't clear up in one visit a week. You better clear it, and you better clear it fast; but my view is, it's the least part of your job. You've got to give these people a reason to live. Oh, hell!" he said. "You'll see. That damned island makes people see. Go round to the Black Widow now and have a drink with McNally."

"The commodore—" said Reis hesitantly.

"Listen." Higgins's tone changed again very slightly. "Listen. The commodore'll tell you that you're going down to stop these people dying because his reputation can't stand two hundred and seventy civilians dying in the creation of a base. You can accept that. It isn't true, but you can accept it. If anybody tells you that he is afraid of a Congressman getting up and asking questions, you can accept that too. It's equally untrue."

He paused for a minute as if debating within himself, and then he said: "Nobody would call Kellie a sentimentalist; but there are times when he sees things in the round, and this is one of them. It's no good trying to explain it to you. You're just fresh from States-side. You'll see what I mean when you've been on the island for a week; or at least"—he looked narrowly at the young doctor— "I think you will. Now go and get a drink with McNally. He'll maybe be a bit sore at you. He's gotten kinda fond of that island too."

Reis shook his head bewilderedly. "I'll try," he said in answer to some unspoken general appeal that he sensed in Higgins's disjointed approach, and went out of the door.

3

Higgins was in his favourite position in the armchair in the corner of the little verandah. He would have preferred a rocking chair, but it was not provided in the Navy Department's estimate of requirements.

"He's gone off," he said, "with a party of twenty Seabees to put up his tents and make a clearing for him and stack his gear and so on. Their orders are to be off the island at dusk. I've given him the best pharmacist's mate I could find at short notice— Watson. I've given him every damned drug I could think of, and he's got instruments enough to do major operations, which he won't. I can't tell you whether he'll bring it off or not."

"Why?" asked Keldon.

"Because I don't know what the necessary qualities are," said Higgins frankly. "But I think he'll try, and that's as much as you or any man can hope for."

Keldon was silent a long while, staring out across the glitter of the lagoon. "They've got food, they've got shelter, they've got medical attention and now they've got a leader of sorts," he said then, and snorted abruptly. "Well, my conscience is clear," he barked.

"What a liar you are, Kellie!" said Higgins gently.

4

A single canoe was standing out wide of the shoal beach above Lolang, and as Reis watched her she hauled her wind to slip in under the lee of the reef towards the northern village of Fassarai. He could see the huts already, their roofs a tarnished silver in the green matrix of the palms. The golden-brown sail of the canoe was bright in the sun against that same darkness of malachite greens; but the hull, lifted slightly on the still water, was black as ebony against the white of the beach.

He had a strange excitement in him. For almost twelve days the *Penasco* had lain to her anchor in the centre of the lagoon. With binoculars the low, green pencil marks around the horizon had magnified themselves into clustered barriers of palms. In the heat of the midday the mirage had lifted them above the horizon so that the white of their beaches was clear, so that on either side of them he could see the bursting plumes of the spray along the reef and the ridged white of the outer sea. But always the picture was evanescent, the image insubstantial in the uncertain quivering of the heat waves. The islands had a thin quality of unreality as if they were seen only in a dream. Nor had his visit to Asor changed in any way the dream quality of the island chain, for Asor had been lifted out of the matrix of the islands, had been changed, Americanised. Its contours had been trained, its softnesses squared off. It was in the lagoon still but not of it—a strange thing and alien. Here on Fassarai was the older Ulithi.

They too were rounding the shallows at the northern end and standing in towards the main village. He could see splashing along the still lagoon beach now and brown bodies rioting in the centre of white spray. He saw the huge, prow-like roof of the *falu* thrust vigorously above the beachward palms, and next to it the high roofs of the canoe sheds, and two canoes pulled up on the white of the sand like sunning crocodiles. He saw figures come down out of the deep purple shade under the palms and, emerging, change from ebon black to a rich, lucent copper. The place seemed secret, inviolate, guarded by its arched canopy of palms. Outside was the brilliant crystal clarity of the sun upon the sea. Close about it was the white girdle of the beach with its fierce intensity of light, and inside its circumvallation was the cool, shaded, interpalmar space, unbroken from one tip of the crescent island to the other—a cool, blue-shaded interior thatched with the living palm fronds, a long, unbroken tunnel of shade that held the whole mysterious life of the island invisible to the outer world.

Reluctantly almost he prepared to climb into the dory to go ashore and break into that still, impenetrable sanctuary.

CHAPTER XIX

≈≈≈≈≈≈≈≈≈≈≈≈≈≈≈≈≈≈≈≈≈≈≈≈≈≈≈≈≈≈

1

PERHAPS he had expected too much from McNally's and Higgins's warnings—perhaps he had built too much of his own picture upon them; but he could see no death here. The children had come down from the north village to reenforce those of the main village. The king himself and the Falalop king (who had resigned his title) were seated, cross-legged, on the terrace of the *falu*. Nine of the old men were with them. The women were looking curiously from behind trees and through the uncurtained sides of the huts. Chickens, driven by the waywardness of a child, ran clucking between the feet of the Seabees, and the dogs were indignant and angry. It was true that there were no young people apart from Teresa and Fayu, Filomena and Fernando. There was an abrupt gap in the progression of heights, in the progression of development; but that did not obtrude itself. There seemed in the village to be a busyness, almost even an excitement.

Yet he had no basis for comparisons, no knowledge to back up his judgment. He could not know that this was a sudden spurt of interest because of the unexpectedness of his landing, because of the number of arrivals, because of the change from McNally to a new doctor, because of the novelty of the Seabees. He could not sense that behind it, underneath it, underlining every motion and gesture of it was fear, because the fear was masked by indifference and by apathy, by the whole strange complexity of the island character.

McNally's interpreter introduced him to the island, made a

short speech telling the people that it was an order that this doctor should live with them and take care of them, that a place was to be provided for his camp, and that the men were to help where he required help, and to obey him where obedience was necessary.

The king accepted order and advantage with a high formality. His speech was sonorous and long, and the Seabees fidgeted and then tramped about, peering under the eaves of the huts and fingering the canoes in the canoe shed and prodding over the nets and the fishing lines and the hooks. And at the end of it the interpreter said, "He says only that he is very glad you are come, and that they will do their best to serve you."

"All right," said Reis. "Let's get going. McNally said the best place would be about midway between here and the northern village. Tell 'em we want someone to show us where that will be."

"The king himself will go," said the interpreter after a brief colloquy.

They went almost in procession: the king with Sebastian and Jesus and four others of the council of the old men, then Reis and the interpreter, then Watson and the children who had attached themselves to him already, and then the Seabees. There was no particular circumstance about the place that the king chose, except that it was athwart the island path, which here ran closer to the ocean beach, and that it was protected from the wind by a thick undergrowth upon the ocean side. The palms were thinner perhaps than elsewhere, and it was necessary to cut down only three or four.

They brought the materials for the little camp ashore rapidly— a sleeping tent and a cook tent with thin metal gauze sides and wooden floors—and put them up firmly and with speed. The tent for the surgery they put further down upon the other side of the path, opposite a small and natural clearing. The children brought coral lumps to mark the paths from one to the other. They built a latrine with immense crudity and badinage, the rough jokes flowing over Teresa's head while she laughed infectiously and said, "Okay, okay."

As Higgins had promised, the camp was ready by dusk; the Seabees tramped back through the village in the half-darkness. And in a little the L.S.I. backed out, one green eye and one red glaring for a while into the secret darkness of the island and then sheering off.

Watson stayed at the tents. Reis, who had gone down with the Seabees, turned now and, suddenly conscious of the severance, walked from the starred half-light of the outer world into the absolute darkness of the island, his flash stabbing a dancing path of light before his feet. It was as if he had turned his back upon a world and upon an age.

2

The island was not silent. It was curious: when the Seabees had been there, he was affected by what seemed to him an almost palpable silence, as if they were an uneasy, uncouth incursion into a pool of quiet; yet now that they were gone he knew the place was not quiet. He could hear always, of course, the bourdon of the reef—that was a background noise like the whirr and vibration of a ship's engines at sea, and not to be considered. Over it and across it he could hear the incessant lesser noises of the island: the rustle of live palm fronds high up above him; the more sinister, higher rustle in the dead fronds of the undergrowth; a woman singing a sad, wailing threnody very far away; a soft, repetitive thudding like a small drum; the groaning of two palm boles together; and once an odd squealing that was beyond doubt rats. He heard a coconut thud close by and the sudden, distressing squawk of an aggrieved and awakened bird.

He found the path and, a little way down it, saw Watson's lanterns in the tents; and, as he came up, saw also silhouetted against the lights the heads and the shoulders of the children, their cheekbones and foreheads picked out in the light and glistening, and their shoulders outlined and bright in it. It streamed out through the gauze, and the palm boles shone like the pillars in a lit cathedral. It made a patch of a rare and mysterious brilliance in the hot velvet darkness underneath the crests. He could hear low giggles as he approached, and Watson's voice. Watson was talking steadily, and the children were answering the innate sympathy of his tone that reached out and through the barrier of the unknown words.

Watson had made ready a meal, and they ate now to an incessant fire of whispered comment and irrepressible laughter from the darkness. Afterwards they sat smoking in the canvas chairs. It was necessary to Reis to find out what sort of man was Watson, for in the strange circumstances of this place they were thrown together more than they could be in any other place. Here they were alien not merely in race but in time, the twentieth century plunged into the prehistoric.

He asked, after a long silence, "What's your home town?"

"Don't know that I can rightly say," said Watson evenly and without embarrassment. "I was born in Maine—little place up north, Muscongus. My father was kinda unsettled—last-war veteran. He moved south to Boston when I was a few months old, and south again to New York when I was about three, and south again to Hillsboro in Ca'lina and then he kinda left my ma. No," he said in answer to an unspoken question, "he came back again; but he wasn't what you'd call fixed. My ma, she headed north again doing jobs on her own. Me, I've lived in the top end of the Bronx last three years before they drafted me but, hell, you can't call N'York a home town!"

"How did you make pharmacist's mate?"

"I been in hospitals, porter, then dispensary assistant. I spika da language."

"Married?"

"No. I got a girl though—or at least I had up to the last letter."

Something in the tone made Reis chuckle, something of comic resignation. "What were you doing before this?"

"Handin' out prophylactics in Baltimore," said Watson cynically, "and then they posted me to the Medical Inspection Unit on Asor. No prophylactics," he sighed gustily, "and I'd worked up such a good before-bedside manner. Hell of a place, this, for women! They tell me they keep a destroyer circling the hospital ships with her guns loaded because of the nurses on board." He stabbed out his cigarette on the wooden floor. "What's this job, lieutenant?"

Reis was silent for a long minute. "I don't know that I can describe it, even to myself. Medically our orders are to stop the people dying; but I think there's a lot more to it than that."

"Queer, the notions you get about South Sea islands," said Watson. "Hollywood and damn'-fool writers—all tits and hula-hula skirts and feasting, roast sucking pig and pineapples and yams. What the hell's a yam, lieutenant?" He didn't pause for an answer. "Waggling their bottoms, and ukuleles, war canoes and fishing on the reefs at night with flares, and making love on the beach with somebody singing in the background. Ain't seen nothin' of that here—flies, old coconuts, and palm trash, biggest rats I ever seen." Suddenly and without particular emphasis he said, echoing Lieutenant Hartwell's unheard words, "The poor bastards!"

Reis measured the words carefully against the velvet background of the night. "Amen," he said.

They sat in silence, considering. Deliberately he initiated no discussion, made no plans. There was the morning, and in the morning a plan would establish itself. Of that, somehow, he was convinced. There was no urgency but only a sense of inevitability, a sense of naturalness. This thing would come shaped to his hand.

They went to bed. As Watson put the second of the lanterns out, there was a smothered giggle in the darkness.

3

Reis woke suddenly in a quick, startling uneasiness that was compound of new sounds and new shapes and unfamiliar surroundings. For a moment he was unsure of his hold on realities, irrationally close to panic. There had been a noise, but it was a noise that had ended even in the instant of his wakening—the thud of a ripe nut, perhaps. Now he could hear a quick, hurriedly repeated sound of gnawing, a crisp *grate, grate, grate* of sharp teeth against something hard. Later he was to know it for the sound of a rat at a coconut. Now that he was awake, there was nothing frightening in it, but only a small strangeness. Over it his unaccustomed ears picked out and registered again the sound of the reef. The wind had fallen to a flat calm, and there was no noise now in the upper palm leaves; but the dry trash of the island floor rustled endlessly and unceasingly, and once and again he heard the whirr of wings.

One part of his brain decided that he should go to sleep again, but the other part remained active; and in the conflict he lay awake exploring McNally's long nervous explanations, running over his list of diseases, trying to remember the personalities as he had described them, the crisp, incisive phrases:

"Jesus—a scrounger, bone-idle but not interested enough even to scrounge properly. Sebastian—he's a bit crazy, I think, but he'll be useful to you because he knows all about the outside world, or thinks he does! That's going to be two-thirds of your trouble, getting them to realise that there is an outside world. You'd better use the four of the big kids. I'd come to an arrangement with the king about them. You'll want help, and they'll learn English fast. Teresa understands more now than you'd think. She'll pick it up in a week or two if you keep at it. They're smart enough, those kids."

And again: "I can't get by with the women, can't get under their skins at all. 'Tisn't that they're just dumb." He remembered McNally's hands beating the air as if to brush away something cobwebbed and insubstantial. "It's just that I can't make contact with them."

These and a score of other judgments and conclusions and asides he would have to fit tomorrow into a mosaic, into a picture of the island as an entity.

[*152*]

McNally had said one thing right at the end. "I'm not sure that I haven't been going the wrong way, treating them as individuals. I'm not sure that they are individuals. I'm not sure that the community is not the thing that matters, instead of the individual. That may be the real root of the trouble; but you'll have to find that out for yourself."

He lay awake, his mind busy and milling over it until the wind rose in the upper leaves again and, rising, pulled the dawn with it out of the east. A cock crew in the south village and it was day.

4

Watson shifted in his bed, groaned, and reached out for a cigarette. "Morning, lieutenant," he said. "You didn't fix no time for a shake. What's the routine?"

"I'm not going to fix a routine yet," said Reis. "I'm going for a swim. Then we'll eat, and then we'll go down to the village and talk to the king. Best thing will be to have a sick call here mornings, somewhere about nine, I think; maybe earlier—we'll see. For a start I think we'll make it compulsory attendance for everybody from the king downwards. What do you know about this king business?"

"There were four of them, I heard Dr. McNally say. Seems a hell of a lot for a dump like this! But one the Japs took—the Mogmog king, I think—and so there should be three on this island. The Asor king's the chief one. He's the king of Ulithi. I suppose we deal with him; the others don't seem to count for much now."

"D'you speak German?"

"Not me," said Watson cheerfully.

"Spanish?"

"Not a word, and no Japanese neither. I can make myself understood in Brooklyn. I've always found that enough."

"Well, you'd better start teaching the kids American, and fast," said Reis. "I'm going for a swim."

He took a towel, slipped on a pair of rubber shoes and struck down through the scattered rubbish under the palms for the lagoon beach. As he passed the surgery tent two children far down the island path saw him and called out, high-pitched and eager. He lifted one hand and shouted, "Hi-ya!" and went on. They reached the beach simultaneously with him and sat down respectfully to watch him undress.

"Scat!" he said. "Get the hell out of it! I'm going to strip." They smiled cheerfully and made no move. "Go on!" he said, and, turning, strode behind a low bush that hung over the actual sand. As he slipped off his pajama trousers they came round the corner of the bush and instantly plumped down respectfully once again. "I give up," he said, and ran naked to the water.

There were seven of them when he came out, and as the eldest of them brought him his towel Teresa came through the bush. He draped himself hurriedly.

"I told you kids to scat," he said. "Get the hell out of it, and leave a man in peace! Don't you know anything about the blue laws? No morals, that's what's the matter with you—no morals at all!"

He shook his head reprovingly, and something in his tone or some light in his eye made all eight of them shout instantly with laughter.

"Don't get it," he said. "You shouldn't laugh. You should be ashamed of yourselves. You're Teresa, aren't you?" he said to the elder girl, who was sitting now behind the others.

"Me Teresa okay," she said, her teeth flashing.

"You've got that much English," he said, faintly surprised. "Well, aren't you big enough to know that you oughtn't to be hanging around when a man's dressing? Aw, hell! What's the use?" He wrapped the towel round his loins, tucked in one end, and, picking up his pajama trousers, started back for the tent.

"Good moarning," said Teresa unexpectedly, dragging out the central *o* endlessly.

[*154*]

"Good God!" said Reis.

As he walked one of the smallest children came close to him, and suddenly he felt a confiding hand in his own. "Now that's funny," he said, and held it gently until they reached the tents. He rinsed himself in fresh water from the Lister bag, and the children gathered round, immensely appreciative and full of subdued laughter. Then he ducked into the tent and put on khaki slacks and shirt. Teresa had disappeared.

Their breakfast was leisurely. Watson, washing up the cups and plates, said, "Hey, lieutenant, what say we hire the big kids for this?"

"Won't hurt you for a while," said Reis unfeelingly, "but I'll think about it." Then, suddenly realising it for the first time, he said: "D'you know, we own this damned place! Asor's too far away to interfere with us, and the commodore, he's too busy anyway." He thought for a moment. "Higgins would only interfere medically if it was necessary." He wondered whether his estimate were just, and decided that it was. "And I joined to fight a war."

He went outside the eating tent, and Teresa came up to him. She carried a wreath of lime flowers beautifully woven on the pliable spines of young coconut fronds. As he stooped to admire it she lifted it with complete naturalness and placed it on his head. His instant impulse was to take it off; his instant reaction was embarrassment; but, impressed somehow by the naturalness of the child, by the fact that here was no giggle, no laughter, he suddenly straightened up with the unaccustomed weight above his temples, and the heavy fragrance of the flowers floated over him.

"Thank you," he said gravely.

"Okay," she said, "okay."

Then he turned and walked back into the eating tent to confront Watson. Here was a crucial test, a moment important in his relations with the other man, that might be the making or the marring of their future.

Watson looked up from the last of the cups and said only, "Hey, that's real nice of the kid!"

They went down the path past the seedy banana trees and approached the *falu* from the rear. One of the boys had gone ahead. The Ulithi king was sitting in the chief place, and the Fassarai king next to him. Ten of the old men sat round the terrace of the *falu*.

To Watson, Reis said: "There's the hell of a lot of ceremonial in these places. I suppose we'll wreck it all. Can't help it. I don't know what we ought to do. Somewhere I remember reading they sit to show respect. More than that, I don't know." He fingered a Japanese phrase book nervously. "I reckon we ought to sit too."

They climbed on to the terrace. No one seemed to take notice of the wreath, yet all had seen it. The king wore only a comb in his hair; but two of the older men wore wreaths on their heads, and three, round their necks.

Reis raised one arm in greeting to the king and nodded round the circle. "Morning," he said, "morning." Then, slightly self-consciously, he sat down close to the king on a smooth coral block. He remembered the necessity for German and said hurriedly and not too clearly, "Morgen, König."

Olimarao caught at the familiar syllables. "Morgen," he said.

Very slowly, painfully, Reis began, "Wir wollen der Volk sehen."

Unexpectedly Olimarao said, "Ja, ja."

"This morning," said Reis. "Oh, damn! I mean 'heute Morgen' —at least I think that's what I mean. God damn it! Does anybody speak any English at all?"

"Me spik," said one of the old men hesitantly.

Reis turned to him eagerly. "You speak English?"

"Allesame forget too much." The old man's brow furrowed suddenly with the effort at the long forgotten words. His name was Kirak, and he had gone from Yap to a plantation near Rabaul for a while and picked up the macabre skeleton of pidgin; but now it was gone. In vain Reis tried him, speaking slowly, clearly.

It needed pidgin to awaken pidgin, and Reis had none. Pidgin is a specialised language in itself. Its relation to English is arbitrary and by courtesy only. Now he could waken no other chords, no useful memory.

He tried the king again. "Der Volk des Dorfes heute Morgen zum Krankenhaus. Verstehen Sie?"

"Ja, ja," said the king. "Verstehe."

Sebastian had come in and sat down now in the circle. He too nodded. "Ich verstehe—verstehe gut, gut."

"I wonder if you do," said Reis. "Todos los hombres— What in God's name is 'women' in Spanish? Todas las señoras—I don't know if that means anything to them either!"

"Sí, sí, señor," said a very old man, suddenly waking up.

"Wait a minute!" Reis put his fingers together and said slowly, "All people." He pointed quickly round the circle, then at the children, then at the heads of the women who were watching round the corner of the canoe shed. "All—everybody—to"—he jerked his arm over pointing towards the hutments—"this morning." He suddenly pointed at the sun, and then made a small movement with his hand and pointed again to indicate the passage of a short space of time. "Understand?"

"Ja, ja, ich verstehe," said the Ulithi king.

"I wonder if you do," said Reis. "I wonder. Let's get back, Watson. This conversation's getting me down. If they don't come we'll send the kids after them. I just want the one village this morning. It's all we can manage, I think."

He nodded ceremoniously to the king, rose, nodded again to the circle, and walked off, the children following at once. Going back up the path he said: "These flies are damn' awful. What sort of D.D.T. spray have we got?"

"Little one," said Watson.

"All right, we'll have to requisition a big one. We'll have to D.D.T. the whole island before we finish, I can see that. You know, I think the first thing we're going to need is a hygiene campaign. This place is dirty, just dirty." A little further down the path Reis said: "We'll make a list of them this morning, a full nominal roll, and we'll keep cards—just get the outline first, name and age and so on. It's about all we'll be able to get out of them. This language business is hell. Going to be hot today. There's no wind now. Was there anything new in the anchorage?"

"Now that's funny," said Watson. "I didn't even look."

They walked on again in silence until Reis said: "All this trash here—we'll get it out to the beach and burn it, make a full-scale campaign of it. Look at those half-eaten nuts! Rats, I suppose. I heard one last night. That's what it was, rats at a nut—queer sort of noise. That's where the flies breed, and round the village. We'll go up to the north village this evening perhaps and tell 'em to come along tomorrow morning."

He came to the tents athwart the island path and turned towards the surgery tent. "We'll get the kids to clear some of this trash away from here for a start," he said. "Hey, you!" he called to Fayu. "Come here!"

The boy came, his muscles lithe and firm and quick-moving under the shining skin. Reis kicked at the old, decaying palm fronds and the unhusked nuts.

"Take 'em away. Pick 'em up, make a pile over there." He bent down and picked up a handful and thrust it into the boy's arms. "Take them over there," he said, pointing.

Fayu nodded, comprehending at once. He moved over towards the point that Reis had indicated, calling out to the other children as he went, and they began to gather fronds and nuts and broken wood and the hard spines of the leaves, and put them over in a pile. Teresa bent down a young palm and broke off half a dozen fronds. Then, stripping bark from a little bush, she bound them together at the top and improvised a broom. As the boys cleared she began to sweep behind them, and from the door of the surgery tent a clear space spread out by magic among the palm boles, floored with a mould that was half coral sand and half the fine residual decay of the palm fronds.

Reis, inside preparing cards, was surprised when he came out to find twenty yards of the frontage clear and seemly and the children toiling on at the pile. He called Fayu to him. He had

made a note of names that McNally had mentioned at the Black
Widow. Now he scanned it; the children's names were there.
Teresa, he had recognised from McNally's description. The other
girl therefore was Filomena. One of the boys was Fayu, and one
Fernando.

He said, "You Fernando?"

"Me Fayu," said the boy instantly.

"Good. Come here!" Reis brought a folding table out in the
open with a chair and sat down with the cards in front of him.
At the top he printed "Fayu" in clear letters, and he called the
boy close. "Your name," he said, "Fayu."

"Me Fayu," said the boy again, grinning widely. "Me Fayu."

"How old are you?"

The boy shook his head uncomprehendingly. Reis held up his
hand with the fingers outstretched twice and then with four
fingers only. The boy looked at him, his brows together, his
face puckered in the effort to understand. One of the smaller
children was going past. Reis grabbed at her arm and motioned
her to stand. Then he pointed to her, held up five fingers and then
three. Then he said, "You," and doubled the five fingers and held
up four.

Instantly the boy comprehended. He was fourteen years old.
Reis's guess was near enough. He followed out the gesture with
the hand, counting up to fourteen, and Reis put down his age.

Methodically he went over the boy. He was sound, but along
the inside of the thigh were three of the telltale ulcers of yaws.
His chest was sound enough, and there was no sign of malnutrition. Reis prodded the new-healed bullet scar in his buttock. It
seemed sound and healthy.

"Hookworm count will have to come later," he said over his
shoulder. "McNally says they've all got it, just about; but we'll
have to get the language business straightened up a bit before
we can get on to that sort of thing. We'll put this kid down for
yaws, and he needs one eye washed out. Can't say what it is at
the moment—they pick up a hell of a lot of things in this lagoon

water. Otherwise I'd say he was okay. We'll look at teeth and ears another time."

To Fayu he said: "Okay, you can go. I want Fernando—Fernando."

The boy ran off calling, and the small children, who had gathered round for an inspection, scattered for a moment as if fearful that they would be called upon. Fernando came from the rubbish pile with Fayu gambolling round him and shouting a long explanation, or perhaps a warning. He stopped in front of the table.

"Your name Fernando?"

"Me Fernando," agreed the boy.

Reis wrote it down on the card and showed it to him. "Fernando," he said, and started on the pantomime with the hands. Fayu stepped forward and thrust his hand over the table: two fives and a three—thirteen years. Slowly Reis repeated it and wrote down the age.

He went through the examination carefully. There was perhaps the slightest evidence of a patch on one lung. He marked it in as doubtful and went over the boy again. He was clean of yaws, but had an ugly coral sore on one foot and a long series of scars up one groin and out across the belly. One ear was suppurating.

Reis looked at it. "Not pretty, but I don't think that's serious. We'll start on that tomorrow. The big thing is to get 'em all down today. . . . Teresa!" he called out.

Behind him a voice said softly, "Me name Teresa."

"Ha, you've picked that up all right! Well, the quicker the better. How old are you?" He said the words very slowly and then repeated them, "How old are you—fourteen?" and held up his fingers to make fourteen.

Instantly she said, "Me old fourteen."

"Now how the hell am I to tell her that that's wrong?" he said aggrievedly. "Oh, well, we'll get over that somehow! She's quick, and that's going to help."

He completed the cards of the four older children. The two

girls, except for slight yaws and, he suspected, moderate hookworm infection, were sound enough.

He grabbed at one of the smaller children and turned to Teresa. "What is her name?"

"Name Rtep."

"Say again."

Teresa shook her head.

"Name again?"

"Rtep."

"Well, I'm damned if I know how you spell it!" He put down Retep, ignorant of the name of the orchid. "How old is she?"

"Old—" Teresa held up nine fingers, using both hands.

"That's all right, we've got a start now."

Reis handed over the cards to Watson and began to work uninterruptedly at the examinations. His interne work at Cicero had conditioned him for just this sort of quick superficial examination. As he went on he was dismayed at the results of his hurried diagnoses. Yesterday and this morning the children had seemed so full of life, so full of energy, that he had forgotten McNally's dicta. It was clear that they were all in need of treatment of one sort and another. Malnutrition showed with some of them, and vitamin deficiencies. Almost without exception they had yaws—some of them to an extent that would have crippled a European child, with the great raspberry ulcers, the framboesia of the medical term, angry and suppurating. Ear trouble seemed almost inevitable, and five of them had sore eyes. As he worked he talked incessantly to Watson.

"Have you seen yaws before?"

"Not me," said Watson. "I ain't been in the tropics, and what I see now don't make me like 'em any."

"It's a spirochete. Next best thing to syphilis, and so damned like it it's hard to tell even under a microscope. 'A thick viscid ichor'—I'll say it is. Jesus, look at this one!" Reis parted the grass skirt of one of the small girls to show an enormous cluster of ulcers in the groin. "That'll be what Fernando's scars come from," he said.

There was a shriek of laughter all round the circle of the children. He disregarded it and went on with the examinations.

It took them almost an hour to go through the children, and then he realised suddenly that some of these children must be from the north village. He had meant to keep the two groups separate, and now he tried to divide them; but though Teresa and Fayu strained at his meaning it was impossible for the time being to get it across. After a little he gave it up. Going back to the cook tent, he fetched out a box of candy and handed it round, two pieces to each child. Rucinski and the others had taught them the sweets of candy. They took them with rippling laughter and pretty gestures of thanks.

"Damn' kids," said Reis, "they'll get in our hair before we've finished. Hell! D'you know I've forgotten completely about the adults, and not a one's showed up yet? Where are they?" He looked at his watch. "Goddam! It's near twelve, and I told them to come this morning."

"Ain't never a nigger yet that had a sense of time," said Watson.

"They're not niggers, but you're right at that. Hey you, Teresa! Listen here." Reis picked up an empty card and pointed to the name space. "I want name Sebastian; I want name Jesus; I want name Olimarao, *der König*, I want *der König*; I want everybody." He made a wide, impressive gesture with his hand. Suddenly from a boys' book came a memory of pidgin, of *bêche-de-mer*. "I want Mary belong him Sebastian, Mary belong him *König*. They come here. . . . Jesus! Doesn't it make you feel a damn' fool speaking something that you know they don't understand? . . . You fetch 'em. Give 'em candy. Aw, hell! Anyway, you fetch 'em!"

The child remained poised like an intelligent dog questioning its master's will, with her head lifted up and her eyes fixed on him.

"You fetch—you fetch Sebastian, *der König*, Jesus, everybody." After each word Reis jerked his head in the direction of the village.

Suddenly she seemed to get his meaning. A torrent of words poured out, and then, clear as a bell at the end of it, "Okay, okay." Turning, she began to run up the path, Fayu at her heels, throwing words at each other until the sound died between the palms.

CHAPTER XX

1

IT TOOK four days to get both villages on the cards—four days and a hut-to-hut inspection. The medical record did not come up to his hopes: tuberculosis and hookworm, filariasis and gonorrhea and the all-pervading yaws. Since Christmas three of the old people had died. Four more looked as if they might die at any moment. McNally had warned him about Li-kanot, wife of Tol, who was patently in the last stages of tuberculosis, wasted with a heavy fever and the continuous hemorrhage; but the other three were dying causeless and without reason.

He remembered what McNally had said: "If they decide they're going to die, they'll die all right."

He had examined each one of the three—two men and a woman—with a meticulous and a bewildered care. There were no symptoms that could account for their condition—or they admitted to none. There was only a deep listlessness, a lack of response in their reflexes, a lack of life. There was nothing more to it than that. Life was flowing out of them, and he could only watch the flow. It bred in him sudden bursts of anger, but they served no purpose either.

The D.D.T. spray had made the area about the camp free of insects now—that and the clearance of the rubbish. He took the D.D.T. with him when he went into the village, spraying some of the more obvious breeding places and the interiors of the huts of the sick. There was already a perceptible improvement in the fly situation.

He had not yet got order into the sick calls, for the days had been taken up with the preliminary examination. Higgins had promised to send the interpreter down at the end of the first week, and Reis made copious notes of things that required eluci-dation.

The routine of the days otherwise had settled itself without volition on his part. At breakfast time the children brought him a wreath of flowers for his head. On the fourth day they brought a second wreath for Watson, who said: "Hell, I've been waiting for that! Reckon we're friends now." They wore their wreaths carefully like insignia. It was not necessary to wear hats in the deep shadow of the palms.

On that day Reis remembered that, except for a glance in the mornings when he bathed, he had not looked out over the an-chorage. He had a quick feeling of guilt at the realisation. The an-chorage was war, and he repeated without preamble and without consciousness a phrase that he had used earlier, "Hell, I joined to fight a war!"

2

He began a movement to clean up the main village on the fifth day, attacking the more offensive piles of refuse. With Fayu and Teresa acting as interpreters—it was astonishing how rapidly they acquired understanding—he called out the fittest of the old men. From the cards it was possible to prepare a list of those who were capable of work. Olimarao came after an hour and stood beside him, watching. He had nothing to say except a guttural answer to Reis's salutation, and in the end he walked back to the *falu* and the shade.

To Watson, Reis said later: "I think the king's mad at us. Wish I could explain things better. Higgins ought to let us have the interpreter down here for a month or so. Aw, hell! We'll get along."

On the late afternoon of Thursday, Reis was making notes of the morning's sick call when he heard Watson's voice from the surgery tent: "Christ, Dr. Reis, will you look what's here!"

He looked up through the netting. Partly obscured by the intervening palm boles, a procession was approaching up the path from the main village. Two of the bigger children were in the lead, wreathed and with the extra decorations of festival. Teresa carried bananas, and Fernando a basket of papayas on his shoulder; other children staggered under green nuts. Two of the men carried on a long bamboo pole, slung upside down and incalculably silent, one of the last of the young pigs of the village. Olimarao walked behind the pig bearers with Sebastian on the one hand and Elingarik, the *machamach*, upon the other. A score of the older men walked behind him. All of them carried food of some sort: fish, a fowl, coconuts, taro.

Reis had slipped his shirt off earlier, and now he stood in the doorway wearing trousers only and the wreath around his head that had become almost a part of his uniform in these last days; it had slipped slightly to one side so that it gave him a bacchanalian air. He knew that a long council had begun the previous night; talking it over with Watson, he had decided that the king objected to the cleaning of the village. What this procession meant, he could not see. But the island path cut between the surgery tent and the living tent, and it might be that this was some festival in progress towards the northern village—some ritual of conviviality.

For the hundredth time he regretted bitterly his failure in understanding. The life of these people was secret to him, secret for two reasons: the barrier of language—with all the good will of the children it was not possible to indicate more than the simplicities of necessity; and the barrier of ignorance, the most formidable, insurmountable barrier. He knew nothing of the Pacific save its illimitable distances. He knew nothing of Micronesia save that it was an archipelago of small islands. He knew nothing of Ulithi save what his eyes had shown him; nothing of the complex, delicately patterned life behind it; nothing of the meaning of ceremony and ritual, of custom and of mores.

Fernando turned from the path towards him. This thing was theirs then. What did it mean? Was the king trying to pay them for what they had done? Or was he trying to buy them off from doing more? He had thought yesterday that Olimarao was disturbed by the work on the outskirts of the village. There was no telling what went on in his mind. He had said nothing, and yet Reis had had the impression of discontent. Tomorrow the interpreter would come down with the stores boat again. Perhaps he could put things right tomorrow—but now was the problem.

Watson came over from the surgery tent.

Carefully and with a complicated gesture, a rhythm, Teresa laid the stem of bananas at Reis's feet. The coconuts were heaped on either side of it. The pig was laid squealing down. The papayas and two great jars plugged with the hearts of young palms were placed with it. No word was spoken until the last offering was laid, and then Elingarik began a slow measured speech. The others had seated themselves beyond him, the king in the centre on his mat of ceremony; but Elingarik still stood, swaying slightly as the tempo of his speech increased.

To Watson and to Reis it was meaningless, sounds strung together in assonance and dissonance that to their ears had neither shape nor pattern; and yet Reis, striving desperately to make contact, sensed friendliness and respect, generosity and kindliness. Dimly he remembered somewhere in his reading a description of a food presentation, the Polynesian custom of marking respect. Almost certainly there was here a simple form of that more elaborate ceremony. He waited until after long flights Elingarik came through his peroration to a sonorous end. As the *machamach* sat the king stood up.

"I don't know," said Reis slowly, "but I think if we sat it might be right."

"Ain't no way of telling unless we try," agreed Watson.

They sat simultaneously on the broad step of the entrance to the tent. Immediately there was a little murmur from the seated group—a murmur, it seemed, of approval. Fayu, sitting back among the old men, nodded vigorously.

Olimarao threw back his head and pronounced something that might have been a benediction. Then he too sat.

Reis looked over towards Sebastian and said, "Was ist das?"

"Für Sie," said Sebastian instantly. "Für Sie—zu essen."

Some of the old men had begun to sing, and the children joined in the brief chant. They clapped their hands in time with it and thumped occasionally on the ground, their bodies swaying. Again the *machamach* got up. There was still an ordered part to play. The speech this time was briefer. He sat down. They seemed to wait expectantly. The silence became almost oppressive. It was clear that they were waiting for him to do something, and Reis had no conception of their need.

He heard Teresa's voice suddenly and saw the old men's heads jerk in her direction. She said one word three times over, "Eat, eat, eat!"

"Maybe that's it," whispered Reis sideways. Stretching over, he took a ripe banana from the bunch.

Evidently it was approved. Again the little ripple of words ran through the seated gathering. He took a second banana from the stem and, rising, held it out towards the king; but it was Elingarik whose arm stretched out to take it—the orator's right. He was going ahead well now and handed a third to Watson. He picked a fourth, and this time the king's hand came up at once and took it. The children began to laugh and clap gently. Somebody began to sing again.

Reis peeled the banana and ate it, holding the damp sections of the skin in his other hand.

Instantly, as he finished it, Teresa came forward. One of the old men pulled the plug from a jar, and a kava bowl appeared suddenly. She filled it and, sinking to her knees and then squatting back on her heels, she held the bowl up to Reis.

"I've drunk most things in my time," he said softly. "Here's how!" Lifting it, he drank off the acrid, peppery liquid. It struck at his palate and burned as it went down his throat. "Hell, how I wish I knew what I did next! . . . What do?" he whispered at Teresa.

"Give," she said, holding up her hands.

She refilled the bowl and presented it to Watson, who swallowed it, saying as he handed the bowl back, "Jesus, jungle juice!"

Teresa rose and turned, walked to the king, and again the bowl was filled. Elingarik drank last, and there was another pause.

Reis said: "In all the kids' books I ever read the explorers made gifts in return. There's nothing that we've got that they like except candy. Let's try 'em with canned meat. Get out a couple of cans of beef and a couple of Spam and some soup. We'll see how it goes."

Watson went over to the cook tent and came back laden. As he held up the beef Kirak, with his eyes on it, said, "Bullamacow."

"He's right! That's one I remember—bullamacow," said Reis. And the old man laughed happily to himself at the remembered words.

Watson built up a pile in front of the king.

"Get some crackers too," said Reis, "and, hell, we'll play safe—make it drink for drink."

He rose, went into the tent, and came out with two tooth mugs of brandy and water, which he handed to the king and to Elingarik. The old men drank, gasped a little, and drank again.

Suddenly the formality broke. It was as if Reis had filled, unknowingly, his share of the ritual, as if he had done all that was needed. The pig was taken off to one side, and in a wild flurry of screeching its throat was cut. Somebody set up a stake and began to husk the nuts. It was clear that this was a feast. The food was to be eaten, respect having been paid. Between the trees an audience came stealing up, the rest of the children of the two villages, the men who were not of the Council, until the encampment was ringed.

The low sun changed its light swiftly through gold to amber and from amber to red, and the boles of the palm trees that were open to the rays gilded and shone and blazed with it. And then it went out, racing down below the horizon, and the evanescent twilight succeeded it and hovered over them like a bird and was gone, and only the fire that they had prepared for the pig lit the encampment. Watson went in and trimmed the petrol lamps and brought them out. The hard, white blaze of them spread through the night and lost itself on the diminishing boles, and the work of the feast went on. There was singing now and hand clapping, and some of the children began to dance in the dancing light of the fire. There was a tremendous bustle, purposeful movement from point to point that seemed to accomplish nothing—nothing more than the exchange of courtesies or passing of humour. There was laughter and shrill cries. To one group Sebastian began to tell an endless story that ran on and on with gesture and pantomime and feeling.

The king and Elingarik had come closer to the steps, moving the mat of ceremony, and Watson filled the tooth mugs again and again. He passed one or two glasses out on his own account to Kirak and Jesus and Tol. They seemed to show no change, and yet the excitement worked up. There were three fires going now, and two separate dances. There were women in the audience too; and the children shrieked and ran between the feet of their elders, and raced round the tree boles and came and collapsed suddenly and confidingly against Reis's legs to get their breath, and ran off in a moment, yelling.

Some time later they ate the pig, fragments of it hot and smoking from the roasted carcass on a platter of palm leaf, and partnered by lumps of taro and baked banana. They ate with their fingers, for neither Watson nor Reis chose to break the spell of this enchantment by fetching plates and forks from the cook tent. They ate, they drank palm toddy, they listened to the singing, clapping to the uneasy, difficult rhythm, and they watched the slow, purposeful, inexplicable dancing. They also finished the bottle of brandy.

Long before they finished it the king spoke suddenly from his mat. Someone called, "Fayu!" Fernando, who was close by, came up, and Filomena and Teresa. Over their heads he said, "Diese sint Ihre Sklaven." There was a quick chorus of approval around him that spread out into the crowd to interrupt the rhythm of the singing in a distant group and, rippling up, seemed to break under the leaves of the palms.

It was not possible to say when the party ceased. Most of the older men—all of the Council—had gone by three o'clock. Watson, looking at the groups that remained, said, "Christ, Lieutenant, I'm cut! What say we go to our sacks?"

Reis nodded. " 'Sklaven' means slaves," he said. "I wonder if I got the old boy right. Okay, we'll hit the hay."

"Quite a party," said Watson, "quite a party."

The night was hot, the still air made even hotter by the fires. Reis stripped and lay on the top of his camp bed, coverless and naked. He went to sleep at once as Watson put out the light. An hour later he woke at a noise and, putting out his hand, felt a soft body crouching on the floor close to him. There was no movement. As his hand slipped over the bare flesh and an immature breast he was fully awake.

"Teresa," he said, "what the hell?"

"Me *Sklaven*," she said, and giggled.

"You get the hell out of it!" he said.

Watson was awake. His flash stabbed across the darkness and hit on the crouched figure of the girl.

"Go on! Scat!" Reis let out a hand and slapped her shoulder.

"Okay," she said. "G'night."

Watson switched off the electric torch. "Would you believe it?" he said in the darkness, piously. "Would you believe it?"

CHAPTER XXI

1

Reis stood on the beach below the *falu* as the dory came in from the L.S.I. His wreath was slightly to one side again, but he was completely unconscious of it. As he had watched them climbing down from the L.S.I. he had been almost sure that McNally was with the party. Now, as she neared the beach, he was certain. Mc-Nally, Adamello, the interpreter, one of the officers of the L.S.I., and a Seabee officer came ashore.

McNally splashed through the shallows and came up to Reis, eyeing the wreath. "Looks like you've settled in," he said.

Reis's hand flew up and pulled it off as he became suddenly conscious of the flowers. "Hell, I forgot this damned thing!"

"I take it the natives are friendly?" McNally's voice was sardonic.

"Yeah. We had us a party last night—quite a party!"

"Now that's interesting," said McNally slowly. "I don't think they've had a party since the Japs went."

Olimarao had come out on to the *ailiuth* and was seated in his customary place. They went across the sand towards him as Mc-Nally introduced the two strangers.

"I'm glad you brought Pintada," Reis said, nodding towards the interpreter. "There's a hell of a lot of questions I've got to ask."

They went through the formal ceremonial of the greetings. Then, while Pintada spoke to the old king, Reis said, "I want to make a full-scale examination of the whole island for hook-worm."

"How?"

"That's what I want Pintada to explain. I've got about fifty small tins, and we'll take excreta specimens at the rate of fifty a day."

"What method are you going to use for examination?"

"Salt flotation. It's the simplest. The microscope you gave me is lousy, but it'll do for that. I reckon there's about eighty or ninety per cent of it from the look of them."

"Maybe you're right," said McNally, "but you've got a job there."

"So what? Let's line Pintada up."

The Chamorro listened in a slightly shocked surprise as Reis explained forcefully what he needed. In the end he shrugged his shoulders: the ways of medical men were past him. "They no like it, but I tell 'em."

He was right—they didn't like it. In three minutes there was a heated debate in progress, with old men coming out of the *falu* to join in the indignation.

Adamello had gone off to the church. The men from the dory had come up to sit in the shade of the palms and smoke. Pawlo-wicz, the Seabee officer, came over and asked: "How's the camp going? Is there anything else you want done?"

"I want the whole island cleaned up," said Reis, "but I think it's better that these people do it. Give 'em something to think about. The camp's all right—fine! What the hell's all this row about?"

McNally grunted. "He said they wouldn't like it. Seems like they don't."

The interpreter came back to them. "The old men say their shit their own," he said succinctly. "You take it, you make witch-craft."

"Who says?" asked Reis.

"Elingarik," said Pintada, "three, four others—big-mouthed son-of-a-bitch!"

"What d'you know about that!" said Reis thoughtfully. "I'd a kind of feeling we'd have trouble."

Matlock, the young lieutenant from the L.S.I., looked up lazily. "Tell 'em you'll put a file of Marines on the island and make 'em crap by numbers."

"No. No, I'm not going to scare 'em. We'll get it one way or the other." Reis turned to McNally, who had been watching him. "We'll drop it for the moment. I haven't told you about last night's party. It was a food giving, a food presentation— Hell! I don't know what you call it. Same sort of thing they have in the Polynesian islands. I want to know what it was all about." He spoke to Pintada. "Tell 'em I want to know what was the meaning of the gifts they brought last night and the speeches."

Pintada went back to the *ailiuth*, Reis following, and spoke for a little. Then, as the king answered, he said over his shoulder: "The king says it was to make offer to you. You his friend. You kill flies. You like children."

"All right," said Reis. "Leave it at that for a minute. Now tell him—"

How was he to describe the astonishing penetration of the hookworm larva, its intricate progress through the blood-stream to the heart, from the heart to the lungs, from the lungs to the gullet, from the gullet to its last stage in the intestines? McNally watched him curiously. A silence that was something more than respect, that had even perhaps a tinge of fear in it, spread over the *ailiuth*. The children, who had come down as the argument progressed, stood hushed on the outer circle.

"Tell him—tell him there is a small thing, so small that he can't see it, that comes from an egg in his excreta—"

"What name 'excreta'?" demanded Pintada.

"Crap," said Pawlowicz helpfully, from the ground.

"All right, crap," said Reis. "Tell him that that small thing climbs up his feet and works under his skin, and gets into his blood. Tell him when it's big enough it gets out, and it hangs in his belly and drinks his blood. . . . Fair enough?" He looked over at McNally.

"Hardly scientific, but fair enough," said McNally.

Pintada launched his description with solemnity. He had a sense of the dramatic. He spun Reis's simple words into a complicated saga of sonorous phrases. The thing seemed to lend itself to drama.

Suddenly, in a moment's pause, Sebastian's voice broke triumphantly across the silence, "Senak along belly!"

"Now that," said McNally, "is pure pidgin. But he's got the idea."

"Now tell him," said Reis, disregarding the interruption, "that I must have pieces of what each man, each woman, and each child does to find out if they have the eggs in them, so as to give them medicine to kill the snakes. Tell them that last night I was their friend, and this morning I am their friend also. Tell them that, so long as they do what I ask them to do I will be their friend, and tell them that I ask them only because I wish to make them well."

He broke off and turned to McNally. "I feel like a Salvationist. Aw, hell! One way or another, they'll come to heel. They're not a bad crowd at that." He looked up.

McNally's eyes were resting on the wreath that he still carried. "No, I guessed that you'd found that."

"It's the kids," said Reis half apologetically. Then, with a sudden burst of honesty: "It's not just the kids. I like it."

"Sure," said McNally. "Sure."

A small battle seemed to be in progress on the *ailiuth*, a war of words that swung quickly from place to place in the half-circle. Elingarik was still fighting, but so far as they could judge from the outside he had lost some of his support. Behind them in the village the bell of the church began to ring, cracked and uncertain. And suddenly the warfare on the *ailiuth* ceased.

Pintada turned to Reis triumphantly: "Can do."

"So now you're happy," said Pawlowicz, from the ground. "Well, it takes all sorts. Me, I'd as lief take a bunch of violets."

"If you knew all there was to know about violets," said Reis, "maybe you'd change your mind. . . . Pintada, last night at the party the king said that he gave me the four big kids—you know the ones I mean. I want to know more about that. Ask him!"

Pintada fired a long question. Again he turned to Reis. "They your slaves," he said. "The boys, they get coconuts for you, do your work. You sleep with the girls, hey?"

"Judas priest!" said Pawlowicz. "Why didn't I become a doctor when my mother wanted me to?"

"Aw, hell!" said McNally. "Some guys get all the breaks. 'Tisn't just that he's a medic. He's just a lucky guy—food last night, flowers this morning, and a virgin for his bed!"

"D'you suppose she's a virgin, doc?"

"I doubt it," said McNally. "They part with it young in these atolls. Realists, that's what they are. They say it's just a membrane that gets in the way. Look at it realistically, that's what it is. What d'you say, Reis?"

"That's what it is, and it's inefficient at that." Reis grinned. "I had to slap her bottom to get her out of the tent last night before I knew she belonged to me."

"He had—to—slap—her—bottom!" Pawlowicz, lying on his back, apostrophised the palm-frond canopy above him. "And I haven't seen a woman properly for eighteen months! D'you want an assistant, doc?"

"I've got an assistant, and I reckon that's all we want here for the time being." Reis nodded to McNally. "I'd like you to go over the cards with me. Will you come on up?"

2

After the L.S.I. had gone Reis went through the village to the main path and walked down it towards the south end of the island. Some of the children followed him, but with a sudden impulse to be alone he shooed them like chickens back towards the village. They got his meaning after the second time, and he walked on alone.

The place where the water had swept over the island in the typhoon was clear enough. He remembered the story that had been told. In places the dead fronds of the underbrush had been piled against the bases of the palm boles. In places the mould was washed clear from the surface, and the white coral sand showed underneath in streamers and whorls of brightness. The path had been washed out here, and the lines of coral blocks that had bordered it since the Germans had first ordered the paths to be made were broken and the blocks themselves scattered. He tramped over piles of heaped brush, dead husks, pieces of plank, nameless flotsam, and came to the furthest end of the island beyond the little cove with the splintered palm boles. A sand spit jutted out, virginal and white in the late afternoon sun.

He walked over it, and then for no reason rolled up his khaki slacks and, still wearing his sneakers, waded out, following the sand across the reef towards Lossau. It ended suddenly and, looking down through the clear water, he saw in a constant and variable distortion the live coral beyond with deep crevasses broken through it, and the crevasses filled with aquamarine water and margined with sea anemones and the brilliant purple of sea urchins and the flashing brightness of the surgeonfish.

For a long while he peered down into the mystery of the depths, intent upon its movement and its life, unconsciously escaping from the problem of the island behind him. Then he heard joyous shouts at the edge of the palms and saw three of the small boys racing over the beach. One carried a fish spear and ran towards Reis brandishing it, immensely happy, immensely excited. He was shouting some many-syllabled offer, and as he splashed up he held out the spear.

Reis shook his head. "Hell, no! Your fish, you get him." He pointed down to the water and made jabbing motions and then pointed to the youngster.

The boy crowed with delight and, moving forward on his bare feet over the coral, cautiously approached the pool. For a second or two he waited, every muscle taut, his back ribbed with a strained anticipation, and then his arm flashed. The spear disappeared and came back bobbing to the surface, suddenly alive, full of a movement of its own. It floated and wriggled away in the deep water of the channel in the coral, and the child plunged in after it and came out shouting and holding it up with a bright blue and golden fish wriggling upon the end of it. The other two boys began to shout.

Reis looked at the island. At this distance the canopy of palms closed down over it so that it might have been almost the hull of an old ship upside down and wrecked upon a sandbank, its copper greened with age in the sunlight. There was a blandness about its functioning. For a moment he shivered at something in it that was almost sinister. He remembered that inside it there was the vast problem of the community—two hundred and sixty human problems that in their sum made up the single stark problem of the survival of a whole people. He wondered if he would ever get to know them, ever get to feel with them and see things in some degree with their eyes. The week had been enough only to show him how little he could touch their lives, how little make contact with the complex of their being.

The children with him now were immensely bright, immensely active, excited, happy; and yet he remembered them. Carlos had an ear discharge that was almost certainly mastoiditis; Farik, the smallest, beyond question was tubercular; the third— he could not remember his name, but Watson called him Joe— had an infected jaw that so far had not responded to treatment. All three had in different degrees the inevitable yaws.

Reis began to walk back through the golden-green water towards the shore. He was sure that he was right about mapharsen. McNally had seemed dubious of it; but the old remedies were slow and uncertain, and he had promised to send a supply of it down by the next boat if it arrived in time. It might come by any plane now.

He plunged into the beachward palms with the children at his heels, and Teresa rose in the shadow and followed him.

Watson was stacking the boxes, the small aluminum boxes for the faeces specimens. He was working down the cards alphabetically, taking the main village first, and printing each name carefully on the label.

Reis looked over his shoulder with approval. "We're going to have us a time over this," he said.

"That ol' bastard Elingarik," said Watson. "Aw, hell! He's not a bad guy."

Reis watched the printing. "When we've got that cleared up I'm going for the yaws in a big way—mapharsen."

"I heard about that," said Watson. "Kicks a spirochete's teeth out!"

"It does," said Reis, "by all the literature. The yaws bug's as like *Spirochaeta pallida* as anything I've ever seen under a microscope. I think mapharsen ought to act the same way with it. It's worth trying, anyway."

"What's the old treatment?"

"They used to use salvarsan according to the books, and then neoarsphenamine. Dr. McNally— Don't think he's excited, but we'll try it all the same." Reis grew enthusiastic. "What a place for experiment! A whole community that you can cut off from the outside world—just the right number to handle. You could do anything here!"

For a moment he was back in his student days with the fervour of the novice upon him. He had been going to devote his life to research and to experiment, and he had found that in a small-town practitioner experiment is unpopular, and research impossible.

Watson stopped working on his tins long enough to look at him curiously, but all he said was a flat "Maybe." After a while he added, "There's a plate broke."

"What plate?"

"Dinner plate."

"Oh!" Reis's voice was incurious.

"The kids done it," said Watson without expression.

"How come?"

"Washing up." Watching Reis craftily, he said: "I thought, seeing how this slave business is jake, that they might as well start in. Going to be expensive in crockery, but they'll get over it. We've got the tin plates to fall back on. D'you say anything to Dr. McNally about a radio?"

"I forgot. Remind me next week." Reis went through the cards until he reached L, then pulled out the card of Li-kanot and put it into a special case by itself. On the outside of the case he wrote, "Deaths."

Watson squinted over. "Funny about her. I'd have thought that she'd last a week. Pintada said she timed it that way because she didn't want to waste the chaplain's visit. Hell, I ain't never seen anybody buried so quick!"

"The L.S.I. had to get back," said Reis defensively.

"My guess is that when he gave her— What the hell do they call it?"

"Extreme unction."

"—he scared the daylights out of her."

"Theologically unsound but medically possible," said Reis amiably. "She'd have gone anyway. That makes twelve since the Japs left." He lapsed into a meditative silence. Finally he picked up one of the little aluminum boxes and tossed it lightly into the air. " 'Senak along belly,' " he quoted cheerfully. "There's times when those guys have a better word for it than the Greeks did. Aw, hell! What's for supper?"

"Bullamacow," said Watson sardonically. Raising his voice, he called out, "Hey, Teresa, can you work a can opener yet?"

There was a duet of delighted shrieks from the cook tent.

CHAPTER XXII

≈≈≈≈≈≈≈≈≈≈≈≈≈≈≈≈≈≈≈≈≈≈≈≈≈≈≈≈

1

McNALLY had said, as they stood at the landing place waiting for the dory to be got ready: "You've done one thing anyway. They haven't been so damned excited about anything since we came here as they were when you suggested the faeces specimens. Maybe it's a sign of life—God knows! Maybe you'll know too in a few days."

There was life all right. The first fifty tins yielded thirty specimens at the early Saturday sick call. Reis was still holding to the double sick call: the main village in the mornings, the north village at noon. He and Watson worked through the thirty specimens in a furious concentration. The tests took time. The mixing in the salt solution was simple enough, but the examination under the microscope was slow at first in their unpractised hands, and it was a considerable while before Reis could make his decision swift and certain. The eggs were small and difficult to see. Yet, when he was sure, he found that in the first ten specimens examined there was a positive result each time. The last light was all but gone, and the eyepiece of the microscope was blurred, when they worked through the thirtieth box. There were twenty-six positive cases, one doubtful in the last light, and three clear.

Watson straightened himself achingly from the bucket of disinfectant in which he washed the containers. "Thank Christ, that's done!"

Reis grunted. "Maybe it's just begun. We're twenty cans short. Did Elingarik show up?"

"Did he? Hell!"

"All right," said Reis evenly, "we'll give him the benefit of constipation until tomorrow. If he don't show up tomorrow I'll give him such a dose that he'll stay purged till next Thanksgiving. All the same I think it's a revolt. Check the cards!"

They went through the list. There were six of the very old men in addition to Elingarik, all "agnostics," according to Adamello, men who adhered still to the old gods and the old customs. Two of the women were wives of this group; Elingarik's wife was a third; two more were children of the group. Reis stacked these cards together. Over the remainder he pondered for a little. There was no certainty as to any of them: some were without doubt constipation cases; some might have been ordinary fright; some might have failed through forgetfulness. He put them in a second stack.

"If we don't get one thing we get another," he said. "At least we ought to get out of this a nominal roll of those on Elingarik's side of the house. Might come in useful at that!"

In the cook tent Teresa was rattling the empty beer can with cowries in it that she had set up for a dinner gong. The rattling stopped, and they heard her voice, "Chow up!"

"She's coming on," said Watson pridefully. "She called me a son-of-a-bitch this morning."

2

At the morning sick call five more specimens came in. There was still no sign of Elingarik. Halfway through, Reis called Fayu over to him. "Elingarik?" he said, with a rising inflection.

"Go fish," said Fayu, and made the motion of a swift paddle stroke.

Reis snorted. He began to check on the cards. Three of the old men, all the women, and the children from the stack of cards that represented the noncooperators were present, blandly boxless. He called them together in a group in front of the table outside the surgery tent, held up an empty box and tapped it.

"Where?" he demanded.

The children laughed cheerfully, the women smiled, the men's faces were superbly blank. Then he called the child over, "Teresa, ask them where the hell this is!"

She addressed a long sentence to the group. Then she turned back. "No got."

"Yeah," murmured Reis patiently. "I guessed as much. Ask them why!"

There was a little consultation, and the oldest of the men answered her. Patiently she translated to Reis, "No do."

"Yeah, I guessed that one too. Well, somebody will burst before long—I hope."

Reis dismissed them caustically and went on with the minor ailments of the parade. Though the times had been fixed for the sick call there was inevitably no strict adherence. There was no time upon the island. The eight o'clock call was the call of the beginning of the day. The noon call was the period when the sun was at the summit of the heavens. Within those broad limits they kept fairly closely to the requirements. In the long afternoons only the children came to play around the tents and pore over their shoulders when they worked at the microscope, or to organise odd and irrational games amongst themselves.

They were working on the faeces specimens for the fourth day in succession, this time on the laggards of the north village, when a woman came down the path from the north carrying a child of perhaps five months. She was close to them before Reis looked up. Then his eyes concentrated immediately on the child. It was desperately emaciated, the limbs almost devoid of flesh, the bones showing angular and ugly, the head precariously attached to the body by the pitiful neck.

"Hell!" he said, and asked Watson as he in turn looked up, "Have you seen this kid before?"

"Not me," said Watson.

"Damn! Who is she?" He called Filomena, who was close, and demanded, "What name?"

"Maria," she answered at once.

"Four Marias in the north village," said Watson. "Which Maria?" He looked over at Filomena and asked, "What man?"

"Elapik," answered the girl.

Watson reached towards the filing box and flicked over the cards. "That's that lame bastard top end of the village," he said.

The woman had stopped in front of the table. Now, mutely and with her face grief-stricken, she held out the child towards Reis. As he came round and took it, it moved very feebly. He said, "Well, it's alive anyway."

Watson picked out four cards. "Elapik, wife Maria, two kids, six and four: that's the lot."

"Have we been through the hut?"

"Yeah, but we didn't see this. I give up!"

Reis carried the child into the surgery tent, laid it down on the table, and began to examine it. It had three yaws ulcers, none serious, but otherwise there were no outward symptoms to explain its condition. He could feel no fever. The heart was regular but faint and slow. He said through the gauze to Watson: "Looks to me like sheer starvation. Send the mother in!"

"Hey, Maria!"

She came in and he began, "How come?" and then remembered the uselessness of words. "Aw, hell! Come over here, and let me have a look at you." He put a finger to the lips of the child and touched the nipple of one flaccid breast. "Eat so? Aw, Christ, she can't understand!" He called Filomena in. Again he went through the pantomime. "He eat so?" he asked. All infants on the island were breast-fed, but occasionally a child would be given coconut milk and fragments of soft food. After a little the mother understood and nodded. Slowly and carefully he began to examine her. In a very little it was patent that the child had been sucking at an empty breast—how long, it was impossible to say.

"Why in hell didn't you come here before?" he demanded.

"And how many more of you damn' women have got kids hidden away, and why?"

He raged across the tent, seized cottonwool and began to clean the child's nose and mouth. For a long while he talked, pouring wrath on the woman, who moved slowly away until she backed against the copper gauze of the tent-side and stood, half crouched, with her head against the canvas. Filomena watched, enormous-eyed. After a little he subsided.

"Best thing I can do is canned milk. Jesus, what fools you women are! Canned milk and orange juice and an anal injection of glucose, but I won't bet on it. And why the hell has your milk gone dry anyway?" He turned again on the woman, and then answered his own question wearily, "Aw, hell! I suppose it's all part of the same thing."

An hour later, with the child asleep and fed, he said: "We can't go on feeding for three months with a pipette. I'm going to send a message to McNally and ask him to put a signal through the Fleet for a feeding bottle." He chuckled.

"Holy hell, that'll fetch 'em!" said Watson gleefully. "Do it, doc, do it!"

Reis grunted. "All the same we've got to fix a feeding bottle somehow. Got any ideas?"

"Jesus, doc, I'm not a family man!"

"Nor I. But I want a feeding bottle by sundown. D'you know, Watson, that's the first time one of them's come to us of her own accord? Maybe we're getting places."

3

Watson came through the low brush that grew on the ocean side of the camp, thrusting the leaves aside. They whipped back and slashed at the half-dozen children who followed him, evoking delighted shrieks. Reis was sitting outside the sleeping tent, trying to catch some coolth out of the draught of the trade wind. He was not reading, nor had he the usual pile of cards beside him. He was just sitting.

Watson tossed something at him from five yards away that fell with a soft slap on the coral sand at his feet. "There's yer feeding bottle." It was an old work glove of heavy red rubber.

"Meaning?"

"Washed up on the beach," said Watson. "It ain't damaged. Cut off a finger and fix it on an eight-ounce bottle, and put a hole through it with a hot needle."

Reis nodded slowly as he examined it. "Yeah. Yeah, I think you've got something. I'd been trying to figure it out myself. There's such a hell of a lot to think of. Rubber's good—not perished. Try one of the small fingers first. And sterilise it!" He handed the glove back.

"Sure," said Watson as he went towards the surgery tent. "What's troubling you?"

"Nothing," Reis said automatically, and then added without withdrawing the word: "Elingarik. Have you seen that damned witch doctor?"

"He's still fishing. Lot of guys go fishing times—"

"Times when they're wanted," grunted Reis.

As Watson disappeared through the door of the surgery tent he said, hardly raising his voice to carry the distance, "José is worse."

"The hell he is!" There was a quick sympathy in Watson's voice, but it was not for José. "What's it, doc?"

"I don't know," whispered Reis. "I don't know—and I used to think I knew all the answers."

4

"Yeah," said Watson cheerfully, "he takes it all right. He was a bit balky at the start. Filomena gave him a bit of practice on herself. It seems like he'd been had that way before. He didn't take, but maybe she got a bit of a thrill out of it at that—I wouldn't know. He seemed to get the idea on the finger though."

This was the third attempt. Reis had tried himself twice. The third time he had left it to Filomena and Watson, who had enlarged the hole in the finger-end empirically and put sugar on it.

"He's taken the lot, and he's still keeping it down."

Reis nodded but made no comment. Watson was as pleased as a child with a new toy. He could not leave it alone.

"Reckon we've saved him, doc."

"Maybe," said Reis. "Maybe we can save the kids." A long while afterwards he added, "For what?"

5

He found Elingarik at the *falu* the next day in the sacred sleeping heat of the afternoon. It was an unfair advantage, but he was past caring. Elingarik was inside the *falu* on his sleeping mat, and Reis was in before he woke. The old man looked at him placidly. Reis sat down on one of the driftwood logs that ran lengthwise down the interior of the All Men House and shook his head sadly. Then he took out a spare specimen box and tossed it high in the air towards the doubtful complex of the rafters. He watched it turn over and over and caught it as it came down again. Then his eyes went back to the old man's face. Elingarik was still impassive.

Reis said: "Hell! I'm sorry for you. Six days and you've not passed a thing. It's bad—goddam bad." And he shook his head. As Elingarik eyed him warily, he went on talking. "You're a stubborn old son-of-a-bitch. In fact I'll go further—you're a stupid son-of-a-bitch. Maybe you think you're within your rights, and maybe you're right at that; but I'm settling the rights of this island these days, and it's about time you got that square." He leant forward suddenly and barked, "Verstehen?"

Elingarik shook his head wonderingly. Reis knew perfectly

well that he could not understand the swift English. He went on for a minute or two particularising Elingarik's crime. Then, jerking his thumb at Elingarik, he spoke suddenly over his shoulder towards Olimarao, who had been an impassive observer of the proceedings. "Krank?"

"Nein," said the king surprised.

"He is, you know," said Reis reprovingly, "and I'm going to start making prophecies. He's going to be a damned sight sicker." He called out, and as Fayu came in through the door he pointed vigorously at Elingarik. "Him he sick. Tell him!"

Fayu spoke rapidly to the old man and was met by an indignant repudiation.

"Him he sick, much sick—fürchterlich krank."

Even before Fayu had interpreted there was a vigorous denial from Elingarik.

"I have brought medicine," said Reis, ignoring the denial. He produced three capsules. He pointed to a green coconut on the floor. "Get!" he said to Fayu.

The boy picked it up and hacked the necessary hole in the top. Then, holding the capsules in one hand, Reis took the nut in the other and walked over to Elingarik. The old man pulled away, still sitting.

"Take!"

For a moment Elingarik resisted. Then partly in curiosity, partly in apathy, partly because he seemed suddenly aware that resistance was useless, he accepted the first capsule. In quick pantomime Reis showed him how to take it and to wash it down with coconut milk. He watched the old man place it tentatively upon his tongue and elevate the nut.

"And don't try to hide it in your gums," he said, "because I'm going to sit here long enough to give the capsule time to dissolve and if you get a mouthful of that goddam stuff you'll be sorry for a week."

One after another, he handed the capsules to the *machamach;* and one after another, with a sort of tolerant resignation, Elingarik took them and swallowed them.

[188]

"Okay," said Reis at the end. "I think you took 'em down all right, but we won't take any chances." He sat back on the log and winked broadly at the king. "He'll do," he said. "There's enough jalap there to keep him on the run for forty-eight hours."

He sat on for a little; then he remarked conversationally. "You've got a lot of flies here this afternoon, king." He pointed to the insects that buzzed round, following their motions with his hands and occasionally swiping at one. Then he went through the pantomime of the D.D.T. spray. "Bring here?" he asked.

The king nodded approvingly.

"Fayu, go fetch—" Reis made the motions again. Fayu disappeared.

Long before he was back it was patent that Elingarik had not concealed the capsules in his mouth. When he returned Reis went round the *falu* with the D.D.T. When it was finished he said: "Guten Abend, König. I'm giving him—" He pointed to Elingarik and rubbed his hand on his naked stomach. "He'll probably get the gripes about midnight."

He went out of the door, and as he passed out remembered to himself a coarse joke of his school days. "Me no movee, people next door movee." Chuckling, he went up the village path.

CHAPTER XXIII

≈≈≈≈≈≈≈≈≈≈≈≈≈≈≈≈≈≈≈≈≈≈

1

HE LAY STRETCHED on the bed while Teresa, crouched at the head, waved a palm-leaf fan slowly backwards and forwards creating no more than the illusion of coolth.

Watson lay on the other bed. "The beer's hot," he said in answer to a question. "Don't you thank God sometimes you're not a limey? Hot beer!" He shook his head disapprovingly.

Reis said, "You're damn' lucky to have beer at all. Thank God for the merchant ships!" He lay quiet for a minute and then said, "The store boat will bring the generating plant down next trip. I've got a note from Commander Higgins—he's a good guy, that! He's sending the sterilisers and the plant and enough gear to put light in all three tents, and he says if we need anything more, just ask."

"Two nurses," said Watson reflectively, "one of 'em blonde, about a hundred and ten pounds. Tell him Watson says it's about time he got laid."

"Too hot," commented Reis. "Teresa, go fetch the beer and a coupla cloths! Watson, you go get the bottle of ether on the table!"

"What the hell you going to do, doc? Put yourself out for half an hour?"

"No," said Reis, "I've just got an idea about the beer."

"Going to needle it with ether?" asked Watson, his eyes lighting up.

"Now that," said Reis, "is something that even I hadn't

thought up yet. No, I'm going to try cooling the beer. Wrap it in a damp cloth and souse the cloth with ether. When I've had a drink I'll think out an excuse for getting an icebox out of Higgins. Once we've got the generating plant the rest is easy."

They tried the experiment, putting the cloth-wrapped cans on the step and pouring the ether over them. The heavy pungent smell of it flooded the tent. "I don't know," said Reis once, "that I wouldn't rather have warm beer." In the end, when they poured it out, the beer still had the same colossal head on it and the coolness was barely perceptible even to the imagination. "All right," said Reis, "we get an icebox. Look who's coming!"

Elingarik was walking slowly up the path from the main village. He came across to them and sat down opposite the steps.

"Damned if he don't look better already!"

It was three weeks since the purging. Reis's prophecy had worked with precision. Half the village had stayed away the next morning from the sick call, and the wave of fear was still on them when the Wednesday store boat arrived. Pintada came down with it, and to him Reis explained the position. The Chamorro saw it as an immense and grotesque joke, and as that he translated it to a crowded meeting of the old men on the *ailiuth*. His conviction of the intrinsic merit of the humour transmitted itself through his laboured explanation. The gathering on the *ailiuth* began to laugh, first singly and then gustily in concert. The fear passed. It became clear to them that Reis was not a poisoner but a man of a pungent humour.

It was curious. The thing seemed to add immensely to his prestige and to his power. He suspected perhaps that the *machamach* had at times incurred enmity or at least unpopularity in the village; or it might have been only a savage delight in the discomfort of a dignitary.

Oddly enough, Reis had had no fear of reprisals. The old man had taken both his pains and his discomfiture with dignity. It seemed almost that he had become a friend: Reis was not sure.

The morning after the boat's return the whole village turned out to the work of clearing, though for days past only three or

[*191*]

four of the younger of the old men had come to pick up a desultory frond or a rotten nut. Now the ground under the palms was clear from the lagoon side to the undergrowth of brush on the ocean beach. The flies had disappeared. The big sprays and abundant supplies of D.D.T. had taken the pest from the open palms and from the village itself. A vigorous investigation of the water containers at the base of every tree and the one tiny fresh-water swamp patch that sometimes formed after heavy rains, and a little spraying with kerosene, had cleared up the mosquitoes. From the village there came daily complaints of the growing boldness of the rats, but there seemed to be no other fell results.

Maria's child was gaining weight steadily. She brought him down each morning to the sick call, though there was scarcely need for that now. She herself was improving: She had lost the unexplained fear that had made her hide him. But Reis, looking over the box marked "Deaths," watched the slow but steady accretion of the cards. José was dead. He had seemed about to die three times, and then it was apparently quite certain that he would live; and just because it was certain, Reis thought, José had died in the night, quietly and without disturbing anyone else in the hut. He saw no reason for it. José was dead and the other Jesus, the one from the north village, and there were four more who seemed to be following them.

He finished off the last of the sweet, sticky beer and went outside and sat on the step of the tent. Elingarik raised one hand in patient greeting. Reis smiled at him and asked politely, "How's your hang-over today?"

"Has he got one?" asked Watson, from inside the tent. "Christ! I think I'm going to take to drinking that palm toddy. Lace it with grain alcohol, it ought to be okay."

Reis said: "You leave the grain alcohol alone! I'm not going to explain your thirst to Higgins." The old man watched him uncomprehendingly, and he called out, "Teresa, ask Elingarik what he wants!"

Teresa called out, still inside the tent, and the old man nodded once and then began to speak volubly. There was a little silence, while Teresa arranged the English words in her mind. Then her voice, disembodied from behind the copper gauze, said flatly, "He want canoe go to Yap."

Reis jerked upright. "The hell he does! Now what in creation does he want that for? He knows perfectly well that the Japs are at Yap. Teresa, tell him Japonesey at Yap. He can't go."

Teresa's voice ran on for a little, and the old man spoke again. His voice was apologetic, explanatory, and insistent. From behind came Teresa's voice again, "He say canoe go every year pay Yap king."

"Wait a minute!" said Reis. "I remember somebody saying something about that. They used to pay tribute to Yap—did it all through the Japanese occupation as far as I can make out."

Elingarik spoke again, and Teresa said, "He want you tell Yap king why not go."

"Ah," said Reis, "I've got it! He's covering himself against trouble with the Yap king when peace comes. Tell him—" He paused for a moment, considering. "Tell him I'll give him a paper to say that it was my order that the canoe should not go." He wondered for a moment if Teresa would understand the sentence, but she said imperturbably from behind the screen, "Okay."

Elingarik nodded at the end, his face satisfied.

Reis rose and strolled to the surgery tent, looking for an impressive form. When he found it he typed: "This is to certify that I, Lieutenant John Reis, (MO) USNR, have this day, February 10, 1945, forbidden the departure of the annual tribute voyage to the king of Yap. Signed . . . . ." Underneath, on reflection, he typed "Witnessed . . . . ." Signing his name, he took the paper to the surgery tent and handed it to Watson.

"Hell, if I'm to be governor of a Pacific island, I'm going to be governor! Witness this state document!"

Watson signed, grinning, and Reis took it to Elingarik. The girl followed him.

"Tell him," he said, "to show this to the Yap king if the Yap king is angry." To himself he added as the girl began to translate, "And if the Yap king is still alive."

The cane chair creaked as Reis tilted back to take the drink properly. "Ice," he said, lingering over the syllable. "You don't know the hardships of life on a Pacific island, McNally. Real ice!" He looked appreciatively round the amorous frescoes on the walls. "Civilisation," he said, "bright lights. Would there be a movie tonight?"

"There would," answered McNally. "Good picture, too—Hedy Lamarr."

"As long as it's not Dorothy Lamour, I can take anything tonight," said Reis.

McNally looked at him curiously. "Beginning to get island-happy?"

Reis considered for long enough to drain his glass. "No, no, I don't think so."

"Here's the boss," said McNally, and rose to greet Higgins. Reis rose also.

When Higgins had got his own drink he turned to Reis. "I've read your report. Now tell me what really is happening."

Again Reis hesitated for a long time, and when he spoke it was slowly. He said, "They're still dying."

"Yes," rapped Higgins. "I told you I'd read the report. Why?"

"I've given all the causes of death I could see," Reis smiled half apologetically, "but they don't mean a damned thing. The only thing I can really say is that the rate has slackened. If I can take a line through the ones that are sick now I'd say it was going to slacken still further; but it's not stopped, and I can't say that it's going to stop." He paused, then said softly, "Maybe I'm not a good enough doctor."

"Maybe," said Higgins noncommittally. "What's on the credit side?"

Reis stared meditatively at the bubbles rising in his drink. "I've cleaned the island up. I've cut down the flies, and I've wiped out the mosquitoes. I've got them all evacuating themselves below the high-tide mark now, and I've got the old king convinced enough to make sure that they do it. I think I've got the hookworm controlled, and if there are no mosquitoes the filariasis won't get any worse. I've got the gonorrhea straightened out—I hope. There's not a case on the list at the moment anyway. As far as the T.B. goes, all I can do is feed 'em up; and that's not easy. Still we get some sort of results. I think the vitamin tablets are beginning to work with some of them." He waited for a little and then said, "But the biggest thing of all is the yaws."

"Mapharsen?" asked Higgins.

"Mapharsen," said Reis nodding. "I've given about eight hundred injections so far, and about two-thirds of the kids are clear already." His voice was suddenly strong. "At least we'll clean that up."

Higgins nodded slowly and began to ask searching technical questions. When he finished he said: "I want a full report on that —detailed—every aspect you can think of. You've got plenty of time for it."

When he went over to the bar to fetch another round of drinks McNally said: "The Old Man's interested. That report had better be good." Reis nodded.

Higgins came back with the highballs and sat down again, watching Reis. Suddenly he asked, "Are you getting anywhere at all?"

Reis fumbled for words and then thrust his fingers into the pocket of his shirt and pulled out a crumpled and slightly sweat-stained paper, a carbon copy of his order to Elingarik. He opened it and handed it over to Higgins, who read out, "This is to certify" and went on reading in silence. Finally he looked up.

"What the hell's this nonsense?"

"I don't know," said Reis. "I don't know at all. Maybe it's the first sign that I'm doing a bit of good."

"How come?"

"Elingarik—he's the *machamach*—"

"Mean the one you dosed?"

"McNally told you? Hell, yes, I dosed him! He's all right

[*195*]

now. He came to me—as far as I can make out, because he wanted protection in case the Yap king should cut up rough about the tribute after the war."

"What tribute?"

"Seems that they send canoes down to Yap every year about this time with the February trades, and they take down the tribute from Ulithi because the Yap kings conquered 'em—maybe a hundred years back, maybe five hundred."

"I don't see—" began Higgins.

"Well, I look at it this way. He's the *machamach*, he's the head of the old-fashioned, he's the religious leader in the old ways, and he's the biggest headache I had at the start. If he's worrying about 'after the war' it means he's looking ahead."

Very gravely Higgins nodded. "Maybe you've got something there."

"Maybe." Reis shrugged his shoulder. "Hell, I'm no nearer understanding them!" Again he hesitated. "Then there's the kids. I think I've got them. The four big ones are all right, and the others take a lead from them." He looked thoughtfully out through the windows towards the tumbled waters on the reef. "If we let the old people die off maybe we could stock a new island out of the kids."

"And who would teach the kids?" asked McNally.

Reis sighed and lifted his glass again. "There's a hell of a lot of angles."

Higgins spoke again, his voice rasping. "Your job is to save the old people as well as the kids, for the reputation of Commodore Keldon and the credit of the U.S. Navy. And by God, you'll do it!"

"Big Chief Thunderbolt," said McNally derisively.

The last embrace ended in the last ribald whistles from the enlisted men, and the screen turned white and flaring in the darkness. McNally and Reis stepped down from the little gallery at the back and walked in the warm darkness towards the officers' country.

"Like to stay up for two or three days?" asked McNally. "There's a Bob Hope movie Friday—I forget the name!"

Reis considered a moment. "No," he said, "I think I'll be getting back tomorrow."

"There's always boats going down to the southern anchorage," said McNally. "Stay if you like. Watson'll manage."

"He'd manage," agreed Reis. "Still I think I'll get back. You keep on at Higgins about letting me send the mastoid cases up to a hospital ship for operation, and the hernia."

"Oh, he'll give in," said McNally easily. "He barks like hell, but he's all right. Pity he's going."

"Going?" asked Reis, startled. "When's he going?"

"Pretty damn' soon."

"D'you get it?"

"Me? No, I haven't got enough seniority. They'll probably bring in some guy from the States."

"Some guy who doesn't know his ass from a hole in the ground," said Reis bitterly.

McNally looked at him humorously. "Six weeks ago you were Johnny-come-lately yourself."

"Sure," said Reis, "six weeks ago!"

CHAPTER XXIV

≈≈≈≈≈≈≈≈≈≈≈≈≈≈≈≈≈≈≈≈≈≈≈≈

1

WATSON said, "Dory from one of the merchantmen tried to come ashore at the north end yesterday."

"What did you do?" asked Reis.

"Told 'em to get the hell out. They argued a bit, but they went in the end. One of these days they won't bother to argue."

"I've asked Commander Higgins to get it put in Atoll Orders that there's no landing on this island," said Reis. "Maybe it'll do some good, maybe it won't. We've just got to keep on at 'em. What the hell have you been doing in front of the surgery?"

Watson grinned. "That's a swing, I thought the kids—"

"Now that's one hell of a good idea!" said Reis wonderingly. "Why didn't we think of it before? We'll put up a couple of swings, and—hell, what else do they have in a kids' playground? A seesaw! We can make a seesaw—split down a palm log easy enough. What about one of those revolving things? What the hell do they call 'em?"

"I wouldn't know," said Watson. "I think we can run to a seesaw. D'you suppose these kids'll know how to work it?"

"They can learn," said Reis cheerfully, "they'd better learn! How was the sick call this morning?"

"I fixed the injections all right, thirty-six this morning and forty-two noon. It cleans some of 'em up pretty well in a night, that stuff. Fat Mary brought her kid down again. He's got ringworm—at least it looks to me like ringworm."

[*198*]

"Tinea," said Reis, "fungus infection—there's not been much of that. Well, maybe we can fix it. Anything else?"

"One burn and two cuts. Hell, they'll be coming to us for headaches next! What did they do before they had anybody?" Watson looked up suddenly and doubtfully at Reis. "Ifalik's dead. Died last night. I can't see anything wrong. Doc, d'you suppose Elingarik or someone's putting a bee on them?"

"No," said Reis shortly.

"Well, put it another way. You don't suppose he's poisoning them off?"

"Why the hell should he? Which was Ifalik? I know, he was sick last week. He's the one from the north village—about the fourth hut up. He'd been down about his back. There was nothing wrong with his water, with his kidneys. Now what the hell would that be?"

"He didn't come for his yaws injection yesterday noon. I went up to the hut to check, and he was on his mat; but he didn't look bad to me. He said his back was bad again, but that was all."

"God damn!" said Reis acridly. "God damn!"

2

"Where's Filomena?" asked Reis over the breakfast table.

"She sick," answered Teresa.

"Sick be damned! She's sulking," said Watson. He grinned at Reis. "She came to me 'bout ten o'clock Wednesday night and said, seeing as you were away, she reckoned best thing would be for her to sleep with me."

"Filomena bad girl," said Teresa virtuously.

Watson flicked out and slapped her thigh. "You mean she's a bad girl because she thought of it first. You've got the morals of an alley cat, Teresa. Hell, now I'll have to explain what an alley cat is!"

"Filomena's growing up," said Reis soberly. "Well, they've got to grow up some time. Did she sleep with you, by the way?"

"She wouldn't be sulking yesterday if she had. I satisfy my women. She didn't come near the camp."

"Hell, if every girl who didn't get laid knocked off work the world wouldn't get very far!"

"Oh, wouldn't it!" said Watson. "My guess is it wouldn't make a hell of a lot of difference."

"That," said Reis carefully, "is a most immoral doctrine."

"Hi-yi! Come down and look at the generator, boss. She's a honey."

The generator had been installed, close to the nearest cooling water, by half a dozen ribald Seabees the day of Reis's departure for Asor; it had taken only a few hours. Since then the light at night had made an immense difference. He strolled with Watson down the path that led first past the surgery and the playground and then past the latrine towards the beach. Watson showed him around the shed with thatched sides and sloping corrugated roof.

"I'm going to collect rain water off that," he said. "They brought a bit of guttering down."

He explained the working of the plant, the gasoline cocks, and the starter switch. He started it up, with a loud coughing that changed to a steady purring. Over the roar he said:

"The old men don't like it. They say the Japs had one on Asor. What the hell! It can't be helped."

"Well, switch it off now. They'll be coming along for sick call. I'm not going to scare 'em away. Where are Fayu and Fernando?" Reis asked with a quizzical look. "They're not sulking too?"

"Hell! That's contrary to good discipline, lieutenant. That's a scan'lous suggestion!" Watson laughed. "No, they're fishing."

They strolled back to the surgery tent, and Reis began to prepare for the day's quota of injections. "You were asking about a blonde nurse the other day. Well, four nurses are coming down next week. Maybe there'll be a blonde among 'em. I didn't make any rule about colour. You can't have everything."

[200]

"Four—nurses!" Watson straightened himself and gaped through the gauze.

"Four. White nurses—four white nurses."

"Jesus, I didn't know there was that many left! How come, doc, how come?"

"Seems they asked Higgins if they could come down and see the natives. I said yes, provided we might send up our mastoid cases to a hospital ship—changee for changee. They'll take the mastoids back with them. Higgins agreed just as I was leaving. And we'll slip Tarik and his hernia on board the boat—they won't just chuck him over the side when they find him."

"Now that's something," said Watson admiringly. "That is something. But Teresa won't like it."

3

The village was silent. Only down by the All Men House was there the sound of voices, low and irregular, as Fayu and Fernando and half a dozen of the older men got the canoes ready for the fishing. There was no particular point in watching the canoes, but Reis had waked early and was sleepless. He strolled down the path between the houses, scuffing at the dust with his slippers.

For a quarter of an hour he sat unseen on the edge of the terrace as the boys moved backwards and forwards between the canoe shed and the two small fishing canoes drawn up just above the tide. Their bodies shone in the light of the coconut-oil lamps that wavered only a little in the windless, pre-dawn hush. It was reflected also by the black polished sides of the exquisite hulls, and there was a gradation from gold to brown, and from brown to black where it lost itself against the woven pandanus leaf of the sails. He could see the dark apex of the triangle silhouetted against the stars. There were two more lamps in the canoe shed; but one of them was obscured to his vision by the heavy uprights of the shed, and the other by one of the great travelling canoes, whose delicate bow curve was outlined in a halo of uneasy gold. The second unseen lamp cast shadows and facets of light that made an irregular, uncertain Picasso effect of shapes and planes.

While Reis watched, the boys got the last of the lines, the drinking coconuts, the food, stowed in the canoes. Fayu called to the older men in the canoe lodge, and they came down. They pushed out the first canoe with some ceremony and followed it with the second. Reis noticed that the canoes took the water without splash in the perfection of their fitness for their element. Only when the boys pushed off and climbed in was there a little flicker of green phosphorescence where their feet splashed. The impetus of the pushing carried the canoes a long way. Then he saw a paddle blade move, and they went out silently, and at last invisibly, to catch the dawn wind.

When the old men had gone back to the canoe lodge Reis rose and walked down the beach past them, still undetected. He realised suddenly that for the first time he had seen the people of the island himself unseen—that for the first time in the seven weeks on Fassarai he had, for a very little, seen the old island, the ancient life, unmarred, untouched by his own impact on the community. It was a sobering thing, this—doubt-making. How far, he wondered as he walked along the soft coral sand, his slippers sinking at every footfall, were his judgments sound? How far were his opinions justified? The report to Higgins had begun to assume the proportions of a nightmare. The necessity to formulate his views, to discipline his optimisms and his enthusiasms had brought with it a chain of related doubts.

His mind went back to the canoes: two going out on the morning fishing for the whole island; two for a community of two hundred and fifty souls. There should have been twenty: in the old days for that number there must have been twenty. This island had been balanced to a point of perfection before the Japanese came. Slowly, stumblingly, he began to see something of that perfection. Even in their dirt and their disease that perfection was maintained—even perhaps because of them. There was dirt enough to spread disease enough to take off enough of the surplus population and keep the people of the island inside that delicate balance of sufficient coconut palms to provide the basic food for sufficient men to man sufficient canoes to provide the necessary fish. These numbers were modified by the marsh patches of Asor, Falalop, and Mogmog. The harvest of the yams and the taro was balanced with an exquisite precision against the mouths they had to feed. This was a thing worked out over countless generations; not static; varying always in little, upwards and downwards, but maintaining over the centuries a perfect level of sufficiency for all. Now there was no sufficiency.

He struck away from the beach and on to the hard soil under the palms, and was lost instantly in absolute darkness; but even before he reached the further fringe he could see a delicate, still light between the boles and between the intersticies of the leaves of the fringing scrub. The dawn was coming.

He began to wonder what he was doing on the island, began to wonder whether—even if he could check the death rate—he would ultimately accomplish anything worth the accomplishment. The old king still said, gently and without apparent regret, in a strange perfection of resignation, "We are a dead people." Perhaps he was right. Reis began to question his own work on the island. The rubbish up and down the length of it was mostly cleared now, and the areas that he judged were infected with hookworm had been sprayed to a bleak sterility. So far as he could judge there were no mosquitoes alive, and the flies had disappeared also. He had begun a detailed inspection of the island for his report to Higgins. He began his report too with these basic facts. To them he appended with a fundamental honesty a concluding note:

"Only by experience over a term of years can one be certain that this is the correct procedure. The natives tell me, now that we have completed the work, that the dead fronds and the scrub under the palm trees act as a kind of breakwater in typhoons and prevent, or mitigate, the free sweep of water across the island and thus save the soil. It is possible that in cleaning up the island we have prepared the way for a disaster. Possibly some agricultural expert could advise on methods of preventing this, though I am doubtful of the value of any further interference with the island's natural vegetation.

"With regard to the D.D.T. used in dealing with flies and mosquitoes and also used on the ground in hookworm-infected areas, I should be glad of information as to the extent to which it will affect the general insect life and so interfere with the pollination of palms and other food-bearing trees and bushes."

When he had finished that section of the report he passed it over to Watson, saying: "I share my headaches. It comes easier."

When he dealt with the yaws he was on happier ground. He was certain of his results now. The immediate efficacy of the mapharsen was in some cases startling. Small lesions disappeared almost overnight; and the skin came up clean and unscarred save in the very worst cases. From the children there had been lifted the intolerable discomforts of the night, the endless necessity for scratching. He could see no ill results attendant on this.

4

"Is it lonely?" asked the youngest nurse.

"No," said Watson, "ain't got time to be lonely. There's plenty to do."

"But there's only the two of you."

"We get by. There's two hundred and fifty others."

"Natives." She added tolerantly, her eyes wandering over Filomena's slight shoulders, "They're cute, the kids specially."

Watson regarded her cynically. "We get by," he said again.

"When did you last see a movie?"

"Quite a while back." Watson was imperturbable. Then his voice became defensive. "Hell, we ain't so far off civilisation at that! We get the radio since we got the generator, and if we want to take a canoe out to a freighter in the anchorage any night we can see a movie if we like. Hell, I can live without movies! We're busy here."

"Oh! I didn't mean anything like that," she said vaguely. "I just wondered, that was all."

"Yeah," said Watson, "I know . . ." (He had been about to say: "You were wondering what we did about getting laid. I ain't answering that one." But she was an officer. He resisted the inclination.)

Oddly they had built much on this visitation, speculating in the warm darkness as they smoked outside in the mosquitoless air in the night before the Wednesday boat. Making plans to separate one of the girls, Watson had chosen "the likeliest-looking blonde," sure that there would be a blonde in the party. There was a plan to keep one in the surgery showing her the steriliser while the others were taken down to the generator or up to the ocean beach or something—elaborate cigarette-smoke plans. Watson had volunteered to take the whole party, less one girl, to the north village. Reis developed a plan for posting the children as sentries round a selected love-nest.

The fulfilment had fallen far short of the vision. The nurses were pleasant-looking, and there was one who was just Watson's weight. It would, of course, have been impossible—or nearly so—to achieve anything in the few hours they were ashore, for with them came two doctors from their hospital ship and the navigating officer, and two cipher officers from Asor, in a chattering, inquisitive, morbidly interested clatter of voices. Ingenuity might have made it possible; and yet Watson found himself not interested enough to make a pass. As the chatter went on he became almost taciturn. They were so horrified at the problem of the island, so properly indignant at its circumstance, so tremendously admiring of Reis's efforts, so respectful at the results of the mapharsen; and so palpably untouched by everything in its deeper implication, so superficially sympathetic. The island was a show.

Once Watson growled to Reis in passing, "D'you think they're good for half a buck for the guide?"

Filomena and Teresa posed for a score of pictures—"tit pictures," the navigator called them to the delightedly shocked squeaks of the youngest nurse. Fayu climbed palms for coconuts, and Fernando husked them. The girls plaited leaf mats in token of village industries.

Watson said in an aside, "Next party, I'll have my flea circus ready."

They both went down to the landing place when the time came for the boat to leave. Half the village was there, silent on the *ailiuth* and in front of the canoe shed, to watch Tarik and the two mastoid cases go aboard the landing craft. As the last dinghy-load pulled off Reis called across the water, "Don't forget you've got to make love to Kellie and get that water tank for us!" And a rich voice came back: "Sure, we'll get your old tank. We won't forget. 'Bye now, 'bye."

Before the dinghy was out of earshot Watson said, "Bet you five bucks she forgets before they're halfway up to Asor!"

"No takers," said Reis. He waved formally and without enthusiasm, and then, turning back through the low-hanging trees, pulled off his shirt. "That's better. Now we can get back to a bit of peace and quiet."

"Suits me," said Watson as they strolled up the path together. "Not but what that youngest nurse had a neat-turned ass."

CHAPTER XXV

≈≈≈≈≈≈≈≈≈≈≈≈≈≈≈≈≈≈≈≈≈≈≈≈≈≈≈≈≈≈≈≈

1

"No TANK," said Reis, putting down the papers on the surgery table. "Can't be spared for the time being. 'Consider you should endeavor to improve existing methods of water collection.'"

"Hell!" said Watson. "Maybe we can at that."

"We can not!" said Reis. "I'm going to get that tank or bust. We've got to have a central reserve of water that I can chlorinate, and that will last through a dry spell." He paused for a minute, thinking of the weird assortment of containers that clustered round the base of the palm trees near the village, each with a bunch of leaves to catch the rain-water from the boles: earthenware pots, five-inch cartridge cases that had come somehow ashore, an oil drum in one place, and a variety of cans elsewhere. The cases and cans and the drum were a tribute to war. The islanders used them only because trade had broken down and there were no earthenware pots, and no clay on the island from which pots could be made.

Reis, on his return to Asor, had seen large sectional tanks, twenty-five feet and more in length, being erected for water supply near the landing place. It was one of these that he had determined to bring down to Fassarai to put an end for all time to the fear of water shortage on the island and to ensure also a sterilised supply.

Reis turned over two or three more papers. Then he said as if he had been stung, "Hell, Kellie's gone!"

"Bad-tempered old bastard," said Watson indifferently.

"I wonder." Reis pulled his lip. "I wonder. Maybe he had a duodenal. We wouldn't be here if it wasn't for old Kellie, and that's something anyway."

"D'you ever see him morning after a party, doc? He used to get in a jeep—"

"I know. I know all about his mess boys; but their mortality rate was low, I noticed, and they seemed to stay by him. My theory is that old Kellie was a sentimentalist, and he covered up. Hell, I'm sorry he's moved! I could have gone direct to him about my tank."

"Where's he gone?" demanded Watson.

"Doesn't say, but I heard talk about Manila last time I was there. I expect that's it. Ever heard of his relief?" He threw a sheet over to Watson.

"I don't know much about the heavy brass. Take it as it comes."

Reis dropped the rest of the bundle of papers into a basket and climbed to his feet. " 'Now there arose up a new king over Egypt, which knew not Joseph,' " he quoted soberly, and walked out of the surgery tent.

2

"Teresa doesn't want any more nurses," said Watson.

"Teresa is going to get her bottom smacked fairly soon," said Reis irritably. "She's getting a damn' sight too many opinions these days. What's the matter?"

"I reckon she's jealous," said Watson maliciously.

"Well, the nurses are coming down again next week. The operation on Tarik is completely successful, and the mastoids seem to be all right. They'll come down same boat. We've got to put up with nurses and all the rest of it from now on, I think." Reis waved his hand vaguely. "One of the sights of the atoll. Myself, I think if we dressed up as beachcombers—and got our liquor supply as efficiently organised—we'd make a better show of it. What did Teresa say?"

"Oh, nothing! Just she didn't like the white nurses. She said the long dark one had too much behind, and her legs were knock-kneed."

"True enough. Can't object to straight reporting. She's had a row with Elingarik again, and I'm not sure she's not in Dutch with the king." Reis called out to Teresa, pitching his voice high, and she came out of the cook tent with her lava-lava swinging defiantly. "What's the matter?" he demanded. "You quarrelled with Elingarik and with Olimarao, and you're grumbling about the nurses."

"I don' like photo," she said quickly.

"Ha! You're the belle of the village. All belles of all villages like being photographed. You'd better like it. They're coming again Wednesday."

"Nurses?"

"Yeah, nurses."

She looked at him searchingly for a long minute and then said, "Teresa don' like nurses."

"Teresa don' like a damn' sight too much!" said Reis. "What you want is a good larruping. Now go get me a cold beer!"

"What she wants is a good laying," suggested Watson speculatively.

"Oh, for Christ's sake, shut up!" Reis's tongue had a sudden edge. "Quit that sort of talk, d'you hear!"

"Sure, doc, I hear." Watson's voice was penitent, but his eyes had a bright glint of malice. "Elingarik's getting quite talkative these days," he said, apparently changing the subject.

"So what?"

"So he's been telling me quite a lot about the island customs. Fayu translates. I think maybe he's trying to tell Fayu too, the same time."

Reis sat up abruptly, interested. "What sort of dope is it?"

"Aw, a lot of stuff! Fishing customs—how they catch sharks.

They get a kind of coconut rattle, and they hit it against the side of the boat, and the sharks come. A lot of stuff like that."

"Make notes of it," said Reis. "Make notes of it while you remember it, each time he talks. I want that stuff. It's going to be useful. Sounds like maybe he's trying to pass something on."

"Maybe he's only trying to get something off his chest," said Watson. "He was telling me day or two back how the kings and the medicine men and the big men of the village used to have all the young girls soon as they qualified."

"*Droit de seigneur*," said Reis idly, and then looked over at Watson. "Is that what he's got on his mind?"

"Hell, doc, I wouldn't know! You can't tell what that guy's thinking."

"Is that what Teresa's got on her mind?"

"The questions you ask!" Getting up leisurely, Watson strolled over towards the cook tent. "Make it snappy with that beer, Teresa—and one for me too. Come on, jump!"

3

"Have you seen the poop sheet anywhere?" asked Reis lazily.

"I saw it somewhere." Watson wriggled over in his chair until he could reach the table and fumble amongst the papers without getting up. "Perhaps it wasn't here. Aw, hell, leave it! There ain't any news anyway. D'you know we haven't listened to the radio news for best part three days?"

"I was wondering what was happening on that place Iwo Jima. What the hell is Iwo Jima, anyway?"

"Another goddam island," said Watson without feeling.

"There's a hell of a lot of islands in the Pacific," asserted Reis. "This one's cost ten thousand men so far. I hope it's worth it."

"If every island's going to cost that much . . ." Watson made the speculation automatically, not believing in it—not able to believe in it.

"The war's a long way off," Reis paused to contemplate the distance, "and the United States is further. Looks like we ain't going to get to either."

He lay silent in his chair, balancing the beer on his knee. Once or twice lately he had become conscious of his lack of interest in the outside world. It was as if they on their tiny secret island were divorced not only from war but from the whole world of men outside. It was curious—he was hardly interested even in the mail now, the letters from home. He had written nothing for this week's boat. He realised it again with a faint stab of conscience. Watson still looked forward to his mail, but only because he conducted in his own mind an immense and erotic campaign over the virtue of his girl in the Bronx. Sometimes he would speculate aloud for half an hour on end as to the possibilities of her faithlessness, as to the methods known rivals would adopt for her seduction. He was alarmingly frank.

Reis came back from the girl to the war again as if his mind were unwittingly driven to its realities. But here on the island there were no realities. The whole place was sited in a dream, and the back cloth to the dream was the endless, changing panorama of the ships. A fleet had sailed three weeks ago for Iwo Jima; another fleet would come in, a week hence. Freighters came and went. They had an importance only as points to be raided for supplies of fresh meat and beer, and the occasional bottle of Three Feathers or Old Grand-dad. Cigarettes and post-exchange supplies, they had in plenty. They had never contemplated an evening canoe voyage for the movies. Ships meant only steak and pork chops and liquor. They had ceased to think of them as bringing ammunition and engineers' stores, guns and rations, uniforms and jeeps and alligators and radio sets, hospital equipment and drugs and furniture for officers' clubs, and bombs and torpedoes and aircraft parts and materials for air strips.

They had only one other aspect that was of importance: whether their discipline was lax enough to let their men come exploring in motor dories.

On first coming down to this place, Reis had felt foreign.

He had felt as if he were penetrating into something hidden, elaborate and mysterious under the Romanesque canopy of the palms. Now he realised—without caring—it was the outer world that was foreign, the war that was strange, the United States that was remote and secret. He sat up in his chair with a sudden jerk. "Hell," he said, "I'm getting island-happy."

"Sure," said Watson soothingly, "we're both of us island-happy. It's as good a neurosis as the next. Have another beer. Teresa, bring two more beers!"

Reis sat bolt upright until the girl approached. Then he sank back in his chair. "Ah, hell, we've got cold beer anyway!"

Teresa filled his glass, handed the other bottle across to Watson, and settled at his knee with one arm over his thigh. She watched his face, her eyes brooding and curiously intense.

4

"There's something up in the village," said Watson. "They've had the kids picking green coconuts all the morning, and they've stripped the papaya trees; and the old men were out fishing last night. I think there's another feast on."

"Is that where the girls have gone?"

"I saw Filomena in Jesus's house."

"God damn it!" said Reis. "There's a packet of dressings to be washed and sterilised. They haven't cleared the breakfast plates yet, and looks like we'll have to fix our own lunch. I'm going to give those kids a lamming. What the hell's the use of having slaves if you've got to do your own work?"

"The genuwine Simon Legree," said Watson admiringly. "Wait a minute, lieutenant, an' I'll call up the bloodhounds."

"Did you ask Filomena what it was all about?"

"I did not. I asked the king, and he said it was to eat."

"Nobody's dead," said Reis. " 'Tisn't full moon or new moon. There's nothing I know in the season. Ah, well, maybe we'll know, maybe we won't. I've got to finish that report on the water supply anyway. I'm going to get the tank out of those bastards if it's the last thing I do!"

There was no sign of the girls at lunchtime. Fayu and Fernando were still away with the canoes. Watson opened a can of chopped pork and a can of beans, and they ate these with crackers, grumbling. In the middle of the afternoon Reis sat down and began an acid commentary on the island water supply. He wrote it at Higgins, aiming at known chinks in his medical armour. He was two-thirds of the way through when he heard Watson's voice:

"Told you it was a feast. Same as last time but more so—both villages."

In the distance Reis heard the sound of singing. He went out of the surgery door to watch and saw the singers approaching from the main village, a procession something like that of the earlier feast day, only now it seemed that every man in the village was there carrying. After them came the women, wearing the necklaces and the ear pendants, the wreaths and the flowers of full ceremony. The women were singing, the men joining in a deep harmony at long intervals. With them were running the children. It seemed as if the whole of the main village had come *en masse* to the camp. Then in the opposite direction, through the gauze of the tent, he noticed singing coming from the north.

He looked down suddenly at his hand and saw that he still held his pen. "The hell with it!" he said, and tossed it through the doorway on to the table where it spluttered ink across the sheet. "Come on!" he called to Watson. "Let's have us a real party."

5

The whole space of the encampment was packed now with people. The crescendo of the singing had risen to some climactic point. It was clear that they were achieving the node of the ceremony. The women's song went into a final high-drawn note, and the rhythmic handclapping ceased with the voices; for a long moment even the children were utterly silent, and there was no more than the drone and drift of the trade wind in the palm fronds and the bourdon of the reef outside.

Then Olimarao and Elingarik and four old men of the council rose, and Olimarao, coming forward, put over the triple wreaths about Reis's neck a necklace of sennit and shark's teeth and plaited palm fronds. Elingarik, moving up on his right, placed before Reis's feet a mat of ceremony. One of the old men from the left put forward a carved canoe paddle. Then, stepping back, Olimarao began to speak sonorously and long, and Elingarik spoke antiphonally, and the men began to take up the responses and the women to answer them till the whole place was in a deep uproar of exciting words thrown backwards and forwards, thundered over by the king—resonant, staccato, immensely exhilarating.

Again there came a pause, and in halting English Olimarao said: "Me king. You king too."

From behind him the girls brought flowers. Already he had more wreaths than at any time previous, but now they brought flowers that all but smothered him. They must have stripped the three frangipani trees of the island: they must have gathered almost every other flower that grew. His head was piled with blossoms, and his shoulders and the mat beside him were heaped with petals.

He heard Teresa say: "Now you king too. You and Olimarao all the same. You king of Ulithi."

The bourbon was beginning to take effect. There had been an hour's steady drinking glass for glass with Olimarao and Elingarik before this moment. Reis rose, faintly unsteady, swaying a little as if the wind had come down through the baffle of the palm fronds and was rocking him gently on his wide-spaced feet.

"Sure," he said, "I'll be king too, and I'll take it for an honour. By God, I've cursed you and dosed you and broken your habits and cleaned you up, and I don't know whether I ought to laugh or to cry at this, but hell, I feel like crying! Sure I'll be king, and to hell with the Navy regulations!"

He sat down abruptly and reached for the bottle, and the women began to sing again, a sad, sweet song that was like the swelling of the wind through the fringing scrub of the ocean beach, with a single girl's voice in it, Teresa's voice, that drowned the melody—not sweet to hear but wailing like the cry of the distant gulls. He filled the glasses of Elingarik and Olimarao and the nearest of the old men and his own and Watson's.

"Sure," he said, "I'll be king—and my mother's a Daughter of the Revolution! I wish," he said, "I wish I had enough liquor here to make every goddam man on the island drunk tonight, but we'll do the best with what we've got."

In the early evening half-light the fires began to rise between the tree boles and under their flickering brilliance the place became again the nave of the shrine of an ancient faun. Watson, with some curious delicacy, forbore to switch on the electric light, and the feast went on, roaring, into the night.

CHAPTER XXVI

1

REIS looked over the entries in the diary with a glint of bitter humour. "Since those damn' nurses set the fashion in February we've had twenty-six rubbernecks on the Wednesday boats, three semiofficial boats from Asor, and five unofficial boats from the merchant ships." He amused himself by adding up some figures. "One admiral, one commodore, a general of marines, three commanders, two colonels, nine nurses, four war correspondents, and a hell of a lot of merchant seamen. We've changed chaplains twice— I like this guy Minchin—and we've had one bishop and three stray parsons. We do keep up the class!" He went back to the papers. "Four attempted seductions of Teresa, two of Filomena—what's Teresa got that Filomena hasn't?—and one attempt at rape. And with all that brass we haven't got our tank yet! It's a hell of a life!"

"Can't Higgins stop it?" asked Watson.

"Why should he?" said Reis drily. "We're the show place of the atoll. Besides, I think he gets a percentage on the nurses. Hell, it's only us that suffer! There's a lot of water in the Pacific and mighty few holiday resorts, and if we don't have the big brass down, ain't nobody we can ask for favours. We don't do so bad at that. I've got a promise that we can send Mau up to get that cyst shifted next Wednesday boat. That's our dividend. Besides, I don't think the villages mind. Olimarao's taken to the idea of a shop for model canoes and carvings and cloths and baskets and things like a Navajo Indian trader. I don't see why, quite, but he has."

He put down the diary and looked out through the vistas of the palm boles. "It's a good idea," he said, half to himself and then more directly to Watson. "Way I look at it is that it gives the old men something to do and some excuse for living. Maybe that's what they want. It's no good pauperising a whole community. If they learn that they've only got to sit back and the rations come down with the Wednesday boat, there's nothing left for them to take an interest in." He turned abruptly to Watson. "We've only had one death in the last eleven days. It links up—it links up."

He picked up the pile of correspondence that had come down with the previous day's boat and started to thumb through it. "Higgins says there may be changes in his department in the near future. Hell, he's been saying that for the last two months! I hope he don't go. He wants a closer examination of the filariasis suspects and all their family contacts. That means a lot of micro-, scope work. Well, it'll be something to do. I wish I could make a trade with him—give him all the filariasis dope he wants for a tank."

Becoming conscious of a dozen of the village children who were playing wildly on the swings and the seesaw, he rose to his feet and called, "Teresa, tell those damn' kids not to make so much noise!" He heard her go out and shout until her voice dominated the uproar. "That's right," he grumbled. "Bawl 'em out! You're worse than the kids."

There was a sudden chorus of laughter. It was clear that Teresa had given the children some undignified reason for his irritability.

All of a sudden he smiled to himself, "Aw, to hell with paper work! It always makes me mad." And he walked into the golden shade. Instantly two of the smallest children precipitated themselves from a swinging bar and charged him, hanging round his legs.

"You're a worthless lot of good-for-nothing little bastards," he said affectionately. "I'm going to gag the whole damn' lot of you when you come to play here. Aw, hell, what's the use! I'm going down for a swim."

Immediately the rest of the children abandoned the swings. They followed him in a chattering, compact troop to the beach.

2

He woke to the rapid slapping of hands against the copper gauze of the side of the tents. A low, urgent voice was saying, "Wake up, wake up!"

Watson roused at the same time and called out, "What in Christ—"

A voice said: "Falifi hurt. Falifi hurt bad!" Another voice spoke in the island tongue, a deeper, older voice.

Reis slipped out of bed and into his trousers almost in the same movement. "Where?" he demanded. "What the hell's happened?" He groped for a flashlight as Watson switched on the electric light, and walked out into the warm night. "Where?" he said. "Show me!"

Watson followed buttoning himself and swearing, and they went at a jog trot down the island path, past the village and down towards the south end, and branched off two-thirds of the way to the end of the island, heading towards the ocean beach.

The child who had called him was too breathless, too excited, to say more than "Falifi hurt, Falifi hurt." It was a constant rhythm to his running.

They came through the low palms and the scrub on the ocean side, and Reis's flash, stabbing across the darkness, picked out a group of brown figures poised and bending above something that lay upon the ground. He moved towards it as fast as he could through the sand. Heads turned towards him, and the gleaming white of eyeballs answered the light of the torch.

Falifi was lying on the ground, and his body showed a red and bloody envelope to the searching beam. His chest and abdomen were covered with multiple lacerations from which blood oozed until it was impossible to see where one cut ended and the next began. One thigh was shredded to the bone in lumps and tatters and strips of torn flesh.

"Christ!" said Reis involuntarily. "What's done this? Shark?" There was a quick chorus in the unintelligible island dialect. "Ah, hell," he said, "never mind! Watson, what have we got for a tourniquet?"

He reached up impatiently, grabbed at the lava-lava of the man nearest him and pulled it off. There was an indignant squawk and then, macabre across the bloody face of the tragedy, a chorus of laughter. He ripped the cloth, twisted it and, with Watson holding the flesh, began to work quickly, feeling for the femoral artery in the slippery, bloodstained mess of the upper part of the thigh.

To Fayu, who could be heard coming through the darkness of the beach, he shouted, "Get something we can carry him on—quick! He'll die if we don't."

Privately he could not understand why Falifi was alive now. There seemed no reason for it. By all medical laws he should have died long since of loss of blood. With quick, silent work, at last the spurting of blood from the chaos of broken flesh was stopped.

The wait for something to carry him on seemed interminable. It could not have been more than seven minutes at the outside, yet Reis, stooping over the unconscious man, was reduced almost to biting on his knuckles in his impatience to get him into the light where he could work with surety and faith. Fayu and Fernando and Olimarao came back with a rough litter of poles and palm matting, and they placed Falifi on it and carried him fast through the palms and then along the path towards the camp.

The moment they had him on the litter, Reis strode ahead towards the camp. All along the path the villagers were coming down as the word spread. He sensed rather than saw Filomena and said, "Get the hell up to the camp—go on! What are you doing down here?"

At the camp he switched on all the lights till the place was an oasis of brilliance in the darkness of the palms, switched on the steriliser, stretched out for the case of surgical instruments, and groped desperately in his mind for memories of amputations. Over his shoulder he was giving voluminous instructions to Filomena, who worked to put the two surgery tables together, to cover them with a sterilised sheet, to get out the chloroform, the disinfectant bottles, the swabs and the towels. They were almost ready when the litter came. A dozen men crowded in with it, and a dozen pairs of hands lifted Falifi to the white sheet that reddened instantly.

"Now get the hell out of it," said Watson. "Come on, all of you—every one of you! Out you go—out!" Teresa had come in by this time, and he said, "You stay, and Filomena—over there in the corner. Now wait!"

Reis was bending above the body with the shade of the light in his hand, turning it this way and that. He went quickly over the chest and abdomen. There were lacerations that crossed and cut at every angle, but they were for the most part superficial. After a quick examination he disregarded them. The right leg was cut too: long abrasions of the upper part, deep cuts above the knee and along the calf. But the left leg was shattered. He could see the white of the bone sticking through the tortured flesh. From halfway down the thigh it was shredded, and three separate splinters jutted from the fracture. It was fractured again above the ankle. Quickly he adjusted the tourniquet, releasing it for a little and tightening it again.

"We'll amputate about here," he said, drawing his finger across the thigh. "Nothing we can do to save that mess. Have you got the chloroform mask?" He began to scrub up in the hand basin and, when he had finished, walked over to the steriliser and picked out his gloves. Not until he was putting them on did he ask: "What happened? Have you got it yet?"

"Fishing," said Watson. "He cut down from the northern end outside the reef and he went too close in and got caught. Tonio was with him. They went over at the edge of the reef. I don't know what happened. Tonio got clear and got the canoe upright again, but Falifi went on the reef and got caught under a fringe of coral and the surf did the rest. No sharks—all coral cuts."

"Then he'll die of coral poisoning," said Reis softly. "But we'll amputate all the same."

With a sober anger he began to make the first incision, cutting above the worst of the open wounds. The surgery tent was brilliant with all the light that Watson could concentrate. The two girls stood at one corner close to a pile of towels and swabs. Outside Reis could sense, though he could not see, the ranked faces against the gauze.

Two hours later he was still working over the half-conscious man; cleaning, disinfecting, sewing up wound after wound.

3

The noise of the radio drowned almost everything except a shouted conversation. Higgins seemed to be inured to it, but to Reis it had an unpleasant metallic timbre, a brutal stridency that he had never realised before. He had described Falifi's injuries carefully and conservatively in medical language. Now he burst out suddenly: "Hell, he looked like he'd been passed over a bunch of buzz saws! I've never seen anything like it. Apart from the stump I put in a hundred and thirty stitches: Watson counted them—I didn't care round about the end." In answer to an abrupt query he said: "Sure he'll live! I told him as soon as he was conscious enough to listen that if he didn't live he'd let me down with you." He grinned, and in a pause in the music he said softly: "No, he's going to live. I don't know why—can't see that he's got much to live for."

The radio changed a disc and began to play sweet, and Reis's voice was plainly audible. "Ifalik died, and I don't know why. Pablo from the north village lived—and I don't know why either. But I think we're getting on top of it. Falifi would have gone straight out a month ago. He may go now, but if he dies he'll die for surgical reasons and nothing else. He's doing his damnedest to live, and I think he's going to. There have been two or three other cases. I wouldn't say it to anybody else, commander, but I think we're getting on top of it."

Without comment Higgins passed the grey club card over his shoulder to the barman and said, "Fill 'em up again!"

Over the new drink Reis came back in a curious concentration to his story. "We couldn't have done it if it hadn't been for the plasma you sent down by the last Wednesday boat—that and the penicillin. We've justified the icebox, commander."

"What you want," said Higgins, looking at him judgmatically over his glass, "is a week up here. You can stay at the hotel and get drunk every night."

Reis shook his head. "No can, I've got too much to do. Hell, I haven't finished your filariasis examinations yet!"

"You take a week off. A week now is better than a month later."

"I couldn't," said Reis simply. "Things like this are cropping up all the time, and I'm just getting on top of it now."

Higgins shrugged. "Isn't anybody we could send down in your place. Well, it's your own choice; but you're getting too tied up with this thing. I don't want you getting island-happy, and you've got the signs of it." He leaned forward and tapped Reis on the knee. "I bet you five bucks you can't tell me a damn' thing about the war. Have you heard of Okinawa?"

"Sure I've heard of it."

"Have you heard the British are over the Rhine?"

"One war's enough," said Reis.

"You'd better keep in touch," said Higgins grimly. "I don't want to have to send another doctor down after you. Is there anything you need down there?" And quickly, before Reis could answer, "No, you can't have the tank! I've talked to the Seabees about it, and they ain't got one to spare. There's another consignment next month. I'll see what I can do then." He drank and added, "If I'm still here."

Reis grinned. "There's four of them down by the landing. Hell, they can't want all that amount!"

"They can," snapped Higgins with finality.

McNally joined them. With Higgins he watched the curious nervousness, the aloofness that seemed to have grown over Reis in the last months. Like Higgins he made no comment.

Twenty minutes later the new commodore came in. Higgins rose. "You haven't met the commodore. Come along! . . . Commodore Raglan," he said, "meet the King of Fassarai. What'll you have?"

4

In the full glare of the sun Reis stood studying the pile of steel plates. The big tanks consisted of twelve sections bolted together. It was easy enough to identify the end sections. One of the Seabees had told him the cabalistic markings. He judged its weight to be in the neighbourhood of eighty pounds. He wanted to try the heft of it, but there were two Seabees under the shadow of the nearest palm and two more in the shadow of the decaying All Men House. He studied it, making a mental picture of the positioning of the bolt holes and trying to estimate the over-all dimensions. A plan was forming in the back of his mind, but he wanted to be sure of his ground.

After a little he strolled away from the pile down to the beach. The ground was clear all the way to the sand, and the beach beyond seemed to have clear water up to it though no boats used it. The landing place was on the other side of the little pier, but most boats used the pier itself now. There was a hut and a police post at the base of the pier and a shelter towards the end. The steel piling leant over drunkenly on one side, but otherwise the pier was solid, the coral packed hard, and the surface sound. The beach was close to the base of the pier; he walked along it, watching through the translucent water for coral heads, but the water seemed clear for fifty yards.

Finally he walked up the slope of the bank, found the rough road that the jeeps used beyond it, and walked down that to the steel pile again, counting his steps. In the end he seemed satisfied and looked at his watch. It was almost time for dinner. He walked back towards the mess hall.

Watson, Fayu, Filomena, and seventeen children met him at the landing place on Fassarai. It was like coming home. Asor was a crowded and dusty wilderness now. The tree boles were grey with coral dust, and the shacks and the surfaces of the Quonset huts were grey with dust too. Each jeep in the island was followed by a perpetual cloud. They had cut down so many of the palms that the island shone now, always white and incandescent in the sunlight. It was hot and achingly dry and intolerably noisy. Always there was a radio blaring close at hand, and always its music was punctuated with the hoarse stridencies of the squawk-box, and the air was cacophonous with commands and requests and instructions, and it smelled of gasoline and stale lubricating oil.

But Fassarai was cool and green and silent except for the happy laughter of the children, and there was all over it the scent of frangipani—the scent of the fresh wreath that they had waiting for him in the shadow beside the *falu*. And it was calm with the still gravity of the island people, and sweet with the drift of the spray-laden trade wind that came in over the reef.

He put his arm round Filomena, and they walked along the path, Watson a pace ahead and talking slowly over his shoulder.

Reis said: "I met the new commodore. That old bastard Higgins introduced me as the King of Fassarai. He's Annapolis. He didn't laugh. Old Kellie was a human sort of bastard. I think this one goes by clockwork. He didn't drink more'n a coupla rye."

"Did you get the tank?"

"I did not," said Reis, "but I'm going to!"

"Is Higgins—"

"He says he'll do the best he can when the next consignment comes in if he's here, but the Seabees say every last one of the next consignment is earmarked. New commodore don't like Higgins. I think the old man riles him—maybe because he wants his move, I don't know. How's Falifi?"

"Fine," said Watson, "fine. You know, doc, you could have made a lot of money betting me against his livin'."

"You could have made a bit yourself," said Reis frankly. He grunted. "Doc Higgins reckons I'm island-happy. He wanted me to stay a week up there."

"Hell, doc, why didn't you?"

"And leave you here with the girls! Any of them sleep with you last night?"

"Is that an official question?" asked Watson happily.

"Any other troubles?"

"Not a trouble," said Watson. "Old Sebastian's been hanging round again—says his back's bad; but he only wants tobacco. I gave him some. Back's cured till the supply runs out. There was only ten for the morning sick call not counting the kids, and you know, doc, I reckon that was all the ten that had reason to come."

They reached the camp, and Reis went directly into the shelter they had built for Falifi. The old man grinned and raised his arm and spoke rapidly. Behind Reis, Filomena translated automatically. "He says he glad you back. Now he fine. Now he okay."

CHAPTER XXVII

1

THE boat came down on a Tuesday, and the children were so intrigued—those who remembered that it was a Tuesday—that they forgot to run back to the camp to tell Watson and Reis. Watson was asleep in the living tent with Filomena fanning him to keep away the now non-existent flies. Reis was working in the surgery tent, checking cards. He came out when he heard an American voice call. He saw the brass hat first, then the medical oak-leaf, and last of all the face thin, untanned, and with eyes set close together. The corners of the mouth were irritable. The voice matched it, acrid and flat: "Where's Lieutenant Reis?"

"My name is Reis," he answered automatically.

The thin nose wrinkled, and the voice said, "You are not dressed as an officer should be dressed."

Reis looked at him, trying to find something behind the thin malice of the tone, but all he could think of to say was, "Who are you?" He suppressed a quick, almost overwhelming desire to say, "Who the hell are you?"

The voice said: "I am Commander Holtzen. I have replaced Commander Higgins. Get dressed! I wish to talk to you."

For a perceptible moment Reis stood; then he shook his head. Watson had come out of the living tent. Reis heard the slam of the screen door to his left. Holtzen heard it also. He turned instantly and barked, "You too!"

"Now what," said Watson out of the corner of his mouth to Reis, "would you know about that?"

Reis pulled on a shirt and looked around for his almost forgotten overseas cap. He went back to where Holtzen still stood in front of the surgery tent. All the way back he was wondering whether he should salute or not. He decided against it.

Holtzen's voice immediately showed him that the decision was wrong. It rasped, "Is it not your habit to salute your commanding officer?"

"Sure," said Reis as his hand came up, "sure."

Holtzen said: "I took over from Commander Higgins on Saturday. It seemed clear from your reports that it was time this island was inspected. I have come to make an inspection. Let me see the surgery."

Brusquely, acridly, the man went through the surgery, through the living tent and the cooking tent. The children's playground, he disregarded. Reis wondered why there were no children there. Then he asked to see the north village. The whole thing was over in an hour. Throughout the time he showed no signs of thawing.

At the end, when Reis went with him to the landing place at the *falu,* he said: "The condition of the surgery is disgraceful. For the rest the island seems clean and the people reasonably healthy. I shall report in those terms to Commodore Raglan. I think you have forgotten that you represent the United States Navy on this island. In future you will be properly dressed at all times. That is all."

Reis fumbled for a moment with a protest and then said instead, "Yes, sir."

The motor dory grounded on the sand. Holtzen clambered in. It pushed off, reversed, and went out toward the L.C.I.

Reis remained perfectly motionless until he saw the dory hoisted inboard, the anchor come home and the L.S.I. turn and head north. At last he turned. Watson was standing behind him.

"Christ!" said Watson feelingly.

"Would you believe it? It did happen?" Reis looked quizzically at him. "Jesus, and I laughed about Higgins's going, so help me God!"

Fayu came out from behind the boat shed, where he apparently had taken refuge. "Goddam son-of-a-bitch! He tell me go away. He tell Olimarao go away. He tell the kids go away." He grinned happily. "So we go away. Sailors from the L.S.I. want to come ashore. He tell them damn' quick go back to L.S.I. Who is?"

"That," said Reis softly, "is the new senior medical officer for Ulithi atoll." He looked at Fayu. "Fayu, I think you are improperly dressed. You are a pharmacist's mate, third class. Next time I see you without your trousers I'll derate you. Judas priest, would you believe it?"

He began to laugh softly and helplessly, walking up the path, and the children began to come out from behind the palms and behind the huts; but Olimarao was sulking in the *falu*.

2

That night Reis went down to the *falu* with a bottle of bourbon. When half the bottle was empty he said to Olimarao, "Is the big canoe fit for the water?"

Fernando was acting as interpreter. He translated and then answered the question himself. The big canoe was sound.

"Right," said Reis. "What's the weather going to be like tomorrow?"

Olimarao and Elingarik consulted. After a placid discussion and another bourbon they said cautiously that the weather would be all right—light breezes.

"Good! I want the big canoe, and I want one of the fishing canoes. I want the two boys and Sebastian and Tonio and one other man. We're going up to Asor, and I want to get there about nine o'clock while the movie is still on. Tell them that, Fernando! Hell, he won't know what a movie is! Tell him nine o'clock anyway—nine!" He waited while the translation was made.

"Olimarao say you start seven o'clock perhaps," said Fernando.

"Okay. Tell him to have everything ready half-past six. I'm

going to get that damned tank for this island if it's the last thing I do!"

He went back to the camp. Watson, on his back reading an elderly *Life*, asked, "What have you been doing down the village?"

"Arranging for a sea voyage." Reis hummed to himself.

"Give!"

Reis hummed on for a little. Then he said: "I'm going to get that tank if it's the last thing I do in this island. Most likely it's going to be!"

"Aw, hell," said Watson, "that sort of guy's all wind! I've served with worse guys than him. Jesus, he's just Annapolis and a stuffed shirt! Why, he didn't even have a tie on! He'll settle down."

"Maybe you're right. But I ain't going to plant any crops—not after this afternoon. We haven't got any security of tenure any more. If old Kellie was still up there maybe we could do something; but the other guy's a frosty-faced bastard too. That's why Higgins quit, I think, and I don't see how *we* can live. Jesus, did you see his eye when he opened the icebox and saw the beer?" Reis laughed again at the memory. " 'Lieutenant, where do you keep your penicillin?' he asked, and I said, 'It's behind the Pabst, commander, behind the Pabst.' No, I don't think we got security of tenure."

"Ah, well," said Watson, "ain't nothing he can do to a pharmacist's mate except kick him up the ass, and we're used to that. Them bruises is kind of occupational diseases."

3

The canoes went out with the sunset. Reis had been out half a dozen times in the little fishing canoes. He was not a sailor, but even he could thrill to their exquisite movement through the water, the speed and the surge of them, the exhilaration of the uplifting outrigger, the golden dynamic curve of the pandanus-leaf sails. This canoe was bigger. He felt, crouching down on the bottom, more secure, less exhilarated. Yet it was faster than the fishing canoe when the diminishing wind of the evening took it clear of the palms and drove it, singing like a harp string, through the quivering water.

The entrance passage was clear. He was anxious to avoid shipping if he could, patrol craft particularly. He had invented a furious need for drugs if he were intercepted; but it was better not to be intercepted.

Fayu, with him in the craft, had passed his instructions to Sebastian, who was sailing her. They headed northeast past Lolang, cut out through the gap in the reef, and already the full darkness was on them. They could not see Lolang by the time it was abeam. They could not see Mangejang at all. They could see only the splintering green of phosphorescence on the nearer reef and the whipping of it below them. The stars were poised on the black velvet pinnacle of the sail and hung around them in a frozen shower. There were lights up in the anchorage to the north, and there was a glow over Asor and Falalop. But they ran on, with the fishing canoe astern of them, divorced utterly from the wartime world of the lagoon, shifting and shuddering uneasily under the stars and heading always and endlessly north. In the grip of the racing surges they lifted up and fell away, the sail coming over and sighing and falling again. Over the side Reis could see the sudden dart of a frightened fish outlined and starred in noctilucans as if the sea were in its depths mocking at the stars that showered over them.

For a long time they sailed thus, suspended in the night peace of the sea.

It was Fayu who saw the ship first, a dark shape, unlit and sweeping fast past the lower stars. He told Sebastian about her even before he spoke to Reis, and the canoe was falling away already when Reis picked her out. She came close, heading in fast for the main gap in the reef, the entrance gate, and suddenly she was outlined clear against the island lights to the north—a destroyer slipping in to the anchorage. She did not sight them.

[230]

Watson was in the fishing canoe. He came up a little later and called out across the water: "Did you see the can? God, I thought she was going to spit us!"

The island lights were clear of the water edge now, bright and growing brighter. The wind held steady, little weight in it but enough to drive the canoes fast to the north. There was no tacking needed. They sailed on a broad reach, free and fast. Reis had given instructions for them to hold out towards Falalop and come in to the Asor landing behind the broken reef that lay to the south of it. The old man commended the approach. The principal danger was from the Falalop boats if any were running from the air strip to headquarters. Reis had small knowledge of the night movements. It was a chance they had to take.

They came up fast now, the fishing canoe dancing on their port quarter. There were lights in the anchorage. He saw the green and the red of a motorboat for a moment as she headed towards them. Then she swung round until only the red showed as she sheered off to starboard. There appeared to be some sort of patrol close in.

He felt the tension rising. This thing was more difficult now than it would have been had Higgins still held his post. He thought that Higgins would have covered him, however unlikely his story of urgently needed drugs might sound. The new man would not. The hairs round the nape of his neck prickled. His thoughts moving on, he remembered suddenly that some trigger-happy fool on the island might open fire if they were seen. The danger area was the water off the gap in the southern reef, for here the lights of Falalop shone across the darkling water and the canoes would show in silhouette to anyone watching from the Asor jetty. In the inner part of the area too the lights from the jetty and the beach, big clusters that made the whole place a pool of brilliance, would be strong enough to outline them against the night's blue velvet.

He had planned that they should drop sail and paddle in the last of the passage, and now he leant over to Fayu and whispered, though they would not have heard a shout on shore, "Sail down!"

The pandanus matting came down rustling, creaking and protesting. The paddles were out, and without losing way the big
canoe headed on for the gap. There was no surf on this reef, for
they were inside from the run of the swells. There were only
rough patches of water where lights from the jetty were broken
and shattered in fantastic fragments. Then they were through
and in the utterly still inner water. To Reis the fishing canoe
astern of them was almost incandescent in the glow of the seaward lights, yet there was no hail from the beach. An instant
later they were in the shadow of the group of palms that he had
marked, and the big canoe went up the beach with a long, rough
sigh. In a second the fishing canoe was up beside it.

Reis and Watson went out across the sand, cut up the beach
and on to the ring road. In the moment that they turned down
it they were indistinguishable from the island's own people—
lawful, proper, correct. On the beach Fayu, Fernando, and Tonio
moved parallel with them, silent-footed on the sand and keeping,
so far as they might, within the shadow. Reis walked slowly to
give them every chance of cover. Very occasionally they could
see in some bright light patch a dark shadow on the sand—that
was all.

They came closer to the jetty, closer to the steel pile. It was
possible that it had been moved. Reis knew that the tanks were
being put up fast. It was possible that the last of the steel was
gone now. Half consciously he shrugged his shoulders and said
to Watson, "I'll look a fool if there's nothing there!"

"Sure," said Watson equably. "Hell, d'you know this is the
first time I've been back to Asor? How about we take in a movie
for half an hour, doc?"

This suggestion scarcely seemed to call for comment: Reis
merely grunted. A moment later he saw the steel pile. He muttered, hardly able to control the excitement and the relief in his
voice, "They haven't touched it, by God!" They walked past it,
talking together, Reis on the outside so that he could examine the
markings as they went by. He said: "There was an end piece on
the top when I was here. I can remember the letters." He paused,

putting his foot on the edge of the steel sheets and bending as if to tie his shoe while he peered at the markings in the darkness. "I think— By God, it is! Okay. We'll walk twenty yards further now."

"Ain't nobody about," said Watson. "I reckon we can do."

Tonio and the boys had stopped at the last patch of scrub bush down on the beach. Watson and Reis walked past the steel, turned, came back again. Standing on the road, Reis called down through the bush to Fayu: "Top piece, like I said. It won't be heavy. You'll lift it easy, the three of you; two take a corner, and the other take one side. Don't make any goddam noise!"

He looked round carefully. As he had guessed, the whole island except the men on duty were at the movie. The place was empty. Deep in at a range of Quonset huts two or three men were moving about, and over by the pier two boats were coming in and one was going out. He reckoned that the men on the pier would be occupied with the boats to the exclusion of anything on the road, and turned his head towards the beach again. "We go now. Come on!"

The two boys and Tonio left the shadow. Reis watched them critically. They moved slowly, matching their pace to his, and he saw that the dark bodies showed hardly at all in the light that came from the nearest lamps. He had calculated that their own khaki shirts and trousers would show so much brighter that any casual eye turning their way would be caught by them to the exclusion of the dark, full shadows beyond. The only fear was that a vehicle with headlights would come past when the men were actually at the steel pile. They walked on steadily, and no vehicle came.

They approached the steel pile, and Reis said without turning his head, "Now—and quick!"

The two boys were at the pile in an instant. The top section was lifted away. Tonio was with them. In a moment it was moving down the beach. A second later, it was lost to sight.

Watson and Reis had turned and were walking back down the road towards the canoes. The end section reached the cover of the shadow and was swallowed up entirely. They were thirty yards along the road when a jeep came up. Reis put his hand up to shield his face from the headlights; Watson turned his head away. It went by, and in the cover of the dust behind it Reis and Watson headed to the canoe. They got there as the boys and Tonio dropped the end section on a framework of bamboos that had been lashed across the struts of the outrigger. Quickly and skillfully they passed sennit lashings through the bolt holes. In a moment it was made fast.

Fayu said, "Okay, doc, okay." He got in and moved towards the stern of the canoe. Somebody pushed at the bows. There was a quick, soft grating under the polished wood. The keel came free. There was a slight splash as one of the boys jumped in over the stern; then the paddle blades dipped, and she moved. Five minutes later they were clear of the reef and the critical light patch. They paddled another five minutes to make sure, and then the sail went up.

Even to Reis she did not move as freely, as delicately, as she had moved coming up; but she went fast and free on the wind, and in a little they were in the deep outer water of the fishing grounds, clear across the Dowarugui channel.

Reis began to breathe freely again.

In the darkness they came again to Fassarai and the beach below the *falu*. To Reis coming in, though his eyes were utterly accustomed now to the sea darkness, there was no slightest thing to indicate the place of the All Men House; no light showed out to seaward, no glow of a cooking fire or thin, red burning of a palm-leaf torch. Yet, when the bows grated on the sand and he stepped over into the oddly warm water, it looked as if Sebastian had put her bows straight into the groove that she had cut down through the sand at sunset.

He stretched himself, bending over and flexing and relaxing his muscles. The fishing canoe was coming in fifty yards astern, and he waited till she was up to the shallows to ask quietly across the water, "How's your bottom, Watson?"

"She's cramped," said Watson, "she's all cramped to hell.

Can I requisition an air-ring if we're going to do more of this canoe riding?"

"Sure. Sure."

Watson climbed out, stretching himself in turn, while the boys laughed at him. They began to fumble at the lashings of the plate. When it was free they lifted it easily.

"Take her down the beach," said Reis, "to the old canoe." He and Watson followed after. When they reached the place, a hundred yards beyond the village, he said, "Now bury her—six inches down or so will do. Above the tidemark! I don't want the water washing the sand away."

"What you make?" demanded Fayu.

"I make same as turtle eggs," said Reis, grinning in the darkness. "Turtle he lay eggs in sand, eggs hatch out, give hell o' plenty small turtles. Okay?"

"Okay, okay," said Fayu, "but this not eggs."

"This all the same eggs. Lots little pieces steel come follow this. Aw, hell, we'll get the tank out of this all right!"

Watson said: "I still don't see it myself. This end piece ain't no good to anyone."

"It's bait," said Reis maliciously, "just bait. If you want to catch a fish you've got to catch a little fish first. When you get a little fish big fish come. This is my little fish. You wait and see! No," he spoke to the boys, "deeper than that. The sand's soft enough, you get on with it! You don't need spades. She's got to be good and covered, or she won't hatch."

"I still don't see," said Watson bewilderedly.

"Hell, you've got to start small," answered Reis. "Haven't you ever read *From Log Cabin to White House?* You start with something, and then you add something else to it, and, by God, you've got something in the end. This is my start. I'm going to be a steel tycoon so the C.I.O. can say rude things about me."

CHAPTER XXVIII

≋≋≋≋≋≋≋≋≋≋≋≋≋≋≋≋≋≋≋≋≋≋≋≋≋≋≋≋≋≋≋≋≋≋

1

THE rain beat down with a heavy, malevolent roar. Every leaf of every palm tree streamed like a fern frond on a waterfall. The ground was sodden, and long flood pools like beaten silver shone along the sides of the path and over the hard-trodden playground of the children; and down the boles of the palms the water ran in endless chromium streams.

Filomena, squatting on the floor, was turning over the glossy pages of *Fortune*. In the cook tent Teresa was singing. She was achieving an island reputation for her singing now, a reputation in the older fashion. Somehow, somewhere, she was absorbing the island legends and the folk tales. Reis was sure that this was an inherited gift, for though the other women sang, he had heard nothing of this spontaneous, inventive flow that she achieved. The others sang only, it seemed, in unison, only according to tradition and to custom; but Teresa sang out of her own heart and, to all appearances, out of her own mind. Her voice was taking on a deeper quality.

The rain stopped as suddenly as it had begun, and the roar of it on the leaves and on the green canvas of the tent roofs was succeeded by the thin pattering of the drops from the fronds, underscored by the deep, slow sighing of the reef. There was little swell running now. The outer sea was calm, and the nearer wavelets were beaten down by the weight of the rain squall. Even as the rain ceased to fall the sun came out. The momentary coolness of the shadow and the rain passed almost while he thought of it, and was succeeded by a sticky, steamy heat. He could see wisps of vapour in the palm fronds. He could see them through the copper gauze ceasing to glisten, dulling as they dried, but turning from the deep, shining olive that had shown against the rain clouds to a fresh green against the renewed brilliance of the sky. He dropped his book and lay back on the camp bed, and Filomena left *Fortune* and began to fan him.

Filomena heard the feet on the path first; the fan stopped in mid-air, and she turned her head towards the entry. Reis, noticing the movement, picked up the noise almost at once. There was the sound of a number of feet running. He could hear the separate, quick-repeated thuds, and he said lazily to Watson on the other bed, "Some boob's cut his finger or broken his neck—"

"Or somepin," said Watson somnolently. "They will do it."

Neither made an effort to get up. It seemed unnecessary to expend the energy until they were certain of the need. Filomena, as if with some premonition of disaster, some foreknowledge of tragedy, remained frozen in the incompleted movement, the fan poised at half-stroke. Queerly, despite Watson's lighthearted response, tension built up in the tent. It might be that Filomena's own anxiety communicated itself to Reis. He lifted himself on one elbow, rapidly abandoning the decision that it was not necessary to expend energy. He could hear confused voices, voices of runners, gasping and panting as they ran—children's voices. There was a wild burst of speed, and in a moment hands were hammering and pattering against the copper of the walls.

Out of the drumming of hands, the breathless gasping and panting, and the thudding feet of the late comers, Mau's voice came clear as a bell: "King, king, put on shirt; Officer come."

Reis lay back and roared. When he recovered he said: "Will you listen to that? Jesus, have I got a bodyguard, or have I got a bodyguard?"

The children's voices broke in urgently, "King, put on shirt, put on shirt! Officer come, officer!"

"Now who in hell put them up to that?" demanded Reis. "Your doing, Watson?"

Watson was sitting up on his bed now. He shook his head. "No, I told 'em nothin'."

"Filomena, did you?"

The girl shook her head.

Watson said: "I believe some of those kids crept up behind old sourpuss the other day. They must have heard him bawl you out."

"Would you believe it?" said Reis happily. "Would you believe it?" He reached out for his shirt, slipping off the noonday wreath of flowers. "My surgery may be dirty, but my Gestapo's efficient. What the hell!" He got up, tucked his shirt in while the children watched him through the gauze. He reached for his cap and strode out through the door. "Now where's your goddam officer?"

With the children yelping delightedly at his heels he walked down the path towards the village.

2

The path was still wet, the pools still not yet drained away through the coral sand. The air was heavy, hot with moisture. It would remain so until the wind sprang up again and cleared it. Reis knew these storms now even as he knew that if he walked out to the ocean beach there would be a giant rainbow splashed across the sky in great sweeps of incandescent light on the drop curtain of the rain.

Ahead of him a khaki uniform was moving between the palm boles, and an instant later, he saw McNally. At once he began to laugh again. He was still laughing when McNally came up with him. "Jesus, I thought it was old sourpuss!"

"No," said McNally, "it's me. You can be glad of that. Your stock ain't high with the new senior medical officer."

"It was the penicillin behind the Pabst that did me in," said Reis. "What's he going to do with me?"

"Nothing for the moment. He's sent me down for a check-up on your health figures. He's got something up his sleeve, but I don't know what."

Reis sobered for a moment. "Do we make 'em good, or do we make 'em bad?"

"If I knew what he'd got up his sleeve I'd tell you. I don't."

"Who the hell is this guy? Where d'you get him?" Reis demanded.

"He's a Grade One son-of-a-bitch," said McNally dispassionately, "but he's a good doctor. He knows his stuff. Maybe we got a little slack under Higgins."

"Maybe we got a little human under Higgins!"

"Have it your way. This guy's in command now."

"All Annapolis and a yard wide," said Reis scornfully.

"No," said McNally, "you can't blame Annapolis for him. He's just ornery. A guy's just that way, or he ain't. Higgins was Old Navy if it came to that. This guy thinks there's been too much dilution with civilian doctors. He told me yesterday."

As they reached the camp Watson emerged from the cook tent with an opened can of beer and a glass. He said, "I waited with a can-opener in my hand till I recognised your voice."

"What would you have done if it had been Commander Holtzen?" asked McNally.

"Moved the penicillin out to the front of the icebox," said Watson instantly.

"You both seem het up about that penicillin," said McNally. "That wasn't what stuck in his throat. It was the flowers in the surgery. He doesn't think frangipani on the forceps is aseptic."

"Ah, hell," said Reis tolerantly, "that's only Teresa. She likes flowers. Ain't nobody died from septicemia since we been here. Did you eat coming down?"

"We ate—kind of."

Reis raised his voice, "Teresa, cut a couple of sandwiches. What d'you like? We can offer you most anything. We've just been out to the freighters again."

McNally's inspection was thorough—it was in the nature of the man; but he made it with sympathy, following Reis's lead all the way through. He had selected the cases he wanted to visit from the cards, and now methodically they went from hut to hut. Once he diverged from Reis's diagnosis; twice he suggested alternative methods of treatment: for the rest he had no comments.

Late in the afternoon they went back to the camp. The wind had come up now. The air was clean, hot, and dry. Enough of the breeze filtered through the trees to make it exquisite in the shadow under the palms. They drank it in while they went over the list of the sick.

At the end McNally said, "Well, I still can't see what he's after. Nothing wrong here."

"My one medical puzzle is the woman Malipa."

McNally rubbed his chin. "I think carcinoma . . ."

Reis shrugged his shoulders. "We'll get her up to the hospital ship next Wednesday boat. I still think it might be a tubercular gland; but if it's a carcinoma she ought to be dealt with at once."

There was a long silence while they sat content in the shadow. Then McNally asked softly, "What would happen if he took you off the island now?"

Reis had expected the question for an hour. Again there was a long silence. He began to speak without looking at McNally. "I'm not a good doctor—I know that! But we're getting along here. When they die now they die for some reason, not just for the hell of it. I think we've got on top of them, Watson and I. They trust us, they like us, and they've come to believe what we tell 'em—and we've told 'em they're going to be all right. Perhaps they'll carry on."

He waited a minute to collect his thoughts. "You know better than anyone else, McNally, what they were like before we came. There wasn't any hope in them. They just didn't have any interest in life—there just wasn't any point in their going on living, so they died. Now they're going on living." He turned suddenly fierce. "You've seen that this afternoon. You've talked to Olimarao, you've seen half the old men of the village, and you've seen a good bunch of the women. I'm not talking about the kids now—they were easy from the start—but the old ones. What d'you think?"

McNally nodded slowly. "What I've thought for a couple of months now, that you've got the nonsense out of them."

"Yes," said Reis. "I don't know how we have. It's not medicine. Sometimes I think maybe it's because I put the fear of death into them. Hell, that sounds crooked, I know. I can't explain myself properly. No, I don't think it's fear."

"Maybe," said McNally very quietly over his drink, "maybe it's love."

Neither of the men looked at the other for a minute. Then Watson said crisply from behind them, "Aw, hell, have another beer, doc?"

4

"Well," said McNally, "the boat crew will curse me all the week if they miss tonight's movie. Let's go!"

They had eaten supper at the outside table in the late afternoon sun, and the three men, followed by the inevitable tail of children, walked slowly towards the landing place.

On the way McNally said, elaborately unconcerned, "That Seabee guy—what's his name? Bernand or something—tells me something's gone wrong with his tanks." And he was looking straight ahead down the path when Reis glanced at him suspiciously.

"Ah, tanks! I've given that one up. I'll never get a tank out of that crab-apple bastard. If Doc Higgins couldn't fix it—"

"Seems like they miscounted or something when the stuff came off the boat." McNally pursued his train of thought without regard for Reis's interjection. "Bernand—or whatever his name is—says they've got one tank with an end piece missing. Everything else is there, it seems; but they're a section short."

"What the hell's the use of that to us?" Again Reis looked suspiciously at McNally.

"Oh, I don't know. But you're a resourceful couple of beach-combers. I thought maybe you could get your friends on one of the repair ships to make an end piece that would fit."

"Can't the Seabees?" asked Reis.

"Oh, they don't work that way! They just requisition two more tanks. They got big ideas."

Watson said from behind, "Seems kind of a pity just to let it lie and rust."

"That's what I think," said McNally. "I thought maybe you had something down here might fit." Suddenly he looked sideways at Reis and caught his eye.

"We'll think it over." Reis was elaborately innocent.

"That's right," said McNally encouragingly. "I guess you could dig something up if you wanted to."

"You wouldn't mean anything by that?"

"Hell, I never mean anything."

As the dory drew away from the beach Reis called out, "Thanks for the tip!"

"That's all right." McNally's voice came back thin and clear. "Maybe we'll see you up on Asor in a few days."

5

Reis walked along the beach in his slippers, the soft sand giving at his every footfall. The water was quite still, yet the star paths shimmered over it in a weaving, uneasy brilliance. The lights of the nearer merchant ships were bright—they were working cargo on one of them—but it was not possible to dissever the low stars from the ships beyond.

They were singing in the *falu*. The sound grew louder as he approached, but when he reached the low overhanging trees just to the left of the great house the singing ceased. For a moment he wondered if his presence had interrupted some ceremony, some rite. Then he heard the slow summoning of a little drum, and the voices came in—men's voices, deep, rugged, inharmonious, but with a forceful rhythm. Then suddenly they became soft, and he heard a girl's voice—Teresa's voice, beyond all question. It came up firm and purposeful, and it continued against the very soft background of the men's voices that was hardly more than the distant whisper of the reef.

He passed the front of the *ailiuth* and the front of the great canoe lodge, passed the fishing canoes drawn high up above the tidemark, and went on towards the south end. And all the while he could hear the girl's voice behind him in an elaborate wailing recitative. Deliberately he did not think about the inside of the *falu* until he had lost the last sound of the voice behind him in the darkness, but when he opened his mind to it he thought instantly of Olimarao, Elingarik, and the *droit de seigneur*. What were they up to in the *falu*? Why was Teresa there? It was the All Men House. It was not a women's place except for—he remembered the wry name—"the women who would have been slaves but for the priests." There were depths in this island that he could not understand, but that were yet a part of its life, of its motion, of its being. It was strange, he was part king of the island—he grinned to himself at the recollection—and yet he could not see more than a little distance inside the eyes, inside the hearts, of these people.

He cut across to the ocean beach and went back to the camp with the reef grumbling and murmuring outside him. Here across the sea there were no lights except the star lights, except the green and luminous glow of the noctilucans in the broken water along the reef. On this beach in the night it was as if there were no war. It was as if he had reached back across time into the peace, the strange, tortuous perfection of this place before the West and the East closed in upon it. He knew now that over in the *falu* they too were reaching back to the past, and the anger that had come to him for a little worked out slowly in the knowledge.

His mind went back to his conversation with McNally. It was difficult to talk to anyone else of what he had achieved here; but to himself it seemed now that there were a score of factors behind the unquestioned success. The children were one. These people loved their children in strange ways, and he was sure that the growing realisation in the old people's minds that the children were safe and secure in their future had of itself played an important part in the salvation of the island.

But there were so many other factors. He thought that the sheer physical comfort that he had brought them—the cleaning up of the yaws, the destruction of the flies and the mosquitoes, the lifting of the curse of hookworm—had made such contrast with the deep, unholy misery of the months before he came that that too had played its part. He could see that he had replaced, almost unconsciously, the slow, unhurried pattern of their old life with another pattern—a pattern that was in part composed of the islanders' own curiosity in him and his doings, in the coming of the weekly boat, in the newness of medicines and of methods, in the strange and often pointless things that he did. He remembered the old phrase that a thousand family doctors used a thousand times a year. He had given them "a new interest in life." A psychiatrist would have other words for it, but it came down to an essential simplicity. Life was no longer worth living for the old people in the months before he came because, with everything that made their life a pattern and an integral whole broken under the inhumanity of the Japanese, they were above all things bored. There was nothing to look forward to and little enough to look back upon. There was nothing to encourage them into a new future.

Watson met him on the ocean beach just clear of the huts, saying, "Thought maybe you'd come back this way."

"Anything wrong?"

"Hell, no! They've got a song fest on, down at the *falu*."

"I heard."

Watson said, "I went down and stuck my head in." When Reis remained silent he went on after a little: "Teresa's leading the choir. That kid's got a voice. Maybe we could take her back and make a torch singer out of her."

"What's it all about?" said Reis at last.

"Oh, I don't know. She's been down there two or three times lately. Haven't you noticed? The boys, too. It's a sort of 'lodge of instruction' so far as I can make out—history of the islands and all that. Same sort of thing as Elingarik spills afternoons sometimes."

Reis in the darkness nodded to himself. He said: "You know the old people don't count for much really. We could have let 'em go and started a new community with the kids. They would have grown up all right. That was in my mind when I came."

Watson grunted but made no comment, and after a little Reis went on:

"But it wouldn't have been any good, because it would have been just a lot of kids growing up. You'd have cut 'em off from the past."

Again he was silent, thinking, and Watson put in, "There's a lot of guys would say that was a good thing at that."

"Yes, maybe they're right. I wouldn't know—but I don't think it would be a good thing with these kids." He looked out over the sea and the dancing stars. "They were born into something that was pretty good in its own way if you look at it right, and it could go on being pretty good for them so long as they knew what was coming and knew what to ask for. But, hell, it wouldn't be any good—way I look at it anyway—if you just let 'em grow up without the things the old people know."

Watson began speculatively, "If you put a teacher on the island—"

"Yeah." Reis was faintly derisive. "You'd do well on the fishing ground under Losiep if you knew the population of North Carolina and the square root of 656! Isn't anybody but the old people who can teach these kids what they need to live in these islands. Seems like they're teaching them now."

"So Teresa sleeps in the *falu?*" asked Watson with an infinitely thin note of mockery in his voice.

"So Teresa sleeps in the *falu*," said Reis gravely.

CHAPTER XXIX

1

As HE WENT ashore past the old Asor *falu*—the thatch was bald near the inner end of the reef now and the ribbing of the bamboo rafters showed naked under it—Reis looked sidewise along the roadway to the pile of tank sections. It was still there untouched as they had left it. He grinned cheerfully and went on.

McNally was in the office with two strange medics. He came over and looked at Reis quizzically: "Some guys are born lucky. He's gone over for a conference on the *Solace*. It will take all afternoon, and I guess he'll stay for dinner. Once that guy's on a hospital ship, he stays."

"I could weep," said Reis satirically.

"You probably would if he was here," McNally answered. "He doesn't love you to any extent."

"How did he take your report?"

McNally shrugged his shoulders. "He has no emotions, and my own private belief is he's got a small electric pump in place of a heart."

"Did he read it?"

"Sure he read it. He read it carefully from one end to the other, and he said, 'Huh!' "

"Just that?"

"Just that."

The two strangers left, and then McNally said: "By the way, your hookworm figures don't square. Medically you may be right. Mathematically you're lousy."

"I'll look 'em over. I never was any good at figures." Reis turned suddenly grave as he asked, "Anything about my going?"

"He said, 'Huh!'" McNally answered. "If I knew anything I'd tell you. I don't know a damn' thing. I don't know a damn' thing about anything. He's the Great White Chief, and I'm low man on the totem pole—or damn' near it. I'm the man the commodore sends for to bawl out, and I know nothing. Have you fed yet? Wait a minute while I finish this check, and we'll go along to the mess."

2

They lifted trays from the rack and joined the chow line. McNally said: "See the redheaded guy at the head of the line? That's Bernand."

"Who's Bernand?"

McNally wrinkled his nose. "John Hector Bernand, of Springfield, Mass.; six foot one; a hundred and ninety pounds at a guess; I should say about twenty-five; married; one child."

Reis grinned and acknowledged the check. "What does he do?"

"He's supposed to control the Seabees," said McNally ironically, "but nobody's ever yet been discovered who can control Seabees."

They had moved up to the head of the line, and they took the helping of wienies and sauerkraut and dehydrated potatoes, and passed on to the tables. Bernand was sitting at the end of a group, and McNally edged Reis to the seat next to him and took his own place across the table.

He said, "Bernand, have you met Dr. Reis, the King of Fassarai?"

Bernand turned and said automatically as his eye ran over Reis, "Glad to meet you." He added after a perceptible hesitation, "I've heard of you."

"It's the only island in the Pacific that's been kept reasonably clear of the Seabees so far," said McNally. "And look what they've done to the rest!"

Reis shook his head. He said, "I've had the Seabees down twice already—once to put the camp up and once for my generator plant. They're all right."

"Thank you," said Bernand mockingly. "I don't get anything except abuse from these guys and, hell, they'd be lying on the sand if it wasn't for us. Helpless, that's what they are! You're the doc that's been pestering us for a tank for the last two months. How come I've never seen you before?"

"I knew a guy called Pawlowicz."

"He's gone," said Bernand. "He was my boss."

"Where?" asked McNally.

"The Ryukus. Okinawa, as far as I can gather. Jeez, those boys are having them a hell of a time there! We had a guy through Monday. The whole damn' front's less than eleven miles across, but they can't do a damn' thing."

"What's he gone up for?"

"Roads, bridges. They're stuck in the mud there. Seems like the rains came early. They can't get the stuff moving. It's a balls-up."

"Situation Snafu," said McNally expressionlessly. "Send for the Seabees. Give those guys a bulldozer and a dynamite cartridge, and they'll carve you out a crucifix in ivory." He grinned across at Bernand, who went on eating. It was evident that this was a stylised brawl.

Bernand waited until he had finished a heavy mouthful before he said calmly: "At least when we make mistakes we leave 'em above ground. We don't bury 'em." He turned to Reis. "Doc, is it true the girls down on your island wear nothing above the waist?"

"Sure," said Reis gravely. "A wreath of flowers, of course, but it don't hide anything."

Bernand shook his head. "Jesus, some guys have all the luck!"

"He's got a racket in nurses too," said McNally. "They come down to see the place where Dorothy Lamour wasn't born."

Bernand was admiring. "And I thought I could work a racket. I used to pride myself!"

"You ought to come down and see us some time," said Reis.

It was clear that this was working up to something. They went back to the line for ice cream and finished together.

McNally said: "You've got ten minutes, Bernand. Come on over to my place." They went into his room in a long Quonset hut, and he opened a foot locker and took out a bottle of rye. "I never drink in the middle of the day unless I've got a good excuse."

"What is a good excuse?" asked Reis.

"Anything," said McNally happily, reaching out for a tooth mug. Over the liquor he said, "I told Doc Reis last time I was down on Fassarai about that tank of yours with a section missing."

Bernand said: "Never trust a doctor when he offers you a drink. I thought there was a catch in this."

"You wait till you go sick!" said McNally.

Bernand contemplated his glass for a moment or two. "Well, I didn't check the stuff ashore myself; but, as I remember the pile, there was an end piece on the top, and next thing there wasn't an end piece on the top."

"Would there be anything to show that it had been there?" asked Reis gently.

"Such as—"

"Hell, everything that I've seen down at the landing gets covered with coral dust!"

"The rain washes it off, most days," said Bernand. "Wasn't anything I could see. There was six tanks landed. We put up four. Next time we went to the heap there was one whole tank and three sides and the bottom of another. That's all I know."

"What does the commodore say?"

"The commodore don't know," said Bernand firmly. "Hell, you wouldn't expect all that brass to be interested in a bit of sheet steel!"

"Not with you around," said McNally.

Bernand laughed outright. "Doc, if you want a tank real bad

you could build those pieces up and sink the one end in concrete. Run reenforcing through the bolt holes and make a good stout wall of it, and she'd hold water. Put a bit of bitumen where the concrete touches the steel. She'll be water-tight all right."

To Reis it seemed that he had hurried over the suggestion— as if it were too glib, too superficial. He saw that both McNally and Bernand were watching him closely. He said, "How about coming down and giving us expert advice on it?"

Bernand's gaze shifted from him, and it was as if he deflated slightly.

McNally said softly, "You've got a nerve!"

Reis was sure that he was on top of the proceedings now. "Nerve? I always use experts when I can get 'em. Bernand, you've been griping about my girls and my nurses. Come on down and see the island. If you come with the Wednesday boat you'll maybe find a nurse or two along with it."

"If I come," said Bernand, "I'll bring my own boat."

McNally was not satisfied. He said: "He's got a graft with the repair ships and all that, Bernand. Supposing he was to get them to work up a piece of sheet steel the right size?"

"It would be better than the concrete." Bernand was not quite sure what McNally was after. Holding his glass up against the light of the window on the sunlit side he stared through it with concentration as he said: "Doc, you can have the tank, and I'll come down and advise you how to put it up and where, if you'll answer me one question at the end of it." He suddenly met Reis's eyes, and Reis responded very slowly:

"That's a deal. I'll answer it."

In the background McNally began to laugh.

3

There was a boat going down to the southern anchorage in the late afternoon. Reis took it over McNally's protests.

"Sure I like the movies, but if I've got to choose between the movies and meeting Commander Crabapple I guess I'll let the movies slide. Sour old bastard! What's he hatching on the hospital ships?"

McNally said: "I keep on telling you I know nothing. When Doc Higgins was here I knew everything. Now he keeps it all under his own hat. It bulges a bit at times. I've given up caring. They'll shift me in a month or two anyway. They always shift everybody on the islands. Might grow into the coral otherwise." He stretched himself and yawned. "Well, when Kellie was here we had fun. Can't expect it always."

"One thing before I go: Can you tell me what's happening on Mogmog?"

"Two softball diamonds, three netball fields; the officers' clubs are about the same. The Seabees are off the island now, but most of the tents and shacks are still there. What was it you wanted to know?"

"Olimarao talks about the women's pool."

"Oh, that's still there! We've deloused it, that's all. Jesus, it was stagnant!"

"What about the taro patches and the yams?"

"Hell," grunted McNally, "you can't expect that sort of stuff to survive three or four thousand enlisted men a day! I haven't looked for it, but I guess it's all gone by the roots now. It could be planted again. I wouldn't know though. Come to think of it, I remember breadfruit trees, and I remember some taro."

"What I want to know," said Reis, "is, *Could* it be planted again?"

"I don't see why not."

Reis perched himself on the edge of the desk and drew on McNally's blotter a rough circle vaguely the shape of Mogmog. Inside it he drew, following the outer curve irregularly, a second circle. He said:

"Inside this line there is a depression—or there should be, from what Elingarik and Sebastian and Olimarao say. The fresh water collects there from the rain. Seems as if it gets enough of a head on it to keep the salt back—I don't know the hydraulics of it—but in that area you can grow things like yams and breadfruit trees and oranges. It's far enough away from the sea to be clear of the salt that comes in with the trade wind and it should be good fresh-water earth. Here on Asor the Seabees filled up the marsh with bulldozers. Have they bulldozed it on Mogmog?"

"No. No. They've done pretty little on Mogmog except build shacks. The Seabees have cut down a few of the palms for the softball diamonds, but I wouldn't think that would matter." McNally fell silent for a minute and then said. "You are thinking about afterwards?"

"I am."

"Well, they could go back at that. They'd have to build a new village. We had to clear all that up—flies and dirt! We've put plenty of D.D.T. on the island, and we've cleared up the pool and all round it, but not enough to stop things growing."

Reis swung his feet for a moment, looking at the coir matting on the floor. "If they had Mogmog and Fassarai, maybe they could live when we go out."

"And when is that?" asked McNally bitterly.

"It don't matter. I'm only thinking in terms of the future—any future. Hell, I wonder what it would be like to live without being able to think forward at all!"

McNally nodded, silent. He spoke suddenly. "Tell Olimarao that the All Men House is all right except that the admirals have had a door cut out of it and a thundering great icebox put up against one end. Oh, yes, some windows! But there's nothing that can't be fixed." After a moment he went on. "Tell him that there's no harm done to the centre of the island—yet. You talk to Bernand when you get him down there. He's a good guy." As Reis reached the door he said: "I think he's got an idea about that tank."

"Sure," said Reis innocently. "Sure. Bit of bitumen and a bit of concrete, and she'll be good as anything I can want."

"It might be that you could play poker," said McNally softly as the screen door closed.

Watson was waiting at the main landing when the boat went in. Behind him were Elingarik and Jesus, and behind them again Sebastian. There was an odd air of tension, Watson's figure very taut and determined. He had his shirt on and no wreaths. As he recognised Reis he could be seen to relax; and he raised one hand in a cheerful greeting. Reis saw that one of his eyes was black in an enormous contusion that seemed to spread half across the right side of his face. There was a scar on the other cheekbone, and his lip was swollen. The children had recognised Reis too. They came stealing out from behind the canoe shed and along the wall of the *falu*.

Watson called out, "Jeez, doc, I'm glad it's you."

The dory grounded in the shallows, and Reis said, "Now what in hell have you been up to?"

"I had me a fight with a guy from a merchant ship. They tried to come in up by the generator. One of them got hold of Teresa. I heard her yell."

"You mean——"

Watson laughed outright. "No, she's allergic to being raped. I had to take that guy into the surgery and clean up the claw marks—but that was later. There was four of them. The one I had the fight with was a big Swede. He marked me all right!"

"What did you do to him?"

"Nothing much. He was too big for me."

"Then how?"

Watson laughed again. "Christ, doc, I been laughing off and on fit to bust since it happened! The king he rescued Teresa and me—the king and Elingarik and Sebastian and Tonio and Kirak—oh, hell, and half a dozen others and every last goddam kid in the village! The old men had the big shields and the spears, and the kids had fish spears and prongs and fish clubs. You never saw anything like it in your life. Hollywood hasn't got it." He said almost soberly through his laughter: "For a minute it almost scared me—yelling and shrieking and shaking their spears, and the women shrieking behind. The noise!"

"What did they do?" demanded Reis.

"Do? They chucked their hands in. Hell, I almost chucked mine in with them. They was good boys really. They just wanted to get themselves laid. Hell, doc, you've been cooped up on a ship six months. You can't blame 'em. Elingarik, he fetched my big Swede a clump on the side of the head with a big club. Jesus, it would have brought down a palm tree! He didn't do more'n shake his head, and I could see I could never have done anything to him if I'd fought the whole afternoon. He gave in. I took him and Teresa's boy friend into the surgery after that and cleaned 'em up and gave 'em a shot of grain alcohol. They needed it. Then I called the other two boys in and gave 'em a snifter too, just for the hell of it.

"Elingarik, he was walking up and down prodding against the mosquito gauze with his spear and rolling his eyes. I tell you, doc, I was scared. I saw a movie once with a cannibal king in it. Hell, it had nothing on Elingarik! Olimarao, he went home; but the others they stayed till I got those guys down to the boat again. We won't have any more from that ship. They were scared all right!" He laughed again. "I just couldn't have faced another one. I've been laughing so much I'm weak. Elingarik, he began to laugh too soon as they'd gone. Teresa, she's just mad."

"And the kids?"

"Hell, they ain't enjoyed themselves so much since we took Falifi's leg off." He nursed his eye tenderly. "She's a beauty," he breathed. "She's just a beauty."

Reis said thoughtfully, "I wonder if they'd have done that three months ago."

"Why?" asked Watson. "Them guys from the merchant ships will do anything for a piece of tail—anything any time."

"No, I don't mean them. I mean the village."

"Now that is something," said Watson. "I wonder if they would at that."

CHAPTER XXX

1

THE tank sections came down in an L.C.T. with Bernand, six of his men, a vast and illicit quantity of rations, three cartons of beer, and two bottles of hard liquor. From the moment of the landing it was clear that this was to be a gaudy day in the history of the island. The Seabees came ashore roaring. Bernand had candy for the children. They began an instant distribution long before they contemplated bringing the steel onto the beach and won the children's hearts at once. Reis had strolled down to the landing with his shirt in his hand on the children's warning. When he knew it was Bernand he did not even bother to put it on; and within the hour the children had a wreath for Bernand and half his men had flowers behind their ears.

The whole village turned to, to carry the steel in, and the men themselves sat back and gave enormous and contradictory directions that somehow were understood through the flood of laughter and horseplay and irregularity; and in well lubricated intervals the steel came eventually to the place that they had made for it. Watson and Reis had worked out the measurements at a spot close enough to the village to carry the water easily to all the huts, far enough away to be a minimum of temptation to the children. They had had to cut one palm tree only. A sufficient number would be close enough to the tank to lead the water into it. They had begun to dig the hole. Bernand had recommended sinking it to a depth of a foot at least.

Teresa from the first had made herself the queen of the festivi-

[256]

ties. She overshadowed and overawed Filomena. There seemed to be a new authority about her. She sang in snatches and chopped logic with the men. She had a quick answer for everything, but she had also always an eye for Reis.

Bernand was all pagan. He wore his wreath with the flush of a young Bacchus tipsily across one ear, and his eyes were hot with laughter. He said once, looking over his crew: "They're good boys. They deserve a break and, by heck, so do I!"

Reis asked, "Was there any trouble about your bringing it down?"

"Aw, hell, we've got a job on at Ealil across the lagoon, that's one of the little ones."

"What sort of a job?"

"A good one," said Bernand flippantly. "I invented it! There's a navigation beacon there—you must have seen it. I put in a report that it wouldn't be strong enough to stand a blow. We're going down to put some concrete over the footing—very urgent work. Hell, how d'you think we'd win the war if we let the navigation beacons wash away? I told the commodore we'd drop the tank sections in on the way down."

"And he said?"

"Well"—Bernand stroked his cheekbone with his forefinger—"he didn't exactly reply. It's just possible he didn't exactly hear. I waited till I was competin' with the squawk-box. But, hell, if you're a commodore you ought to be able to hear two things at once!"

"And Sourpuss?"

"You mean your boss?"

"Who else?" asked Reis.

"He ain't no buddy of mine till I get the bellyache, and maybe it won't be safe to go to him then. I hate that guy's guts. I've never seen a bastard who could look so ornery over the top of a glass."

The whole village was crowded now round the space under the palms. Olimarao himself was seated on his mat of ceremony three yards from where the head of the tank would lie. The old men were scratching in the alley that had been marked out for the sinking. Fernando and Fayu were working solidly at the further end. The last of the steel had been brought up, and the older women were making fires for cooking, carrying up the hearth-stones from the village.

A little before noon Reis called a halt, saying: "Fassarai fire water—guaranteed to kill any thirst and most enlisted men. Any takers?"

He called to four of the smaller boys, who went up the nearer palms. In a moment nuts were thudding down. There was an art in this that never failed to please. Sebastian took the heads off the green nuts with an adze, and to each nut Reis added a liberal jolt of grain alcohol.

"It comes rortier if you leave it for forty-eight hours to ferment, but it's got a kick now, boys, believe me!" And he passed the nuts round.

They ate in the open round the tank. Half the floor of it was bolted together already, and they piled the food on the clean steel. Reis had rooted in his stores, and they ate well. Small boys ran cool beer from the icebox and replaced it with warm from the cartons. The meal became a riot, a prodigious affair of curiously innocent mirth. Teresa slapped the faces of three men who tried to put their arms round her, but there was neither anger in the slapping nor embarrassment in the slapped. The whole thing had freshness and wild vigour.

When the Seabees left for Ealil two sections had been bolted to the floor, and Reis and Watson and the boys understood to the last movement of the wrenches the exact procedure. They went down through the village in procession, singing, while the children rushed between the huts and the women chattered, high-pitched and excited; and at the landing they went aboard in a cheerful uproar. Bernand stayed behind upon the slope of the beach with Reis, and said at the very last, his voice completely expressionless: "You know all you need to know about it now. You can fix the rest." As he went down to the boat, he said over his shoulder, "When you get the end piece out, clean it well before you make the joints." He glanced back, but Reis's face still showed not even the flicker of a smile.

Reis said blandly: "Okay. I always follow instructions."

"And for Christ's sake build a wall of concrete over it just the same, because if anybody comes down from Asor and finds an end piece there I'll catch hell, and so will you!"

"Now how did you—"

Bernand somehow heard Reis above the clamour. He turned and said superbly, "The Seabees have their methods." Then he went aboard the L.C.T.

As she pulled off, with the children shouting, Reis said to Watson: "That guy knew all the time. I had a hunch he did up at Asor, and then I thought he didn't. And making me dig like a fool in that end trench to make a sunk concrete foundation below the tank! Jesus, what a guy! But how the hell did he find out?"

"What's the odds? We've got the tank."

Reis thought for a moment. Then he said slowly: "He was going to ask one question at the end. That was part of the deal. He hasn't asked it. Now I wonder why?"

2

The Seabees were gone, but the feast revived itself as the village returned to the tank. There was food; there was song; there was all the time that God had made. The women began to sing in a little group around the cooking fires.

Watson asked, "Shall I stir 'em up?"

"Ah," said Reis lazily, "there's always tomorrow. You know I couldn't understand the Mexicans till I came to this place. Now I think when I get out of the Navy I'm going to get me a practice outside Vera Cruz."

He lay in the shadow with his head pillowed on the curiously unyielding mass of a bag of cement. Two of the smallest children staggered over and began to drop flowers on him. The fragrance hung heavy round his nostrils, and he shot out a hand suddenly on either side and grabbed a bare ankle. With screams of delighted panic they pulled away. Little gusts of loud talk swept through the group from time to time. Some of the children went for an expedition of their own to the waterside. He could hear the shouts in the distance. The women's singing changed its rhythm and changed back again, and once he heard Teresa's voice leading their music; but she seemed more with the men than with the women. Presently he went to sleep.

He woke an hour later to an insistent rhythm—men's voices and Teresa's, and the harmony of it scored and underscored with quick hand clapping. It was coming nearer to him, although distant still, and when he raised himself and looked out he could see the head of a procession, the men walking, clapping their hands. And then, as it came closer still through the palm boles, he saw that they were carrying the end piece of the tank, the buried piece from the beach. Watson was with them, smiling amiably. Watson was slightly drunk. They brought the end piece up with ceremony, singing it all the way, and dropped it clattering at the far end of the tank where the deep trench had been dug to hold the concrete.

Watson said, "Thought it was time it came to life."

Reis asked: "What was that song? I haven't heard it before."

"Ah, that's the song they sing coming home with turtle eggs when the season of the turtles is on."

"And Teresa knew it?"

"Elingarik has been teaching her," said Watson. "The turtles are due in about a month now, I guess. There's a song going and a song coming. Didn't you hear us going?"

"No, I was asleep." Reis lay back again thoughtfully. More and more the people of the island were looking forward. More and more they were reaching backwards to pass on the necessary tradition to the future.

They started on the concrete in the early morning, robbing the fresh-water containers left and right to mix the white coral sand and the grey cement. They mixed it according to Watson's directions. Reis had forgotten to ask Bernand for quantities. They mixed it and added lumps of broken coral, the boys and the old men wielding the spades after Watson had shown them how to puddle the dry mixture of cement and sand. It took till noon to get the trench filled.

The day before they had bolted home the rest of the sections, making fast the stolen end piece with ritual and with laughter. The turtle had bred. The egg had hatched, as Reis had promised Fayu and the old men. They sang most of the time as they worked, and the burden of their song was a story of a turtle that developed itself interminably, that mixed speculation with bawdry and prophecy with badinage. That too had taken the whole day, for they rested according to custom and custom was generous.

In the afternoon, after a long noon rest, they began to build the dummy wall. They built it upon the inside first. Watson had provided shuttering out of old lumber that had been used for packing their gear down to the camp. It was rough, and the wet concrete oozed through the cracks between the planks; but it held long enough for the mass to set. It made a masking wall six inches thick inside the tank. When it was done they began work on the outside wall. Reis was growing tired of the game. The mixing was monotonous. It was hard to keep the boys—and harder still the old men—to the task.

The wall, when it was finished, was thin and unsubstantial; but after they had piled a sloping bank of sand and grey earth from under the palms against it and had battered it down and rammed it firm, and had banked up the sides to keep the tank cool—as Bernand had advised them—the thing looked solid enough to outlast Judgment. There had been no rain since the tank was raised.

The work was completed at dusk of the third day after Bernand had left. Even then it wanted some of the guttering and the ducts that were to lead the water to it. But in the night the rain came, and with the dawn there was three inches of water on the steel floor: three inches of water covered with dust and scum from the work, uninviting, unhygienic—but water.

That day they scrubbed the tank, and when they had gone over all the interior and washed the dummy concrete of the end, they let the water drain through the stoppered hole in the base plate of the tank.

"Now when it comes it will come clean," said Reis happily. "I reckon we're about done."

Watson nodded. "Maybe. Maybe we are at that."

4

Beyond question it had been a mistake to give reasons for the invitation. The nurses from the hospital ships came down to Fassarai for no better reason than that the place was out of the world, out of the world of ships and war and wounds and sickness and the constant tensions of anxiety. Reis's note had said:

"To attend the opening of the Fassarai and Lesser Carolines Water Conservation Scheme. Come and see the T.V.A. of the Pacific. Come and view the inland sea of Fassarai."

He had been a little lightheaded when he wrote it. Two days and two nights of constant showers had filled the tank with clear water. The scum had drifted over the top when it was full. He had been sure always in his own mind that the tank would answer, but now there was the solid proof of it. The women had taken their pots to it, and now just the normal showers of the day were enough to keep it filled against their borrowing. There was water to spare now—water not only for the cooking and the drinking, but for washing and a score of purposes. He had the feeling of triumph that attends no more and no less the completion of great enterprises, the heady wine of satisfaction. Fassarai was made safe against drought.

The nurses came, and one of the doctors who had come before, and two new doctors, and McNally came with them. It was all very frivolous. Reis was photographed against the tank, sitting on the edge of the tank, standing on the concrete wall of the far end, sitting dabbling his fingers with his broken reflection in front of him. The thing became a game, a contest to see how many and how absurd the attitudes that could be achieved. The twenty-five-foot length of the water surface made possible an infinite variety.

The place around the tank began to fill up with islanders. Chaplain Minchin had finished his service. They had heard the singing in the distance and the shrilling of the sanctuary bell. And now the children came racing through the palms, and after them, slowly, some of the men. The women stayed behind around the church while Minchin went from one to another talking, Fayu translating for him. The interpreter had stopped coming to the island now. The tank had, for the time being, taken the position of the playground in front of the camp as the meeting place. They even ate outside the tank, the children bringing the food down from the camp.

5

It was in the afternoon, when the party divided to look at the villages, that McNally got Reis to himself on the path. He said, "Two things: old Sourpuss heard about this party—somebody talked on *Solace*. I think it was that crack about the T.V.A. You'll have him down in a couple of days to inspect. Will it stand up to inspection?"

Reis shrugged his shoulders defiantly. "You've seen it."

"Sure I've seen it." McNally laughed. "I think it will do. The other thing was Bernand. He said you had promised to answer him a question."

"I promised," said Reis.

"Bernand told me to ask you how in hell you got the end piece down here."

Reis laughed. "It was easy. We took out one of the big canoes. I think that's what foxed Bernand. He thought we only had the fishing canoes. Because the others are up at the big canoe lodge nobody ever thinks they can go into the water. We took the big canoe and one of the smaller ones, and we ran into the island from the Falalop side, beached 'em in the shadow and then, while Watson and I walked along the road to keep a lookout and attract attention, the boys and Tonio whipped it down to the beach, lashed it on the outriggers, and we got away again. Nothing to it."

McNally began to laugh and went on laughing steadily for a long three minutes. Then he said, "Bernand's checked the movements of everything that moved that night and everyone who was on duty and off duty, and he couldn't find a damn' thing out."

"How did he know it was stolen?" demanded Reis.

"You know him. He's a methodical guy. He remembered the serial numbers he read on the top piece when he was last at the pile."

"How did he know it was me?"

"Be your age! Who else wants a goddam piece of sheet steel like that? The Seabees themselves'll steal the gold teeth out of a man's head if they want them; but they've no need to go hijacking steel plate. They can get it without asking. You were the only guy in the atoll who wanted anything to do with a tank as badly as that, so you were the first choice—and the last one too!"

"And he didn't give me away?"

"He's a good guy. He was just interested in how you did it, and he thought the only way he'd find out was to give you the rest of the tank and then ask. I helped to hot up that idea myself."

Reis grinned. "Between you, you've done the last thing that Fassarai needed. I can't say more than that," he went on simply.

"I don't need to talk about being grateful. You can see what it means. Tell him from me."

"I'll tell him," agreed McNally.

6

There was a routine that had developed of drinking coconut milk at the north end of the island. Today Reis coupled it with "Damnation to the authorities" and all the party said "Amen"— even Minchin. They drank separate comminations against Commander Holtzen and the commodore, and Minchin, who had had some trouble with the lieutenant of the boat pool, asked for a special curse against him and volunteered to find one in Holy Writ. It was completely lighthearted. The feeling of relief that had come upon Reis when the tank first filled with water still hung about him like a benediction. It was the seal upon accomplishment.

The boat was to go back at four. At three o'clock they started to walk back towards the camp and the main landing. The children met them halfway down the island, hurtling along the path. They were calling, "King! King!" And when they came up, breathless, with the party—Reis was walking with one of the nurses—they shouted, "King! King! Put on—" They halted abruptly, for Reis had his shirt on in deference to the party.

Mau, quicker-witted than the rest, suddenly substituted for the formula: "King, put on hat! Officer come."

"My radar," said Reis expansively to the company behind him, "thirty-kid-power radar. Nothing ever gets by 'em. Now who the hell will it be this time? Mau, what sort of boat?"

"Fas' boat," said Mau.

"Who's it, McNally?"

"God knows," said McNally cheerfully. "It wouldn't be the commodore. He's got a meeting with three of the carrier captains on the *Hancock,* I think, round about this time. He couldn't get down here."

Minchin said, "You've been invoking the wrath against Commander Holtzen."

"If we've called him up between us," said Reis, "I'll never forgive you, chaplain!"

They walked on towards the camp. When they reached it there was still no sign of visitors, and McNally left the nurses to gather their bags and went on through the camp towards the village.

"My God!" he said suddenly. "It *is* Holtzen."

They saw the commander down between them and the beach, close to the women's hut. "Now for it!" said Reis.

Holtzen seemed preoccupied when they came up to him. He said, "The condition of that hut is a disgrace if it is still in use."

Reis explained its purpose and then said, thoughtfully, "I ought to have done something about it at that." He wondered for a moment why he hadn't, and then he realised that the women were used to it as it was and were intensely conservative. It would never have occurred to them to ask for improvement, and so it had never occurred to him.

Holtzen snapped through his cogitations. "Get it done!"

For a moment Reis's heart leapt. He thought: He's going to leave me on the island. There was an implied futurity in the brusque order. Then he remembered that the reprieve might be no more than a week or two. He answered, "I will, sir," hastily swinging his mind from a laconic "Okay."

"Now let me see this tank," demanded Holtzen.

He talked to McNally as they went to the tank, ignoring Reis. It was technical small talk—accommodation, hospital beds, transport to the hospital ships. Reis felt rather than saw the children stealing up behind them. Occasionally he caught a glimpse of an arm or a leg behind a palm bole. Over and over again he heard the rustle of the girls' grass skirts. Something had inspired them with a real terror of Holtzen, but as the walk went on they grew bolder.

The tank stood lonely by itself now. The litter of their lunch, fortunately, had been cleared. The water in it was clear and utterly still. It looked sober, efficient, and full of purpose. Again Reis felt the curious sense of comfort, of fulfilment that it gave him, and he felt with it a sort of defiant pride.

Holtzen inspected it as if he had been an engineer, peering at the bolt heads, staring down into the water, moving backwards and forwards to get it at certain angles.

The children decided apparently that the danger was not too great, came out from behind the palms and gathered tentatively a little way off, and then gradually, slowly, closed in. The nurses could be heard, laughing and frivolous, and Chaplain Minchin and one of the doctors in a high-pitched argument. Then the party from the camp came up. They saw Holtzen, but could not turn abruptly away. There was a clear reluctance in their approach. Some of the men had arrived now; not the old king, not Elingarik, not Sebastian—some of the lesser old men. The others still had the slight that Holtzen had put upon them on his first landing heavy on their pride.

The children were playing now. They ran up and dipped fingers in the tank. They pressed on it and leant over, admiring their ripple-moulded faces. Mau and four other boys went up to the far end, the concrete end, and one of the nurses said: "What a cute picture! Lieutenant, can I take those kids?" Reis said, "Sure," and the nurse said: "Kids, pile up—come on! Get right to the edge of the water."

Watson, who had come from the camp with the others, said suddenly and almost below his breath: "Christ! There's a crack in the end. I saw it when we were clearing up after lunch."

Reis started forward. Even as he moved there was a curious cracking noise. Mau lurched, stamped hard to recover himself, and then the whole pyramid of children cascaded into the water. There was a single unanimous shriek of laughter. The thing was cleanly done, so instant, so absolutely perfect. At one moment there was a pyramid of little brown bodies above the end of the tank, and in the next there was a floundering complex of shining

legs and arms, of spray and broken water. Then Mau and two of
the other boys broke away and swam to the far end of the tank;
the others clustered on it, gasping, shrieking with joy. The nurses
and the other doctors were rolling with laughter. The thing had
in it the sudden risibility of unexpected slapstick. It was the
exact counterbalance to Holtzen's ponderous officialdom, the
counterblast of laughter to the sin of disciplined dullness.

And then Holtzen walked forward to the end of the tank
and stood staring down at it. Without turning his head he asked,
"Dr. Reis, what is the meaning of this?"

Reis saw the naked steel of the tank end showing through the
broken concrete.

CHAPTER XXXI

≈≈≈≈≈≈≈≈≈≈≈≈≈≈≈≈≈≈≈≈≈≈≈≈≈≈≈≈≈

1

THE children were still squealing, the nurses laughing. No one save Watson and McNally seemed to realise the implications. Reis went forward. There was no point in denial or argument. He said, simply, "I think it means we mixed the concrete a bit thin."

Holtzen swung round on him, tight-lipped, his face white with anger. "Lieutenant Reis, you will report at the Medical Office at the Asor base on Wednesday next." The nurses who had seen his face had stopped their laughter, but the children shrieked on happily. He paused for a long and pregnant moment, and added, "With your gear."

Reis's shoulders twitched slightly. "Very good, sir."

Looking beyond Holtzen, he saw the pain in McNally's face, a strange, deep sympathy. Holtzen turned and took one more look at the tank. Then he stalked past the end of the tank where the children were shaking themselves like little dogs, past the nurses without looking at them, down towards the village and the landing place. As he went one of the doctors from the *Solace* said acidly, "The son-of-a-bitch!"

The youngest nurse, the one who had walked with him along the path from the north village, came up to Reis. She asked, "What's happened?"

"Nothing. Nothing. It was bound to happen anyway."

McNally looked at his watch. "Hell, girls," he said, "boat's waiting. Time we were moving. Come on, let's go!" He drove the little group together like an old sheep dog who knows his sheep.

When they were on the path for the centre of the village he turned back. "I'm sorry," he said. "Damn it all to hell, I'm sorry!"

Reis said crookedly: "And now I'll never know if he meant to keep me or not. I'd half an idea— Oh, it was bound to come one way or another."

"Maybe there's something I can do still."

Reis shrugged his shoulders again. "No," he murmured, "there's nothing anyone can do now—not with that guy."

The still-laughing children were dancing on either side of them, wet and glistening in the occasional shafts of the sun. Behind them the water in the tank settled to a silver stillness shot over with green lights. Only at the far end there was a little scum of concrete dust and dirt.

2

Watson and Reis stood in the traditional place upon the beach to watch the last dory pull out. The nurses had gone calling, as always, that they would be back again, that they would see him soon. Reis was thinking over McNally's last words, in the alley between the *falu* and the canoe shed, where he had stopped to say: "Give 'em something to think about when you've gone. Build up the story of your going. . . . You've got to give them something. You can't leave them hanging in mid-air."

Reis had answered only, "He said nothing about Watson."

"No. We'll try to keep Watson. Maybe I can do that. I'll try." Then McNally had turned and gone down to the dory.

Behind him Reis called out, "See you Wednesday."

"Sure. See you Wednesday."

The dory went out noisily, and they heard the throb of the L.C.I.'s motors starting up. Holtzen and the fast boat had gone long since. It was now only a black speck with a V of white far to the northward. When the L.C.I. had turned and swung up in its wake they moved together up the path between the *falu* and the canoe sheds and past the king's hut and the first of the huts of the villages.

Not until they were clear of the last of them did Reis speak. "Well, that's that! It was good while it lasted."

"Sure it was," said Watson, "and maybe it's not over yet."

"That bastard will court-martial me if he doesn't die of an embolism between here and Asor," said Reis with finality. "Ah, well, I've got it coming."

"What are you going to tell 'em?"

"That," said Reis. "is what we've got to figure out."

3

They sat in the warm darkness long after the normal time for supper. Neither of the men had appetite. Filomena and Teresa sat on the steps of the sleeping tent, and Fayu sat below them on the ground. They had sent the children away of their own volition in the early dusk, sensing that something was wrong. Now they waited for orders for supper in soft human sympathy. Reis and Watson talked over cases.

Mau had cut his head in the fall into the tank. In the excitement he had not noticed it. Just before dark he had come up to have it dressed. He was still breaking out in little bursts of giggling, immensely pleased with himself. Watson cleaned the wound and slapped an emergency dressing across it. The young child of Jesus of the north village came down with an unidentifiable pain below the lung which Reis diagnosed as stomach-ache from an overacceptance of good things from the nurses.

"Nothing else on the books," said Watson. "Come to think of it, we've had damn' little on the books for a week—just the old regulars and oddments."

"Just the old regulars," agreed Reis. A silence followed that he broke himself. "We haven't had a death for thirty-four days."

"That long? By God, it is, you know! Thirty-four days—

jeez, it's a long time anyways you look at it! . . . D'you want to eat, doc?"

"No. I ate too much at lunch."

"Me too," said Watson. "Teresa, scat! You too, Filomena and Fayu. We don't want you tonight. You can go to a movie."

This was an old joke. The three laughed dutifully, and Teresa, coming up to Reis, said, "That old man—me, I wouldn't like to stop in bed with him." And then, as if to emphasize it: "No, sir. No—sir!"

He slapped out at her. "Teresa, your mind runs on one thing these days. I'll tell Chaplain Minchin about you."

"Chaplain Minchin!" She began to giggle. "What use you tell him?"

"Scat!" said Reis in his turn. "You're past praying for. Go on, all three of you—get rolling!"

Filomena said, "He make plenty trouble?"

"Sure, he always makes trouble. Now go!"

They listened to the soft footfalls on the dusty path and the voices diminishing in the distance. In the darkness they could see nothing but the loom of the boles of the nearest palms and, overhead, the flicker of the stars between the fronds. The voices fell, rose again, and died out in a last tenuous whisper of sound, and then the roar of the reef took over the night again.

Reis said, "Well, what are we going to do?"

He got no answer. For almost half an hour they sat in a companionable silence, not even looking at each other, not even smoking. And then Reis began to chuckle. "It was damn' funny at that. Nine kids in the water at one fell swoop! I suppose he'd say we ought to put up a notice: 'This water unsafe pending chlorination.' "

He sat up abruptly and turned to Watson. "Go down to the *falu,*" he ordered, "and tell them I want the big canoe at nine o'clock tomorrow morning. Hell, I'm the second king of this atoll, and I'm going to throw a feast now—and God damn it, it's going to be a good feast! If I've got to go I'll fill every damn' mother's

[272]

son on the island as full as a tick, and I'll throw them a feast they'll remember me by till the end of time!

"Get hold of Fayu and Fernando and tell 'em the fishing canoes must go out at midnight—they're not to come back till they're full. And tell Olimarao to hold a mullet fishing down at the south cove tomorrow afternoon if the fish are running. The women can start drying fish right away. Find out what the toddy situation is, and start stepping it up. We'll have the feast Monday. That'll give 'em time for a number one brew. Beer, whisky, gin . . ." He was ticking things off on his fingers. "I can't get 'em trade tobacco. They'll have to make do with shag, but we'll see if we can lace it with something. Have you got all that?"

Watson had risen to his feet. Reis could not see his face in the darkness, but his voice was vibrant when he spoke. "How long would it take the big canoe to go up to the *Solace*? We can fill her till she sinks from the *Solace's* icebox if we tell 'em the story."

"We'll fill her," said Reis, "we'll fill her!"

4

Reis sat in the only armchair. Two of the doctors who had come over on the Wednesday sat on the edge of the bed, and Marks, who had come over twice before, stood leaning against the bulkhead. Reis told them: "So I'm for the high jump. He'll hack my buttons off with his sword—if he's got a sword—and, by Christ, if he does my pants will come down! So I'm going to give them the biggest goddam feast they've ever had on that island and tell 'em why."

"Right," said Marks. "Now what d'you want?"

"Meat," said Reis, "pig meat. Beef will do if you can't fix pig, but what I want is pig carcasses that I can roast in the open."

"I'll fix the butcher," said one of the two on the bed. "I know they've got pig carcasses. I've seen 'em in the cold store. What else?"

"Fruit. You wouldn't have yams or taro or such like, but you'll have pineapples and oranges and bananas."

"Can do," said Marks. "I'll fix that."

"Liquor," said Reis, "hard liquor—they don't like beer. Grain alcohol'll do as well as anything."

"Can do," said Marks again.

"You want breadfruit and yams?" asked the third man suddenly.

"Yes," said Reis, "but you won't have them. I want papayas too—you might have some of that."

The third man spoke again. "You want breadfruit and yams and taro root. When do you want them?"

"I aim to start the feast Monday noon, and it will go on as long as the food lasts."

The little man said: "I'll bring you down a boatload of yams and breadfruit and taro root and anything else you want in that line noon Monday. Okay?"

"How?"

"Mogmog—the stuff's rotting there. I've been prodding around. I don't get drunk on Mogmog like you bastards"—he turned to the other two—"and there's enough stuff there to keep your feast going three or four days."

"Boy, oh, boy!" said Reis. "McNally said there might be. Bring it along! The two of you come with him." He turned to Marks and the other man.

"We'll come. Girls?"

"No. You haven't seen my people when they're canned. No girls."

"Okay," said Marks, "we'll make it. Look here, we'll bring down the pigs and everything else Monday. We'll get an L.C.T. out of the commander, and it can collect us Tuesday. We've got a day off due to us. We'll go aboard *Respite* too. Two hundred and fifty—two hundred and fifty can put away quite a bit of meat. We'll fix it." He began to laugh, and then bit off suddenly, "The crab-faced bastard!"

Watson said: "They know something's cooking. Elingarik asked me, 'What for feast?' His English is coming on. Filomena wants to know what's the trouble. I think Teresa's making guesses. What do we do?"

"Work it up," said Reis, "work it up!" He took on mockingly the tones of a public relations officer. "There will be an important announcement at the feast." He turned to Watson, suddenly grave. "This is not a joke. McNally was right. We've got to build up my going; we've got to make it into something. That bastard Holtzen won't put anybody else on the island, and I think he'll take you off damn' soon. We've got to leave something for them to hang on to—some big reason for my going."

"Doc, they'll remember you anyways."

"Hell, I'm not thinking of myself!" answered Reis. "It's them. If they get to thinking they're chucked into the discard because of a departmental row there's no telling what they'll do. We can't upset things now." He hesitated for a moment and then said angrily: "We won't upset things now. Damn Holtzen to hell!"

6

From early dawn they could hear the thud of the nuts as the children stripped the palms that Sebastian had marked. The old men were digging pits for the pig roasting, the line of them parallel with the path beyond the children's playground. The women and the small girls were cleaning up the clean earth. Elingarik was marking out a space at the head of the long main aisle of the feast with lumps of coral to platform it with white coral sand from the beach. That was for Reis and Watson and the *Solace* doctors, and for the king and Elingarik himself. All through the morning the preparations went on. The fresh mullet from the evening's fishing was brought up from the cool leaf piles. The fish canoes arrived in the midmorning, and their fish was cleaned and brought up too. The coconuts were piled down the centre of the path, a long wedge of them like a potato clamp in an English field. The papaya trees had been stripped to the last ripe fruit. The few bananas had been plucked. The brews of island stew had begun already with canned meat from the camp store and from the village rations.

The children were intolerably noisy, shrieking all the time an octave above their normal voices, running up and down with fresh nuts, crashing through the old women, bothering Elingarik —riotous, excited, strangely apprehensive. The whole island was apprehensive. The problem of the big talk had been heavy on the *falu* for three days, heavy in the huts, heavy in the women's talk. Even the children were wound up with it, tense.

Mau and the two boys next to him in age were the boat guard. They hung in the tops of the tallest palms on the lagoon side watching the sea. Five times they had sent down false alarms of craft approaching, but it was only the ordinary, orderly traffic between the north and the south anchorages from Asor to the merchant ships, from the merchant ships to the base ships up the harbour. And then in the late morning, half an hour before twelve, they picked out an L.C.T. that kept steadily towards the island. They screamed in unison. They kept on screaming till the other children took up the shout and flocked down to the beach and, unable to see, climbed up the palms themselves, simian and chattering.

The L.C.T. came on. When Reis himself walked down past the generator hut to the beach the L.C.T. was just in sight from the beach level. She needed twenty minutes more to make the island. He ducked into the comparative cool of the palms and strolled down, thoughtfully, towards the *falu*.

Olimarao sat outside it by himself with his back to the wall and his face out towards the waters of the lagoon. He smiled at Reis, and his smile was curiously sad. Slowly, in his halting German, he said, "Gehen Sie fort?"

Reis found himself suddenly shocked at the old man's acuteness. "Yes, I'll tell them tonight when the feast is on." He remembered that even now Olimarao hardly knew English enough to translate that, and he began, "Ja, ich—"

But Olimarao was nodding to himself. Meditatively, quite without rancour, he said in German, "It will be like death again."

Reis started violently. "Nein, nein! Tot nicht!" The old man sat patiently with raised eyebrows, waiting. Reis said in English, "You will be looked after," and again it seemed as if the old man snatched his meaning out of the foreign words. "Listen, there will be Chaplain Minchin and Watson and Dr. McNally. It is nothing that I go—nothing at all. You will hear tonight." Again the old man nodded.

For the first time in months Reis felt the awful resignation that had been the dominant mood in the complex of the island's emotions when he came. Behind him he could hear the mutter of the L.C.T.'s motors as it drifted in with the onshore breeze, a hot thudding that rose and rose until it was a deep roar across the silence of the landing place. Reaching desperately for something that would convince the old king, he found suddenly in it salvation. He said, "Wait!"

The children were flocking over the beach now. Some of the men were coming down the path. He heard voices all round him. Teresa and Filomena came past him, covered in wreaths and riotous. Mau leapt onto the *ailiuth* and ran across it unrebuked. The place was full, crowded, immensely exhilarated, immensely noisy. The L.C.T. came up to the beach with a rush, and they heard the clashing of the door.

Reis beckoned to Olimarao. "Come!"

Marks and Rattigan, the smallest of the *Solace* doctors, came staggering across the ramp with great baskets of breadfruit clasped in their arms, and behind them Blake, the third doctor, bowed double under a net of yams.

Reis watched the old king's face with an immense, an incredible anxiety. He saw his eyes take in the breadfruit and the yams. He saw them flicker beyond to the taro piled on the iron deck and move back to the breadfruit again. There was incomprehension in them, almost unbelief. And Reis said, "From Mogmog, from Mogmog—you will be able to go back to Mogmog when this is over." He said it again in bad German. "You will go back to Mogmog when the war is over." And suddenly relief flooded the old man's eyes.

He went up to Marks very near to tears himself.

7

Every light that Watson had been able to wire into the sorely tried light circuits blazed between the palms. The naked bulbs flung their light upwards as well as downwards, so that the green canopy of the palm fronds was rich in many tones above them, and the blue of the night sky was like a black and velvet curtain over all. The palms themselves shone like silver. There was now nothing of the dim, cathedral aisles; instead the boles were harsh, theatrical, and brilliant in the light; and only far down the path where the smoke of the cooking fires still rose and softened the lights and hung like a mist under the leaves, was there a sense of mystery—there and in the outer lines of the palms where the light died down and ceased.

There was no mystery along the path. There was only riot— the gorgeous, glorious riot of men full fed on flesh—and the hot scent of burnt pig was like the smoke of a hundred sacrifices. There was something religious about this Gargantuan eating; something with the stacked pyramids of coconuts down the path, the lessening piles of bananas, the papayas and the smoking breadfruit, that had in it all the ancient solemnity of feasting full. But between the trees, and out where the firelight flickered, there was no solemnity: only a roaring noise, a singing and a shouting. This was high feasting. This was something out of a hardly remembered past. Only the oldest of the men could remember such full feeding, such tremendous laughter.

There had been palm toddy, enormous bowls and pots of it, but Reis had not brought out the hard liquor yet. These people were drunk enough on their own innocent enthusiasms. And as he watched them from the sanded square of ceremony, looking down the long double row that stretched almost as far as the surgery tent, and that flickered in a constant movement of children passing between their elders, he knew that he would have to speak soon or miss the golden moment. Fayu was missing: Fayu would have to interpret for him. He passed the word for Fayu, and presently the youth came, an enormous rib of roasted pork smoking between his hands.

"My God," he asked, "are you still eating? You've had six men's food already."

Fayu patted his stomach with a greasy hand. "Good," he asserted, "goddam good!"

Reis said, "Tell Elingarik that he must call for silence for the king."

It took four full minutes for the old man to impose his will upon the noise and the laughter and the singing, but when Olimarao rose it was clear that rapidly through the splendid wildness of the night the apprehensions of past days had come crowding back. It was as if behind each tree bole in the outer darkness there was a ghost.

When Reis himself rose he knew suddenly that the speech he had worked on was no good; but in the same moment he knew what it was that he must tell them and he said simply, throwing his voice so that it would reach the furthest end of the crowd, "My people, in two days I leave you."

Beside him Fayu called out the words in the island tongue. For a very brief moment there was a silence, and then out of the silence there was a rustle that became a moan, a moan that was made in many keys, a moan that was made out of two hundred voices. And behind him Marks's voice was saying softly, "Christ!"

He said: "I must go. There is a war." Swiftly Fayu took the words from his mouth and flung them out across the still people.

It became a chant, his baritone against the tenor of the boy's voice.

He said: "We have taken the islands of Guam and of the Philippines, which your old men know. We have taken Iwo Jima in the north, and it cost ten thousand men; but when we took it we killed twenty thousand of the Yellows—and still the war was not over. We have taken the island of Okinawa, and again it cost us ten thousand men."

He paused while Fayu attempted to place Okinawa in their minds, and said to help him: "We have taken the islands that lie round the very reefs of the home islands of the Yellows; and now in the north and here in Ulithi, in Guam and in the Philippines, in Hawaii and in Eniwetok and in Kwajalein we are making ready to storm the islands of the Yellows. We lost at Iwo Jima ten thousand men and at Okinawa ten thousand, and in the Philippines ten thousand; but on the beaches of the Yellows, when the ships go in, we will lose a hundred thousand."

Again he waited while Fayu struggled with the immeasurable conception of a hundred thousand men. Then he went on: "And I must be there with them. I must go with them because my place is with my own people as in these last months it has been with you. You know what the Yellows are. You know what they have done to Ulithi. You know that we must go in and slay them. There will be ten times all the ships that you have seen in Ulithi. They will go there from America and from Australia; they will go there from all the islands to the north and to the south and to the east— and I must go with them, with the first of them, because of what the Yellows did to Ulithi and to Yap, to Tarawa and to Luzon."

The names came off his tongue rolling, immensely rich and pregnant. And far down the line he heard a voice suddenly, Teresa's voice, beginning to sing. Before Fayu could stumble out of the English into his own tongue he heard Teresa telling the names and telling of the ships of the great assembly to the north and, wondering, he stood silent for a little. Her voice stopped and he said again, "So in two days I go." And again it was Teresa's voice and not Fayu's that threw the words across the silence.

He heard Blake behind him say, "By God, that girl!" And again the little moan swept like a wind across the islanders.

He said quickly to Fayu, "Tell the king to tell them that they must do all that I have told them to do, and that they must wait and in the end they will have Mogmog again, and it will be unharmed."

As Olimarao rose Reis sat down again, and the old man's voice cut across Teresa's singing in a high chant. They were reaching back, Reis knew, into some old memory, some ancient custom, and he heard the roll of Olimarao's voice and the name of Mogmog; and then he heard the girl throw back an answer to him, and again the king's voice: and far beyond someone picked up the response as the girl's voice came in again, and then another and another until a score of women sang with her, and her voice dominated them all. And in the breaks of their singing Olimarao's voice went on and on and on.

Marks said: "God Almighty, you didn't tell us to expect this! What have you done to them?"

Reis said, his voice hardly audible above the singing, "I think it will be all right now."

CHAPTER XXXII

THE pier was empty when the boat came alongside save for two petty officers and two tired-looking enlisted men. Reis's gear was dumped near the base of it, and he said, vaguely, "I'll get 'em to send down a jeep or somethin'," and walked off up the dusty road. He did not want to telephone the medical office. There was no reason why: it was simply that he did not wish to do so.

As he reached the main ring road he looked up to the right to where the steel pile had lain. There was nothing there now. He looked away again with a wry smile and walked on. The glare of the place, the stark isolated palms that were left, the staring stumps and the pervading coral dust were ugly to him now after the cool green of Fassarai. The place had an unkempt, angry glare.

There were new clerks in the medical office. They looked at him with an odd curiosity that he felt was mixed with an uncertain condemnation, and he said, his tone brusque, "Where's Commander McNally?"

"In there." One of the men nodded his head towards a door in the light partitioning.

McNally himself had heard the question, and the door opened. "Come in," he greeted him. "Come in." He put his head on one side and said, "What, no flowers?"

"No," said Reis soberly, "no flowers. What gives?"

McNally dropped the bantering tone. "The commodore wants to see you—first."

Reis whistled. "Why?"

"I don't know." McNally shrugged. "I don't know what it means."

Reis shrugged his shoulders. "Hell, they can't hang me. Where do I find him?"

McNally looked at his watch. "He'll be up at his own place. He always goes there a quarter of twelve. Maybe—maybe you'd better go straight there. He said 'at once.' " His voice implied that Commodore Raglan expected his orders to be obeyed—at once. "My jeep's outside." As they went out he asked, "Where's your gear?"

"Down at the pier," said Reis.

"Why didn't you phone for a jeep?"

"I don't know."

"I'll send for it. You'll be in my Quonset for tonight anyway."

Reis turned suddenly as they seated themselves. "You're being damn' good to me. I thought I'd be under arrest."

"Technically," said McNally whimsically, "it might even be that you are."

They drove round the circular road and the jeep pulled up short of the commodore's hut, the old hut that had seen so many of Keldon's wild parties. Raglan was sitting, hatless, on the verandah.

Reis went as far as the foot of the steps and saluted. "Lieutenant Reis, sir," he said.

"Yes," answered Raglan, "yes. Come up." The grey eyes flickered over Reis for a perceptible moment. Then he said shortly, "You'd better sit down."

He was completely silent after that, looking out over the water. Reis had time to hear the roar of the surf to the north, a deeper note here than on the ocean beach at Fassarai. There was surf even on the sand in front of the commodore's hut, the sweep of water coming round over the shallows of the reef. The beach here was more alive, more active than the beach on Fassarai. Birds moved on the edge of it, and the sun glittered.

After a long pause Raglan said, "Did you take the end piece of the tank from the stack pile on the beach?"

"Yes, sir," said Reis evenly. Raglan's eyes were on him again, and in the same moment he was aware that the eyes were not hostile. There was in them a piercing honesty that seemed to recognize the honesty in his own. A spark of sympathy seemed to leap between them.

"Will you tell me why?" asked Raglan.

"I'd like to, sir."

"Shoot," said Raglan, with a little motion of his hand.

Reis waited for a little. Then he said, "I don't know how much you know about the people of Fassarai, sir."

Raglan continued to look out to sea. He answered only, "You have good friends."

"That'll be Commander McNally. Well, he knows about them." Reis dropped the "sir." After a moment he went on, "When I went to the island—I was going to say they were in a bad way, but that's not enough. They were dead. That sounds crazy, I know; but if you had heard the old king say 'We are dead men' the way I've heard it you'd know what I mean. You know the story of how the Japs took their young people? It's true, but it wasn't only the young people that they took—they took everything that these islands mean. I have come to learn—I've come to know—what this place was before the Japs came here. I've come to think that maybe it was one of the few perfect places on the earth. You see, they had just enough—just enough of everything: just enough people and just enough food, and just enough islands and just enough canoes. And then, all of a sudden, they hadn't anything. Oh, I know there was food! I know maybe they could have gone on dying slowly until the kids grew up. But if you rip the heart out of a dog, it dies. That's a physiological fact, and times I think there are psychological facts that are as hard as physiological. The Japs ripped the heart out of"—he nodded down towards Fassarai—"out of them."

Again he waited, wondering if he was saying too much, wondering if there was any purpose in this saying. Raglan gave him no sign either of encouragement or of check, and after a little while the words came to him. "I don't know what I did or even if it was what I did." He looked up with a quick candour. "I'm not a very good doctor. I've got a lot to learn, but I did what I could. I cleaned up their yaws for them." He smiled with a quick boyish pride. "That's something—they can't take that away from me—and I cleaned up the island, although I made mistakes there. Oh! And I cleaned up all the other things for them, the gonorrhea and the hookworm. And I don't know, but somehow in the doing of it they got to trust me; and because they trusted me, and because I said it was all right—I don't know what else there was to it, but maybe it was because of that—they began to think it *was* all right. And then they stopped dying."

Again he smiled a queer, disarming, boyish smile, and this time Raglan was watching him. "It's just as simple as that"—and suddenly, catching a glimpse of Raglan's cap on the table, he added, late and softly, "sir."

"Go on," said Raglan.

"I don't know that there is much more to go on with. I went on looking after them. I set them to work. You can't give people handouts for ever and not expect them to become handout-minded, and so I made them work for their rations. They saw that. Olimarao— He's the king. You ought to talk to him some time. He's a great man in his own way; he's a wise man. Olimarao saw that. And then they began to teach the kids again, to teach them the legends and where the best fish holes were and how the mullet came in in the evening, and how you call a shark up when you want one. It was slow." Reis's voice became toneless, but in its tonelessness Raglan could sense something of the agony that he had gone through on the island. "It was slow, but it came; and when they started to teach the kids I knew that things could go on.

"You see, the way I look at it is this: we could have sent those kids up to Guam; we could have parcelled them out amongst the people there—they're all Catholics. It wouldn't have made any difference, and they would probably have survived. Some of them would have died because they're that way, but I think most would have come through. And we could have let the old people die. They're old, and they've got to die anyway. But I couldn't have it on my conscience that I had broken a thing like that—

[285]

I couldn't have it on my conscience as an American. D'you see what I mean, sir?"

When Raglan made no answer Reis became discouraged, but only for a moment. Then he went on again.

"While there was a chance that we could get them going again—get the life into them again—there was the chance that we could upset what the Japs had done; and as far as I can see that's what this war's about. Maybe I'm a fool—" He hesitated. "But that's what it seemed to me. You see, if we tried to save the kids and just let the old people go and kept the kids here, well, they couldn't have got a community going again. Oh, we could have got a schoolmaster down here, I know that! We could have taught 'em, educated 'em, but it wouldn't be the same thing. As it stands there's a chance. I think we've got over"—he groped for a word—"the gap in the continuity.

"The future of a community like this," he began again after a pause, "lies as much in its past as anything else. These kids have got a chance now of catching up on their past. They're good kids, sir." He watched Raglan's face hungrily. "They're worth it," he insisted. Then, because he could find nothing in Raglan's face, he said, "That's about all, I think."

"No," said Raglan. "What about the tank?"

"Oh!" Reis's voice was almost contemptuous. "They collect their rain water in pots and odd things underneath the trees. You know, you tie a little bunch of leaves round the bole of a palm, and you lead the ends of the leaves into your container, and there's your water supply. It ain't good. Besides, they've got very few pots left. They get broken, and there are no new ones. They come up from Yap, and the trade's bust. I wanted them to have a water supply that would last. Sometimes when it's dry for a few days on end they run out—there's no more margin than that. Oh, they don't die of thirst! They've got coconut milk, but it's not the same thing. They don't wash enough anyway."

He smiled ruefully. "They're not angels. Don't let anyone tell you that! I tried to get a tank in Commodore Keldon's time, but I couldn't—the Seabees wouldn't part. And I tried again when you first came. I don't know if you knew."

Raglan made an impatient little gesture.

"And I tried the Seabees, and they said they needed what they had. But I thought there were enough tanks on this island and on Sorlen, and I was told that they were only backing up what was there already."

Still there was no sign either of approbation or of disapprobation on Raglan's thin face.

"Well, sir, when you want a thing as bad as I wanted it maybe you lose your sense of proportion. I don't know. I'd done everything I could for them except that. It was the last thing I could think of. You see, on Mogmog or here or on Falalop they had water-holes of a sort. They didn't drink the water—it was stagnant, and it was brackish. They didn't drink it, but they could have, and they had enough to wash with. But Fassarai's a long island. There's no swamp in the middle and no water. I knew they needed it." He paused and sighed very faintly. "So I took it."

Raglan's head came round sharply. "How?"

"With the big canoe," said Reis slowly, "the king's canoe: everybody had forgotten about that. They only remembered the fishing canoes. I couldn't have done it with those."

To his unqualified surprise Raglan began to laugh, slowly at first and then with quick, audible chuckles. But he made no comment, and a long silence followed. Raglan broke it. He asked abruptly, "Did anyone on Asor help you?"

"No. It wasn't necessary."

Raglan looked at him sharply. "Would you have told me if they had?"

"No, sir."

Raglan snorted. "Commander Holtzen has asked for a court-martial on the ground of stealing U.S. naval property." He left the words to sink in for a long minute, his eyes roving backwards and forwards across the upper section of the anchorage. "I don't think a court-martial will be necessary." It seemed that he was looking in at himself as he said quietly, "This is all irregular, but then the whole circumstances are irregular." When he spoke again it was not to himself but directly to Reis. "But I cannot stand between Commander Holtzen and the just punishment of a member of his department. I want to know one thing more only. Will you tell me, Dr. Reis, if it is necessary that there should be a full-time doctor on Fassarai?"

Reis flinched almost as if Raglan had struck him. He had difficulty in framing an answer, but at last he said: "No, sir. No, sir, not if they have any hope for the future."

"How much attention will they need?"

"A doctor every week with the Wednesday boat," said Reis quickly, running over the circumstances rapidly in his mind, "permission to bring up more urgent cases to the hospital ships if they need attention, and perhaps an occasional visit between the weekly boats to see that they are keeping up to the mark. The boy Fayu can be trusted with some of the simpler things now. He's quick, he's very quick." He added half apologetically, looking across at Raglan: "Maybe I've lost my sense of proportion more ways than one. You get to forget there's a war on—on Fassarai."

"Yes," said Raglan grimly. "Is that all?"

"No," said Reis, "no, that can't be all. Commodore, on Monday I gave a feast, a big feast, to the whole island. I'm going to ask you not to enquire into this."

Raglan's eyes switched cholerically to him and then turned away again.

"A feast is no good to them unless they have their own food. We got breadfruit and yams and taro down from Mogmog. It still grows there, and when I told them that I had to go—I think I have known all along that I had to go—I told them that they must keep on teaching the children and keeping their way of life alive because when all this"—Reis waved a hand in a gesture that took in the aircraft carriers and the battleships in the anchorage, the ranked Quonset huts on Sorlen and the distant palms on Mogmog, the aircraft swinging round in the Falalop circuit—

"when all this was gone they could go back and there would still be breadfruit and taro on Mogmog at least."

He jerked his head impatiently. "This island is dead except for the palms, and Falalop is dead—the Seabees filled the central depressions. But that's not been done on Mogmog—yet." There was an infinity of pleading in his voice now. "Commodore, if you will leave Mogmog alone—they've got the softball fields they want and the bars and everything—if you can leave that central marsh, then these people can go on living as a community. They know what it means all right. There are so few of the children that it will take generations to populate both islands fully; but they can do it. They can get back into their past and make their future out of it. Can't you see, can't you see what it means to them? There's just no sense in their going on living if they can't have it that way. I don't care about the court-martial, commodore. Commander Holtzen can send me down for anything he likes. I don't count any more. I've done all that I could, and there's nothing else to it. Maybe most of what I did was wrong—but they're alive, and they've got a chance to live. If you save Mogmog for them you will save something that was"—he groped painfully for the word—"that was perfect in its own way; and it may be that that's as much as the winning of a battle."

He sat back exhausted, the tension of his nerves broken now into a dull apathy, and Raglan said, very quietly, "Thank you."

Again there was one of the curious long silences that seemed to be part of the necessary ritual between the two men. Then Raglan said: "I think we can save Mogmog. You will see Commander Holtzen at two o'clock. You can tell him you have seen me. You will, of course, be posted elsewhere. I am afraid that is inevitable."

For the second time the austere correctness of his manner broke. It was clear that he was human underneath, and it was equally clear that he wore his austerity as a duty. He said: "Holtzen defended you when Captain Craik said you were the only man who would have taken it. He said there was no boat that could have carried the tank end down to Fassarai. They have savaged him some over it." From the little edge in his voice it was clear that he did not like Holtzen, but there was no overt hint. He ended: "I cannot, of course, stand in the way of his decision. That is all."

Reis got to his feet and stretched for his cap. To his surprise Raglan rose too, walked across the narrow verandah, held out his hand and said, changing Reis's own words very slightly: "It may be that some things are more than the winning of a battle. I am sorry, but discipline is more than the individual. If it is not, the whole chain of command breaks down."

He watched as Reis went down the steps and turned towards the medical office. He looked at his watch and realised that they had talked clear through the lunch hour. For a moment he thought of calling for the mess boy; then his eyes turned to the anchorage again, but they saw beyond the ships to the low palm-tops of Mogmog and he stood quite still, his mind going back to the hesitant, pain-full voice of the young doctor.

CHAPTER XXXIII

≈≈≈≈≈≈≈≈≈≈≈≈≈≈≈≈≈≈≈≈≈≈≈≈≈≈≈≈≈≈≈≈≈≈

McNALLY strode ashore through the warm shallow water, his khaki trousers wet halfway up the calf. The children gathered round him, splashing and cheerful. He cuffed Mau, the king's son, behind the head with a mock hostility and raised a chorus of delighted shrieks. Emberton followed him, and behind them two of the enlisted men began to dump ration cases on the sand.

Olimarao was sitting on the *ailiuth* in his place of ceremony. His mat was rolled out beneath him. Elingarik flanked him, and Sebastian and Jesus of the north village. Others of the old men were coming down the path between the canoe shed and the *falu,* and down the path on the far side of the All Men House. The children were all there already.

McNally greeted the old man formally and said in German, "Is it good?"

"Sehr gut," said the old man gently, "sehr gut, mein Freund."

McNally's hand went up and flicked away a fly. They sat for a few moments talking. Fayu had joined them, slightly breathless, and made a quick interpreting. When they had done McNally turned between the great huts and went up the path through the village. Again his hand whisked up to brush away a fly. He said: "You see what I mean? The flies are back and the mosquitoes too. But they don't mind. I think they like it better that way."

"How did they come?" asked Emberton.

"Wind probably—wind from the next islands, or maybe from a merchant ship or something. You can't tell. It's dirtier than it was, too. There's trash on the north side of the village." He nodded over to untidy heaps under the fringing palms. "I must talk to Fayu about that."

Fayu behind him said defensively, "I tell 'em."

"All right, we'll deal with it some other way."

They turned up the main path towards the place where Reis's camp had stood. The surgery tent was still there, still stocked with harmless drugs and first-aid gear. McNally went to it always on the Wednesday to check the names of the shaky entries that Fayu had made. He could print in a rough square script now, names or enough of them to jog his memory. Inspection lasted only a few minutes.

McNally said: "You see, there's no real increase in sickness on the island. They're just a bit more slovenly—they've fallen back a little. I'm watching out for signs of yaws, but there's nothing to signify yet. I'm not sure that he didn't clear up the hookworm permanently; but that may show in time too. You can't keep them aseptic—they're not made that way; not by weekly visits anyway. D'you want to have a look at the tank?"

"The famous tank!" said Emberton. "It's a legend over the Pacific now. Where is it?"

"Just outside the village," McNally answered. "He put it there to make the shortest haul for the largest number of women."

They began to walk back down the path, and Emberton said: "The kids are fit, you know. Look at that little beggar! Nothing wrong with them that I can see. What's this one's name?"

"He's the king's son, Mau," said McNally, reaching out at Mau again. The child said: "Me Mau, okay. Got any candy?"

"You'll get your PX ration," growled McNally, mock-angry. "Scram!"

"The kids are all right," said Emberton again. "But what about the old people—those old men at the big house?"

"They're all right. They always look that way. The king's getting old, but he'll last a bit yet. There's nothing to show that they're slipping back. I'd say—" He stopped to consider the question in the round. "I'd say if anything they were easier than they were when Reis was here. They're getting closer back to nature."

"How do you assess that?"

"Rations for one thing. They're using less than they did: I keep a check. They're fishing more. This kid Mau goes out with the fishing canoes now, and one of the other boys. They're running three canoes—four sometimes. They can go a long way with fish, and we get stuff down from Mogmog regularly now—breadfruit and taro; and they'll take that before they take canned goods, every time. They can do a lot with fish and taro and breadfruit and those damn' things." McNally nodded up at the clustered nuts under the palm fronds. "Cut off the path now. It's the short way to the tank."

The children had strung a rope of coir fibre, beautifully made, immensely strong, from end to end across the tank and six feet above its surface. Emberton and McNally stood looking at the water. There was a green scum at one end of the tank, and the water was cloudy. McNally felt in his pocket for a packet of chlorination tablets. He said: "I can't keep it clean at weekly intervals but it doesn't seem to do them any harm. Now what are those damn' kids up to?"

Mau had climbed up a palm trunk to which the rope was anchored and began to climb out, hanging sloth-wise to the taut rope, hand over hand, leg over leg along the line of it. He climbed till he was almost in the centre of the sheet of water and then, with the other children shouting at him, he let out a cry and dropped, back downwards, into the water with an enormous splash. Instantly the children began to yell at the top of their voices, and two of them broke and ran for the tree to repeat the feat. Mau swam slowly to the end of the tank and lay there kicking his legs lazily in the fresh water.

"And they drink it!"

"Sure they drink it," said McNally. "Why should I stop 'em. I'm not a New York City analyst. There's probably 10 per cent of *Bacterium coli* in the water, but it won't do them any harm. They don't drink enough of it for one thing." He turned to Emberton. "Don't you see? It doesn't matter. Nothing matters very much. Nothing ever did matter very much in these islands. They'll get by. Sometimes I think Reis was too sanitary-minded;

but they took that just as they take this: and he had something else—that we haven't got. He wanted it that way, so they let him have it; but I don't think it makes a hell of a lot of difference if they're clean or dirty so long as they're happy."

"That," said Emberton, "is an heretical doctrine."

"Oh, I wouldn't put it in a report! I don't trail my coat. But look at them—you can see they're all right."

"And spiritually?"

"You ask Minchin. I don't answer that one. I never did."

"I don't mean from the religious point of view," said Emberton. "I think you know what I mean."

"Yes," said McNally, honestly, "I know what you mean. They'll do. You see, they believe that he went away because it was necessary for him to go to make certain that we would beat the Japs. That last feast was something. Marks told me about it, and Blake. It was a feast to end feasts. He kept every man on the island drunk for two days, and I think they were all five of them— there were three doctors from the *Solace*—I think they were all five of them cut most of the time themselves. But it worked. It made such a big thing of his going that it—I don't quite know how to put it—that it satisfied their pride. Maybe that was it. Anyway it gave them a sense of importance, and perhaps that's the easiest way.

"And besides you've got to look at it from this angle. He'd done his work before that bastard Holtzen got him shifted. He'd brought 'em as far as they could lift: as far as any man on earth could lift them! I don't think he could have done anything more. Watson thought that way too; he thought they were through. He was quite glad to come away himself, I think. They had brought them up to a point where they had to stand on their own feet, and it's better for them to stand on their own feet than to be killed by—he used to call it 'pauperisation.' I don't like the word, but it means about what he thought it meant. I'm not sure that Holtzen didn't do quite a bit of good in his own way—and he'd be goddam mad if you told him so! And you see at the end that business about Mogmog gave 'em a chance for the future.

We haven't any of us got much more than a chance for the future. I don't think they can ask for more."

"And the girls?"

"Filomena, she's all right. She's moved into the *falu*."

"Teresa?"

"I don't know." He turned to Fayu. "Where's Teresa?"

"Most days this time she sit down at the south end. She sing."

"Let's go," said McNally.

They walked down the southern stretch of the path. The palm-frond trash was beginning to gather under the trees again, and McNally pointed it out. He said: "I'm letting it lie. I think he was wrong to clear it—he thought so too in the end. It's as good a breakwater as they make. The brush is growing again where he cleared it, and that's a good thing too. I don't know what my old professors would say, but the more I see the more I come round to the belief that you can be too tidy-minded. I don't think it suits the Kanaka."

"And Mogmog will be all right?" asked Emberton.

"Ask Raglan. He's got a kind of fixed idea about it now. Holtzen wanted to fill in the women's pool because of the skeeters three weeks back, and Raglan jumped right down his throat. He doesn't love him!"

"And you?"

"Oh, hell, I endure him! I find senior officers interesting psychological material. He's better that way than most. I think he's nuts."

"He lets you have a free hand down here?"

"Now," said McNally. "He tried to interfere in the beginning, but Raglan sent for me. That guy smells things out. It's all right now."

They were coming to the far end where the broken palms were, the south end where the wreckage of the bomb and the later wreckage of the typhoon showed across the sand. Teresa was sitting on a coral rock that jutted into the water. Her back was towards them, and her hair blown in the trade wind. She wore flowers in her hair and round her neck, but under the flowers were strings of necklaces—the necklaces of honour. She was singing though there was no audience, her song low yet clear above the noise of the reef, clear and firm and endless.

McNally said: "She's going to marry Fayu some day but she belongs to the *falu* now. She's the singer to the island. I'm not sure she is not in some way a priestess. Minchin will tell you that's a lot of damn' nonsense, but Minchin doesn't know everything. In these islands you can be a good Catholic and a good pagan at the same time—no difficulty." He called softly to Fayu, who had dropped a little behind them. "What is she singing about?"

Fayu cocked an indulgent ear towards the girl. "She always sing 'bout Doc Reis. All the time she sing 'bout him. She sing how he go to war to kill the Japs."

McNally looked at her whimsically. Then he said, sighing a little, "She thinks that he is going to lead the general assault on the beaches of Tokyo. I haven't had the heart—" He hesitated just for a fraction, and then he said softly to Emberton, "I haven't had the heart to tell her he's Number Two in the dispensary of a boot camp in Baltimore."